PENGUIN BOOKS

DREAMS OF OTHER DAYS

Elaine Crowley was born in Dublin. She left school at fourteen and became an apprentice tailor. At eighteen she went to England and joined the A.T.S. She married a regular soldier in 1949 and spent part of her married life in Egypt and Germany. Since 1963 she has been living in Port Talbot.

Elaine Crowley has six children, three girls and three boys, and nine grandchildren. Once her children were at school she did a variety of jobs – Avon lady, dinner lady and part-time sewing machinist making sleeping bags. In 1969 she went to work in the personnel department of the British Steel Corporation in Port Talbot. After nine years there she took voluntary redundancy and began writing. At first she wrote articles and had several accepted. But this form of writing was not satisfying enough and she began work on the novel which she had had going round in her mind for years. *Dreams of Other Days* is the result.

Elaine Crowley

Dreams of Other Days

PENGUIN BOOKS

Penguin Books Ltd, Harmondsworth, Middlesex, England
Viking Penguin Inc., 40 West 23rd Street, New York, New York 10010, U.S.A.
Penguin Books Australia Ltd, Ringwood, Victoria, Australia
Penguin Books Canada Ltd, 2801 John Street, Markham, Ontario, Canada L3R 1B4
Penguin Books (N.Z.) Ltd, 182–190 Wairau Road, Auckland 10, New Zealand

First published by Century Publishing Co. Ltd 1984
Published in Penguin Books 1985
Reprinted 1985

Printed and bound in Great Britain by
Cox & Wyman Ltd, Reading
Filmset in 10/12½pt Monophoto Photina by
Northumberland Press Ltd, Gateshead

For all who believed in me,
especially Chris

Chapter One

Chapter One

On a fine May morning, in 1837, in the village of Kilgoran, a young man stood in front of a long, low, whitewashed, thatched building, a hand shading his eyes against the sun as he looked for sign of the midday coach bringing the new parish priest. The man's name was Peader Daly, and the building outside which he stood, a public house called Carey's. It was situated where the road divided four ways, a place referred to locally as Carey's Cross.

The sound of men's voices, laughter, and a strong smell of porter wafted out through the half-door. Peader moved into the road a bit for a better view, and thought as he had all morning, of how once the new priest was settled in, himself and Katy O'Donnell would arrange to have their banns called. A rapturous look crossed his face at the prospect of having Katy for his wife.

In his mind's eye he saw her, the shape of her, the way she moved with a swing to her hips. Golden-haired Katy who soon would leave her father's cottage at the Lodge Gates of Kilgoran House, and make her home with him. He felt weak with longing for the night she would lay beside him. Images of her skin the colour of new milk, the narrowness of her waist that he could span with his hands, how her hips curved away from it and her breasts swelled above it caused a sensation in his loins. He dwelt on the feelings aroused by his visions. Then remembering that such feelings before marriage were lust and a cause of confession, he said a silent prayer for the gift of purity, and concentrated on the road ahead.

The sun shone on his hair highlighting the reddish tints in it. His eyes were green, the colour of clean bottle-glass. Men admired his height and litheness. And the girls of the village considered him the handsomest man, except, maybe, for Jamsie O'Hara.

When he saw a vehicle come over the hill, a speck in the distance, he went to the half-door and called urgently, 'Jamsie! I think it's coming. There's something just cleared the rise.'

Jamsie and his brothers, Padraig and Johnny, were seated round an upturned barrel, drinking porter, Jamsie's back to the door. Without turning to look at Peader, he waved a hand dismissively and said, 'You're seeing things. Did you ever know it to be on time? Come in and sit down. You've been in the sun too long, sure your brain must be parched.'

His brothers laughed, so did the men at the counter. And Carey, the landlord, said, 'Aren't you in a terrible hurry to get the priest here altogether, Peader? And sure you know the minute he arrives he'll be laying down the law about drink. If the clergy had their way I'd be out of business.'

Peader took another look up the road. There was no mistake about it, the coach was arriving. Going back to the door he appealed to Jamsie's brothers. 'Padraig! Johnny! Will you shift, and him, too. I tell you the priest

8

will be here in a minute. Won't it be a nice reception with not a soul but myself to welcome him? Come on,' he urged, 'and someone give Tim Coffey a shout. His horse is half-way to Clonakilty with the cart behind her. We'll be in a nice fix with no yoke to lift the priest's things.'

'Eh, Tim!' a man shouted. 'The jennet's bolted.'

Jamsie turned his dark head and smiled indulgently at Peader. 'You're as bad as a woman any day for worrying,' he said good-naturedly. 'But rest easy, I'll be there now in a while.' He returned to drinking his pint.

Then a man at the counter said, 'Whisht! I think I hear something. Be God, he's right! It's the coach.' There was a hurried swallowing, a wiping of hands across mouths, and faces assuming serious expressions, an attempt by way of straightening shoulders to erase the signs of drink, as one after another the men headed for the door. Tim Coffey, coming in from the yard adjusting his trousers, headed after the men and his straying animal who with lowered head was grazing on the move.

They assembled in a little group outside the public house. Those who wore caps removed them, and stood twisting and rolling them for they were ill at ease, more so as they knew the sign and smell of drink was about them.

'Whoa! Whoa there,' the coach driver called to the horses, reining them in.

'Whoa,' he called again, leaning back in the seat, pulling on the reins.

The horses came to a halt; they were lathered in sweat, their bits flecked white. The driver got down, opened the carriage door, tipped his hat, and in a voice loud enough for the waiting men to hear, announced, 'We're here, Father. It's Carey's Cross. Mind the step now,' he continued, and with difficulty restrained himself from helping down the tall black-clad figure emerging slowly and awkwardly, for he remembered how at the staging post his assistance had been kindly, but firmly refused.

Peader, not aware of the driver's earlier experience, thought him the queer, surly sort of a man not to offer a hand, and moved forward, his own outstretched. Then a look about the priest's face, a set to his mouth, made him halt. Feeling foolish with a hand raised he brought it up to his head pretending that the gesture of combing his hair with fingers was his original intention, and watched the priest negotiate the step. Saw his swollen knuckles whitened by strain grasping the door frame, as one stiff-kneed leg after another was lowered from step to ground. Then the driver unloaded the luggage, tipped his hat again, and bid the priest goodbye.

'Father Bolger,' Peader said, 'we were waiting for you. We have the horse and cart. Will you put on your things, and maybe ride with them? The chapel's a good walk.'

'God bless you for all your kindness, all of you,' the priest said, looking from one to the other, seeing the men still nervously twisting their caps. Peader introduced everyone, and for each the priest had a word of greeting, and thanks. When the introductions were done he exclaimed, 'Well, well, that's grand indeed! I never expected this, and a conveyance, too!'

His face, that at first sight appeared stern and forbidding, took on a kindly humorous appearance, his deep-set, pale blue eyes smiling, the skin at the corners creasing into lines furrowing the pale flesh. He pushed back his tall hat and massaged the red crease made by the too-tight band, a strand of ginger greying hair escaping on to his forehead.

'Well,' he said again, 'that's grand indeed. I never expected the like. If all my days in Kilgoran are like this I'll have no cause to complain.'

The watching men beamed at the praise, and were glad Peader's father, Michael, had organized the meeting, and persuaded Tim Coffey to come with the cart. It was wonderful to have a priest again in their midst. Three months they had been without one since Father Mullen died suddenly.

'Right then,' said Father Bolger, 'put the bags on, but myself I'll foot it with you. Walking keeps the joints moving, nothing like it for the rheumatics.' Tim Coffey who, since recapturing the horse, had not let go its straw bridle, backed it closer to the group. Padraig and Johnny loaded the cart, while Jamsie at the priest's request undid the blackthorn stick tied to one of the bags and handed it to him. Tim exchanged bridle for reins and mounted the cart, its wooden wheels creaking as the procession set off to walk the four miles to the chapel.

The road was narrow and winding, hedged with hawthorn. The cart sides dragged at the leaves, crushing the white May blossom so the summer morning was heady with the sweet smell. Here and there along the way old men, old women, and children had gathered to see the priest. He spoke a few words to them and gave his blessing. Jamsie and Peader pointed out little whitewashed cottages, some clearly visible, others only glimpsed at the bottom of boreens, saying who lived where. 'That's the Widow Murphy's. In the next field Statia Tierney lives, she's above now in your house seeing to things. And over there is Mary Doyle's. Mary has lumbago, she's the one who'll look after you, but Statia's agreed for the present.'

The priest listened, thinking that in time he would remember all the names, meet the people to go with them. After a while he asked, looking from one of the young men to the other, 'Tell me now, which one of you is which? I was so overcome with the unexpected welcome I didn't take in half of what was said.'

They identified themselves. 'I'm Peader Daly, Father.'

'Ah, yes, Peader.' A fine, serious-looking man, better dressed than the others, Father Bolger noted.

'Jamsie O'Hara, Father.' Taller than the other one, heavier, too. A divil-may-care expression about his blue eyes. A different type altogether to Peader, the priest felt sure.

'Them's the two brothers behind, Padraig and Johnny,' Jamsie said.

The priest glanced back. 'You're the spit of each other, more like twins than brothers. You're not, are you?'

Johnny moved up alongside Father Bolger. 'We're not, though the mistake is often made. Padraig's the eldest. He's nineteen. Jamsie's a year younger, and I'm seventeen.'

'Is that so? And yourself Peader, what age are you?' the priest inquired.

'I was born the same year as Jamsie.'

– Well, I've got them fixed in my mind now, and your

man on the yoke, an oul sour puss if ever I saw one, is Tim
Coffey, Father Bolger thought.

They went on for a while until they came to a place
where the hedge was scant. The priest stopped walking,
the men did too. One of them called to Tim who pulled
up the horse and sat smoking a short clay pipe, brooding
over the few shillings lost because Peader's father had
pressed him into carrying the priest's traps instead of two
churns for a farmer beyond the village.

'That'll be Lord Kilgoran's house, I suppose?' Father
Bolger asked, looking across the fields to where rising from
landscaped parkland there was a pale-stoned mansion,
flanked on either side by curving wings. From its many
windows and conservatories the sun was reflected.

'It is,' Peader confirmed. 'Once it was the seat of the
O'Sullivans. Their castle was there long before the English
came. Part of it is still there at the back of the house, and
their dungeons beneath it.'

'Is that a fact?'

'A fact indeed, as it is with many of the big houses. Built
on the ruins of something else, someone else's. This one
goes back to the time of Henry VIII. Though as you can
see it's been altered over the years. Changed, the way
Kilgorans themselves changed, for they were Catholics
when they came, and are Protestants now. That's how
they held on to what they have.'

'You know your history well,' Father Bolger said approvingly.

'He does that – Peader's the great scholar,' Jamsie
said, as they started again on their journey. 'Him and me
went to the same hedge school. His father let the master

teach in his house. Peader had the gift for learning all right.'

'And yourself?' the priest inquired.

'Ah, no, not me,' Jamsie laughed deprecatingly. 'I've a head like a brick. And you could say the schoolmaster didn't take to me, nor me to him. One day after he hit me, I hit him back. Fighting you can do for nothing, my father said when he heard tell. Out you come, I can put my twopence a week to better use.'

'Jamsie's the hard man,' Peader said with affection for his childhood friend.

'I'm told Kilgoran's a good landlord.'

'He is that, one of the best,' Peader said.

'Are you all his tenants?'

'All except the O'Haras, here,' Peader explained.

'Oh, and whose tenant are you?' Father Bolger asked.

Johnny O'Hara, the youngest of the brothers, took from his mouth the grass he was chewing, and spat on the road. 'Dano Driscoll's.' He uttered the name with contempt.

'I see,' said the priest, and thought he knew the sort of man Dano was. Irish and a Catholic, if the name was anything to go by. A regular at Mass and the sacraments, generous with offerings and oats for the priest's horse, making sure of his place in Heaven. He knew the sort well. A small farmer maybe, that had come up in the world. A grabber of land, able now, from whatever source, to afford expensive leases. Wanting big fields for pasture, never mind that to get them he ran out the occupiers of small tilled ones, depriving them of a home and their living. He was sure he would hear more of Dano. But in the meantime he would give Johnny no more encouragement to vent his spleen so, bringing the conversation back to Lord Kilgoran, he asked, 'Tell me now, has the Lord many in family?'

Answers came back from all sides. 'Four, Father. Three girls and a son.'

''Tis a great week for Kilgoran – yourself arriving, and Miss Catherine, the eldest, marrying tomorrow. Great goings on altogether.'

'Great excitement indeed,' Father Bolger agreed. The men were gathered round him, he saw their shabby clothes, the worn frieze coats, breeches stitched and patched, stockings that had seen better days, brogues, handy shoes fitting either foot, scuffed and battered by long wear. All showing their badges of poverty, except Peader, with a comfortable cut to him. Poor men who seldom handled a penny, and when they did, as often as not spent it on drink. Blaming their plight on drink was an excuse, he knew, ever on the lips of landlords, officials and priests. Not that he condoned its misuse, but drink wasn't the whole story, he thought, detaching himself from them, walking to where he could look out over the little fields. The men, thinking he needed to relieve himself, walked on a bit.

His head ached from the tight hat, he pushed it back, and again the gingery grey strand of hair fell forward. What unfortunate people were his countrymen, he mused. Their land in the hands of strangers, governed from England, soldiers in the King's uniform barracked in the towns.

In front of him were the plots of potatoes, their green leaves growing well, the fields planted with barley and corn. Behind him a way, the big house with the women slaving to have everything ready for the wedding. Washing and cleaning, mending and dairying. Always it had been the same. 'Yes Sir,' and 'No Sir,' bending the knee and touching the cap. Preparing for weddings, hunts and balls, shoots and weekend parties. Rocking the stranger's cradle. Turning the houses inside out while the gentry had their season in Dublin or London. Conditioned to think themselves lucky to earn the few shillings that stretched the price they got for their grain.

What an existence they had! Seldom anything to eat but the potato washed down with buttermilk when they could afford it. Maybe once a year, at Christmas, a bit of fat bacon or salt fish. All over the country the same. People in little cottages with one field, two if they were fortunate. Dividing them up when a son married. It was that or he'd be out on the road. Exhausting the bit of ground with too many mouths to feed. And even with the rent paid – no security. Anytime the humour took him a landlord with the law behind him could evict: anywhere except Ulster that had a system like England and an agreement between two parties was honoured.

Jamsie, Peader, and the men came back, but left the priest undisturbed gazing at the fields, thinking his thoughts. The fields that were tilled, planted, that were prayed over for sun and rain, for the frost not to be too hard. From which children picked stones and frightened the birds. And all for what? he asked himself. So that the fruits of their labour, the corn and the barley, cattle and pigs, the firkins of butter, went down the road to the ports – and England. And the people ate potatoes, depended for their life on them, a vegetable that was as contrary as the weather. Was it any wonder they sought solace in drink?

A breeze blew across the field sending ripples through the grain. Looking at the undulating crops soon to be plundered he felt a surge of hatred rise within him, a flood of anger and bitterness for the English who had so treated his people. An emotion first experienced long ago in his home town of Enniscorthy on the day he saw the man being flogged. He prayed daily for God to take it from his heart.

A touch on his elbow, and a voice inquiring, 'Are you all right, Father?' brought him back to the present. The waiting men looked concerned. He assured them he was fine, sighed and indicated he was ready to continue the journey.

When next they stopped it was at a stone, slate-roofed house belonging to Peader's father who was outside waiting to greet the priest. 'Come in Father,' said Michael Daly, who looked like his son. 'You'll be tired and thirsty after the journey, and wanting to rest.'

'Thanks all the same, but I won't, for if I sat I'd not rise again.'

'Sure you can stand, so, but out of the sun,' Dinny Crowley, beside Peader's father, said. He was small and thin with a cranky face.

'You'll have a drink?' asked Michael Daly.

'A drink would go down well. A drink of water.'

'Ah, Father, sure you can have that, too,' Michael protested.

'Water will do fine.'

Dinny wrinkled his face in disgust, and went to fetch the water.

Michael spoke to the priest. 'I needn't tell you how delighted we are to have you, Father, three months without a priest in the chapel was a terrible long time. The house has been put to rights, and a few things sent up. I doubt if you'll want for anything. I'd have had your horse down at Carey's waiting, but at the last minute I thought she'd gone lame. Myself and Dinny stayed to doctor her. But, sure, thank God I was worrying over nothing, and she's grand. There she is.'

Father Bolger's eyes followed Michael's pointing finger and saw the brown mare grazing. – A beautiful creature, and a more than generous gift, he thought, but one I'll have to refuse. The man will think bad of me – a churlish individual. First refusing his hospitality, then his fine mare. But it can't be helped.

He explained how unless there was always someone to hand, he could neither mount nor dismount. Michael's face fell with disappointment, then showed concern and sympathy when he heard the reason for the refusal.

'God comfort you, the rheumatics is a terrible affliction. But how will you manage, especially in the night for sick calls?'

'I'll have to put my trust in God,' the priest replied.

'Then that He may answer your prayers,' said Michael.

For a while, the priest, Michael and Dinny discussed Daniel O'Connell, Michael commenting that nothing but good seemed to have come from the granting of Catholic Emancipation. And wasn't it a grand thing that paying tithes to support the Protestant clergy had been reduced? The priest said it was, and expressed his hopes that one day O'Connell would secure Ireland's total freedom. 'God bless and spare him to us. A man that hates violence and has achieved what he has without shedding anyone's blood.'

'A clever man, that's what he is,' Dinny said. 'Look at the way he's after uniting the people and clergy in the struggle. And wasn't his penny a week Catholic rent a stroke of genius. There's few that can't find it, and the paying of it makes everyone feel they have a say in what's going on. Which reminds me, Father, there's been no collection since the priest died. You'll be seeing to it?'

'I will that,' Father Bolger said. 'We'll call a meeting first thing.' He bid Dinny and Michael goodbye and, accompanied by the band of men, set out on the last stage of his journey, Peader telling him as they went, that further along the road was a small gate into the estate, and some of the women working in the House might be there to see him.

Chapter Two

In the cool, dim, dusty dairy at Kilgoran House, Katy was churning extra butter for the wedding guests. It was strenuous work, her thick golden hair was disarranged from the effort, a fine sweat beaded the upper lip of her full mouth, and her usually serene brow was marred by a frown. Occasionally, without stopping the churning, she raised her head to look at a spider descending an invisible thread spun from one of the many cobwebs festooning the ceiling. The thread grew longer, the spider hovered above a pan of milk set for the cream to rise.

However, the frown on Katy's forehead was not a result of her labour, but of the worry going through her mind. For with the new priest's arrival there was no longer an excuse for not getting married. The sudden death of Father Mullen, on the very day she had realized what she felt for Peader was not love, seemed as miraculous a happening as the miracle she had experienced during the old priest's last Mass. To think so about someone's death was probably a sin, she had told herself several times, and wished some other happening had given her the opportunity to put off the calling of her banns and Peader's. That very Sunday after tea they had an appointment with Father Mullen, but the poor man was gone to God by then, and she madly in love with Jamsie O'Hara.

The thought of him made her tremble and feel hotter than she was already so that she sweated more profusely. She bent her face and wiped it across the sleeve of her blouse, and began to relive again the moment she fell in love. It happened in Mass. On the men's side across the narrow aisle, one row up from where she was sitting, Jamsie O'Hara knelt as he did every Sunday. The warning bell rang before the elevation of the Host. Katy bowed her head. The second bell sounded, she raised her head to look at the priest with his back to his congregation, arms uplifted offering the sacred bread. Out of the corner of her eye she noticed Jamsie as if seeing him for the first time. His head was bathed in a shaft of the hard bright February sunshine slanting through a narrow window; she saw how the hair she thought was black had a bluish tinge to it, and as the priest lowered his hands, found herself remembering the colour of Jamsie's eyes and thought how strange and sinful it was to think about such things at this moment. She she again bowed her head, and closed her eyes, trying by squeezing them to distort the image of his face clearly visible as if imprinted upon her lids. Again the bell was struck, the chalice offered. Katy's head came up, but as if they had a will of their own, her eyes were cast in Jamsie's direction instead of at the vessel whose wine had now been transformed into the blood of Christ. And within her heart another miracle occurred – she fell in love with Jamsie O'Hara, with the shape of his reverently bent head, the vulnerable exposed skin between the rough, shabby frieze collar and the hair that curled on the back of his neck. She was possessed by a longing to cross the aisle, bend and kiss the pale skin. It would feel soft, she was sure, like that of a baby. 'Holy Mary, Mother of God, don't let me do any such thing,' she prayed, alarmed at what was happening to her.

– I must be losing my mind, me that's promised to Peader. My heart leaping out of my breast, my head light, a feeling maybe that I'll faint, only it's nice, and not a sick feeling at all. And all because of Jamsie O'Hara that I've seen most days of my life passing the Lodge Gates. One of what her mother called the rough dirty crowd from up on the bog, that before this minute she had never given a second thought to.

So lost did she become in the wonder of this strange and delightful emotion that she continued to stare at the one to whom it was directed, until a sharp dig from her mother's elbow, and a hiss to 'stop gawping, and pay attention to her duties' brought her to a temporary reality. But from that moment on she thought of Jamsie all day as she went about her work in the House; when she opened her eyes in the morning, last thing before she closed them – and sometimes God granted her bedtime prayer, and she dreamed about him.

A shout from Nan, the dairymaid, recalled her from her thoughts. 'I said, aren't we fortunate getting a priest? I think you're losing your hearing. Three times I spoke to you.'

'I was miles away,' Katy said. 'It's grand isn't it? I was just thinking maybe I could slip down to the gate and see him pass by.'

The old woman said nothing and returned to stamping patterns of cows and leaves on moulds of butter, and Katy to thinking wouldn't it be great if Jamsie was with the crowd walking with the priest? And wondering how she

22

would break the news to Peader that she didn't love him? And then angry thoughts about her mother's refusal to let her go dancing at Carey's Cross.

She remembered how, the week after falling for Jamsie and knowing he danced there, she broached the subject.

'Have you lost your mind? Dancing above at the Cross – you, a girl about to be married! Only tinkers and the like dance there. Buzzing and leaping, screaming like the demented, and their clothes disarranged exposing their limbs,' her mother had replied.

'Peader goes,' Katy had said, by way of persuasion.

'Not since he's been courting you. And anyway, a man can do what he likes, and not one thinks the worse of him. On the nights Peader doesn't call you'll sit by the fire.'

– Sit by the fire one night, the next with Peader, never allowed to go dancing – where will I ever see Jamsie except a glimpse of him outside Mass, Katy thought. That's how I'll spend the rest of my life till I die. But if I never lay eyes on him again I'll not marry Peader, and tell him so tomorrow.

Anger and frustration surged through her, unconsciously she channelled the emotions into her churning, so the paddle turned faster, the sound of the swishing milk changed as it became less liquid.

Nan stopped stamping the butter. ''Tis coming,' she said. 'I can hear it. You're the great butter maker, nearly as good as myself.'

'Indeed I'm not, sure's there's no one to beat you.' Katy believed what she said, but at the moment would have said it anyway, for she wanted Nan to wash and salt the butter, then she might see Jamsie.

The old woman preened at the praise, wiped her greasy hands on her skirt, sat down and began probing with a long finger nail between her remaining two front teeth. 'There's something there. I can't get at it. It has me tormented,' she said.

'You'd want a bit of thread,' Katy advised. 'I was thinking,' she added, 'you might finish the butter. I'd love to see the priest. I wouldn't be a minute and tell you all about him when I come back.'

'There now I've got it,' the dairy woman said, extending her nail with an atom of something attached for Katy's inspection. She rubbed it off on her skirt and answered Katy's question. 'I will. You can go and welcome. If I had the power in my legs I'd run with you.'

Katy left the churn and rolled down her sleeves. The woman went to look at the cream. She skimmed her fingers across the pan. Some fell back, she licked the rest, skimmed again and offered it to Katy, who hastily refused and put on her cloak, noticing as she did so that the spider was drowning in the milk pan.

On her way to the small gate well away from the main one, she saw Charlotte Kilgoran. The child was bowling a hoop along a narrow path, her hair streaming behind her as she ran to keep pace with the hoop. The path, Katy knew, led to a drainage ditch. After the wet spring it would have a depth of water. It was a place forbidden to children.

'Miss Charlotte,' she called. If the child heard her, she pretended not to, so that Katy had to call again, louder this time. Charlotte looked round, the hoop went rolling down the slope, veered, collided with a tree, and fell over.

Katy beckoned and the little girl came across the rough grass which separated the path and road. Her face was red from exertion. She smiled shyly at Katy who reached out and touched her affectionately. She felt sorry that the child's mother was dead, and that her brother and sisters were so much older, and often thought that her life was lonely and sad, especially since her old nurse died, and no one came to replace her.

'Hello, Miss Charlotte,' she said, looking at the eyes which reminded her of a startled deer. 'You shouldn't be down here, not near the ditch rolling a hoop. Who said you could come?'

Charlotte shrugged her shoulders.

'They'll be looking for you,' Katy said, and thought how slight the child was, a puff of wind would blow her away.

'They won't,' Charlotte said. 'No one will, they never do.'

'Ah, now that's not true. Anyway, Miss Catherine will.'

'No she won't. Not any more. Not since Edward. And no one else will, everyone is too busy about the wedding.' She started to cry.

Katy's heart went out to her. She knelt in the grass and pulled the child close. 'My poor lamb, don't be crying. Of course she cares.' She patted the thin back and thought – she feels like a little bird, as fragile as a bird. 'Miss Catherine loves you, you know she does.'

'No she doesn't,' Charlotte sobbed. 'She only loves Edward and is going away forever. And I'll never see her again.'

Katy rocked her and stroked her fine brown hair. The child clung closely. 'She'll be back in no time, wait'll you see. She'll be back at Christmas. There now, don't cry, sure everyone loves you. You're a little dote.'

'I wish I could live with you,' Charlotte said. 'Could I Katy? Could I live with you in the Lodge? I'd never be frightened then in the dark.'

'Ah, sure I wish you could. But what would your father do without you?'

Charlotte stopped crying to consider what she thought was a serious question. She said nothing for a minute then her eyes lit up as she thought of a solution. 'I could come up every day with you to the House, and see him.'

'I don't think he'd like that. Would he not be lost without you?'

'He wouldn't, Katy. Papa wouldn't miss me one bit. He's very busy all day. Olivia wouldn't, nor Charles, they have so many things to do. Nobody would. Please, Katy.' She began to cry again. 'I wish Catherine wasn't getting married. I don't want her to go away.'

'Hush now, astoir, it'll be all right. I'll tell you what, every day when I come to work I'll see you, and sometimes we'll go down to the Lodge. Will that do? And I'll get something for you so in the dark you won't be frightened. Wouldn't you like that?'

Charlotte nodded her agreement, wiped her eyes, and gave a big sigh. 'I do love you, Katy.'

'Then you'll be a good girl and go this minute for there's your brother and sisters coming back from their ride. Look! Aren't they lovely? Like a picture with the colour of the horses, and the grand habits on the young ladies. Miss Olivia's as blue as a harebell, and the green of Miss Catherine's brighter than the grass.'

26

'They are horrid, and I hate them,' Charlotte said.

'You do not, so don't say it,' Katy scolded. She retrieved the hoop, kissed the side of Charlotte's face and sent her off. Watching for a minute to make sure she went, then walked on down the road to see the new priest – and Jamsie, she hoped.

Across the field came the riders in a flash of brilliant colour and movement. The women riding sidesaddle, the white veils wound round their hats streaming behind them. On they galloped, hooves pounding, heading for the plantation. Nearing it they slowed to a canter, to a trot, then eventually to a walk as they took the bridle path between the horse park and the front lawn. One behind the other they rode along the narrow tree-lined track.

Charles, leading on his white stallion, waved his crop before his face. 'Damned flies!' he exclaimed.

Olivia behind him on a dappled grey filly called out, 'It's the sweetness of you, it attracts them.' She laughed. Her eyes were blue, the same colour as her brother's and her features resembled his.

'Then there's no fear of them bothering you,' Charles replied. They continued calling bantering remarks to each other. Following them on a chestnut mare Catherine was silent, her face pensive, for she was thinking sadly that today was the last time she would ride with the others for many a long day. Sadness and shyness were always thus reflected in her face, so that strangers meeting her thought of her as being aloof – a notion quickly dispelled once she felt at ease, and smiled. For she had a smile that lit her face and showed the warmth of her disposition.

She heard Charles complaining that luncheon would be tiresome. 'All those aunts and uncles come for the wedding. Sizing me up. Telling me I'm the image of this one or that. Tut-tutting about me being sent down from Trinity. Especially Uncle Monty, stuttering old idiot.'

Olivia, an excellent mimic, impersonated to a tee the uncle's stammering speech. Charles rocked with laughter on his saddle. And Catherine thought it cruel of them, then told herself it was thoughtlessness more than cruelty.

They left the bridle path, and emerged on to the drive. Soon they were by the steps and terraces that led up to the house. A groom and stable boy waited by the mounting block. They saluted the riders, helped the women down, then led away the horses.

'It must be one of the loveliest houses in the country,' Catherine said, gazing at the white stone mansion with its columned porch and pedimented portico. 'Great-great-grandpapa did us all a favour when he had it rebuilt in the Georgian style.'

'A pity he didn't go the whole way and do the inside as well,' Olivia said scornfully. 'Imagine going to all that trouble, then keeping something as ancient as the Great Hall.'

'But the Great Hall is beautiful. It goes back to Tudor times, back to when the house was first built,' Catherine protested.

'That's what I mean. It came out of the ark,' Olivia said. She began to climb the steps. 'It's a draughty barn of a place. It gives me the shivers. All those suits of armour and blood-stained battle honours. It's probably haunted. The servants believe it is. They say that

O'Sullivan walks there once a year, staking his claim, don't you know.'

'That's not news. We've grown up on that tale. I think the servants put it about to remind us we're interlopers,' Charles said.

'They do no such thing,' Catherine said. 'They believe the ghost appears to warn of trouble. Hannah swears she saw it the night before Mama died.'

In the hall Mrs Cummings, the housekeeper, was waiting for them. She inquired if they had enjoyed their exercise, then told them she would have hot water sent to their rooms immediately, and took her leave. Charles looked after the tall gaunt figure dressed in black and made a face. 'What a frosty countenance she has. If I came upon her at night she'd pass for a ghost,' he said.

Olivia took off her hat. Her hair was golden. Catherine looked at her, and wished as she often did that her own hair was the same colour instead of brown, and that she had been blessed with Olivia's tiny feet and hands. Then she told herself it was a vain, useless wish, and put the thought from her mind. 'Ghosts and draughts, I'm still going to miss it all frightfully,' she said, as they began to ascend the stairs.

'For Heaven's sake, you're only going to England when you marry Edward, not being transported,' Olivia said. 'I'd be dancing for joy if I were in your place. Wouldn't you Charles, if you were getting out of Ireland?'

'Rather,' Charles replied, racing on up ahead of his sisters. 'See you at luncheon,' he called back.

On the first landing, portraits of the Kilgoran ancestors looked down on the two girls. One, a woman in Elizabethan costume, bore a striking resemblance to Catherine.

'There she is, your kinswoman,' Olivia said, pausing to look at the picture. 'Put a ruff around your neck and it could be you. All dark and brooding, the image of you and Papa. I'm glad I take after Mama's side and not the Kilgorans.'

'Some people, Edward for instance, prefer dark women,' Catherine could not resist saying.

'Love, they say, makes people blind,' Olivia retorted. 'I'm only teasing,' she quickly added. 'But one thing I don't understand, if you are so besotted with Ireland, and Kilgoran, why choose to marry an Englishman?'

'Love not only blinds one, it makes you do strange things, takes away your choice.'

While Catherine talked, Olivia's face took on a dreamy look. 'You are so lucky,' she said, 'loving someone as handsome and nice as Edward.' Then her face resumed its usual bright pert expression, and lowering her voice she confided to Catherine that she had a secret. 'It's about Peter Melrose. After I've bathed and changed I'll come to your room and tell all.'

'Oh do tell me now,' Catherine coaxed.

'No,' Olivia said, and hurried down the passage to her room. Catherine followed her, wondering what there was to tell about Peter. A nice young man, eighteen, the same age as Olivia, the son of a Scottish peer, over with his family for the wedding. The truth of the secret dawned on her – Olivia's set her cap at him! But she would pretend surprise, she decided as she entered her own room.

In a few minutes her maid, Bridie, came, and with her a young girl carrying a copper jug of hot water. The girl put the ewer on the wash stand and brought from a cupboard a hip bath which she filled with cold water from a china jug on the stand, adding afterwards the contents of the copper jug. Bridie put a screen round the bath, sent the young girl away, then helped her mistress to undress. While Catherine bathed the servant inquired which dress she would wear.

'The beige, sprigged cotton, I think. Yes that, the one with the cinnamon-coloured flowers, and my Kashmiri shawl.' With her maid's help she dressed before the fire, then moved to sit in front of the looking glass while her hair was arranged.

'Do you know, Miss, your hair and eyes are the same shade of brown, beautiful, God bless them,' the girl said, as she brushed the long lustrous tresses.

'Thank you, Bridie.'

'I wish I was coming to England with you.'

'So do I,' said Catherine, 'I'm sure I don't know how I'll manage without you. But I couldn't take you. It wouldn't be fair. The regiment might go at any time to India, and then what about your sweetheart in Ireland?'

'Ah sure, we'd have managed somehow,' her maid replied.

The girl finished Catherine's hair. 'That looks lovely now. Though myself I think it would suit you better not brushed back so tight, but 'tis how you like it.'

'It is. It's grand. Thank you, Bridie.'

The young girl came back, emptied the bath water into a pail, dried the bath and put it away, then staggered out of the room with the heavy bucket. Bridie moved about collecting the soiled linen, inspecting the riding habit to see if it required brushing, hung it up, then put the riding boots outside the door for the boot boy.

'Will there be anything else, Miss?' she asked.

'Thank you, no. You can go now.'

While Catherine waited for Olivia to come, her face once again resumed a sad expression as she thought how this was the last day she would spend here. She looked round the room seeing the familiar, loved objects soon to be left; her satinwood writing desk where she had spent many hours writing romantic poetry – verses she had never shown to Olivia or Charles, knowing well the howls of derisive laughter they would have provoked. She rose from before the mirror and moved about the room, touching things. Fingering the embossed roses on the three-leaved silk screen, the intricate carvings on the clothes press. She opened the press door, and inhaled the smell of oak, and the scented sachets hanging amongst her clothes. She noticed a peacock-blue dress she had intended to be passed on to Katy O'Donnell, and forgotten until this moment. She took it out and laid it on the bed.

Most of the things, she thought, have been here for hundreds of years. The press and chest going back to the time of Henry VIII. The writing desk and work table to the eighteenth century. She found the link with the past comforting. One day my daughter may sleep here, open the press, finger the roses on the screen, draw the curtains round the bed and say to herself, this was so in my mother's time, in my grandmother's and before that too. Nothing would be changed, all remain as it was. The descendants of the Kilgorans would stretch out into the future. Maybe the house would be altered through the years, but the essence would always be the same. Her eyes lit up as she saw down the years, the women, daughters, and granddaughters, sons, too, of course, all the succeeding generations.

The Estate would go to Charles, but not for many years yet, she hoped. And by that time his attitude to Ireland and managing the property would have altered. Maturity would surely bring a sense of responsibility such as her father had. Though, so far, she had to admit, there was no sign of it. Charles was lovable and charming, she had a great affection for him. But that didn't blind her to the fact that he was sowing his wild oats with a vengeance. His drinking and carousing, and the debts he was running up worried Papa dreadfully. She knew he feared that Charles had inherited his grandfather's rakish tendencies. All the years and hard work it had taken to pull the estate out of near bankruptcy! How Papa had worked at improving matters. What a tragedy if Charles were now to jeopardize it again.

Then she took herself to task for being such a pessimist, and let her thoughts return again to a pleasant view of the future. Charles would settle down, marry and have a family. Her children and Edward's would come to Kilgoran for holidays. Aloud she said, 'My children and Edward's.' She smiled, her eyes shone, and she told herself how blessed she was to have fallen in love with such a wonderful man, and how twice blessed she was that he loved her in return, and that tomorrow she would become his wife.

She remembered her attempts at writing romantic poetry. She who had known nothing of love except at secondhand, from novels, and verse. How infinitely more exquisite was the real thing, how intensely more pleasurable a single kiss, an embrace from the man you loved.

Then as if a candle had been snuffed out, the light went

from her eyes, and her expression became pensive, a pensiveness that was quickly replaced by a look of fear. For headlong after her thoughts of embracing and kissing came the knowledge that there was another side to love. One she knew nothing about. Fearfully she recalled the tales told in whispers, only half-heard, as giggling girls who came to house-parties passed on secrets learned from married sisters.

'Absolute brutes! The ones you least expect behaving like stallions.'

'It hurts like anything!'

The fears had plagued her before now, but on previous occasions she had controlled them, telling herself that no matter what anyone said Edward wouldn't suddenly on his wedding night be transformed into a ravishing brute. Time then had been on her side. Her wedding was still distant. Now with the ceremony almost upon her she could draw no such comfort, and gave way to her panic, so that when Olivia came into the room, she blurted out her fears. Immediately she regretted having done so. Olivia was a year younger than her, and unmarried. What comfort or advice could she offer for all her pretence of being worldly-wise?

'Nerves, that's all it is,' Olivia said dismissively. 'All brides suffer from them.' While she talked she looked in the mirror, rearranged her curls and smoothed the folds of her grey silk gown. Then she remarked on Catherine's hair style. 'It's much too severe. I hope you'll tell Bridie to dress it in a more becoming style tomorrow. Like that, beneath your veil, you'll look bald.'

'Oh, for Heaven's sake be serious, Olivia. I didn't intend

telling you or anyone else. But now that I have at least take me seriously and don't prattle on about hair styles.'

'Don't work yourself up. You'll be bedded, that's all. And don't blush at the mention – you'll be married, it's allowed.'

'But what if all they say is true?'

'What if it is – it won't kill you. And anyway if you're no good at it, you won't be bothered for long. Once you've produced, Edward will take a mistress, they all do.'

The regret Catherine had felt after confiding in Olivia was replaced by indignation and anger. 'How dare you say such a thing about Edward!'

'Sorry, darling,' Olivia replied flippantly. 'But all the same, it's true. Being bedded won't kill you, it might even be nice. I haven't noticed many new brides going into a decline for all they complain. And whether you like it or not, men do take mistresses.'

For an instant, curiosity overcame Catherine's anger. 'How do you know?'

'I keep my eyes and ears open. Listen to the gossip. Anyway I've seen the goings-on at house-parties, here, and when we've gone away. You'd be surprised how many people move about in the night and who sleeps where.'

'You horrid little weasel! You disgusting thing, ferreting about like that. I'm absolutely appalled. I wouldn't dream of doing such dishonourable things.'

'Of course you wouldn't. You'd only dream of knights in shining armour, all that stuff, like your romantic poetry.'

'Romantic poetry, what do you mean?'

Unabashed by Catherine's question Olivia began to recite. *'When the moon her mantle spreads ... In the vale my love and I,'* then unable to continue, she burst out laughing.

'You read it! You read my poetry! And showed it to Charles I suppose. Olivia, how could you? It was mine, it was private.'

'I'm sorry, honestly I am. Anyway it was ages ago. Don't let's quarrel.' She came to Catherine and put her arms around her. 'Remember what you said about going away, and how you'll miss everything? Well, I'll miss you, too. And don't worry about the other thing. I'm sure Edward isn't a brute.'

Catherine, who always found it impossible to remain bad friends with Olivia for long now accepted the apology, returned her sister's embrace, and snatched at the crumb of comfort. 'I expect you're right, and I have just worked myself into a state. Nerves, that's all it is. What about this secret you had to tell me?'

They sat together on the bed, and Olivia confided that she had fallen in love with Peter Melrose. Catherine pretended to be surprised, then reminded Olivia that she hardly knew him.

'I shall soon remedy that,' Olivia said confidently. 'Then Papa and Lord Melrose can work out the details. We'll be married. Won't that be wonderful? I'll be saved. Able to leave Ireland. I'll never come back, except for holidays. The Melroses have a place in Scotland, one in Surrey, a house in London, but nothing here. You've no idea how relieved I am. I've always been afraid Papa might have arranged a marriage for me with an Irish landowner.'

'You silly little goose, Papa isn't like that. He believes in marrying for love, otherwise he could have objected to me marrying Edward. The Synges are a good family, but haven't a penny.'

'I'm glad the Melroses aren't poor. I'd hate that. Imagine not being able to have new gowns when you wanted them. I think I'd die. How ever will you manage? But, then, of course, you're different. Not so interested in clothes and things. Anyway, I expect Papa will have been generous with your dowry.'

'I'm sure he will,' Catherine said.

Olivia who never concentrated for long on a single subject then suggested that until the gong sounded for luncheon they should play a hand of cards.

'Good idea,' Catherine agreed, and so they occupied themselves for the time being.

After leaving Charlotte, Katy ran all the way to the gate, praying as she ran, please God let him be there, let him be with the men. Let him see me. Let him say my name out loud. Say, 'Father, this is Katy O'Donnell.' She opened the gate, stepped out to look in the direction from which the priest would come. Maybe I've missed him, she thought. They might have passed while I talked to Miss Charlotte. Her mood swung between hope and despair – she had only stayed a minute with the child, surely they couldn't have gone?

Then she became conscious of what a sight she was, her hair coming down from the running, her face stained scarlet from the thumping of her heart's anticipation, and her skirt stuck with sticky grasses from chasing after Miss

Charlotte, and despaired more than hoped. Then she saw the cart, and behind it the men, just raising the brow of the hill. She stepped in behind a bush, able to watch the group approach.

Now she was able to pick him out. *He was there.* Oh thank God, he was there. – Let you smile openly at me, she willed. Smile so that I know for sure the message I think your eyes tried to tell me outside the chapel. But as they came nearer, despair again overwhelmed her. He wouldn't, he'd hang back in the crowd. Let Peader do the talking, would let on he didn't see her. And what good would hearing Peader speak her name be, or smiling at her either? Couldn't she see and hear him every day of the week, talk to him whenever she liked. 'Oh, Jamsie O'Hara, I love you,' she whispered into the hedge.

They were nearly here. She would step out into the road, let on she had just come. He must have seen her, the others had, they were looking in her direction but he was pretending interest in a lark soaring, his head turned up watching the bird. As if he couldn't do that any time, she thought, then sadly wondered if he had not looked at all in the direction of the gate, did not hope she would be there. Maybe she imagined that his eyes tried to tell her things. Maybe she was just a foolish girl, and he had no notions of her at all.

Jamsie, before pretending interest in the lark, had seen her, wanted to go running down the road, leave behind the priest, Peader, his brothers, everyone. Wanted to kiss her mouth that smiled shyly at him outside Mass. Tell her, 'I love you Katy O'Donnell. I'd marry you tomorrow if you'd have me. I'd stop poaching his Lordship's salmon

38

and snaring his rabbits. I'd even give up the drink for you, I'd marry you if it wasn't that you love Peader.'

Katy stepped into the road. She would say 'God Bless you, Father,' and they would stop. Tim Coffey's cart drew level with her, he nodded and drove by. She drew in her breath, dipped her knee and bowed her head, and called out the blessing. Raising it she saw the face of the priest smiling at her, and beyond him Jamsie looked down at his brogues – How gorgeous he is, she thought.

'Good day, child. God bless you.' The priest made the Sign of the Cross and, as she feared he would, Peader stepped forward.

'This is Katy, Katy O'Donnell, Father.'

I knew it, I knew he wouldn't come forward, Katy thought, as she replied to the priest's questions, and noticed with irritation that Peader was still smiling at her, while Jamsie now talked to another man with such interest that she was convinced he didn't know or care it was she standing there. The priest bid her goodbye and went on his way. She stayed out in the road looking after them, hoping that Jamsie might turn round, but though she waited until there was no sight of the walking men, he never looked back. With a heavy heart she returned to the dairy, got a twig broom and vented her feelings on the cobwebs festooning the ceiling.

Below stairs in the vast kitchen of Kilgoran House, Hannah was issuing orders to her army of assistants, many of whom had been brought in for the week before the wedding. Some she put to scrub potatoes, others to peel vegetables, and the ones she had no faith in at all to wash pots in the wooden sink. She was nearly demented with all that had to be done before tomorrow. Her face was flushed from bending over the range, and rushing round trying to supervise everyone at once. The aggravation deepened creases above her nose, and down the sides of her mouth, and her wiry pepper and salt hair was disarranged. In between scolding the women, who immediately her back was turned made faces at her, she was instructing her assistant cook how to jug hares, and wanting to know where was Paudeen with the carrots, ten minutes ago she had asked for them.

'Isn't it great all the same the young mistress getting married tomorrow, and us having a feast after. God bless the master's generosity,' said a woman scouring pans.

'Great for them that only has to eat it. They mightn't be so pleased if like me they had the cooking of it.'

'Ah, sure, go on Hannah, aren't you well able for it?' the woman bantered.

'I don't know about that. There's a side of beef to be cooked for the tenants, and finishing touches to the wedding breakfast to be done. I've glazes to see to, fowls to be boned and stuffed, sucking pigs for roasting, and three salmon for poaching. Which reminds me, where's the fish kettle, and where's that young Paudeen? I'm run off me feet. And now there's the lunch to be sent up.'

'Take the weight off your legs for a minute,' another advised.

'I couldn't – not till everything is done,' Hannah replied, and then caught sight of Paudeen coming in with the carrots. 'What kept you, and me waiting for eggs and cream? Run down to the dairy and, when you come back

– no, on the way, here take this.' She ran to a dresser as long as the wall, laden with delft, pewter plates and tankards, cheese dishes and two baskets, one for hens' eggs and the other for duck eggs. 'Take the baskets with you to the henhouse, and tell young Noreen to have them ready when you've brought back the cream.'

In her apron pocket the keys of the dresser presses jingled, for Mrs Cummings, in honour of the busy occasion, had undone them from her waist and let Hannah have them for the day. 'And make sure in your possession they stay, for I wouldn't put it past one of them women to be at the sherry and port, to say nothing of what might happen to the tea,' she had instructed. This minute with her head in a twirl from all the goings-on, Hannah was tempted herself; a mouthful of sherry would put her to rights in no time. But she resisted the temptation, and dispatched Paudeen, calling after him, 'And don't take all day about it, I've another message for you to do.'

The women called after him as he went, 'There's great you're looking, Paud. Don't you wish you were getting married tomorrow?'

Paudeen blushed, but wasn't short of an answer. 'I do not, wouldn't I be the right eejit to do such a thing.'

'Ah, you won't be saying that in a minute. Wait now till another few years, wait now till you're fourteen.'

After Paudeen had gone, the women continued to talk to each other. Hannah's bark, they knew, was worse than her bite. So long as they did the work, she was easy, not like Mrs Cummings who, thank God, was above in the house kept busy. If she appeared on the scene there'd be no talking.

One, peeling potatoes, said to another, 'My sister married a man from Captain Synge's regiment. He says the Captain is a gentleman. On Spike Island they were stationed, 'twas near there at a ball Miss Catherine met him.'

'Is that so?' a woman at the sink said. 'And is the regiment there still?'

'It's not. It's gone over to England, to a place called Aldershot, 'tis where Miss Catherine will live.'

'She'll do no such thing,' Hannah informed them. 'Miss Catherine and the Captain have a house in Frimley Green a good way from the barracks, maybe seven miles or more.'

'Look at that now,' the woman said, and began to talk of something else.

Hannah went to the long range, poked it, adjusted a damper and, lifting a ring, put on shovelfuls of coal. Cursing silently the black filthy stuff, regretting the day the Master ever got the newfangled range that didn't do well on turf. The top of the cooker was covered with simmering pots and pans. But none cooked as slowly as the one furthest back. Early that morning Hannah had placed in it a small chicken and not quarter a cup of water, with pepper and salt and the scraping of an onion and left it to simmer in its juice. She took off the lid and with a spoon tasted the stock. It was delicious and done to a tee, would lie easy on the stomach of Father Bolger, and the Master nor Mrs Cummings never miss it. She transferred the contents of the pot into a bowl, covered it with a clean cloth and called Paudeen who had returned from his errand to the dairy and henhouse.

'Take this up to the priest's house, Statia Tierney's there. Tell her to keep it warm till he comes, and don't let me hear tell that you picked it on the way.'

Up the stairs from the kitchen, along a warren of passages, and through the baize door came the procession of servants. Maids and footmen, carrying tureens, entrée dishes, sauce boats, silver trays of roast meats, platters of fish, and bowls of vegetables. Throughout the house the sound of the gong announcing luncheon reverberated. Lord Kilgoran, his family and guests came to the dining-room, were seated, and waited upon. The great table was covered with crisp white damask, crystal goblets sparkled and the plate gleamed. Lavish baskets of hothouse fruit waited to be plundered.

Unobtrusively the servants attended, carving and serving; watching, waiting to step forward, remove a dish, replace it with another, replenish glasses, retrieve dropped napkins or cutlery. The atmosphere was festive as Edward and Catherine's forthcoming marriage was toasted.

Peter Melrose was being attentive to Olivia who smiled and nodded demurely. Little does he know, Catherine thought, watching the pair, that every glance, every word of hers is calculated to enchant him. I hope she succeeds. He seems a nice boy. I think they would be suited. He's handsome, too, in a fair way. But not as handsome as Edward.

She turned her attention back to her fiancé and caught his eye across the table. They smiled at each other. – I love you so much, she thought, gazing at him, and was sure his dark eyes returned her message. From further down

43

the table she heard the stammering tones of her uncle giving advice to Charles, gently admonishing him for being sent down from Trinity. Her father attempted to change the conversation, but the old man was not to be deflected, and continued in an avuncular manner to advise Charles on his shortcomings.

His face, she noticed, was assuming its sullen expression, and she saw, too, that he was drinking copiously, constantly having the footman replenish his glass. – Poor old Charles, she thought, always in hot water of one kind or another, and absolutely unable to stand being criticized. Seeking refuge in alcohol. Before the meal is over he will be paralytic.

She hoped he wouldn't do anything foolish like riding up to the bog. Lately he had been doing that. Bridie had told her so, adding that the younger master had been seen talking to that wan who was going to marry Johnny O'Hara. A bold hussy, no better than she should be. 'You'd want to warn the young master against the likes of her.' – Much attention he would pay to anything I said to him, Catherine thought. All I can hope is that he drinks so much he falls asleep and is put to bed.

The meal was almost finished: plans for spending the afternoon were being discussed. Some of the guests chose to avail themselves of Lord Kilgoran's excellent stables, and ride. Fishermen took advantage of a beat on the fine salmon river. Olivia and Peter were going on the lake. Catherine asked Edward to play croquet.

'What about you, Charles? What are you doing?' Olivia asked.

'I need exercise,' he replied, rising and swaying slightly,

making a tremendous effort to appear sober. 'Exercise, a long hard ride over the bog. Nothing like exercise,' he said and left the room.

Out on the bog a young girl with a basket was collecting turf already cut that had been left to dry. She was alone, having lingered after the other girls left, for in the distance she had seen the man on the big white horse. Her red petticoat was torn at the hem, so the white skin and slim ankles were exposed, her bodice was too tight and above the frayed neckline her breasts showed.

She bent her long tangled head of black hair, pretending great interest in the turf, not raising it until the horse was beside her and a voice said, 'Hello'.

Then she looked up, her hand flying to her bosom, knowing well his eyes would follow it. 'Oh, Sir,' she said, 'you gave me a fright.' Her long narrow eyes looked up at him, her lips parted, and in a single glance she took in everything about him. The black polished top boots resting against the white coat of the animal, their turndown tops the same colour as his fawn breeches, his cutaway brown coat. He dismounted, and came towards her. She backed away pretending to be frightened.

'You're the most beautiful girl in Kilgoran,' Charles said, catching up with her, reaching a hand for her.

'Ah, now, Sir, you shouldn't be saying that, I'm promised to Johnny O'Hara,' she said, but her eyes gave him the come-hither. 'You shouldn't be touching me.'

'Only a kiss, a little kiss. Johnny will never know. You've kissed me before.'

'God forgive me, I have. I didn't know what I was doing.'

45

Charles took off his coat, threw it and his riding crop on the springy ground, then held her fast. She struggled, half in earnest, inflaming him, enjoying her power. At last she raised her face for the kiss. His hand went to her breast. For a moment she allowed it to linger, then quickly and with surprising agility wrenched herself free, picked up the creel and ran away.

Charles looked after her and smiled. – You little vixen, he thought, you know how to excite a man. But one day I'll have you. He remounted and rode back the way he had come.

'Oh, it's you,' Statia Tierney greeted Paudeen when she opened the door. 'With such hammering I thought it was the priest himself. Didn't your mother ever teach you how to knock on a door?'

Paudeen, who was afraid of Statia, didn't know what to say. He had never seen such a big face on a woman, like a man's it was, hairs on it as well, above her lip and sprouting out of her chin, black and thick, which was a queer thing, Paudeen often thought, when she had so few on her head and them grey. But it was her eyes that frightened him most, they had a way of staring at you as if they could see what you were thinking. And that's why it was no good trying to tell Statia a lie. Them little brown eyes of hers knew. – I hope to God, he thought, she doesn't look at the chicken before I'm away. For though I've hidden well the bit I've picked, she'd spot it.

Statia continued to regard him, with what he thought of as a glower, then said, 'Well don't be standing there like a big thick – come in.' He had to squeeze past for she was fat and he holding the dish in front of him. Once in the room he continued holding out the basin not sure where to put it.

'Yerra, put it down on the table,' Statia said impatiently. Then taking pity on the soft-faced boy, apologized. 'Don't be paying any attention to me at all. I do be in the divil's own humour when I'm woken out of my sleep. And you gave me a fright – me thinking it was himself, God bless him, and me stretched out in his chair. Tell me now,' she continued, 'is there great goings on in the kitchen? Is Hannah up to ninety?'

'Oh, she is that. There's so much going on 'tis like a fair.'

'I'm glad I'm not there, so, I don't like being ordered.'

'No,' Paudeen agreed, for he did not know what else to say. Statia went on to enlighten him.

'Nobody tells Statia Tierney what to do. I bring children into the world, and wash and straighten the limbs of the dead so they can face their maker decent. And I tell you a corpse nor a woman in labour gives no orders.'

Paudeen said he was sure they did not, and Statia continued, 'I brought you into the world, and a fine big lump you were, too, and smacked your arse till you roared like a jack-ass. Did you know that now?'

'My mother said you were there,' Paudeen replied, not knowing which way to look, then made an excuse about going back, remembering before he left to tell Statia the chicken was to be kept warm.

While transferring it to a pot she saw it had been picked, and took a piece herself, put the saucepan on the side of the fire and returned to her chair. She had the potatoes washed, ready to put on the minute the priest arrived.

47

There was plenty of everything to take his fancy. More food than she had seen this long time. Milk and butter sent down by the Driscolls. Tea and sugar sent from Connolly's shop, God bless the man, who wouldn't give anyone else the time of day if he didn't see the money first. And everyone from the cottages had come with potatoes.

To the best of her ability she had swept and cleaned the parlour, made the bed with clean sheets, and kept in the fire. Tidying and cleaning was a fool's work, she thought. No sooner was it done, than it wanted doing again. Service would never have appealed to her, and she thanked God she had her mother's gift that could ease a woman in her hour of travail, and lay out a corpse better than anyone in the county of Cork. It brought her enough to live on, and willing hands to dig and plant her potatoes. She had a grand life since her husband was laid to rest. No, not for all the money in the world would she wash and clean for anyone. Putting the house to rights for Father Bolger was an act of charity, which, when Mary Doyle was over the lumbago, she wouldn't have to offer again. A grand life, she thought again, and grander still if the seal on the whiskey sent up with the tea and sugar from Connolly's was broken. She looked longingly at the bottle on top of the press, but decided that interfering with the chicken was one thing – tampering with the bottle another altogether.

Jamsie and his brothers left the priest outside his house and took the bog road. For a while they discussed his merits then lapsed into silence. Jamsie cursed himself for hanging back like an amadhaun outside the gate instead of saying something to Katy, if it was only 'hello'. He wouldn't lay eyes on her again till Sunday. That was no way for a man to exist – waiting from one week's end to another, and then only be able to make sheep's eyes at her. Every waking minute she was in his mind, and came to torment him in sleep. There in front of him, mouth smiling, inviting, her arms stretched out, and he'd go to her, and she'd back away, and him following her, led on by her glance. And when his fingers touched her and he thought he had her she'd vanish.

Johnny detached himself from his brothers and strode ahead. He, too, had a girl in mind, she was willing to marry him, but first his father had to agree to a share of the acre, or what was left of it, since Padraig married last year and slung up a cabin. If he said 'yes', then three ways the potatoes would have to go. Thank God, he thought, Jamsie was not courting for the acre would not split in four. It was a terrible way people had to live. Not enough land to feed them, going away every summer to lift potatoes in England and Scotland, or working on the diggings. God blast them that caused it.

His thoughts turned to Driscoll. A grabbing bastard! Made his money working in a shop in Cork city – him and his boss, fleecing people one year in a scarcity. Buying their pitiful possessions for half their worth. Selling them meal when there wasn't a potato to be had, at double the price. Then charging three times what he had paid for the clothes, blankets and spades, once things improved. Dano, who had been reared begging, putting the money, and what the robber of a shopkeeper left him into land. Finding himself a good match, and now after the big fields. Fields

49

to graze another head of bullocks, for grazing was where the profit was. The robbing bastard, him, and all the bloodsucking landlords! 'Fuck them all to hell!' he said aloud, and kicked viciously at a stone, sending it spinning in front of him. 'And the likes of me for lying under them. One of these days I'll join the Society.'

Soon a smell of pigs and manure wafted on the warm summer afternoon in the direction of the three young men. They recognized it and knew they were nearly home, and in a while saw the cluster of cabins, windowless and without chimneys, their walls made of mud, the roofs thatched with sods of grass. Women, young and old, were gathered, gossiping around one of the cabin doors. Babies slept, smiled or cried in their mothers' arms, swarms of their brothers and sisters ran round playing, their bare feet coated with dung and dirt. Two black-and-white nanny goats surveyed the scene from on top of a drystone wall.

'That hoor of a big one ate the only shirt I had to my back this morning,' Johnny said, as they neared their cabin. Their mother's sow was stretched on the ground, six bonhams along her belly, suckling blissfully, eyes closed, lashes pale as their flesh. The brothers separated, Padraig making for his own house and Johnny heading to where the men, well away from the women, were gathered. Their crop of potatoes was long since planted, growing well, and needing little or no attention. They had all the time in the world to stand and talk.

Jamsie went into the cabin. It was dark and smoke-filled. His father was asleep by the fire, on a stool with his back propped against the wall. 'Which one of you is it?' he asked, opening his eyes.

' 'Tis me, Jamsie.'

'You're back from meeting the priest, so? I never thought I'd see the day.' He got up from the stool, and stretched. He was a big man, dark like his sons, but broader in the chest and shoulders. His belly hung over the trousers held up by a piece of straw rope. He yawned and scratched his stomach. 'No, be God, I did not. An O'Hara down to walk with the priest! You might as well have gone to walk with Kilgoran, sure what's the difference, aren't they both gentry?'

'This one's not like that.'

'Hasn't he a tall black hat, and a horse? Aren't them the hallmark of the gentry? And won't he be laying down the law?'

Jamsie laughed. 'Ah, he has the hat all right. But he refused the horse. He has rheumatics.'

'Well it won't get worse for lack of comfort,' his father said, and spat into the fire. 'Priests and landlords, they're all the same, hand me down that bottle like a good boy.'

Jamsie took from a niche in the wall a stone bottle and handed it to his father, who pulled the cork with his teeth, drank a long drink, then passed the bottle to his son. Jamsie drank a mouthful of the poteen, and returned it.

'That's a good drop. Poteen's the greatest comforter a man ever had. I'll have another sup, then take it out and hide it. Today might be the very day the polis would come looking.' He drank again.

'Padraig went to meet the priest,' Jamsie said.

His father paused in his swallowing. 'Sure nothing would surprise me about him. I sometimes wonder if he's a son of mine at all. Wasn't he ever an eejit, and worse since he married – a big soft eejit.'

'Johnny came as well,' Jamsie said as his father began to drink.

'*What?*'his father roared, spluttering so he coughed, and the pale spirit ran down his chest. 'Be Jasus, what's the world coming to?' He pushed Jamsie aside and went to the door. 'Maggie O'Hara,' he shouted, 'come in here till you hear about your son!'

In the Lodge at the gates of Kilgoran House, Eileen O'Donnell awaited the return of her daughter. Once she must have looked like Katy, but now her fair hair was faded, her skin bleached and withered looking. This evening she was very tired for all day she had run in and out, opening and closing the heavy iron gates as carriages with guests for the wedding arrived. Several times a pain had stabbed near her left breast. It was wind or her heart, she didn't know which. But in case it might be her heart, she had decided when Katy came home from work to send to Statia's for the medal – a sure cure for pains near the heart.

The small room in which she sat was very clean and neat. There were wool-embroidered cushions on the wooden settee, a white cloth on the table, in a glass-fronted, home-made cupboard, six china cups and saucers, pink-flowered and gold-edged. Folded in the corner by Eileen's chair awaiting the finishing touches was a quilt on which she had worked during the winter. That, the china, a pair of linen sheets, and a damask cloth folded away were for Katy when she married – all, except the quilt, gifts once given to Eileen from the House.

At this moment, although tired, she was very happy thinking how her only child, her ewe lamb was set up for life. In no time now she would be the wife of Peader, mistress of a comfortable home, daughter-in-law of a strong farmer with thirty acres, every foot of it good land. And no mother-in-law looking over her shoulder, for the woman, God rest her, was dead this long time.

'Amn't I the fortunate woman,' she said to herself, 'and wasn't all the care I lavished on Katy paid back treblefold. Where in Kilgoran, or in the whole of Ireland is there a girl as beautiful? Is it any wonder Peader loves her so much he forewent the dowry? Isn't she dowry enough for any man, God knows.'

She heard Katy's step, got up and opened the door. 'You're back sooner than I thought. Your father's still out – some guest to be picked up from Macroom. I declare to God the coach will collapse with all it's done today.'

'I have a headache,' Katy said. 'It was that bad, Mrs Cummings said I could come home and lay down.'

'Headaches are terrible things, but sure you can lie down when you come back. And maybe the fresh air will cure it. I want you to go down to Statia's for the blessed medal. Will you do that like a good girl?'

'Do I have to? My head is awful bad, every time I put a foot to the floor it throbs,' Katy lied, as she had to Mrs Cummings, for she wanted to go to bed and sleep, forget until morning that Jamsie had passed her, never even glanced at her. If she was lucky she might dream about him, sometimes she did. Lovely dreams which, when her mother called her in the mornings, she tried to recapture by closing her eyes and attempting to coax sleep back.

'I had a pain myself today, that's why I thought I'd get the medal. But sure if you're not well, astoir, I'll not ask you to shift. We'll stay by the fire, and have a grand chat. We could talk maybe about you and Peader putting in your banns.'   .

– In that case, Katy thought, I'd rather go to Statia's, otherwise my mother might pull out of me things I don't want her to know. She said her headache was better.

'Isn't that grand,' her mother said, pleased and unsuspecting. 'You'll go to Statia's so. Tell her I won't forget her. And don't delay, like a good girl.'

Katy took her time walking to Statia's, thinking as she went about Jamsie, wondering what he was doing, and wasn't it a pity his father wasn't a tenant of the Master's, for then she would have seen him tomorrow at the party after Miss Catherine's wedding. Statia was delighted at her unexpected arrival, and told her the priest had asked the men who had escorted him into the house. They had all, except Tim, and the O'Haras, come in. 'If only,' she said, 'Connolly knew where his tea and sugar went he'd be leaping.' Then she said how the priest, because of his complaint, wasn't able to take Michael Daly's mare, and she wondered how the unfortunate man would get round his parish.

'It's hard enough for the likes of me with the power of all my limbs. The poor man walks terrible slow. I wouldn't like to be dying and waiting for him. But tell me now what brings you here, I'd have thought you'd still be at it above in the House?'

Katy told her about the supposed headache, how it was better and she had come for the medal.

'You're in love,' Statia said, 'and impatient to be married. The blood running hot in you. It can give young girls terrible headaches. Ah, sure Peader is the fine man, and light about you, I'd say you'll be his wife in no time. I'll dance at your wedding, and ten months after, with God's holy help, bring your first child into the world.'

Katy blushed, and Statia laughed. 'Wait till you see I'm not right.'

'My mother says she'll give you something for yourself during the week.'

'She'll do no such thing,' Statia protested. 'I wouldn't take a ha'penny, you know that.'

'I do to be sure,' Katy lied, knowing well that the payment would be given and accepted, once enough refusals had been made by Statia: it was how things were done.

'I wouldn't mind one for myself as well,' Katy said before Statia went into the bedroom where she kept a supply of medals, scapulars, and Agnus Dei, each one of which she attested had the power to cure ailments, droughts, barrenness, and anything else that ailed man, beast or weather. – I'll give it to Miss Charlotte, tell her to keep it a secret, and teach her a Hail Mary to say each night, and kiss the medal. Then she'll have no more fear of the dark, Katy thought.

'Tell your mother it's blessed and lay next to the bones of a saint,' Statia said returning from the bedroom with two silver-coloured discs, wrapping the one for Katy's mother in a piece of flannel. 'It's the miraculous medal, if she pins it to her shift over her heart, she'll have no more trouble with the pains. Our Lady will see to that. I only have the one of them left, but this other is a grand medal altogether. Sleep with that under your pillow, and you'll get your heart's desire.'

Katy took the medals, thanked Statia, and decided she would delay giving the one to Miss Charlotte but place it instead beneath her own pillow.

'Don't go for a minute,' Statia pleaded when Katy prepared to leave, 'sure there's no hurry on you.' So they stayed talking until Katy, noticing that the light was beginning to go, and that her mother might be worrying, bid Statia goodnight, and began the journey home.

At about the same time Jamsie began walking down the bog road. He whistled as he went, and jingled the four coins in corduroy breeches, the price of two pints of porter. Carey might let him have a couple more on score. But in any case, he thought, being in the public house talking and listening to whoever was there would ease the torment of his mind that never stopped thinking about Katy O'Donnell.

He looked about him as he went. Over to the right, where the river was, the sun was down, bands of pink and dark grey clouds above the water. He stopped to watch a Johnny The Bog. 'Isn't it well for you,' he said aloud, gazing at the bird fishing. 'Not a worry in the world except where the next meal's coming from. Not like myself at all, always wondering and worrying if the woman I love gives me e'er a thought.' The bird waded gracefully through the water, rose and flew out of sight.

Jamsie continued towards a place in the road where a hawthorn hedge was growing, came to the end of it, there was a bend now to his way ahead, a curve ascending, the

56

hills beginning. In the fading light their edges were blurred and a bluish tinge was about them. Looking up at them, Jamsie thought how they seemed to fold one into the other, and how beautiful they were. Everything around him changed, softened by the twilight, even the stones of the walls separating the little fields softened and seemingly melted into each other. Then he spied a figure in a blue cloak and moved back to the hawthorn, and stepped into it. A nesting blackbird clacked its warning as he pushed into the hedge. He heard the footsteps coming nearer and his heart pounded with anticipation for he had recognized the cloaked woman – it was Katy O'Donnell, and she was coming his way.

Chapter Three

Katy was in no doubt that it was Jamsie. Who else in the parish walked as if he owned the world, who else was as tall? So great was her disappointment when he swivelled round and went back she almost cried out. She hurried on, hoping to catch a glimpse of him going down the road, turned the bend, and stared in amazement – he had vanished! But where, she wondered, and why had he not come on? Had he recognized her? Was she so unattractive to him he couldn't bear to meet her?

The blackbird in the hedge called. She knew the sound – it was alarmed. Then she saw the branches move slightly though there wasn't a breath of wind. So that's where he was. Hiding in the bush. Hoping she hadn't spotted him. She felt a sense of despair at this further proof of his lack of interest, and slowed her pace considering what to do. Should she let on she didn't know he was there? Or say with a bite in her voice, 'Were you afraid I'd eat you?' But she knew she would say no such thing. For wouldn't he have the great laugh, and little he'd care what she said.

There was another way home, she would take it, she thought as her feet dragged her to the place he was hidden, but her heart quickened, and as she neared the spot was certain he would hear the sigh of her breath and know the reason. She didn't think her legs could carry her one step further for the trembling and weakness in them. Then at the moment when fear and excitement nearly caused her to collapse, he stepped from the hedge, blocked her way, and with a smile that made the faint more imminent said, ' 'Tis a fine evening. You're out late.'

She took a deep breath, and another, before answering. 'You gave me a fright. I didn't know you were there. I wasn't expecting anyone.'

'Where's himself? What's come over him letting the girl he's to marry roam on her own?'

She laughed to hide her nervousness, and for the same reason began to talk quickly. 'I wasn't seeing him this evening, you know, because of working late, then I didn't, and my mother sent me to Statia's. She delayed me.' As she talked she was looking at him, noticing the length and blackness of his lashes. Talking too much, for her heart still pounded, explaining about the medal and its miraculous powers, she took it from her pocket and flannel wrapping, holding it towards him, hoping he wouldn't see how her hand shook.

'Isn't that the grand thing all the same?' he said, moving so close she felt his breath on her cheek as he bent to look. 'Imagine that now – no more pain in the chest!'

' 'Tis wonderful,' she agreed enthusiastically until she realized he was codding her. 'It is so,' she protested indignantly. 'Wasn't it blessed by a priest that's now a saint.'

'I wouldn't doubt that,' Jamsie said, attempting to be serious. But he could not resist adding, 'The same saint of a man blessed one Statia gave my mother for a different complaint entirely – I think she buys them by the score at the fair . . .' He put a hand lightly to her waist, steering her round a rut in the road, removing it once they were by. Her flesh tingled where his touch had been, and she wished the depression had gone on for ever.

He said no more for a while, and she searched for something to say, but could think of nothing except to admonish him for what she considered blasphemy. 'It's a sin to mock something blessed – a cause of confession.'

'Ah, sure isn't everything a cause of confession? Everything that's a bit of life, or love, or enjoyment. You wouldn't want to pay attention to all they tell you.'

And while Katy grappled with this new irreverence, he caught hold of her and kissed her. 'A mortal sin, and you to be married shortly and to my best friend,' he said when he let go her mouth, though he kept his arms around her.

'I'm not so sure that I am,' she said.

'Am what?'

'About to be married. I've changed my mind.'

'What made you do that? Isn't Peader a grand man, and will make a fine husband. What caused you to change your mind?'

'I took a liking to someone else,' she said looking away from him.

'Did you now?' He took a hand from her waist and turned her face back to his. 'I wonder who took your fancy, and when?'

– Should I tell him, Katy wondered, as his hand was replaced on her back, his fingers caressing her spine. I won't, she decided, not yet anyway.

'Oh, so it's a secret.' He let go of her. Her back felt naked

60

and cold without his touch. They began to walk on. The hedge was thick with white blossom, the smell of it sweet and heavy. Jamsie began to pull handfuls of it, eating it. 'Bread and cheese,' he said.

'That's unlucky,' Katy told him.

'It's not,' he contradicted. 'They don't mind a man eating it. They're decent enough about a man's needs. It's bringing it indoors for useless decoration they don't like. Here, have a bit.'

She refused, afraid, not sure if he spoke the truth: the little people might well object to humans eating the May flower.

'Tell me now, does Peader know about your secret?'

'He does not. Not yet.'

'When will you tell him, so.'

'Tomorrow, tomorrow at the party, maybe.'

'It wouldn't do to let him go on living in hopes. Living in hopes is a terrible thing.'

Was he trying to tell her something, Katy pondered. Was he living in hopes of her? Was that what he was saying, or just making a remark? She cursed herself for a fool, for not, while he was holding her, having put her arms round his neck and said, 'I love you, Jamsie O'Hara.' The moment had passed, she couldn't say it now.

'I'll see you again, so,' he said as they neared the Lodge. She wasn't sure if it was a question, and as ambiguously answered, 'Yes.' Then she asked, 'Would you walk no further till I go in? My mother might be watching, and think it queer that I was with a man.'

'A woman given to pains in the chest, and not partial to the O'Haras would surely think so. Goodnight then.'

'Goodnight,' she hesitated, thinking he might kiss her again. When he did not she went on quickly till the road curved and she was out of sight. She touched her lips: they felt hot, swollen. 'Oh Jamsie, Jamsie!' she said to herself. 'I love you. I could die in your arms with you kissing me, and not mind at all. I'll never marry Peader now, not even if you never asked to court me. Not if I stayed an old maid till the end of my days. I'd rather sit by the fire remembering the way it was, how you held me, the kiss you gave me. Remember forever and ever, than be another man's wife.'

She began to skip along, full of joy at the thought of their meeting, the memory of him holding her, of the body he had pressed against hers. 'I love you, I love you,' she repeated aloud, stretching out her arms, spinning round in the road, until a thought came into her head that was beginning to go dizzy – if her mother was by the gate she would think her mad, bewitched by the fairies, deranged by the May moon. Stopping the spinning she walked slowly home, thinking – I am, too, stone mad. Why didn't I tell him my secret instead of shouting it to the trees and the moon, and any creature listening? The joy she had recently felt ebbed and doubts took its place. Maybe the kiss meant nothing, no more than his passing remark, 'I'll see you again, so.' Wasn't it what everyone said? By the time she had entered the Lodge she was dejected.

She woke in low spirits the following morning, and told herself as she got ready for work, that she was no further ahead than the day before. But as she walked up the tree-lined drive to the House, and heard the quarrelling rooks, began to find consolation in the memory of Jamsie's kiss, and the possibility that his parting remark might have been more than a casual one. Maybe he would try to see her again.

Now she was nearing the beginning of the landscaped sward ascending to the steps and terraces of Kilgoran House. The drive divided, each half-circle sweeping round the green to come together beneath the flight of steps leading up to the front entrance. Katy followed one of the halves, stopping a little along, looking to her left where in the horse park Paudeen and a group of men were erecting a large tent. She continued, looking up at the sky, hoping the fine weather wouldn't break: rain at a wedding was unlucky, and the tenants' party would be destroyed, everyone packed into the tent on top of the refreshments, and no room to dance. 'Ah! anyway,' she said to herself, 'sure what do I care about the party. Jamsie won't be there.' She went on round the back of the House where the entrance to the basement kitchens was.

Later in the morning, Mrs Cummings marshalled the servants and led them upstairs into the Great Hall. Here they waited to see Miss Catherine before she left to be married. Katy as she stood in line looked round the room at the arrangements of yellow and white flowers. How clever Miss Catherine was with flowers. The mass of bloom in the vast fireplace looked as if it were growing there and not standing in the biggest stone jar, for she had draped ferns and green stuff around it. All sorts of flowers she noticed, pale lemon early roses, tulips white and yellow, primroses, wallflowers, and white candytufts. There were bowls, she saw, and ewers, vases and jugs on the dark carved chests, and black bog oak furniture. She thought they looked gorgeous and made the Great Hall that had a cold dreary feeling about it seem warm and bright.

Her eyes turned from the floral arrangements to the furnishing of the Hall itself, the suits of armour, shields and swords on the walls, faded tapestries hanging beside them, she glanced down at the flagged floor, then up at the arched beams, and thought how old the room was, knowing it was from the time of the King who gave the Master the land – the one who brought the Protestant religion.

Then her glance went to the long carved mahogany table on which some of Catherine's wedding presents were displayed. She saw in front the silver tea and coffee service with the three-legged sugar bowls given by the servants and better-off tenants. Behind the service, the drinking cups, silver mounted, and knives and forks from officers in the Captain's regiment – All silver, she thought, the cruets and salvers, and dish rings. Irish silver, too, so Mrs Cummings said. Wasn't Miss Catherine lucky, all them lovely things, and in a minute going out to marry the man she loved. If only it was me, me going out to marry Jamsie. I wouldn't care if I didn't have a bed to lie on.

The intake of everyone's breath made Katy look to the stairs leading from the galleried end of the room. Miss Catherine she saw standing at the top, and waiting at the bottom Lord Kilgoran who must have entered while she was looking at the presents. 'Oh! Miss,' she involuntarily gasped, too enchanted by the vision of white gleaming satin and lace beginning to descend to hear Mrs Cummings' hiss of admonition. Open-mouthed she stared at the white satin gown, the shimmer of it rippling beneath the net over-dress, at the satin slippers pearl-encrusted, the train of gown and veil sliding in folds down the stairs after Catherine.

Hannah, standing next to Katy, squeezed her arm and whispered, 'Look at that for lace, Brussels, the real thing. It was her mother's and hers before her. There's a veil for you, and a beauty of a wreath, look at the orange blossoms.'

The bridesmaids, Olivia and Charlotte, wore simpler versions of Catherine's gown and Olivia carried a white satin swansdown trimmed cape for the bride in case the day became cooler. 'God bless you, Miss,' Hannah said, as, on her father's arm, Catherine made her way through the Hall.

'God bless you,' the assembled servants echoed, looking after her, following the wedding group out to where the carriages were waiting. All marvelled at the bride's beauty, the loveliness of Olivia and Charlotte, and remarked on how handsome the Master was in his blue dress suit with gilt buttons, the grand white waistcoat. He was a picture, they said, a gentleman, and a proud father.

They waved and called blessings after the carriages before returning for final touches to the wedding breakfast. Katy's head was full of dreams about Jamsie, and white wedding dresses, occasionally troubled by the thought that at the tenants' party Peader would bring up talk of putting in the banns, and she would have to tell him she could not marry him.

On the route to the church, villagers waved and called good wishes, remarking to each other that it was only like yesterday Miss Catherine was a child passing in the cart.

They invoked blessings on her and the Captain, wished them a long happy life, and many fine children. One woman was saying to her neighbour, 'Wouldn't it be grand to see them married?'

'Yerra, that's wishful thinking. Sure we wouldn't be asked, and couldn't go if we were. One foot in a Protestant church and you'd be halfway to hell,' the neighbour replied.

In the bridal carriage Lord Kilgoran patted his daughter's hand. 'Don't be nervous, darling, the practice was perfect,' he said reassuringly.

Dear, sweet Papa, Catherine thought, covering his hand with hers. He refers to the ceremony. Afraid I shall trip or stammer – some such thing. How could he know my real fears? How I dread this evening when Edward and I reach Kerry, when we retire and are alone.

Olivia in the following coach thought about Peter Melrose. Last night he had kissed her, she was sure he was smitten. And this morning he gave her such an adoring look at breakfast. She wished he were taller. But still, one couldn't have everything, and he was handsome in a boyish way. Not unlike Charles actually, except that his mouth wasn't as full. She was glad about that. Charles's lips were like a woman's.

In Kilgoran church, where generations of the family had worshipped, been baptised, married, and had their deaths commemorated, Captain Edward Synge waited for his bride. Beside him in the front pew on the right-hand side of the aisle knelt a brother officer, his groomsman. Both men wore ceremonial uniform, scarlet tunics laced with silver braid, silver stripes along the seam of tight-

66

fitting dark blue trousers, epaulettes of fine chain mail rippling like fish scales on their shoulders. Captain Synge's hair was dark brown, straight, his face long and narrow, his nose aquiline, his eyes as deep and serious-looking as those of the girl he was soon to marry.

The pews were packed tightly, more people present for this occasion than any other in living memory. Relations and guests seated according to degree of kinship and rank. Brass commemorative tablets, candlesticks, an eagle on the lectern gleamed from recent assiduous polishing. The air was redolent of the flowers with which Catherine, assisted by the vicar's wife, had filled it.

Occasionally while he waited for his bride, Edward nervously touched his tunic, and once appeared to ask a question of his groomsman, who nodded affirmatively, indicating his pocket and smiling. In the last pew on the right-hand side knelt eight officers from the Captain's regiment attired in the same splendid uniform; on the floor in front of them their dress swords with which they would form the triumphal arch for the bride and groom. At the lychgate an usher watched for sight of the bridal carriage. On its appearance he signalled a man by the church door who passed on the message.

The minister's wife, seated at the organ, played a Bach fugue, her eyes straying from the keyboard for indication that the bride was about to enter. Then began the wedding march and the heads of the congregation turned to watch Catherine, on the arm of her father, walk up the aisle.

Edward, standing before the altar, turned too and saw the tall figure in shimmering satin and cascading lace, the face he so loved obscured beneath the veil, and prayed he should be worthy of her. Lord Kilgoran's genial face and shining silver hair belied the sadness he felt as he prepared to hand this most beloved daughter to another man. The music stopped, Catherine stood beside Edward. Olivia, Charlotte and the groomsman took up their positions. Olivia stepped forward to receive Catherine's bouquet of lemon and white flowers, passed it to Charlotte, then lifted the bride's veil to reveal in all its sweet gravity her sister's face. The minister began their marriage service.

The tenants and servants lined up, this time outside the House to watch Catherine and her husband leave in the Master's best coach, flanked by two outriders, for the journey to Dargle House. Family, tenants, servants and guests waved and called after the departing carriage. Then it was time for Lord Kilgoran to declare open the retainers' party. Keeping a respectful distance they followed him to the horse park and the big tent where barrels of ale and porter, a side of beef, bread and butter, and cordials were arranged. Lord Kilgoran made a speech, thanked everyone for their help in making it such a wonderful day, a memorable occasion. Drinks were served, a toast drunk to the newly-weds, and the party got under way. For a while Lord Kilgoran, Olivia, Charles and guests mingled with the villagers; making polite conversation, inquiring about crops, old parents' health, and commenting on how kind the weather had been. Then, as was the custom, bidding them goodnight, and returning to the House.

Eileen O'Donnell, seated near the tent with Statia and Hannah, said it had been a grand day, and Statia, into her second glass of porter, said it would be a grand night as well. Eileen looked to where Katy and Peader stood, and thought what a lovely couple they made, and wondered if she would be a laughing stock for attempting to copy Miss Catherine's dress for her daughter's wedding. Regretfully deciding she would, she consoled herself with the surety that Katy would be a beautiful bride, was getting the finest man in Kilgoran with a good stone house and thirty acres.

Food and drink was passed round, games organized for the children. Then two fiddlers took up their stance. 'We'll put the banns in next week,' Peader said as the music began.

'I'm dying to dance,' Katy said catching hold of his sleeve, pulling him to where the dancers were collecting. Interpreting this as an expression of delighted agreement Peader allowed himself to be led. The warming-up music finished, the fiddlers played a jig. The dance began. Those not doing the jig gathered on the side and clapped in time to the music. Steps were danced, intricate movements to the centre and back performed. Passing Peader in the middle Katy whispered, 'Slip away with me, I've something to tell you.' He followed her from the dancers. Having decided there was no easy way to say it, as soon as they were out of earshot she told him, 'I can't marry you.'

'Don't be codding me,' he laughed and went to put an arm round her.

'No,' she replied, restraining him. 'I'm not codding you. I'm awful sorry, but I can't.'

'Move away,' he said, the colour draining from his face, 'everyone is watching us.'

Katy looked back, and saw her mother and Hannah smiling benevolently in their direction. They went over to the trees and Peader said, 'Ah, Katy, you're having me on. Sure we're getting married, it's arranged except for the banns.' His eyes pleaded, and she wished she could laugh and admit to the cod. He looked as if he might cry. She had only ever seen a man cry once, the father of a child at a funeral. It was a terrible sad thing to see a man cry. The sight of Peader's face almost made her change her mind. But the love she felt for Jamsie was stronger than her pity. The memory of her heart racing, pulses throbbing in parts of her body she had never seen, had no name for, parts that were sinful to dwell on, gave her the strength to say, 'I wouldn't want to hurt you for the world, and I'm sorry, but I can't marry you. I don't know how to say it better than that.' Her voice was full of genuine sorrow. She had never meant to cause him grief. He was kind and good. It pained her to see the dejection in his lovely green eyes that had always regarded her so tenderly.

'´Tis a whim come over you, that's all,' Peader said. 'Yesterday you loved me. Yesterday everything was all right.'

'But it wasn't. It wasn't this long time. I should have told you, but I didn't know how.'

'Why Katy? What's happened? Is there someone else? It couldn't alter just like that.'

'No,' she lied quickly. 'No one else.' Then she began to explain, hoping to lessen his hurt. 'Don't you see how it happened, Peader, how we thought we were in love? We were thrown together. My mother wanted you for

70

me. "He's for Katy," she would say to herself. "He's the best catch. Look at the stone house, the acres his father has."'

'That's not true. Your mother wouldn't say that.'

'How little you know her, she would so. Oh, she was cautious while your mother lived, knowing she'd expect a fine dowry. Fifty, or maybe a hundred pounds; cows or land in kind. And where would we get that? But the minute she died, my mother went to work. Getting the right side of your father, throwing us together. Inveigling you into the Lodge every five minutes, putting me before you. And you that broken up after your mother wasn't it only natural you'd look for love somewhere else? And me that flattered that the best-looking man in the parish was paying me attention I thought what I felt was love. Sure I knew no better.'

While she talked, Peader watched her face, listened enchanted to her voice, quiet-spoken, husky, so you had to lean close to hear every word. Saw the expressions on her face changing from minute to minute, and thought – I love her. I can't let her go. 'Katy,' he said, 'I love you. Maybe your mother did all them things, sure what matter, I'd have found you anyway. And so long as there's no one else I'll never lose you, I love you, and I'll be here, waiting, always . . .'

Katy was so moved by his words, and guilty at the deception she practised, her eyes filled with tears, and she whispered, 'I'm going back to the dancing, Peader Daly, or out of sorrow I'll be relenting, and that's no grounds for a marriage.'

'We'll go back so,' he agreed. 'But I won't take seriously

71

a word of your talk. Talk, sure that's all it is,' he said, attempting to be light-hearted.

They joined the dancers, stood in opposite lines waiting for the music. When it began, they stepped in to each other, stepped out again, danced facing each other, repeating the movements, the music quickening, feet matching the tempo, excited loud whooping from dancers and spectators.

Couples moved to the centre for the final burl. Peader and Katy placed a hand under each other's elbow, supporting the raised forearm, joined hands and began to spin. She gave herself to the wild music, the frantic twirling. Faster and faster Peader spun her. Her feet were leaving the ground, her head dizzy, faces, trees, the tent went out of focus, became distorted. Abruptly the fiddling stopped. Peader let go the hold on her elbow and hand, his arm encircled her, pulled her to him. She pulled away, closed tightly for a minute her eyes, opened them again, but the face did not go away. It was not dizziness making her see things – Jamsie was there in the trees, beckoning her. She ran from Peader to where Jamsie was, to the tree behind which he had stepped, hidden from anyone looking after her.

'I'm here,' he said when she got into the little wood. She went to him, he enfolded her. 'Katy, Katy, I couldn't wait. I had to see you. I love you.' He was kissing her, his arms straining her to him. She tasted drink on his mouth, it was a new taste, not unpleasant. Her blood raced. She burrowed closer to him, returning his kisses passionately, murmuring when, for brief seconds, his mouth released hers, 'Oh, Jamsie, Jamsie, my love.'

Peader waited for her return, vaguely wondering why she had chosen the trees and not the bushes where the other girls went. When she didn't come back he went after her, calling as he approached the trees, 'Katy, are you all right?' He heard movement, became alarmed. There was someone there. 'Katy!' he called again, then casting aside decorum went into the trees. Incredulously he saw two figures, Katy and a man – she was in the man's arms. 'Katy!' he ran towards her. The man let her go, turned. *Jamsie! It's not, it can't, he's not here, his father isn't a tenant.*

Jamsie began to walk towards him, staggering slightly, explaining.

'It's all right, Peader. Wait'll I tell you . . .'

Peader ran at him, swung his fist, Jamsie ducked.

'Ah, now, hold on. Wait . . . don't.'

Peader ignored his placating entreaties, hit him on the side of the head, and Jamsie began to fight back.

Dusk was falling. Lunging at one another, landing hard blows on face, head and body, the antagonists fought out through the trees into the clearing. Peader's fist caught Jamsie on the mouth, split his lip, and the blood poured from him. Katy screamed, half from fear, half from excited pride that two men were fighting for her. From all directions of the horse park, people came running. Word was shouted: 'There's a fight. Peader and Jamsie are pucking the daylights out of each other.' Everyone assuming, as Peader had, that Jamsie, drunk, uninvited, came upon Katy in the trees relieving herself, and made free.

'Go on, Peader,' the women shouted encouragingly. A few young men exhorted Jamsie to stick up for himself, and yelled at Peader to fight his match, couldn't he see Jamsie was stocious. 'Jesus, Mary and Joseph!' Eileen O'Donnell exclaimed, a hand going to her breast. 'It could be the cause of killing me. The cur! The dirty cur! My lovely daughter. Smather him, Peader.'

The fighters were tired, staggering, clinging to each other. But anger spurred Peader. Jamsie had taken liberties with Katy. Jamsie, his best friend! Drunk or sober there was no excuse. He drew away from Jamsie and punched him on the chin; Jamsie staggered, dropped as if felled.

Katy's piercing scream rang out silencing for a moment the excited crowd. 'You've killed him. You've killed Jamsie.' She ran and knelt beside him, cradling his head, crying, stroking his face, kissing him, repeating over and over, 'Jamsie, love, don't die on me.'

Peader stared in disbelief at the girl that not an hour since he had promised to love for the rest of his life, crooning over the bloodied, swollen face of the unconscious Jamsie. He felt a hand on his shoulder, and heard his father's quiet voice. 'We'll go home now.' He turned and left.

Another hand fell on Katy and dragged her up. 'You whipster!' her mother screamed, and hit her across the face. 'You've brought shame on your good name, and broke a decent man's heart. Get home. When I get you in I'll kill you. I'll dance on you.'

Katy tried to free herself from her mother's grip, imploring as she began to pull her away, 'Someone help Jamsie. He's dead. Peader killed him, he's dead.'

'He's far from dead,' Statia said and tipped her glass of

stout over his face. 'Look at that now, there's life in him.'
Jamsie stirred, sat up holding his head, looking round in
a dazed fashion, seeing Katy in her mother's hold, the
alarmed face of Hannah. He shook his head like a dog
shaking a wet pelt, black liquid trickled down his face. He
saw Statia's upturned glass, put out his tongue, caught
the drops of stout, and grinned at her.

'Be God, Statia, that was a terrible waste of good drink.'

'It was so,' she agreed, grinning back.

'Oh Jamsie! Are you all right?' Katy asked, wriggling in
her mother's hand like a caught fish.

'I am. I'm all right, Katy,' he said, and called after her,
'I'll see you again, so.'

Never loosening her hold for an instant, Katy's mother
berated her all the way home, and once in the Lodge gave
full vent to her anger, shame, and bitter disappointment.
'There's bad blood in you. 'Twasn't from me you sucked
it – you're an O'Donnell all right. I'll kill you so I will.
Letting one of them O'Haras lay a finger on you! Losing
a good man, a life where you'd never know want – and
for Jamsie O'Hara!'

'I love him,' Katy said, for the first time in her life daring
to defy her mother.

Taken aback by this new departure her mother was
momentarily silenced, then said, 'Love! Well, we'll soon
see about that. First thing in the morning I'm up to the
priest. I'll have your name called from the altar, we'll see
about love after that. When your father hears tell, he'll lay
Jamsie O'Hara low. Oh! If only he wasn't driving Miss
Catherine to Kerry he'd fix him.'

Despite being frightened by her mother's threat to tell

the priest, worry about Jamsie's injury, and a sneaking feeling of shame that he hadn't won the fight, Katy could not but smile at the thought of her little mild-mannered father laying anyone low.

'You'll laugh the other side of your face on Sunday at Mass. Get to bed now before I lose myself and do something I regret,' her mother ordered; and Katy went.

The master bedroom in Dargle House faced a wild beautiful bay; nothing but seabirds, the sun, and the moon by night overlooked the chamber, so only when fierce Atlantic winds blew did servants draw the curtains. On Catherine and Edward's wedding night, the air was balmy, the moon shining, bathing the room, the great four-poster bed and the two figures in pale light. Languorously Catherine lay, her hair spread over the silk, lace-trimmed pillow, looking with wonder at the face of her husband bent above her. Tenderly her fingers caressed his face, lingered, tracing his lips.

'I was so frightened,' she said. 'For months, since we became engaged, filled with dread about tonight.' She sighed contentedly. 'And all the time there was no need, no need at all. I never imagined ... I never knew it could be so.'

'Neither did I,' Edward said.

'Didn't you, darling? But I thought all men did.'

'I think most do, or say they do.'

'Then I'm glad you never did – it makes it even more beautiful. Lie beside me.'

He lay down, put an arm under her and arranged her head on his shoulder. She began to talk. 'How marvellous it is that two strangers, because actually we were strangers, not family or anything, once they are married know one another so intimately.'

'I love you,' Edward said, his hand caressing her breast, turning her to him, his mouth silencing hers. Eagerly she responded, and when their love-making was done, and once more she lay with her head on his shoulder, whispered, 'You'll never take a mistress, will you?'

'Never,' he promised.

The moon sailed by, the room darkened and the new lovers slept.

'Take this bit of chicken, I've diced it, and there's a junket, take them to the Widow Murphy's,' Hannah told Katy the morning after the wedding. She was glad of an excuse to get out of the kitchen, away from the young servants inviting confidences of last night's happenings, and Hannah's almost total disapproving silence.

Walking to the cottage where the old woman lived, she wondered how Jamsie was this morning, was his lip sore, and was he thinking about her? Her mother had said not one word this morning until she was leaving for work, when she called after her, 'I'm up now to see the priest, I'll put a stop to your gallop.'

Statia, who was in her field earthing up potatoes, called to her as she neared the plot, 'How are you this morning after all the excitement?'

'All right,' Katy replied.

'You don't look it. And how's your mother, wasn't it as well she had the medal pinned to her shift – you could have been the cause of killing her.'

Katy shrugged and said nothing. Statia put down the spade and asked what was in the basket.

'Food after the wedding for the Widow Murphy.'

'The poor creature, what would she do without the Master's charity, and her neighbours? Out long ago, another landlord would have put her. 'Tis two years since her sons went to America with promises galore, and not tale nor tidings of them since.'

'Hannah says maybe they died on the way.'

'More likely they forgot they ever had a mother,' Statia replied dryly.

'I'll have to be going, there's oceans to do above,' Katy said – then asked about Jamsie. 'What way was he after I left? Was he hurt bad?'

'His face only destroyed.'

'Oh!' Katy gasped. 'Will he be marked?'

'Black and blue round the gills, no more. I plastered him with cobwebs to staunch the blood and stop the poison. He'll do.' Statia went back to the potatoes and Katy on to the Widow Murphy's.

The cottage was at the bottom of a sloping boreen with well-grown hedges either side. Katy noticed how the air was warmer along the track, and knew the house was sheltered except when the wind was fierce. – It's a long time, she thought looking at its peeling, yellowish walls, since that saw a coat of whitewash or anyone took a rag to the windows. She peered in through the dirt and spiders' webs: the old woman was sitting by the fire. By the door, she called to her, 'It's only me, Katy, I brought you something lovely.'

The widow woman looked round, and stared at her vacuously.

'Don't you know who it is?' Katy spoke loudly, somehow hoping her raised voice might register, bring a light of recognition to the empty eyes. When it did not, she spoke in her normal tone, telling the woman about the chicken, putting down her basket, stroking the brown-spotted hand, her fingers recoiling as they touched the raised, dark-blue veins.

She fed the woman the chicken and watched her chew with relish, swallow and reopen her toothless mouth. Afterwards, spoon-feeding the junket, having to prise the spoon from lips fastened to it like an infant clamped on the nipple. While she rinsed the plate, holding it above the slop bucket, pouring water from the kettle over it, the widow began to talk. 'You're a very bold girl. I called you this long time. You never came.' Then the voice pleaded, 'Ah, don't go. Don't leave me. Not the two of you. Don't go away over the sea. Sure I'll never see you again. Don't go to America.'

'I'm going now,' Katy said. The woman did not answer her. Outside she saw the two fields, not planted. Two good fields. It was a lovely cottage. — Wouldn't it be a grand place for a young couple like me and Jamsie if we could get married. I'd clean it and sweep it. I'd make a garden, and Jamsie would put in potatoes and barley. It would be a lovely place to live, we'd be happy in it till the day we died.

She continued to day-dream about her future and Jamsie's on the way back to the House. Then began to wonder if her mother had yet been to see Father Bolger, and how would she live through Sunday when her name was called from the altar.

Chapter Four

The congregation made with their thumbs the Sign of the Cross on brow, lips and breast: they believed, proclaimed, and loved. The priest began to read the gospel. Katy, standing beside her mother, felt weak with fright. When the gospel was read and preached she would be denounced from the altar.

Her name might not be mentioned, but everyone would know it was her the priest spoke about. A girl who had deceitfully led a man to believe she would marry him, while all the time she was ensnaring and tempting another man. A man who was the childhood friend of the other. With the snare of her body she had enticed two decent men to fight like wild animals. Oh, she could imagine every word. It wasn't two years since she had heard such preaching, and seen the girl it was meant for nearly die of shame when every head turned to look at her.

She was sure she would faint, or run out. Run and keep running, never cross the chapel door again. Peader was over the way from her, next to his father, not beside Jamsie the way he used to sit. Jamsie was at the back. She had glanced at him when she came in. His lip was swollen and his eye black. He smiled at her, and it gave her some comfort to know he was there. For a moment when the priest began interpreting the gospel, she let herself imagine that at the first word spoken against her he would storm up the aisle and rescue her. But imagination she knew was all it was, for hands would reach to stop him before he was halfway there.

The priest was concluding his sermon. Sweat trickled between her breasts, her heart beat quickly – now, he would call her. In one minute she would be shamed. All that was beautiful about her love for Jamsie would be ridiculed, made to sound dirty. Made to sound as if she had played a game between the two men, and it wasn't like that at all. She had never meant Peader to find her in Jamsie's arms. She would have had it different. Had Peader reconciled to losing her before Jamsie was mentioned.

Terrified she heard the priest clear his throat: now he was beginning.

'My Dear People, since arriving on Thursday I've met most of you, and a grand welcome you gave me. I was quite overcome with your generosity, and I thank each and every one of you for your gifts. I know the sacrifice the giving of many entailed. Some I was unable to accept, but let it never be thought they were appreciated one bit less. May God bless you for your charity. He has called me to minister to you, pray for me that I may succeed ...'

He paused, shifted his position slightly, and massaged one hand in the other. To herself Katy said – when he starts again it'll be about me. So tense was she her breath was short.

'I wanted to mention something else. Something that concerns everyone here ... Eight years ago Daniel

O'Connell won his fight for Catholic Emancipation. Don't let time dim the memory of his struggle, or take for granted the liberties we now enjoy. They were taken from us once before; until we have a parliament of our own they could be snatched again. Demonstrate your faith in the Liberator, your Counsellor, by remaining members of the Association, don't neglect your penny a month subscription. This evening at five o'clock there'll be a meeting in the presbytery to discuss the collecting of it. May God bless you.' He made the Sign of the Cross, returned to the altar and the murmuring of Latin began again.

Katy let out her breath, stared ahead, not daring to glance at her mother. Dizzy with relief she said prayer after prayer of thanksgiving. Mass ended, the congregation – once the priest departed – began to leave. Mrs O'Donnell indicated to Katy to stay where she was, saying in a low voice, 'I want no one gawping at me, let them go.'

When eventually they came out only one old woman was in the chapel yard talking to the priest. He motioned to Katy and her mother not to leave, and they waited. The weather had changed since yesterday, it was cold and blustery, the wind whipping Father Bolger's vestments round him. In the sky clouds raced, it looked as though it would rain.

'Come to the house,' he said, when the old woman went. Mary Doyle's eyes glinted with curiosity as they passed the kitchen where she was slicing bacon. She nodded and they followed Father Bolger into the parlour. Katy looked about at the books, and the priest's breviary open on the table, coloured ribbons down the centre. On the wall was a crucifix, and on a shelf another cross, small and roughly carved, no figure on it. It was a penal cross made in the time when there were few chapels in the land, when Mass was said in fields and hidey-holes, stones used for altars and men on the look-out for soldiers.

'Sit down,' the priest invited, indicating the chairs. They sat and he did the same. For a minute he said nothing, and Katy thought that whatever his reasons for not calling her, her mother would not question them, nor would he be likely to give an explanation.

'Now then,' he began, 'wasn't it a very foolish thing you did last night?'

She did not answer.

'Come on now,' his voice was brusque. 'Your mother tells me you had plenty to say to her. Let's hear it.'

'I love Jamsie O'Hara,' she mumbled.

'Love me eye!' her mother said.

'That'll do,' the priest warned. 'Go on, child.'

'Well, the way it is, Father, Peader was put before me this long time. I was going to marry him one day. It was just something ... you know ... something that was bound to happen, I never gave it much thought. Then one day it was as if I saw Jamsie for the first time and knew I couldn't marry no one else.'

'Wasn't that a very hasty decision?'

'That's the way it was, Father. It came into my mind.'

The wild handsome Jamsie, he thought, while she spoke. The one who hit the teacher. 'Things come into your mind. Sometimes you have to blot them out. It wouldn't do at all to follow every inclination that comes into your mind. You must know that surely?'

Not giving Katy time to answer, her mother pleaded,

'You'll make her see sense, won't you, Father? Don't let her throw herself away on an O'Hara.'

Katy didn't know how to argue with him. Bad things you had to put out of your mind. But loving Jamsie wasn't bad. She remained silent.

'You went a cruel way about treating Peader. Don't you think it was a cruel thing to do?'

'I never meant it to be like that.' She began to cry. 'Honest to God I didn't – it just happened.'

'Ah, now, come on, you have a will of your own. If you let things just happen you're playing into the hands of the devil. They're not just happening as you say, he's making them come about, and you're aiding and abetting him. Isn't that so? Your mother only has your interest at heart. She wanted you to marry a good man. A man that could look after you.'

'Jamsie's good, Father,' she said.

'I'm sure he is. But for the time being you're to put him out of your mind. Pray to the Blessed Virgin to help you. Now like a good girl, you'll promise me that. No more letting things into your mind that shouldn't be there and you'll not attempt to see Jamsie. Will you do that?'

No, I won't do any such thing, Katy thought, but didn't have the courage to say so.

'Will you?' the priest insisted.

Her 'yes' was hardly audible. But he accepted it. It was unwillingly given, he knew. At the moment she believed she loved Jamsie, and maybe she did. But a breathing space would do her no harm. Let them all cool down. Let her stay from him. He'd talk to Peader, see how he felt. 'Listen,' he said, addressing them both. 'I'll have a word with Peader and his father. Things could be patched up I don't doubt. But only on condition you keep your promise, Katy.'

She heard her mother's sigh of relief. She looked at the priest, he was smiling at her, thinking how everything was grand. Not knowing she was lying, had no intention of putting Jamsie out of her mind, and if there was a way of seeing him, she would jump at the chance. God forgive me, she said to herself, he can patch up anything he likes, but I'll never marry Peader.

'Well, that's that,' Father Bolger said, rising. 'I won't keep you any longer. I'll come and see you after I've spoken to the Dalys.'

'God bless you, Father, and thanks very much. I'll see she doesn't set eyes on him again.'

'Goodbye, Father,' Katy said.

When they were gone he went in for his dinner. Mary had boiled the potatoes and cabbage in the bacon water the way he liked them. – Somehow, he thought, as he began to eat, I don't think much of your chances, Peader.

During the week he called at the Lodge. Katy told him truthfully she had not seen Jamsie, neglecting to add, 'A chance would be a fine thing, my mother never lets me out of her sight when I come in from work.'

'Good girl,' the priest said, encouragingly.

'Did you have a word with Peader, Father?' Mrs O'Donnell inquired.

'You might say I tried. But the way it is, his pride took a great blow. I'd say it would take a while to heal. He'll want a bit more time, his father as well. We'll leave them alone for a week or two.'

'Whatever you say. The poor unfortunates, I can understand their feelings, though not that they pass me. Sure what happened wasn't my wish.'

'The Dalys are a proud lot, that's all it is.' He was telling her the truth, or as much as he thought necessary. He couldn't dash her hopes completely, tell her what Peader had said. *I don't want to talk about it, Father, never.*

Earlier that morning Charlotte had seen her father's agent going to the library carrying the account books. Later, in the kitchen, she remarked that it was a strange thing.

'Not a bit, the Master has a cold, the poor man is choking, he couldn't be traipsing to the estate office.'

Charlotte accepted the explanation, and listened while Hannah lamented to another servant that the new priest was crippled, could neither walk nor ride. She had visions of him in great pain, curled up, wriggling across the floor as once in Cork she had seen a beggar squirm across the pavement. She was sure Papa didn't know. Papa helped anyone who was ill, she must tell him. But not while the agent was there, Papa didn't like being interrupted. Soon she heard Hannah remark that the agent was leaving without the books, and that it was a shame when the poor Master should be in bed with his cold.

'I shall go now, Hannah.'

'Do then, but if you're going out put something on, May is a treacherous month,' Hannah called after her.

Charlotte climbed the stairs, thinking that Papa was

sure to be interested in her news. And as Olivia and Charles were riding no one else was likely to come. She would have him to herself. They could talk, he might take her on his lap. She would like that. But Papa seldom did any more. Sometimes she felt he forgot all about her. But of course he was always busy, or angry and quarrelling with Charles. Charles was horrid. Even Hannah who liked everyone didn't like Charles. Once she heard her call him a young pup, and say his drinking would ruin Kilgoran.

She left the kitchen stairs, went along a passage, through another door and into the main part of the house. At the library door she hesitated before knocking, then did. There was no response, so she quietly opened the door and went in. She noticed the funny smell in the room, it tickled her nose as it always did. Hannah said it was dust from the Master not letting anyone disturb his papers or run a cloth over the books.

On tiptoe she approached the desk, hoping she wouldn't sneeze and spoil the surprise for Papa who had his head bent over the accounts.

'Do you know, Papa, Hannah says the priest cannot walk nor ride. Isn't that dreadful?'

He did not appear to hear, seemed lost in concentration on the ledgers before him. Charlotte quietly moved to stand behind him, looking over his shoulder at the accounts. She read across the headings: *Tenants. Arrears. Half-Year's Rent, due 1st May 1837. Half-Year's Rent, due 1st November 1837. Rent & Arrears. Rent & Arrears Received. Arrears due.* She recognized the names of tenants, people she knew living in the cottages, but the figures were a jumble. – Poor Papa, how difficult it all looks, she thought, perhaps I should not disturb him, sums are very hard. She began to move away, not aware that her father's mind was far from figures, that he was thinking about Catherine.

Pondering how much he missed her, how lonely the house was without her: wondering if every father felt so when another man took their daughter. His lovely sweet Catherine with whom he had been so in accord that they sometimes guessed each other's thoughts, often at the same moment saying the same thing. It was uncanny. With what frequency she had asked his opinions, quoted them. In future she would seek Edward's, use his name to lend weight to her arguments and discussions. – I'm suffering from the green-eyed monster, I'm a . . . The thought was not complete when he became aware of a presence behind him. Turning, he saw Charlotte.

'Good heavens, child! Where did you come from?'

'I was here for a long time, Papa.'

'And I didn't notice you! I'm sorry. Did you want something?'

'Only to tell you about the new priest. Did you know he cannot walk, nor ride either, Hannah says.'

'Charlotte, that is nonsense! You've been listening to the servants' gossip. I've told you, you mustn't do that. And certainly you mustn't repeat it.'

'Yes, Papa,' Charlotte replied meekly.

'You understand, otherwise I shall forbid you the kitchen.'

'Of course, Papa. I promise.'

'Very well, dear, then run along now.'

She came to him and he kissed her cheek perfunctorily,

thinking when she was gone that really Olivia must take more interest in her. She was a dear, sweet child, lonely no doubt with such an age gap between her and Olivia. He had to rack his brains to remember exactly how big it was. Eight years, he said to himself, is it really that much? How the years flew, ten since Charlotte was born, and his beloved Julia died. He remembered how disconcerted they had both been at the prospect of a baby so late in their lives, then how secretly proud – it quite rejuvenated them. – Oh my darling Julia, little did we know that was our last summer. What a joy you were, how smooth you made my life. What a wonderful mother you were. How cross you would be at my neglect of Charlotte, how sad that your adored Charles behaves in such a way. And how you would chide me now. 'David,' you would say with mock asperity, 'do stop moping and do something positive instead. You gloomy old thing, put right the things that worry or sadden you.'

And, of course, she would be right. Positive action, that was the remedy. He began to think of ways to improve Charlotte's life. Olivia must be made aware she had a duty to her, encourage her to ride. He must engage a new governess – keep the child occupied – she spent too much time in the kitchen. How woebegone she had looked when he admonished her. But it wouldn't do to have her repeating kitchen gossip. He continued to make resolutions as to how he might enhance her life, in the middle of which he vaguely wondered what she did with herself all day. He must find out. Must do something to take the waif-like look from her remarkable eyes.

Then there was Catherine – she was happy, had a

wonderful husband. He would cease to mope about her. England wasn't at the ends of the earth – he would visit her, she would return for holidays. He rose from the desk, went to the window and gazed out over the park. – What a beautiful place it is, he thought. How I love it. He saw in the distance Charles and Olivia riding. – She rides well. She does everything well, yet gives the impression of being helpless, and how self-sufficient she really is. Her mind quite set on marrying young Melrose. Determined to leave Ireland for which she had no liking.

The riders went on out of his sight. He continued to admire the view. The greenness of it all, surely there could be no other country so verdant. The soft, fine rain that fell so frequently was a little price to pay for such lushness. Then gloom once more penetrated his musings, and his mind returned to the accounts. How Kilgoran swallowed up money. What an extravagant lot they were. Bills, always bills. Rents still owing from the November gale, more arrears incurred since this one just gone. Mrs Cummings' account up to August last year – six hundred pounds. Donations to the fever hospital. The cost of three coffins and burials – couldn't have tenants buried as paupers. Monies for coals and apothecaries. Twenty-two pounds for coals. An exorbitant amount. Yet, he sadly reflected, the cost of tea, sugar, veal, whiskey, all the sundries was as nothing to the debts Charles was running up; the notes he was required to buy back from moneylenders. Sowing wild oats was one thing, all young men did that, but squandering the family fortune another. If the fellow did not change his ways he would ruin them.

He returned to his desk, began perusing the columns of

figures, then suddenly exclaimed, 'My God! I meant to send a carriage. I made a note, I'm sure I did.' He reached for his diary, turned back the pages to 20 May. *Catherine's wedding* was printed in large letters. 'The day before,' he said aloud and went back a page. There in his normal hand was written *Father Bolger arriving, send a conveyance.* 'And I didn't, forgot all about it. It was some garbled version of that Charlotte would have heard. The servants complaining the priest had to walk, didn't get a ride, something like that. The fellow must have a horse by this time. Daly would have seen to that as was the custom. Still, perhaps it would be wise to have Hannah come and explain exactly what has been said. No smoke without fire and all that.' He went to the fireplace and tugged the bell-pull and sent for Hannah. She explained about Father Bolger's infirmity and refusal of Michael's horse. After thanking and dismissing her, he hurried to the carriage house.

Katy's father, Seamus, and a groom were leisurely polishing harnesses. They jumped up when Lord Kilgoran came in.

'I want something for the priest, something he won't have difficulty getting in and out of.'

'Yes, Sir,' the men said, and accompanied him along the row of coaches, dog-carts and high-sided gigs.

'That one, I think.' He indicated a small trap. 'It seems the right size, the step not too high.'

'Not too high at all, Sir, he'd have no trouble mounting that.'

'We'll want a suitable pony.'

'What about the black one?' O'Donnell suggested.

'No, not her,' the groom said. 'That one, given half a chance, takes her head, and sure with the way Father Bolger's hands are he couldn't hold her.'

'The grey one so, I'd say,' O'Donnell proposed.

'Would you agree with that?'

'I would, Sir, the grey one's a lamb,' the groom said.

'Very well then, arrange to have them sent up immediately.'

'For me?' Father Bolger stared in astonishment at the highly polished black trap and silver-grey pony. He walked round it exclaiming delightedly, 'What a grand yoke! Look at that now! Look at the variegations on it!' and tracing the fine red lines bordering the brim. 'Look at the lamps! I'll be seen a mile off at night.' He opened the door and ran his hand over the black-buttoned leather upholstery.

'Let's see you get in and step down, Father,' the groom said.

With little difficulty he got up, sat for a moment, his face wreathed in smiles, then descended. 'I'm speechless,' he said, and remained so for a moment before adding, 'May God bless his Lordship, he's been the answer to my prayers. Give him my heartfelt thanks, and tell him I'll pay my respects when it's convenient for him.'

'Will I undo him?' the groom asked, nodding in the direction of the pony.

'You'll do no such thing! Him and me are going to get acquainted. We'll step out in style, and then I'll unharness him myself, thanks all the same.'

The groom and Seamus, as delighted as the priest, bid

him goodbye. When they were gone he talked to the pony, fondled it, stroking the silver hide, letting it nuzzle him. 'I'll call you Acushla. Acushla, that's who you will be. And isn't it a fitting title – the heart's blood, the pulse without which I couldn't minister to the parish.'

'Katy! Commere, Katy!'

Katy, walking down the drive from work, saw Maura, a scullery maid who lived up on the bog, running after her. She slowed to let the girl catch up.

Out of breath Maura gasped, 'I thought I'd missed you – all day I've been trying to see you, but couldn't leave off for a minute. Jamsie said he'd wait for you beyond the lake, you know, near the trees. He'll be there now, you'd want to run.'

'Oh, I will, Maura, thanks. If my mother's by the gate say I'm delayed in the House. And mention it to no one.'

'I'll not breathe a word.'

Katy ran back the way she had come, past the stables, and hoped her father wasn't there. Leaving behind the outbuildings, she crossed an uncultivated patch of ground, ploughed through stinging nettles, crushed dandelions and daisies beneath her eager feet, no thought in her mind except that in a minute she would see Jamsie, be held in his arms, kiss and be kissed by him. Down the slope that led to the lake she went, not glancing at the water advancing in small waves, the reeds bending before the light breeze, not hearing the moorhens call from the island. Round she ran along the shoreline towards the trees. He was there, she rushed into his arms.

'I thought I'd never see you again,' she said in between kisses. 'I cried myself to sleep every night.'

'Well, you'll cry no more.' He kissed her. She closed her eyes, let him part her lips. His tongue explored her mouth, its tip touching hers, sending the blood racing to her breasts, to the nameless parts which came alive and throbbed with an aching sweetness. She squirmed in an attempt to place her body closer to him, her hands parting his frieze coat, pushing it aside to be nearer. She was vaguely aware of pleasurable pain, that his arms crushed her, that his mouth hurt hers. Then his hands were everywhere, attempting to undo her blouse, ruching up her long skirt. Reluctantly she took away her lips, opened her eyes.

'Don't, Jamsie! Stop it!' His eyes she noticed had a glazed look, not like himself, a madness in them. He did not seem to hear her, his mouth reached for hers.

'No,' she pushed at his chest. 'No, stop.' Then he came back from wherever he had been – the wild look replaced by one she knew.

'Oh, Jesus, Katy, you do terrible things to me.'

'Well,' she smiled coyly at him, 'you're not doing terrible things to me. You should be ashamed of yourself.'

'Oh, I am, ashamed all right,' he said in the tone he had used to mock Statia's medal.

'Let go of me then.' He held her at arms' length, his hands clasped behind her waist. She leant back on them looking up at him. 'Your poor eye, it's still black.'

'Kiss it better so.' He pulled her towards him.

'I'll have to go, my mother thinks I'm working.'

'All right, but we'll meet here every night when you finish.'

94

'And have you savaging me, I will in me eye!'

'No more of that. I'll be the soul of decency.' He kissed her gently. 'Like that every time.'

'Like that till we're married.'

'You'll marry me then?'

'Well you didn't think I threw Peader over to die an old maid!' She lowered her voice. 'I'll marry you. I love you.'

He held her tenderly, stroked her golden hair, and told her of his love.

'Your poor eye,' she said again, reaching up to kiss it gently. 'I'll go now. Till tomorrow then.' She ran back the way she had come.

In their hiding place the following night she asked if he had seen Peader. 'Not since the fight, except outside Mass when he never recognized me. God, wasn't it a terrible way he went about it all the same? He must think bad of us.'

'You're not regretting it?' Her voice was alarmed.

'I'm not.'

'And wasn't it worth it?'

'Oh, it was, a thousand times worth it.'

'Will you kiss me goodnight, so?' She held up her face, and he kissed her. She allowed his hand to encircle her breast for a moment, no longer. Then she said she must go or her mother would get suspicious, and not to worry about Peader, he was sure to get over it.

The sound of someone rattling the chain on the gate woke Katy. She knew by the light that it was very early, not yet dawn. She listened to hear if her mother or father was up, but heard nothing, only the rattling chain. Whoever it was, it wasn't gentry, they would pull the bell. She rose and slipped on her cloak before going outside.

'Statia!' she exclaimed when she saw who was there. 'What brings you at this hour of the morning? Come in.'

They were no sooner in the kitchen when her mother joined them. 'I thought someone was dead when I heard all the commotion. What is it?' she asked.

'You know the brown mare the priest refused, well didn't I see it now, and me coming back from a confinement, with Peader galloping it, and pucks of things hanging out of it.'

'I've been expecting it. He hasn't been outside the door only to Mass since the happening. The poor boy could face no one. His heart broken, deceived on all sides,' Eileen pronounced, and Katy was afraid she would start again the way she had the night of the fight, and wished Statia had kept the news to herself.

'I was wondering,' said Statia, 'if I shouldn't knock Michael and tell him?'

'Are you looking for more information?' Eileen said, and before Statia could defend herself continued, 'Anyway what could he do? If he knows he knows, and if he doesn't leave him sleep. I'm going up now to get dressed.'

'I'll get the blame for Peader running away. I wonder where he's gone?' said Katy, seeing Statia to the gate.

She didn't find out until dinner-time. Tim Coffey came to the House with a package when the servants were sitting down, and told them. 'Peader's gone to Dublin. He left a note for his father, the first thing he knew about it.

96

Said he'd leave the mare with a relation in Cork and take the coach on up.'

She had difficulty swallowing, every lump of food sticking in her throat as one after another the servants expressed their sympathy for Michael, and pity for Peader alone up in Dublin. No one criticized her openly, but she was in no doubt how they regarded her. She was the cause of it all. Keeping her eyes lowered she pushed the food round her plate, deliberately delaying, letting the others go until only she and Hannah remained.

Hannah, looking at her bowed head, felt sorry for her. She was young and impulsive, and maybe had never loved Peader. Love was the strange thing, no accounting for how it took you, she thought, and went to Katy putting an arm round her. 'Starving yourself won't alter anything,' she said, her mild blue eyes and soft creased face full of concern. 'What's done is done, and though I'm not saying I approve of it, maybe you weren't meant for each other. There'll be talk for a while – talk is cheap, but in no time it'll be about someone else.'

Katy turned to Hannah, put her arms round her waist and laid her head against her soft round stomach. She began to cry, and Hannah smoothed her hair, soothing and telling her to whisht now. 'I'm sorry he went – sorry for him and his father.' Katy's voice was muffled by the folds of Hannah's clothes. 'But I couldn't help it – honest to God I couldn't. I'll pray that he'll be happy up in Dublin, but if I had to do it again I would. Jamsie . . .'

'That's enough now – tell me no more about him.' Hannah stopped stroking her hair. 'Putting your mind at rest about people talking is one thing – but you're getting no encouragement in anything else. Like a good girl get up now and go back to work.'

On the way to Dublin, Peader thought about what he had done and why, of the sleepless nights he had spent since Katy threw him over. How he had lain wondering where he had gone wrong. Had he talked too much about Ireland, the terrible wrongs it had suffered? Had he moidered her with news about O'Connell and what he could yet do for the country? Was that it? Was he talking, and telling her about history when he should have been making her laugh? Was that what she liked about Jamsie? Jamsie who was never serious for five minutes, always able to see the funny side of things. He had admired and envied him that ability, but since finding him with Katy, and himself rushing to her defence, he feared Jamsie would also have seen the funny side of that.

– Maybe, he speculated as the coach rolled through the plains of Kildare heading for the city, I could have borne my loss if Katy loved someone other than Jamsie, though God knows it would be a hard thing to have to look at her day in, day out with anyone else by her side. But then at least there would have been Jamsie to talk it over with, to take my mind off it. Losing them both was more than I could stay and face.

In Dublin he found lodgings, and the next day a job, labouring. The lodging house was dirty, the bed infested with vermin, the room shared by many others. Katy's face was constantly before him. Sometimes walking through the crowded streets he saw someone who resembled her. Once he hurried after a woman, his reason telling him it

couldn't be her, but his heart hoping for a miracle. He
would think of her when, after a disturbed night's rest in
the flea- and bug-ridden bed, he opened his eyes. During
the day he pictured her walking up the drive to the House;
when it was time for Mass, see her in the little chapel. He
wondered if she was still seeing Jamsie.

As Katie had feared, her mother became suspicious
about her working late every night.

'What keeps you till all hours? Isn't the clearing up after
the wedding done this long time?'

'Oh, it is to be sure. But Miss Olivia's going to stay with
the family of a young man who came to the wedding, and
I've been doing a bit of sewing for her. Her maid asked me.
Why that one's a lady's maid when she can't thread a
needle I'll never know,' Katy said, all nervousness,
making up the lies as she went. 'And there's things as well
to be done for Miss Charlotte.' Her mind worked quickly
as she sought another excuse for being late. 'Mrs Cummings said I'll be wanted tomorrow night, too. You know
like, with the Master and Miss Charlotte, the young Mistress and Master Charles all off, there'll be clearing up to
do.' She sighed as if full of discontent. 'I wish I was one
thing or the other, a dairymaid, lady's maid, or a cook, so
I knew where I was.'

'You will one day,' her mother replied. With Peader
gone there was no one she considered suitable for Katy in
Kilgoran. 'You won't be marrying and that's for sure, so
you'll be kept on permanent above. You might learn the
cooking, though you have a fine hand for sewing, and a
lady's maid is a superior sort of position. And for that

again you might rise one day to be the housekeeper. Mrs Cummings, God spare her, won't live for ever. That's the highest job anyone could wish for.'

'That would be grand,' Katy agreed, humouring her mother's ambition. 'Anyway things will slacken after tomorrow.'

'They will surely,' her mother replied.

'Please God,' Katy prayed when she went to bed, 'don't let my mother talk to one of the servants and find out I've not been working late, and let me find a way to keep seeing Jamsie.'

The idea came to her when she was in the kitchen saying goodbye to Charlotte, who was off to Dublin with her father. As Charles and Olivia were already gone there was no evening meal to prepare, and Hannah was taking her ease, making lace. She put it down when the child was about to go, and while she rooted in her pocket for her bottle of Holy water, Katy picked up the piece of work and examined it. Hannah sprinkled the Holy water over Charlotte, and made the Sign of the Cross. 'That'll protect you on the journey, astoir. Goodbye now and God bless you.' She kissed Charlotte, and Katy hugged the little girl.

'The lace is lovely,' she said, when she and Hannah were alone. 'Where did you learn it?'

'A lady from the Big House in Galway had what you could call a school for the lace-making, and the girls from the village went.'

'Would you teach me?'

'It's very trying on the eyes, but I would.'

'I could come up of an evening.'

'Your company would be welcome, maybe your mother would come, too.'

'Ah, no, not my mother,' Katy said, alarmed. Then she decided she would tell Hannah the truth. 'You see the way it is – I thought I could do a bit of lace, then maybe slip out of the back door and see . . .'

'If it's Jamsie you're thinking of seeing then the answer is *no*.'

'Please, Hannah, there's no other way. I love him.'

'Your mother's my friend, I'd be deceiving her.'

'Oh, Hannah, *please*,' she pleaded, went to her and put an arm about the comfortable waist. 'If you only knew what it's like loving someone – you'd help.'

Hannah moved out of her embrace, and busied herself by the fire, keeping her back turned, raking the coal, rattling the poker. Her skirt, hitched from bending, exposed her black woollen stockings, wrinkled round swollen ankles. Her voice when she spoke seemed to come from a long way off, and was sad. 'I wasn't always old. Once there was a boy. I loved him, he was gorgeous. We were sixteen. I can see him still as if it was yesterday. My mother put between us.' She turned from the fire.

'Hannah, you're crying!'

'Ah, don't mind me. It was just for a minute you reminded me how time goes.' She lifted the hem of her apron and wiped her eyes. 'I'm an old fool. My mother, Lord rest her, thought she was right. So does yours. But they're not always, so I'll aid you in your deception, God forgive me.'

Her mother said lace-making was as good as another way of putting in time, and didn't question Katy's nightly excursions up to Hannah. She worked hard learning the rudiments of the craft for ten to fifteen minutes, then went out the back way and sped to join Jamsie, congratulating herself on the ease with which her plans were working. Everything was grand. Even Peader's father was talking to her mother again, partly reconciled to the loss of his son, relating news of him from Dublin.

A bit more time was all that was required, Katy believed, before she told her mother she was seeing Jamsie, that she intended marrying him. Sometimes when he got too passionate and she removed his straying hands, and shifted out of his arms they talked: one evening about Peader, Jamsie regretting he had not made it up with him before he left, that he was sorry he was gone.

'It's as well, for now there's no obstacle,' Katy said. 'While he was here my mother would have kept hoping. Now she has to get over it.' She reached up and kissed him. 'Take that frown off your face, haven't you got me?'

'I have, oh I have, and I wouldn't swap you for the world.' He returned her kiss, and fondled her breast through the stuff of her blouse. She allowed him to do that sometimes, though she believed it was a sin, maybe a mortal sin. But more than the sin, she feared if she left his hand there too often, or too long, he'd have his way with her. When he touched her she melted, it was as if every bone in her softened, and her will dissolved, the most gorgeous feeling of melting and floating. But she knew it was dangerous for sure, and if she didn't take his hand away this minute, God only knows what would happen.

'Listen,' she said, imprisoning his fingers, lifting them to her lips, kissing them, 'isn't everything going well for us?'

'It would be better still if we were married. Johnny's getting married, putting up a cabin, we could do the same.'

'Four families pulling out of the acre! I'll do no such thing,' she said, not adding that if there were no one sharing the land she wasn't moving on to the bog. Didn't want her children, when God sent them, reared like wild things, nor herself stretched by the side of an old sow, not a window, nor chimney.

'What else is there then, except America or conacre?'

'Not them either! Not conacre certainly! Be at the whim of a leech who'd let us the ground, prepare it and give a bit of seed for a crippling rent; have you at his beck and call in exchange for leave to sling up a cabin, and after all that the crop could fail and us slung out.'

'I'd risk it, risk anything to have you in bed beside me. I'm demented with wanting you.'

'There's the Widow Murphy's cottage. I was thinking we could move in.'

'The woman's not dead yet, are you mad or hoping she'll be evicted?' He let go of her, sat down, patted the ground, coaxing her to join him.

'I'll do no such thing. Once lying beside you was enough. You nearly had me stripped. Get up and listen or I'll go.'

'Come on, only for a minute. I'll keep my hands behind my back.'

'No, I'm going.' She began to walk away.

He was up, pulling her back. 'All right,' he said. 'We'll prop the tree. Tell me about the cottage.'

'If my father asked the Master he might let us have it. I could mind the woman. You could plant the field. There's two, and two rooms. We'd sleep in the kitchen not to disturb her.'

'What about her sons in America? They might walk back.'

'After two years and not a word! They died, or forgot they had a mother,' she said repeating Hannah and Statia's opinions.

'There'd be no harm trying, I suppose.'

'No harm at all. I'll ask my father.'

'Would he do it?'

'I could make him.'

'How so?'

'Let on if he didn't that we'd go to America.'

'There'd be no harm in the lie I suppose.'

'Not a bit.'

'We'll need a few shillings. I'll go over the water, there's work on the railways. I'll do that for a few weeks.'

'Oh Jamsie, I love you.' She showered kisses on him. 'We'll be together every night.'

'You forward strap. I'm not sure I want you for a wife.' He gave her kisses, fleeting ones on eyes, the tip of her nose, then a lingering one on the lips, adding when he finally let go her mouth, 'I have my doubts about marrying you, but not one about laying beside you in the widow woman's cottage.'

Chapter Five

Father Bolger, returning from a sick call with the reins loose, Acushla walking easy, looked at the scenery and the beautiful evening it was. He was on the top road, below him the lake rippled, shimmering the golden path of the setting sun. He reined in the pony, and sat enjoying the view. He could see the river and on its banks the lichen-covered ruins of an early Christian church. All that long ago, he mused, there were priests here, preaching the gospel, ministering to the people. Maybe on an evening like this in cells bent over parchments they inscribed the strange fishes, the birds and coiling serpents in colours of the rainbow. Was it, he wondered, the same men who gave the village its name, combining the Irish word *Kil* for church with *Goran*, the name of the river?

He let his mind dwell on the early monasteries, the exquisite illuminated manuscripts the monks produced; the time when Ireland was a land of saints and scholars. The time when the same monasteries were dissolved, when Ireland felt the weight of the oppressor: and he felt the familiar surge of hatred. The strength of his emotion distressed him physically, made him sweat, become aware of his bodily discomforts.

He took off his hat, flapped it before his face. Hatred was

a destructive emotion, it served no purpose, he wished to be rid of it. Silently he said an aspiration, calling on God to cleanse his heart, but the feeling persisted, and once again he was transported into the past, to the day of the flogging. Saw it as if it was happening, the crowded street, felt the clutch of his mother's hand, and heard the intake of breath as the cart entered the square.

It was noon on a hot summer's day. There were flies everywhere, dancing in swarms, descending on filth in the gutter, flying up to rest on faces. One landed on his cheek, near his eye. The hand not held by his mother was pinned to his side by the pressing crowd, he shrugged his neck in an attempt to dislodge the fly, but it remained.

Soldiers in red coats and white breeches lined the route. A drummer boy led the procession tapping out a slow rhythm. Behind them came the cart. The man for flogging was naked to the waist, bound to the tailboard of the cart, his feet hanging, dragging on the ground, the flies swarming on his sweat-soaked skin. Behind the cart rode the town's magistrates and behind them in an open carriage the major of the regiment who would direct the flogging.

'Hate them. Grow up to hate them.' His mother's voice was insistent. Her hand clenched and unclenched on his, the fly irritated his skin. The sergeant-major and the farrier sergeant were by the flogging post; they saluted the major who got down from his carriage. The man on the cart was being untied, dragged to the post. The drum stopped, the crowd drew in its breath. 'Hate the murdering English bastards.' His mother's whisper was low. The man's bound hands were stretched above his head, tied to the frame, then his elbows were secured against it. The major gave an order, the drum rolled and the farrier sergeant stepped forward holding the cat-o'-nine-tails; the drumming stopped.

He raised his arm and swung the whip twice above his head then brought it down. The knotted strands hissed through the air, landed on the man's back, lay for an instant, before the whip was lifted, its thongs run through a cloth in the Sergeant's left hand to cleanse them. Along the man's back long, ragged red seams which split and frayed appeared.

'One,' the sergeant-major counted. Above the sergeant's head the ropes spun before descending to widen the gouges from which blood flowed. The smell of it was heavily sweet on the warm air, the flies buzzed frantically, hovering out of reach of the spinning ropes. Flesh, skin and congealing blood made the thongs stick together, they took longer to pass through the cleaning rag. 'Two,' called the sergeant-major.

Again and again the ritual was repeated until after the count of nine the man screamed an agonizing scream, then sagged; the life seemed to have run out of him. Like a crumpled sack, red-soaked, he hung against the post.

A little wind blew off the lake, found its way to the top road where Father Bolger sat in the trap, it teased his hair. He remembered that was how the fly on his face had felt. Clearly he could recall the irritation, yet could not picture the man's face nor whether he was young or old. Only the scream and the mauled back criss-crossed with crimson split seams.

He had felt sick and pulled on his mother's hand asking to go.

'Whisht,' she hissed, 'don't make a sound.' He closed his eyes and kept them closed till the sergeant-major shouted, 'Fifty,' and his mother whispered, 'Thank God.' Then he looked and saw the man untied and thrown on to the cart. He lay face down, his arms spread out not moving, the flies clustered on him. The major gave an order, the procession formed up and they moved away to the smart tap of the drum.

His mother took him home, hurrying him through the jostling crowd, past the drunken people, telling him all the way, 'Never forget today. That man bore his pain for Ireland. Grow up to hate them.' Dragging him, for the sickness had not passed and his legs were weak. Pushing him before her into his father's shop as if he were a culprit she had captured.

On this fine evening, thirty-five years later in a county miles from the shop near the banks of the Slaney, he could see it as it was then. The shelves from floor to ceiling with bolts of grey frieze, black kerseymere, rolls of white bawneen, scarlet jackets for altering. The goose heating on the fire – the hot smell of it, the bucket of water with the ironing cloth draped over it and his father sitting cross-legged on the table stitching at a scarlet jacket.

'May God forgive you, Declan Bolger, sitting there taking in and letting out their jackets and breeches, stitching on stripes and crowns and gold braid. And not ten minutes since in the square Timmy Hanlon was nearly flogged to death and the child here watching it all,' his mother said holding him in front of her, her hands on his shoulders.

108

His father's voice that always had a hint of mockery in it so that one never knew when he was serious, replied, 'And did you have to stand and watch? Were you paralysed all of a sudden that you couldn't walk away and take him with you? And sure I suppose someone dragged you there in the first place?'

'I was not. Clever talk, that's all you can do. I went. I wanted him to see. To remember and not grow up like you – an oul lick-spittle.'

'Shame on you, woman – he's nine years old! Away out to the kitchen and let me earn my living. Leave the child with me.'

His mother went and his father laid down the jacket. 'Come up here beside me.' He patted the work table. 'You'll be a tailor when you grow up, you'll have to learn to sit like one. Make yourself useful, pull the tackings out of that.' He passed over a finished coat white with basting thread. 'The bodkin's there in the box.'

Father Bolger recalled the smoothness of the blunt-headed bone bodkin and how he had wielded it, imagining it was a dagger, that the coarse, white thread was skin and the red cloth the heart of the sergeant with the whip. Again and again he thrust and twisted and all the while his father's quiet patient voice talked.

'I'm sorry you saw it. 'Tis a terrible thing to witness. I saw one once. It was not less terrible because the man being flogged was a soldier and not a poor misguided Irishman belonging to a Secret Society. It was your first sight of what men do to each other. But there's nothing new about it. They flogged Jesus, other soldiers long ago. Soldiers like those today, in a land where they didn't belong either. Crucifixion, hanging and flogging, they've been with us a long time.'

He talked as if to himself, pausing now and then, repeating something. ''Tis a strange thing – they draw big crowds. Women like your mother, crying and praying. Farmers' wives, fine ladies and their men too. All sorts of people. Wasn't it like that today?'

'It was, father.' The tacking was nearly all out. Only a few small stitches near the collar remained. He probed them, concentrating, dragging them out. He would kill them, every one. Grow up to hate and kill them.

'Promise me then that you'll never witness such a thing again, that you'll never choose to go. Did you hear me?'

'Yes, father. I won't.'

'You're a good boy, Declan. Don't be led astray. Men have a savageness in them. They do things to each other no other creature on earth does. That's grand, you've taken them all out. Throw it over there for pressing. All men everywhere do them. It's the devil that's born in us. 'Twas the devil that sent the English here to pillage and murder. 'Twas the devil that made them change their faith and want to change ours. It's him that makes a man flog another, put a rope round his neck and break it. If you watch his work you pay him homage. Keep from it. Keep from it lest you become contaminated. Grow up and fight injustice but not with the weapons of the unjust. Sure if you do, what's the difference between you? There's only one way and that's the way of Jesus. Do His bidding. His word has lived for nearly two thousand years. It'll live long after the soldiers are forgotten. Love God. Your soul and the soul of men is what counts – the spirit within you.

No one can touch that. Not even if they take your life in the attempt. Isn't that an awful lot for one small boy to understand and remember on a hot day, and you no doubt dying for your dinner? But remember all the same. And now till your mother calls us I'll teach you the tailoring. Hand me over that bit of cloth and you'll practise stitching. Your only weapon then will be a needle and the drop of blood spilled easily sucked off a prodded finger.'

He remembered his father teaching him his trade, speaking often against the violent ways of men. Placidly plying his needle, talking to his customers. Treating them all with the same courtesy – the comfortable farmers and shopkeepers, the officers and sergeants, even the beggars who came. Never displaying annoyance or anger, not even with his mother who daily castigated him for trying to ruin her son, making him into a white-livered man.

His poor, fiery, passionate mother. Urging him when alone with her to be a man. To fight for Ireland. Never to forget his people murdered down the years by the English. To mind his religion. Grow up to run the Evangelists out of the country, to light bonfires with the books of the Hibernian Bible Society, feed the flames with their tracts.

He had loved them both – God be good to them. And pleased them both when he announced he thought he had a vocation. 'Glory be to God, a son of mine a priest! It's what I've always prayed for,' his mother said, her eyes full of wonder. His father had told him something he had not known before. 'I once thought that God called me too. He hadn't as it turned out. But for a long time I thought it was so. 'Twas as well he hadn't for my father had nothing to pay for a seminary in France or Rome. But it's different now. Since the Relief Act we have our own. What I've got is enough for any one of them.'

He went to Carlow to study for the priesthood. With him went the memory of the flogging, the hatred that had flared in him that day; the feelings fostered by his mother, nourished by his reading, the evictions he had witnessed, the degradation of his people. It was all there buried in his heart. But in his mind were the lessons his father had taught him. When the irrationality of his nature warred with his reason and the life of Christ he tried to imitate, he prayed.

Acushla, attracted by a patch of lush grass, moved forward jolting the priest from his reverie. The evening was cooler now, the light going. Father Bolger gathered up the reins. He felt at peace again. Knew that his father's message had been the right one. That in the long run his father's way was the one that would triumph. Violence and hatred achieved nothing. Hadn't Daniel O'Connell proved that? Hadn't his protests, every one within the letter of the law, achieved more since 1832 than all the bloody battles waged in the past? Daniel had brought Ireland Catholic Emancipation. He was an educated man, a barrister. He had united the people, involved the clergy. His Monster rallies were a sight to make England quake. His fight by the same means would one day achieve Repeal of the Union, then Ireland would have her own parliament – a say in her own affairs. And with God's help there would be no room for hatred in people's hearts.

'Well,' he said to the pony, 'I've kept you long enough away from your stable, come on now.' He took a last look round, and saw two figures emerging from the trees down by the lake. They were shadowy, but he was in no doubt as to who they were.

'So that's how you kept your promise, Katy O'Donnell!' he said out loud. 'Didn't I let the grass grow under my feet? It's a month tomorrow since I arrived, four weeks come Sunday since I extracted your word, and I've hardly given it a thought since. Well, Miss, it's time I had a talk with you.'

'From the priest,' Mary Doyle said, handing Katy an envelope.

'For me? Are you sure?' She felt weak with fright, sure that somehow the priest had found out about her seeing Jamsie. Her face went scarlet, and she could feel everyone's eyes on her, all full of curiosity. She kept turning the letter over in her hands until Hannah took pity on her confusion, and told her to go back to the dairy. Relieved to escape, she went quickly, opening the letter as she ran. It was only a line asking her to come to the priest's house after work. It worried her all the afternoon so that Nan told her to take the sour puss off her or she would turn the milk.

'Sit down,' said Father Bolger, and she sat with hands in her lap, nervously fidgeting with her fingers. It seemed hours before he spoke again. 'Last evening I was above on the top road looking down on the lake, and I saw a strange sight. I couldn't believe it, yourself and Jamsie coming out of the trees.' His eyes seemed to bore into her, to know her every thought.

'I was there,' she admitted, 'but we did nothing bad.'

'You lied to me. Promised you wouldn't see him, that's

bad enough. But alone with him at the hour of the evening I saw you is dangerous as well as bad. And your mother, of course, is being deceived the way you deceived me. For a young girl you're accomplished at the deception.'

She hung her head, ashamed, resentful, not knowing how to answer, except mumble, 'I'm sorry, Father.'

'Sorry you should be. You've caused enough trouble in the month I've been here. Now you listen to me. I'm not asking for promises – I'm telling you what you will not do.' She raised her head and stared, a look of defiance on her face. The priest ignored it, and continued, 'You will not see Jamsie O'Hara again. You won't go near the lake again. I'm not having you add a hasty marriage to your list of faults.' He stared her out.

She said nothing, and with lowered eyes thought – I wish you'd called me from the altar, then I'd have run away. I'll still run away if Jamsie will run with me. I'll never stop seeing him, never, not even if I go to Hell, for I don't believe loving someone is a sin.

Father Bolger waited for her to speak. She remained silent, knowing she could never make him understand the impossibility of his command. How on the Sunday after the fight so relieved she was not to have had her name called, she had promised, told lies. But not now. Not after the weeks she had spent with Jamsie, not now when she loved him more than her life. To say she would never see him again, to put that into words would be flying in the face of God. Like letting on you were sick when you weren't, inviting ill luck, so the things you pretended happened. Ill luck could attend her, something happen to Jamsie, the false promise come true.

For the priest to ask such a vow she instinctively felt was wrong; loving as she loved Jamsie, wanting to be his wife, that couldn't be wrong. So, though terrified of openly defying him, she raised her head and said, 'I can't, Father. I could no more stop seeing him than stop breathing.'

'Then you'll be relieved to hear he gave the same answer.'

'Jamsie! You saw him? When?'

'Never mind that now. Hold on, I haven't finished,' he said when her relief and excitement made her want to interrupt. 'You'll still not see him. Not until you've told your parents, and he can come courting you the way a respectable girl should be courted. Then make arrangements to be married. There's nothing to stop you, and you'll be a comfort to each other. And stop crying, isn't it what you wanted all along?'

'Oh, it is, Father, indeed it is. But how'll I tell my mother, she'll kill me.'

'She won't. She'll give you the length and breadth of her tongue, no more than you deserve. Go home now and face the consequences. I'll expect the two of you at confession. Away you go now, and let me have my supper.'

'What did the priest want with you?' Eileen O'Donnell asked when Katy returned. She was on a stool by the fire, her face creased with annoyance, her body rocking to and fro. 'Well?' she demanded when Katy did not answer immediately. 'Was it about Peader? To tell you how you broke his heart and left his father in old age without a son? A man that was willing to welcome you without a dowry? The more I think about it the more I feel like streeling you round the floor by your hair.'

'I thought you were over it,' Katy said. 'That you knew how it was. It's a while now, and Peader's gone.' Her voice was wheedling, trying to get round her mother. Wanting her in a better humour before she broke the news about Jamsie and what the priest said.

'Till my dying day I'll never get over it. You made a show of me in the parish, a laughing stock! You'll finish up an old maid, for who'd have you now? And that you may. That you may go to your grave a dry oul woman and give to the maggots what should have been Peader's.'

'Well I won't! I'm marrying Jamsie. And what's more, the priest says I can,' Katy retorted, driven to tell her news sooner and in a more forthright manner than she had intended.

For a minute her mother did not appear to have heard. Then, as though she had been struck heavily, a dazed look came on her face, and a hand went to her head as if searching for where a blow had landed. Her mouth hung open, foolish-looking, then she screamed: 'Jesus! What did I hear you say?' Katy told her again. Her mother screamed louder. Her father came running from the bedroom, startled-looking, clutching the waistband of his long flannel drawers. 'What ails you? What's up?'

His wife ignored him. She was up from the stool, running at Katy, grabbing her hair, shouting, 'Say that again! Say it and I'll kill you!' She tugged and pulled at the golden hair. 'Go on, say it, let your father hear!'

Katy, in an attempt to defend herself, raised a hand and struck her mother's face. Immediately Eileen let go her hold on the hair, the fury on her face wiped out, replaced by horror. 'You struck me! You raised a hand to them that bore you! That hand will wither, and your arm stick out of the grave for eternity! For mortal man can't straighten the arm that strikes a parent!'

'In the name of God will you sit down and shut up. I'm torn out of my sleep with the shouting and bawling. Find you like a tinker swinging out of Katy and I still don't know what's up.'

'A tinker is it?' his wife flashed back, momentarily recovered from the sacrilege committed by her daughter. 'Tell her about tinkers. She's marrying into them. Marrying an O'Hara – his mother's a tinker. Dirty Mag – with the legs roasted off her from sitting in the ashes. And Fintan, good for nothing except making children. Ask her about tinkers.'

'They're not tinkers, and I'm marrying Jamsie, not them. I love him.'

'They come with him, the seed, breed and generation of them. And love will fly out the window, if they had such a thing on the bog. All he wants you for is to make children. Love indeed!'

'Will you shut up and sit down.' Seamus O'Donnell dragged his wife to the stool and forced her to sit. 'Now Katy, tell me what this is all about.'

Katy told him about Jamsie, that she'd been seeing him, not mentioning Hannah's part in it, and her conversation with the priest, that she was marrying Jamsie.

'I knew it, you're having a child,' her mother shouted and became hysterical again.

'I am not, God forgive you accusing me of such a thing.'

'Have you thought of where you'll live?' her father asked.

'Up on the bog,' Eileen shouted. 'And the day he puts a ring on your finger you'll be dead to me, I'll forget I ever had you.'

'I'm telling you for the last time to shut up. I've never laid a finger on you in anger, but I will. Take out your beads and say them if you can't be quiet. Tell me, child, where will you live?'

'I was thinking, Dada, if you had a word with the Master we could live in the Widow Murphy's cottage.'

The worried, inquiring expression with which her father had been regarding her was replaced by a look of incredulity, then repugnance. 'The woman's in it – how could you move in? Were you hoping the Master would evict her, change his ways of a lifetime for you? Well you're mistaken, and I wouldn't lift a finger to help even if he would.'

Her mother crowed with satisfaction. 'Amn't I telling you what you reared? That's your daughter in her true colours. A deceiver – telling lies to the priest, wanting a defenceless creature thrown out – a child that raised her hand to her mother.'

'I only wanted to move in *with* her. I'd mind her, and Jamsie'd see to the ground. But it doesn't matter. He's away to England in a while. With what he earns we'll go to America.'

Katy watched their faces as she spoke. Saw the fight go out of her mother, the indignation fade from her father's eyes, leaving him drained and old-looking. Neither of them spoke for a moment. Katy waited.

'You wouldn't do anything hasty like that, would you, aghillie?' Her mother began to cry quietly. 'Sure you're all we've got. Not one in the parish a drop's blood to us. You wouldn't cross the sea and leave us?'

Knowing she now had the advantage, Katy pressed it. 'What else could we do? If we couldn't get the cottage we'd go all right. I'm going to bed now.'

She left and went upstairs. She could hear them talking, the quiet mumble of their voices coming up. They might come round to her way of thinking, maybe her father would ask for the cottage. She was sorry she had threatened them with America. It was what they had always dreaded. I shouldn't have afflicted them so, she thought. Haven't I seen the grief of others? Gone to the bits of nights thrown when someone was going. Seen the brave face put on it. The few drinks, and the songs, the dancing. Everyone pretending it was an ordinary night, a celebration. Then when daylight was coming the pauses longer between one song and the next. The mothers huddling nearer the fire, fathers drinking the last drop. All the young ones crowded round them that were going, shaking hands, kisses and loves. Promises to send word. And the tears. Then the crowd walking a bit of the way with them. The sun not yet up, the women rocking backwards and forwards, the awful wailing that made you shiver and think of the dead. Faces you would never see again. And on whatever bit of a rise there was, the father climbing it, standing and looking down the road.

The sound of her parents' voices was still drifting up the stairs when she fell asleep. In the morning she saw her mother's face was puffed and knew she had cried for a long time. She nodded to Katy and made porridge. Her father ate his standing, and went to work. When he was gone her mother spoke.

'Your father will see the priest, we'd want his opinion before we did anything about the cottage. Then if Father Bolger doesn't object he'll ask the Master when he comes back from Dublin.' She put out the oatmeal, and said no more until Katy was leaving. 'I suppose the lace-making was more of your deception. I'm surprised at Hannah, but there, there's no fool like an old one. I'll say no more about it. We'll do what we can, and tell Jamsie O'Hara he can call for you.'

She was beside herself with joy. It was settled, she was sure the priest would approve of them moving into the cottage.

She wanted to throw her arms round her mother's neck, tell her she was sorry for the way she had gone about it, the fight, and letting on about America. Tell her she'd never regret having Jamsie as a son-in-law. But she knew that though her mother wasn't spiteful, it would take a while before she welcomed such signs of affection – a while before she was completely forgiven.

Father Bolger saw no reason, if Lord Kilgoran agreed, why Katy and Jamsie should not have the cottage.

'But mightn't the neighbours think bad of it?' Seamus asked.

'Some will, them that had the same thing in mind. If there's too much talk, tell them it's with my approval. And what's more by next year there'll be Poor Houses in Ireland, so tell them if it wasn't for Katy looking after the widow she might finish in one. That'll shut them up.'

Eileen thawed considerably when she heard the priest's verdict, but Katy knew it was still early days, and left for the time being suggesting alterations to Miss Catherine's peacock-blue dress in which she would be married. She was nervous about Jamsie's first visit to the Lodge, how her mother would receive him. But it went better than she hoped, for to a guest in her home Eileen could be nothing but hospitable.

Jamsie talked to her father about England where he was going to work labouring for the railways. They discussed how much he would earn. 'Two shillings a day,' Jamsie said. 'Great money.' Her mother inquired after his parents, and how was Johnny settling to married life, and that she liked Padraig. That he was a nice quiet boy, and though the image of Johnny, not like him at all.

Jamsie came to the Lodge most evenings, and Katy was very happy, though she missed their time alone by the lake. Sitting in the room with her mother and father they could not even hold hands, and when she went to the gate to send him off, her mother kept the door open and, if she lingered, called her to come in. On the night before Jamsie was going to England, her father went to bed early, and each time her mother left the room they snatched kisses. 'I'll die of loneliness,' Katy told him, 'what'll I do without you?'

'Maybe you could see Johnny's wife, she'll be lonesome too, with him gone.'

'Sure my mother wouldn't let me out,' – and even if she would, Katy thought, I'd keep far from that brazen hussy who, according to the talk, had been seen tricking with Master Charles when she was supposed to be collecting turf.

*

121

While Jamsie was away working, the Master and Miss Charlotte came back from Dublin. Katy's father put the case for the cottage, and Lord Kilgoran thought it was a good idea. He asked when they were to be married and, when Seamus told him October, added that Katy was a sensible girl and the Widow Murphy would be in capable hands. They could move in as soon as they married. In the meantime if Katy wished to clean or whitewash, there was no reason why she shouldn't: the old woman would not notice what was going on.

'Thanks very much, Sir, I'm much obliged.'

'Not at all, O'Donnell, delighted to be of help. One other thing ...'

'Yes, Sir?'

'I'll see that the agent adjusts the ledgers, gives Katy a clean slate, no arrears, eh?'

'God bless you, Sir.'

'Well now, that's done,' Eileen said when her husband returned, and then to Katy, 'I suppose you'll have to have something to wear.'

'Miss Catherine's dress, if you'll alter it.' Katy brought it out and tried it on. Her mother made her turn this way and that, pinned up the hem, said the waist needed taking in, and round the bust letting out. 'It will do,' she said, 'and the colour is becoming.'

That night in bed Katy thought about being married. How herself and Jamsie would have a palliasse in the kitchen, and lay with the spark from the fire shining, and they would be in each other's arms, stripped except for her nightdress and his shirt. Laying close together, able to do anything they liked. The thought of it made the melting feeling come, she hugged herself with the pleasure of it.

Then she thought of ordinary things: how she and Jamsie would manage to live, and that it was a pity the Master didn't let married women stay on, the money would have been grand. Now she would only be called for special occasions when extra help was needed. Still, she was sure they would be all right. Her mother would help, and there'd be the money Jamsie earned in England. She did sums in her head. Fourteen shillings a week was a fortune, even after he paid for food and lodgings, enough left to give them a good start, he would bring home at least two pounds. Everything was going to be wonderful, they would live happily in the cottage for the rest of their lives.

He was drunk the night he came back. Drunk as she had never seen him before, foolish with it, laughing all over his face like an eejit, not noticing or caring that her mother was looking daggers at him. Full of talk, engaging her father in conversation, demanding that he listen, repeating himself, his words slurred, not making sense. He kept forgetting where he was, attempting to put his arms round her, to kiss her, until her mother ordered her off the settle to sit by the fire, and put her father beside Jamsie.

To make matters worse he started to explain what had delayed him. 'We had a grand time, me and Johnny. We'll just have the one, I said to him, at the first place we stopped. Then we got talking, and had another. A fellow we knew came in, and sure, before I looked round the night was half gone. But the craic was great, all right.' He smiled fondly at Katy. 'It was the excitement of being home, and knowing you were here waiting for me, made me not notice how the time went.'

Her mother sniffed, a thing she did when displeased, and suggested he must be tired, mightn't it be as well if he went home. He demurred, he wasn't a bit tired. What would have tired him, he asked. But her mother insisted, and when Katy rose to accompany him to the gate, indicated she was to stay where she was. 'Your father will see him off.' And when they were gone. 'What did I tell you? Cat after kind makes a good mouser. And you threw over a sober respectable boy for him. You won't see him again until he's spent the remainder of whatever he earned beyond, that's if there was a penny of it left after the night's carousing.'

But the next evening he arrived, sober and repentant, reminding her father they were going to whitewash the cottage. When her mother and father disappeared to find brushes and buckets, he held and kissed her. 'I'm awful sorry over last night.'

'You were a disgrace, made a show of yourself,' Katy said, not too harshly for she was overcome with happiness to be in his arms, to look into his lovely face. His kiss filled her with longing for more, but still she said, 'I hope you'll never do that when we're married.'

'Never,' he said fervently. 'Not a drop, what would I be doing in a public house with you to come home to?'

She could hear her mother returning, and quickly asked, 'Did you manage to save much?'

'I didn't. Sure, wasn't I robbed? Between what I paid for food, candles and a bit of tobacco, the few shillings were owed before I handled them.'

Her mother was back before she could ask, 'What about the few shillings that paid for last night's porter?' He let go of her. She sat down and kept looking at him. His skin was darker than when he went away – brown as a berry, it made his eyes bluer, and his teeth like new milk. Sure, what matter if the few shillings were gone. She had a golden guinea from Hannah, and five more promised from her mother and father, wasn't that a fortune, and she had him as well. When he came back from painting the cottage and they said goodnight by the gate, he whispered, 'It won't be long now, love.' She clung to him until her mother banged on the window.

'It will be a quiet wedding,' Eileen O'Donnell announced the night she finished altering Katy's dress. 'I'll have Jamsie's parents, not his brothers. I can't very well ask Peader's father and, without him, I couldn't ask Dinny Crowley. Statia can come, and Hannah if the House can spare her, and that's it. No drinking and dancing for two days and a night like it was for Johnny O'Hara's wedding.'

'All right,' Katy replied, for she didn't care what sort of a night they had, so long as she was married, and in the cottage with Jamsie. Anyway the O'Haras would do their own celebrating, she thought. Her future father-in-law needed no excuse to get out the poteen, dance and sing as the humour took him, nor his wife either. Maybe a quiet wedding was as well – for then Jamsie would go home sober with her.

As the time of the wedding approached, Katy packed her belongings to take to the cottage. Amongst them she found the medal meant for Charlotte. 'Sleep with it near you at night, and you'll never be afraid of the dark,' she told the child when handing it over.

Charlotte thanked her, left the kitchen and returned soon afterwards with a lace-trimmed handkerchief. 'For you,' she said, proffering the gift, 'a wedding present.'

'You kind child.' Katy was delighted with the dainty scrap. 'I'll keep it always.'

As was customary when a servant married, Katy was invited to choose something from the attic as a gift. Accompanied by Mrs Cummings, she looked at the vast array of objects relegated, tables and chairs, beds, chests and presses. At things she could imagine no use for, nor put a name to, at fishing rods, and nets, gaffes and disused croquet sets. So many things she did not know where to look.

'Is there anything takes your eye?' Mrs Cummings asked when Katy made no choice.

'Oh, there is, Ma'am. There's oceans. But with the Widow Murphy having her own bits of things, I've room for nothing, though I'd be glad of a pair of pillows, and that wooden chair.' And Katy thanked her and went back to work.

She woke on her wedding morning and saw the blue dress hanging on the door. Her mother called from downstairs telling her to get up. She called back that she would, but stayed where she was, looking at the gown wishing it was white satin and lace like Miss Catherine's, and that in the parlour, spread so as not to be crushed, was a long veil.

'Are you up yet?' her mother shouted.

126

'I am,' she replied, swinging her legs out of bed, stamping on the boards, then getting back into bed. The smell of bacon boiling for the wedding breakfast wafted into the room making her hungry.

Her clean underclothes were laid on a chair. – Tomorrow morning, she thought, they'll be in the cottage, and me beside Jamsie in the bed. She smiled at the prospect. Tonight and every night I'll lay in his arms for ever and ever.

The sound of her mother's feet on the stairs made her leap from the bed.

'I might have known,' she said, entering, carrying a jug of warm water, looking at the unmade bed. 'You've only this minute left it. Get yourself washed and dressed or you'll be late for your wedding.' She continued to scold while she poured the water into a basin, then plumped the pillows, smoothed the sheets and pulled up the covers.

When her mother was gone, Katy stripped off, and washed herself all over. Soaping her breasts and belly, her thighs and in between her legs, down as far as her knees, rinsing and drying herself. Put on her calico shift and drawers, moved the basin to the floor by the chair, sat and dipped in her feet, her fingers cleansing between her toes, weeding out the dirt and fluff. When she was in her dress she called her mother to fasten the row of hooks and eyes down the back.

She walked with her mother and father to the chapel. In honour of the occasion he had a new pair of stockings, and had spent a long time brushing his hat. They said nothing to one another on the journey. When they got to the door her mother hung back to let Katy and her father enter first.

Katy's eyes sought Jamsie, he was there in the front kneeling next to Padraig. She thought how in a few minutes she would become his wife. Then she noticed with disappointment how bare the chapel looked. It was, she supposed, because there were only a few people. You never noticed of a Sunday, that except for the Stations of the Cross, and the statues of the Sacred Heart and Our Lady, the walls were the same as a cottage, plain and whitewashed.

She saw Statia, Mary Doyle, and two girls from the kitchen. Hannah couldn't leave the House. She was sorry, she would have liked Hannah there. Jamsie's parents were there, but not Johnny nor his wife.

'Did you see the cut of them,' her mother whispered walking up the aisle behind her. 'The dirty bare feet of her. They come so seldom, it's a wonder they're not struck dead.'

Katy let on not to hear her. Jamsie looked round and smiled at her. Her heart was lifted. She forgot the bareness, the chill, and could think of nothing but that he was hers.

Her father handed her to him: they walked to the altar. Maura and Padraig stood by them. Father Bolger began to pray in Latin. Then in English, proclaimed, 'I join you together in marriage, in the Name of the Father, and of the Son, and of the Holy Ghost, Amen,' and sprinkled them with Holy water. Padraig put the ring bought with the money from Katy's parents and a silver shilling on the prayer book held by the priest, who blessed them. Following Father Bolger's instructions, Jamsie offered Katy the gold and silver, repeated after him, 'With this ring I thee wed, this gold and silver I give thee; with my body I thee worship, and with all my worldly goods I thee endow.'

His fingers were rough and scarred from the recent labouring. Awkwardly he placed the ring on Katy's left thumb, his voice barely audible, repeating as he moved the ring from finger to finger, 'In the name of the Father, and of the Son, and of the Holy Ghost,' uttering the final 'Amen', placing the ring on Katy's wedding finger. The Latin prayers commenced again, the priest blessed them. – *We're married. He's mine, I'm his. I love him. Oh, thank you God*, Katy thought.

She lay on the palliasse and watched him undress. He kept his back turned. – *How beautiful his legs are*, she thought. *I never knew men had nice legs. Come to think of it, you don't see the legs of anyone, except your own, and a baby's and them of the old woman, thin shanks with little flesh*. Her mind for a minute settled on the woman, fearing she might get up from the bed in the other room and, maybe, wander in on top of them.

Then she stopped thinking. Jamsie was slipping in beside her. They were in bed, and it not dark yet. He lay for a minute propped on an elbow, looking at her. 'A ghille mo croidhe,' he whispered, then kissed her. Her hands clasped his head, tangling in his soft curly hair. His hands were on her breasts, his mouth fastened on her nipples, then his fingers stroking her secret places that were no longer sinful, never sinful in the hands of your husband.

Her nightdress was pushed up, the folds of it obscuring her face, getting in the way of his mouth. She pulled handfuls of it away. A thought went through her mind – thank God we're here on the floor, and not in my mother's, I'd have died from shame. It was quickly lost, as strange, sweetly painful sensations occurred deep within her, her teeth bit into his shoulder to stifle the moan of pleasure.

He left her body and lay beside her, his breath still rapid, a hand on her belly. 'You're my husband now,' she whispered. 'I love you.' She turned on her side, settling the nightie down round her. He kept his hand where it was, his fingers making little circles on her soft warm flesh.

'Would you take it off for me?' he asked.

She considered for a minute, then sat up on the pallet, and pulled the nightgown over her head.

'Let me look at you.'

She lay back on the pillow. He raised himself, and gazed at her body, at her hair, one half of it like a shawl covering a breast, he moved it aside. 'You're that beautiful. I wish I was clever with words. You're like hawthorn and dog roses, your skin like the May blossom, and your nipples pink like the rose.' His palms circled her breasts. 'They're like soft hills, and your heart is a fluttering bird beneath my hand.' He kissed each nipple, then her lips. 'Your mouth tastes like wild sweet strawberries, and I love you.' He lay on her and loved her.

When he slept, she thought of what had happened. How she was a woman and knew the secret now. Though she was sure no other woman in the world had been so loved. Nowhere on all the earth was there a man like Jamsie, no man with his strength and beauty. He had turned from her in his sleep, she moved into him, fitting her knees under his thighs, her arm round him, and she slept.

News came from his father to Peader in Dublin that Katy and Jamsie were married. He was overwhelmed by a sense of loss and grief. His intention when he first came to the city had been never to return to Kilgoran. Months of loneliness in a strange place had weakened that resolve; until word of the marriage he had begun to contemplate going back. Returning to all he loved and missed, to see again his father, and the village. To work the land, breathe clean air, be surrounded by people he knew. Walk on the white sands of the shore, feel the wind coming from the ocean, the clean freshness of the wind that had blown across miles of sea. How peaceful it was there, not a soul on the strand, just an occasional gull swooping. How different from the city; cities were terrible places in which to live, like being constantly at a fair without the good humour.

Sitting on the bed, still holding the note from his father, he realized that all his nostalgia for Kilgoran had Katy at its source. Without her what use was the clean sweet air, the green hills or the silver strand? What comfort would he derive from familiar faces when hers was turned to Jamsie? In Mass he'd see the golden hair curl from under the hood of her cloak, and know it wasn't his to loose. And of an evening in Carey's he would look across the room, see Jamsie and know he was going home to lay with her. He could not bear that. To return was to invite torture and torment. He would love Katy from a distance, never let a day pass without remembering her.

He would remain in Dublin, make the best of the place. He looked round the filthy room, saw the bodies of squashed bugs on the walls, the thin streaks of their blood in brown spatters, the greasy pillow ticks, ringed with spittle dribbled from sleeping mouths. Day and night the room was filled with the stench of dirt, or porter, or urine, and the sweetish smell of the bugs. Tonight, he resolved, was the last night he would sleep there – tomorrow he would find new lodgings.

'Like me you're getting old,' Lord Kilgoran said to the pair of labradors following him to the library. The dogs looked up at him with adoring eyes, and wagged their tails. 'Sit now, there's good boys.' Toby and Tara seated themselves before the fire, and Lord Kilgoran sat at his desk to await Charles' arrival. He dreaded the coming interview, and wasn't sure it would achieve anything. But something had to be done about Charles. Some attempt made to make him see sense.

'You wanted me?' Charles said, coming into the room. The dogs rose to greet him, he made a fuss of them.

'Down Tara, down Toby,' Lord Kilgoran commanded. He wanted the business over as soon as possible. He felt ill-at-ease, and avoided looking directly at his son. He cleared his throat and invited him to take a chair, forced himself to regard his son and began, 'I'm sure you're as delighted as I am that Olivia and Peter are to be married.'

'Delighted,' Charles said, his expression amused and puzzled. 'Is that what you wanted to talk about?'

'In a way, yes. Olivia's marriage settlement will strain my resources, so I'd appreciate it if you were a little less extravagant. You do seem to run up the most exorbitant bills. Isn't your allowance enough?'

Charles lolled back in his chair. 'Enough for some things, not for all.'

Lord Kilgoran felt the first stirring of anger. 'Well, it's time you tried cutting your cloth according to your measure.'

'I try, my intentions are of the best – trouble is I never get the measure right.' He shrugged and spread his hands in a helpless gesture.

'Then you must try harder.'

'Oh, for Heaven's sake, Papa, you sound like Mrs Cummings lecturing the servants for using too much tea. I had bad luck at cards, that's all.'

'Bad luck, you blame everything on luck. Being caught cheating at cards and the ensuing fracas which had you sent down from Trinity, was that bad luck, too?'

As soon as he uttered the words, Lord Kilgoran regretted them. Charles's colour rose and he jumped up from the chair. 'I wondered how long it would be before you raised that subject.'

'I never intended to. I preferred not to think of it. It disgraced the family name. Now I'm not sure that brushing it under the carpet was the right thing.' As he spoke, Lord Kilgoran wondered how events had taken this course. His intention in asking Charles to talk with him had never included reference to the incident at Trinity. They were supposed to have a rational discussion, find ways of resolving Charles' spendthrift ways. Instead they were both seething with anger. He made an effort to regain control, to steer the conversation into safer waters.

'Charles, I'm sorry for bringing that up. What I intended talking to you about was the estate, ways of keeping it solvent. After all, it's for your benefit, it will be yours one day.'

'Damn the estate!' Charles pushed back his chair, making it fall over. 'That's all I've ever heard since I was born – the estate, my duty to it. Don't you understand – *I don't want it.* That, as the servants say, I've no gradh for it. In other words I've no love for it, nor Ireland. I'm leaving, going to England, and I'm not staying here to be lectured any more.' He kicked the chair out of his way and left the room.

The dogs came to Lord Kilgoran as he sat thinking how badly he had handled the matter. All he had done was antagonize Charles. There was good in him, he was sure of that, if only he knew how to reach him. He probably would go off to England, but not for long. He would be back. He wondered if he should have made it clear to Charles that Kilgoran, unlike most of the estates in Ireland, was not entailed. He was sure Charles was unaware of that. Unaware that the estate could be left to the girls. Though that, he reminded himself, was unthinkable. From the beginning the land had passed from father to son. Perhaps, though, he should have pointed out to Charles that not having an entail on the property meant that it could be seized for debts. If Charles continued to gamble away his inheritance what then of Kilgoran? The remedy presented itself to him – he could change his will. Let it be known that he had done so. Word soon got around. Would reach the ears of money-lenders, put a stop to Charles issuing post-obits. But such a step, at least for the present, was unthinkable. Charles must be given more time to redeem himself. He would come to his senses, he would reform. There was still time.

Chapter Six

'Only that much,' Katy pleaded, spreading out the wet sheet to bleach on the grass, 'go on, only the size of the sheet.'

'For a garden! Are you mad? You'll be made a laugh of.'

'I don't care. I want one, and the gardener at the House has slips and seedlings ready for me, and Paudeen will carry them down.'

In the end Jamsie agreed, for he knew it wasn't good to thwart a pregnant woman, even though the same patch would have grown a good few potatoes. When he agreed, Katy hugged and kissed him, so that he wanted to throw down the spade and take her inside, but could not for the old woman was there. Morning, noon and night the old woman was there, sometimes wandering in on top of them when they were making love, and he having to stop while Katy led her back to bed, and talked to her like a child, many times scolding her.

He held Katy to him remembering what she had told him last night. They were in bed at the time trying to find a way that was comfortable, for her belly was big, when she said, 'After next week Statia says I'm to have no more to do with you until the child is born.'

'To hell with Statia, that's more of her piseogs. Even the priest would tell you it's a sin to refuse your husband.'

'A lot you care about the priest except when it suits you,' she had teased. 'And it is one of the times when it's not a sin. But in any case, who's refusing you until next week?'

How would he last three months without her? It was a terrible sentence, he thought as she leant against him talking about her garden. He put her away from him. 'Go now before I scandalize the widow woman, and let me get on with planting the potatoes.'

She set off for the House, thinking as she went about the child, and how Statia said it would be a boy because she was thriving, that a girl stole her mother's beauty, made her skin like tallow candles, and her hair like rope. And how her own mother said not to fly in the face of God talking about boys or girls when only a whole, healthy child mattered. And as she neared the Lodge gates she wondered could she hold out against Jamsie for three months. The kiss he gave her now in broad daylight made her weak with longing. What about the nights laying next to him in the bed?

Her mother asked how she was, and said she hoped Jamsie got the potatoes in before Good Friday; it was an unlucky sign if you didn't. Katy assured her they would all be in. Eileen gave her a shilling and told her to keep it for a poor day, and not let Jamsie get his hands on it. Katy knew she was referring to the drink. 'Only twice since we've married has he come home with the signs of it on him,' she said defensively.

'Twice is two times more than he should,' Eileen replied tartly.

Katy said nothing, for if she did they would row, so she let the remark go, then changed the subject to that of Miss Olivia's marriage. 'I believe it's to be in England. When?'

'September I think. Isn't it a disgrace not marrying from her home . . .'

Katy agreed that it was and bade her mother goodbye.

Up at the House, Hannah had something for her. Paudeen shouted when she came to the kitchen door, 'I have the plants in a basket, give me a call when you're going and I'll carry them down.'

Hannah gave her a mug of new milk, and bread and butter. 'Eat that, it'll do you good,' she urged, at the same time packing Katy's basket with food.

'What would I do without you and my mother. I never knew it was so hard to live,' Katy said sitting down.

'So long as it's here you'll have it, there's more thrown out than would feed a nation. Food coming down from the dining-room not touched. Get that into you, you're feeding two.'

They sat by the range and gossiped. Hannah told her the latest: how Miss Olivia was going over to London to choose her wedding dress, that Charles was travelling with her, and that Miss Olivia intended visiting Miss Catherine.

'Won't it be strange all the same, not one in the House but Miss Charlotte and the Master,' Katy said.

'Terrible strange,' Hannah agreed, 'but maybe the child will come into her own. Sure now she doesn't get a look in. Thrown to the winds, poor lamb. There was a governess supposed to come last month that didn't. Maybe now with the others gone, the Master will have more time to think about the child.'

Katy supposed it was with having no Mistress in the House – a man couldn't be expected to see to everything.

'He could not, the poor man. God knows he's been sorely afflicted, rearing a pup like that for a son on top of losing the woman he loved. It was a terrible day for him, the day Miss Charlotte was born and her mother died.'

'Didn't *you* see the ghost the night before?'

'I did that, as plain as I'm seeing you. I'd gone into the Great Hall for something I'd dropped there early in the day, a handkerchief, I think it was. Anyway you know how cold it is there? Well this night, it was worse, an unnatural coldness altogether. I felt the shivers running down my back. The candles were lit, but the draught was making them flicker so you could hardly see at all.'

'Was it then you saw it?' Katy asked, her voice hardly above a whisper.

'It was. Down under the gallery, a tall figure walking with a kind of glide, so you wondered if the creature's feet touched the floor.'

'Would you say it was a man?'

'From the size I would. A fine big man. Oh, it was the O'Sullivan all right come to warn of a death in the family.'

Katy moved closer to the fire. 'Isn't that strange all the same, you wouldn't think he'd be bothered about a death in the family that ran him out.'

'You could say so, though it's my belief that in Heaven old scores would be forgotten, and that the O'Sullivan thinks only of the one who is to die as a human being, and isn't bothered about names or things like that. Anyway I blessed myself, and said, "God spare everyone", but I knew someone was going to meet his maker. And the next morning, the poor Mistress, God rest her, went into her travail.'

Hannah described the day. The screams of the woman that went on for hours. The doctor there, and another coming from Cork. Every servant on bended knees saying the Rosary. Then God seeming to answer their prayers for the screaming stopped, and word came down that the child was born. The prayers of thanksgiving no sooner started when there was a great commotion; the menservants being sent for to prop up the ends of the massive bed for the life's blood was pumping out of the Mistress. Hannah started to cry, and Katy let her. Neither of them saw or heard Charlotte, who had been standing by the kitchen door, tiptoe away.

The air was full of the sound of birds, the song of larks, and the constant pheet-pheet-pheet of meadow pipit. Johnny's wife crouched in a hollow, well hidden. She heard none of them, only the hooves of the galloping horse. When she judged it to be a certain distance from her hiding place, she briefly showed herself, then crouched again.

She had heard tell the young Master was going away, and had come to give him a present. The lovely present of herself, and not one would be the wiser except her mother who would have half the golden guinea Master Charles might give. Once before he offered a guinea. A bright dazzling coin, holding it between finger and thumb.

'I'll give you this,' he had said. A week after her wedding that was. 'I couldn't, Sir, sure I'm a married woman. Johnny'd kill me,' she had said. Laying in the hollow, hearing the horse come nearer, she remembered it wasn't fear of Johnny hearing tell, for he would split open man or woman who said such a thing. But the young Master might give her a child, a child with the Kilgoran stamp. Then Johnny would surely know and maybe kill her. But now with an O'Hara child inside her, she could have Master Charles and the golden guinea.

She stood up again. The breeze pulled at her tangled hair, whipped her petticoat into her flat belly; only a more pronounced blue veining and swelling breasts signs of her pregnancy. Charles saw her, raised his whip. She went down again. When he came to the hollow she protested and struggled. 'Ah, don't, Sir, don't take advantage of me.' She made him fight for her, revelling in the passion she unleashed. And when it was over, thinking that for all his fine ways, clothes, and speech, he was only a man, laying beside her like a floundered fish.

'I'll have to go,' she said arranging her clothes. 'Is it right you're going over the water, Sir?'

'I am.'

'It'll be terrible sad. I hope you'll be back. The place wouldn't be the same without you.'

'Here, take this.' He held out the guinea.

'Sure I couldn't, Sir, it wasn't for money I did it.'

'Go on, take it.' He flicked the coin, and smiled sardonically when he saw her frantically search the grass. 'You're worth more than one,' he said when she had retrieved it. 'I'll give you two next time.'

'You'll be back, so?' She made her expression expectant.

'I'll be back,' Charles said, fastening his breeches, rising, brushing himself down, picking up his hat and crop. He mounted the white horse. 'You give good value, I'll be back.'

A rumour reached Father Bolger about Johnny's wife and Charles Kilgoran, brought to him by Mary Doyle. 'I thought you'd want to know, Father,' she said after relating the news. – She brings me every tittle tattle of the parish, the priest thought, looking at his thin sharp-featured housekeeper, and tells it with relish.

'Do you know this for a fact, did you see them yourself?' he quizzed.

'How could I do that, and me here all the hours God sends, but it's a fact all right. And doesn't everyone know it, except Johnny O'Hara.'

Father Bolger assured her he would look into it. There was no use, he knew, reminding Mary not to repeat unfounded gossip, he had done so many times. And on each occasion she had regarded him as if he was simple, and asked, 'Sure how else would I know anything if it wasn't by word of mouth? If I had to see proof of everything I'd know nothing.'

Though wildly exaggerated, and frequently attributed to the wrong person, there was usually a grain of truth in the news she brought, so her accusation that Johnny's wife was seeing Charles Kilgoran could not be dismissed. And if they were it wouldn't be discussing the crops or admiring the flowers on the bog they'd be. No, Father Bolger said to himself, that young woman would be entering into the occasion of mortal sin, and that he would have to prevent.

He pondered how best to go about it without making Johnny the wiser. If it was any other woman in the parish, he wouldn't hesitate going to her house, asking to speak with her – no father, husband, or brother would question his right, or inquire the nature of the business. The O'Haras would, Johnny, Jamsie, the father, too, maybe not Padraig, but certainly Johnny. In his attempt to save the girl from sin he might drive her husband to take some-one's life. How was he to balance one sin against another? What he wanted of course was that one in confession. How to get her there was another thing, once only since he'd come to the parish, the day before she married, had she confessed.

While he was still wondering how best to tackle the problem Mary poked her head round the door and an-nounced that Johnny and Padraig were here to see him. – Glory be, isn't that the strange coincidence, he thought, then told Mary to bring them in.

'We want your help, Father,' Johnny said, approaching, brandishing a piece of paper. 'Look at that – Dano's put-ting up the rent from November.'

'Sit down, calm down,' Father Bolger exhorted.

Padraig took a chair, Johnny remained standing, exuding an air of angry belligerence, not waiting for the priest to finish reading the notice before continuing, 'You know what he's after – it's not extra money – he wants the fields – he wants us out. Asking for money he knows we haven't got gives him the excuse he's been looking for. I'm telling you if he's not stopped there'll be trouble.'

'Trouble, what sort of trouble? What do you mean by that threat, Johnny?'

'Ah, don't mind him, Father, that's just talk. Just his talk, but maybe you'd have a word with Dano, make him hold his hand,' Padraig said.

– They're like peas in a pod, Father Bolger thought, looking from one face to the next, and yet as different as chalk and cheese. Padraig nice and easy, no violence in him, a good man, happily married to a good woman – the other fellow the complete opposite.

'Well, Father?' Johnny's bellicose tone recalled the priest.

'I'll have a word with him certainly, not that I think it'll do a ha'porth of good. I've had words with Dano before. He quotes the law at me. He has it on his side. Remember that, Johnny, when you threaten trouble. Dano has the law behind him. Patience, prayer and hope is our only weapon.'

'Sure, I might have known,' Johnny said mockingly. 'It's not only the law he has on his side, it's the clergy as well. Come away out, Padraig, we're wasting our time. I told you didn't I – I didn't want to come in the first place.'

In sorrow Father Bolger watched them go. He knew well what Johnny's threats implied. If he wasn't already in one of the Secret Societies he soon would be. And if Dano went ahead with an increase or eviction one night he would have a visit. His cattle would be harmed, his house maybe razed, himself injured, even killed. He had to try and stop Dano's planned increase, stop him unleashing violence in men like Johnny O'Hara.

He rose and went into the chapel, knelt before the altar

144

and implored God's help. Prayed for Johnny; for his wife entering into the occasion of, if not already committing, mortal sin; for Dano, that God might touch his heart; for himself that his hatred for men like Dano, the agent who leased him the land, the English absentee landowner, who was at the back of it all, should diminish.

Dano's house, a small, country Georgian one, had the look of prosperity about it, Father Bolger thought as he drove up in the pony and trap. He noticed the new roof, the doors and windows freshly painted, and saw a servant answer the door to his knock. Behind her, coming up from the hall, Mrs Driscoll was greeting him profusely.

'Good day, Father, God bless you, sure isn't it an honour to have you call. If it's himself you were wanting, he's in the parlour.' She sent the serving girl away and led him to the room. 'It's Father Bolger,' she said opening the door, putting her head round it, standing back then to let him pass.

'Good afternoon, Dano. Don't stir, don't get up,' Father Bolger said. Dano was by the fire, his jacket off, his stomach bulging at his waistcoat. There was a brown and white dog at his feet who growled at the priest's approach.

'All right, all right, easy now.' The dog relaxed. 'This is a surprise,' Dano said, getting up from the fire, his voice amiable but his eyes wary. 'You haven't been this long time. Will you have something?'

'I won't, thanks, it's not what you'd say a social call.'

'Oh, and what sort of call might it be, Father?'

'You're putting up the O'Haras' rent. They've been to see me.'

'I am, times are hard.'

– He's like a bull, the priest thought, surveying the thick-necked, powerful-shouldered figure, a red-faced bull, even to the little pale eyes, and pale lashes. 'For the poor times are always hard. The people are afraid. They say you want them out. It's the fields you want, that you'll evict.'

The colour went up Dano's neck into the red face, deepening its floridness. Father Bolger half expected to see a foot paw the ground, but Dano kept his stance and the little pale eyes did not flinch. When he spoke there was a sneer in his voice. 'Aren't you very concerned about the likes of Fintan O'Hara, a man who never darkens the chapel door?'

'There's more to being a Catholic than that. There's charity, something you haven't got.'

Dano lowered his head, took a step forward. 'Now listen, Father, I respect your cloth. I don't mind you giving me a going-over in confession. But in my own house I'll not have you say how I conduct my business. And as for charity, name one in the parish quicker to put his hand in his pocket. Go on, name one!' He was sweating with anger, puce in the face.

'Is that what you think charity is, Dano, Mass offerings, paying your Easter Dues? What'll you do when you die, Dano? Do you think God'll say Dano gave five pounds at Easter and Christmas, he goes to Heaven? Or Dano gave ten pounds and made eight families homeless? Dano caused men to hate, to plan vengeance, to commit violence, send him to Hell!'

He watched the florid face pale, heard the voice bluster. 'I'm making a living like the next one. There's a market for cattle – I have a family, three sons and three daughters, I'm providing for them.'

'The men on the bog have families, they're trying to provide for them. The fires of Hell are hot, Dano. Eternity's a long time. I'd think about that before November if I was you. Now I'll be going. I'll see myself out.'

When he opened the door Mrs Driscoll was behind it, a terrified expression on her face. Nervously she escorted the priest to the hall door, and bade him goodbye.

On the way home he saw Statia walking along the road. He reined in Acushla, and asked was she going in his direction.

'I am, Father.'

'Get up so,' he said opening the trap door, 'and save your legs.'

'May God bless you,' Statia said, clambering in, nearly taking the door off its hinges with the way she banged it. She talked as they drove along, about the weather, the child she had just delivered, and how it was so big it looked like a man beside its mother in the bed. And then remarked that tomorrow Master Charles was off to England, for good, and not one in the parish would be sorry. When he dropped her, Father Bolger thanked God for answering one of his prayers. With young Kilgoran gone the salvation of Johnny's wife was assured. And thought that if his sermon on Hell went home to Dano, so maybe was the salvation of Johnny, and the homes of them on the bog secure.

'Olivia!'

'Catherine!' The sisters embraced each other.

'Oh darling, how good it is to see you,' Catherine said, delightedly. 'I've missed you so much. I want to hear all about Papa, Charlotte, Kilgoran, everything.' Catherine released Olivia. 'But do come in, darling, you must be exhausted and me prattling away. Was the journey over dreadful?' she asked, leading the way into the house.

'Absolutely appalling. The boat was pitching at anchor in Kingstown, so you can imagine what happened once we cleared the harbour. Do you know, for hours after we disembarked I could still feel the horrid movement. Each time I cross in a storm I say never again. And definitely, once I'm married I shall return to Ireland seldom.'

'You poor thing – you always were a bad sailor. Let me take you upstairs – you must rest before luncheon.'

'No, I'm quite recovered. I slept well last night in London, but some tea would be nice.'

Catherine rang, and while they waited, the sisters talked, Olivia explaining why she was being married away from home. Peter's family were long-tailed, simply hundreds of them, all being invited – London was much more central, Saint Margaret's the place for fashionable weddings – it was as simple as that.

'I expect Papa is very upset,' Catherine said.

'He was, initially, but the fracas with Charles rather took his mind off it.'

'Poor Papa. And Charlotte, how is she?'

'Growing into a sullen, moody girl. She was never very outgoing, but recently – I don't know, she sits round all day moping.'

While the maid served tea, Olivia complimented Catherine on her house, the gardens she could see from the window, how magnificent the rhododendrons were. Surrey, she said, was such a pretty county, such sweet little villages, not at all like Ireland. Everything so ordered, clean and tidy, the people, too.

'Not at all like Ireland,' Catherine agreed, and thought wistfully of Kilgoran with its straggling cottages, its wild beauty, of the bare-footed women working in the fields, raising good-humoured faces to call, ''Tis a fine day, Miss Catherine,' when she rode past, the shy, polite men who touched their caps, every face one she had known all her life.

'Do you realize,' Olivia said breaking in on her thoughts, 'I haven't seen you since your wedding – more than a whole year. I've been dying of curiosity. What did happen on the night? Were your fears fulfilled or was I right?'

'Really, Olivia, you can't ask such things, you shouldn't,' Catherine said, going scarlet.

'Why not? I'm about to become a bride myself for heaven's sake. Do tell, no secrets.'

'I'd rather not. I can't – I can't talk about such things. You look so beautiful, your gown is lovely.'

'Changing the conversation, eh! Oh well, all right, I won't pursue it,' Olivia said, then stood up to display her dress. 'It's the latest mode. See how much softer the shape is, the skirt right to the ground. Isn't the sloping shoulder becoming?' She pirouetted for Catherine to have an all-round view. 'And isn't the shade of blue divine?'

Catherine agreed that it enhanced Olivia's colouring.

'I knew you'd like it. I say, isn't it exciting having a Queen on the throne, and one so young. I can't wait to see what influence she'll have on fashion, can you, Catherine?'

Catherine shrugged. 'You know how uninterested I am in clothes, not like you at all. But it is wonderful to have a Queen so young, younger than either of us.' She became silent. 'My daughter shall be called after her.'

'Why you sly old thing! You're having a baby.'

'Oh, but I'm not. I only meant – oh I am such a fool leading you to believe that. What I should have said was, that if I have a baby, a girl, I shall call her Victoria.'

'Well, I must say you've disappointed me. At last, I thought, I was to be an aunt. But not to worry, I'm sure you'll have dozens. By the way, when will Edward be home?'

'He won't, he's dining in tonight, and will sleep in barracks.'

'Oh!' Olivia raised her eyebrows. 'Oh, yes, I see. Pity, I'd like to have seen him.'

Catherine explained the reason for Edward not being at home. 'One has to dine in once a month. It's unfortunate it coincided with your visit, but the army is the army.'

'Yes, of course,' Olivia said.

Catherine began to wonder why she had felt compelled to justify Edward's absence. Olivia knew very well that dining in was a normal part of an officer's life. Then why the raised eyebrows? Was she implying something? Had she misinterpreted her reluctance to discuss her married life? With a sinking feeling she remembered how Olivia, on the day before she married, sought to console her fears by saying Edward would one day take a mistress. Was that what the quirk of her eyebrows was suggesting? The thought had never crossed her mind, not since that wonderful night in Dargle House when she had extracted a sleepy promise from Edward. For a moment she regretted that Olivia had come, had engendered such a suspicion. He was dining in, of that she had no doubt, but what about afterwards? Who was to know where he went then? She remembered how definitely on the day before she married Olivia had said that *all* men take mistresses. – How would one know? Catherine asked herself. Was an unfaithful husband less attentive? What exactly were the reasons Olivia had given for a man straying? Wasn't it to do with a wife being unresponsive? She recalled her sister's words. 'If you're not good at it, once you've produced he'll take a mistress.' Well, she certainly wasn't unresponsive, nor was Edward inattentive. And they had no children, yet. Perhaps she had just let her imagination run away with her. That was a fault of hers, like her ridiculous fear that she was barren. It came of not being fully occupied, she must take herself in hand.

'Come back, come back from wherever you are,' Olivia's voice cut in on Catherine's thoughts.

'I'm so sorry, I was thinking.'

'Well,' Olivia said with mock severity, 'I must say that's a nice way to treat your sister. Now listen attentively, I want to describe my wedding dress.'

Catherine smiled, and relaxed and enjoyed enormously the remainder of her sister's visit.

'What did I tell you – ten months to the day you were married I'd bring home your first child.'

'That's not till the day after tomorrow,' Katy said.

'Well,' Statia replied, 'often the first takes its time arriving. Lay down and let me look at you.'

Katy obeyed and while Statia's hands did things to her, thought of the night Statia had forecast this day, and how then she was referring to a child that would have been Peader's.

'Get up,' Statia said as she finished her examination. 'You've started. Keep moving, keep on the go, but don't go far, I don't want you dropping the child in the field. I'll let your mother know, and be back later on.'

'Is that all?' Katy asked.

'What else do you want?'

'I thought it was happening?'

'It is, it will in its own time. Carry on with what you were doing.'

With Statia gone, Jamsie came in and, seeing Katy down in the mouth, he asked what ailed her. She told him what Statia had said. He put an arm round her.

'Sure didn't you know it would take a while?' He held her close.

'I'm not an eejit altogether. I didn't mean immediately, but soon, and I didn't think Statia would leave me. And don't be doing that,' she pulled away when he tried to kiss her. 'Leave me alone. Statia says I've to keep walking.'

She was sorry for being short with him, yet she couldn't help herself. For all of a sudden she hated him. Blamed him for what was happening to her. For the pains that each time they came were getting worse, not terrible, but unlike any pain she had ever had. It was all his fault. She was afraid, remembering the stories she had heard about childbirth; the story Hannah told about the Mistress; the woman her mother had taken her to see, dead in a coffin, a baby at its foot. And the women telling each other, 'Yesterday she was in the whole of her health, walking round like you or me.'

It was all his fault, she thought again. I never had a thing wrong with me before I married. I was that healthy I could jump over the moon. Another pain encircled her, she paced the kitchen till it went, then continued with her thoughts. And for the last nine months I've not known what it is to be right, sick and not sleeping, waddling like a duck.

'I'd say from the look of them we'll have a good crop of potatoes,' Jamsie said when she put before him his dinner made of scraps of meat and bread sent down from Hannah. She spoon-fed the old woman a mixture of the same.

'You'll bring bad luck on us mentioning the crop without saying, please God,' she said. 'You're always doing that.'

– I'll go up the field, Jamsie thought, for if I don't, in a minute in labour or not I'll lambast her if she keeps on at me. 'I'll be above if you want me,' he said.

She sniffed as much as to say, what would I want you for. And when he was gone, sat down by the old woman, held her hand and cried. 'You know what it's like, I wish you could tell me,' she said, the tears spilling down her cheeks. The old woman smiled foolishly at her.

Her mother and Statia returned, and she felt better, safer. Later on Hannah brought a bowl of chicken soup, and though she wasn't hungry, Statia made her eat it. 'You'll need to keep up your strength.' Jamsie came in and ate a cold potato then went out again out of the way of the women. The pains got bad enough to take her mind off her earlier fears. Before it got dark Statia sent Jamsie up the bog to get poteen from his father. 'I'll make sure she sleeps tonight,' she said, nodding in the direction of the old woman. 'I don't want her falling over me when I'm delivering the child, please God.'

Katy sat while the women said the Rosary, offering it up for her safe delivery. Hannah went home. The quality of Katy's pains changed so that she bent double and cried out. 'They'll get worse before you get better,' Statia said, and herself and her mother linked their arms through Katy's and kept her walking.

Hours later laying on the pallet waiting for another wave of pain to engulf her Katy said wasn't Jamsie a long time coming back. 'Don't waste your breath talking,' Statia kneeling beside her said, 'the old woman's asleep without the drink.'

'Isn't it a long time coming?' she heard her mother say in the brief respite between contractions, when for a moment it seemed as if they had never in reality existed, as if they belonged in some terrible nightmare. She drifted into seconds of blissful oblivion, brought back to consciousness by sharp slaps on her bare buttocks, and Statia's exhortations to 'Wake up, to come on now, it wouldn't be long!'

She didn't know whether it was morning or night, didn't care that once she had heard Jamsie talking at the door, that he was drunk, and gone again. Only thinking that if she didn't die, never again would she have another child. Her mother gave her a hand to hold and pull on,

Statia rubbed her back, and put cloths on her burning head.

She couldn't endure it any longer, she would die. She wanted to die. No one could endure such agony and live. The bones in her back were being wrenched asunder, she could feel them tearing apart. 'Oh, Holy Mother of God help me,' she cried.

'It'll soon be over, astoir, only a little while. Suffer it a little while longer,' her mother said, her face etched with the pain of watching Katy's pain, and the wrenching of her arm nearly out of its socket.

'Oh Jesus! Oh God!' Katy's nails dug into her mother's hand, drawing blood. Statia was bending over her, forcing her legs apart, telling her to keep her knees up, that the head was crowned, that when she told her, she was to push.

'Come on now, push hard. Go on, you're a big strong girl – push.' She clenched her jaws, let go her mother's hand and bore down, conscious of nothing except the uncontrollable urge to expel.

'Don't! Stop! You'll reef yourself. Don't push till I tell you.'

She was deaf to Statia's instructions, heard nothing, only her own animal grunting, raising in pitch, in protest against the cleaving of her body, it was being parted, an enormous hard mass was splitting her in two.

'Good girl, the worst is over, the head is out. Come on now, don't go to sleep on me. Come on now, another push. Press down on her stomach, Eileen. Push now, Katy, it's nearly over.'

Again her body was assaulted, forced open, her voice

155

cried out involuntarily, and she pushed, and pushed. Then as if within her there was a fish slithering and wriggling, attempting to escape, and succeeding, the remainder of the child slid out.

She had delivered, she was free, and the pain had gone, was as if it had never been.

Her mother was crying, then laughing, crying again, holding her hands to her face, her eyes filled with wonder. She heard the child cry, and Statia saying, 'It's a girl.'

'A girl! Are you sure?'

'Do you think I can't tell the difference?'

'You were wrong, so,' Katy said, raising herself on an elbow.

'Lay down and don't move – it was bound to be one or the other.'

'Where's Jamsie?' she asked. She wanted him beside her. The fear and the pain were gone, gone too the inexplicable hatred of him she had felt. Now she wanted only him. To show him their child.

'I sent him down to sleep in the Lodge, I'll take word to him,' her mother said.

No sooner was she gone than Katy cried out, 'Oh Jesus! it's starting again. I'm getting another pain.'

'Stop bawling,' Statia commanded, and pressed the heel of her hand on Katy's belly. 'It's the after-birth. Push again.' Katy did, and to her great relief it required only a little effort to eject the soft mass.

'All in one piece,' Statia proclaimed. 'Thanks be to God that's come away for until it does your life's hanging on a thread, you could bleed like a stuck pig and be dead in no time.'

Katy felt wonderful, and lay with the child on her breast looking at the tiny fair head. By the time Jamsie came, Statia had tidied up, collected the washing, and had the Widow Murphy dressed.

'That's everything for the time being,' she said, looking round the kitchen. 'I'll take herself to my place for a night or two.'

'A ghille,' Jamsie said when they were alone. His voice was low, hoarse with emotion. 'How are you? Are you all right, are you better?' He kissed her, and then timorously touched the baby's head. Katy laid her down and put her arms round him.

'I love you,' he said. 'She's beautiful, she's like you.'

'We'll call her Bridget, and Eileen and Margaret after your mother and mine.'

'Whatever you like,' he said, and kissed her again. Holding each other tenderly they fell asleep. She woke before him, and lay looking from him to the child. She compared the two faces, searching the child's for a resemblance to Jamsie's – she wanted it to be like him, but had to admit it wasn't.

One day after Statia said she could get up, she took from a box under the old woman's bed her wedding dress, and tried it on, thinking, as she slipped it over her head, she would wear it when the baby was baptized and herself churched. Her hands reached round the back for the hooks and eyes, but to her surprise and disappointment the edges were inches apart. She was amazed! She had been so sure that once the baby was born she would be the same as before. After taking it off, refolding and putting it back in the box, she lifted her petticoat and furtively

157

looked at her stomach. – And I thought it was gone, she said to herself, picking up handfuls of wrinkled silver-streaked flesh. Sure it was only that it seemed so after the way I was, big and swollen. While she stood looking down at herself her milk came in and leaked oozing through the bodice. I'm like a cow, she thought, a good milk cow, and it'll be many the long day before I'll wear peacock blue.

Six weeks after Bridget's birth, her stomach had gone down, the flow of milk regulated itself, and one night when Jamsie, as he had done for several weeks, put his hand on her breast, instead of scolding him, and telling him, 'No, not yet,' she felt again the race of her blood, and turned to him, her mouth hungrily seeking his.

The potato crop was not as plentiful as Katy and Jamsie had hoped. Three rows yielded roots the size of marbles. The same thing happened to many of their neighbours, and they consoled each other, that God was good. Next year it would be a different story – plenty always followed scarcity, and somehow they would manage until then. There was no fear of them starving – Hannah would see to that.

The baby thrived and slept long. Katy had never felt happier, occupied during the day cleaning her little home, minding the child, and the old woman, gossiping with her neighbours, and at night laying in Jamsie's arms. Then one morning she got out of bed and felt sick. She thought little of it the first time, but when after a week she still felt an urge to vomit when she rose, decided to ask Statia's advice.

'You're in the way again.'

'Ah, no, Statia, sure I couldn't be.'

'Unless you've been sleeping with your two legs in the one stocking I'd say there's nothing surer.'

'Oh I can't be, Statia! I can't be having another child. I've just had one. All last summer I carried one. I can't do that again, not yet. Not yet, Statia.'

'It's no use pleading with me, astoir, to tell you you're not. You'll have to make the best of it.'

'But I can't. I'm sick. I'll swell up again and be lifeless, not able to sleep, to lay comfortable in the bed. What'll I do?'

'Go home and make the dinner. Think no further ahead than you have to. Go about your business a bit at a time. The sickness will pass, and everything else happen so gradual you'll get used to it ...'

But Katy was unable to take the advice, fretted, woke each morning with the thought of pregnancy uppermost in her mind. The child became cranky, and slept badly. When the breast did not pacify her, Katy, bleary-eyed, walked the floor nursing her. In the mornings she was irritable with Jamsie.

One night Johnny came to the cottage, a jubilant expression on his face. 'Driscoll's withdrawn the notice, the rent's not going up. I'm going to Carey's to celebrate, are you coming?'

'He is not,' Katy said, before Jamsie could answer. 'We've no money to squander on drink.'

'Go on you,' Jamsie said to his brother. 'I'll be after you.'

'Oh, no you won't,' Katy shouted.

'Listen to that now,' Johnny said, laughing as he went out the door.

'*Don't ever do that again,*' Jamsie said, walking towards her. For a minute Katy thought he was going to strike her, and backed away. She had never seen him regard her with anger, never heard him use such a tone.

'Do what?' she asked, genuinely puzzled.

'Shame me in front of my brother. I only married you. You don't own me. You'll not tell me what to do.'

She was so astounded that he was gone before she could think of a reply. While he was out she sat by the fire and nursed the child. The widow woman wouldn't go to sleep either, and talked all the time to her sons who were long gone. Katy wished she would die, then said a prayer for God to forgive her such a thought.

Her mind kept returning to how Jamsie had spoken to her, the way he looked at her. Never in all the time she'd known him had he been so. And now he was down in Carey's with his scut of a brother, drinking. But wait till he came back; she would have something to say.

He was drunk when he returned, full of plamais, all over her. She was determined to show her displeasure, pulling away from him, turning her head when he tried kissing her. But he cajoled, persisted, placing kisses anywhere he could, on her neck, cheek, eyes, while his hands caressed her so that she melted and in the long run willingly surrendered herself. Afterwards he slept quicker than usual. He snored and the smell of drink hung heavy about him turning Katy's stomach, reminding her of her pregnancy. The straw beneath her felt lumpy, she sat up and teased it flat. And, as her fingers worked smoothing and

160

separating, unbidden into her mind came a memory of Peader. Clearly she saw him, the red-gold gleam of his hair, the pale green of his eyes. She lay down and nurtured the memory, recalling his gentle ways, the respect with which he had treated her, how he never got drunk, and thought just before she fell asleep – if I'd married him, it's not on the floor I'd be laying, but in comfort, in a good bed up in his father's house.

Chapter Seven

Katy's second child was a boy with black hair and blue eyes like Jamsie. She called him Thomas. Eleven months later she had a girl, Mary Kate, brown-haired and grey-eyed, neither as robust as Thomas, nor as pretty as Bridget. In the agony of each of her labours she vowed never to have another child, a vow that diminished hourly after delivery, and was forgotten within weeks, so that she responded to Jamsie's touch, hungry for him after the long abstinence, and welcomed him passionately into her body, no longer stifling her cries of pleasure, for the old woman had died shortly after Thomas' birth.

In his arms she forgot her perpetual weariness, the demands of the babies, the worry over crops and food. For the time it took to make love she transcended her cares, her ordinary life, was conscious only of her body, of Jamsie's, of the delightful experience, and wanted it to last forever.

Then a night came when the magic was dispelled. About to drift into sleep, she heard a child cry. She rose and saw to it, it took a long time to settle. Returning to the pallet before the fire where Jamsie snored, she felt resentful. Became aware of a desolate feeling. Of having been used as if she was an animal – covered, then discarded. Was it always to be so? she asked herself. Jamsie was sleeping, lost to her. Such an abrupt ending. Gone from her, he who had been part of her. Was there never to be cherishing?

On another night when her mind pondered such things her thoughts wandered to the days before marriage, and to Peader. She remembered how he had courted her, his tenderness. She was sure he would have cherished her, and never come home drunk, as Jamsie frequently did. Himself and Johnny always in Carey's. Johnny calling for him. She bitterly resented that.

Johnny continued to come, Jamsie to drink, and Katy to resent. But remembering his reaction the once when she tried to stop him she curbed her tongue, until the night she knew she was once again pregnant; then so distraught was she when Jamsie came in she screamed.

'I hate you! *I hate you!* My mother was *right*. You're no use, no good. All you want me for is making children. The O'Haras were never any use. Lookit you, just look at yourself, you get more like your father every day ...' On and on she went, pouring out invectives against Jamsie, his mother and father, dead this long time, driven by rage and misery.

'Let my parents rest in peace.' Jamsie swayed towards her. 'Don't bring them into it. Do you hear me now? I'll kill you if you do.'

'Go on, do it, I don't care. I'd be better off dead. Better off any day than married to the likes of you.'

He hit her. She screamed, and he hit her again, with an open hand across the face. 'You asked for that,' he said, 'you're like a demon.' Then he sat on the chair she had chosen from the attic and fell asleep.

It wasn't how she wanted it to end. It was over too soon. Her face stung from the slaps, she massaged it, and kept thinking that he shouldn't have gone to sleep. He was supposed to say he was sorry. To kiss her, hold her close. Tell her he was sorry for getting drunk, and wouldn't, never again. Tell her he knew she was tired, worn out with three babies and another on the way. He wasn't supposed to fall asleep on her.

She went to him, bent over him. 'I hate you. The smell of you. You're like an animal, like a pig.' He snored. She pounded him with her fists. He shrugged as if a fly irritated him. 'Oh God, I hate you, I hate you,' she sobbed. She saw how his beard was growing, black, darkening his chin and cheeks, and remembered the smooth goldness of Peader's skin, how he had never smelled of drink. 'Oh! the fool that I was to give him up for you,' she said. Then she sat by the fire and cried quietly. After a while she too slept, her head lolling against the wall.

When she woke her body was stiff, and her neck ached from the awkward way she had leant by the wall, but her heart felt lighter than the night before. It was thinking about Peader that had done it, she was sure. The reminding herself that someone else loved her, and always would. It was a great comfort. Jamsie was still sprawled on the chair. It crossed her mind that like herself his bones would be aching, and she almost called him to say, 'Throw yourself on the pallet for an hour, it's early yet.' But didn't, saying instead to herself, 'Let them ache, 'tis the price of him.'

After every drinking bout Jamsie was contrite, for he never meant to grieve Katy. Never when he set out for

Carey's did he intend to get drunk, but two pints led to three, and then he was done for. After that all thought of Katy and the wasted copper vanished from his mind. When he woke on the morning after the row he knew something out of the ordinary had happened. There was a vague recollection of something unpleasant, what exactly he couldn't remember. But he had no doubt what sort of humour Katy was in, and that Prince the black and white dog was bearing the brunt of it.

'Did I do anything last night, I have a feeling I did.'

'Nothing at all, only hit me twice.'

'God! I didn't,' his voice was incredulous, his face shocked. 'I wouldn't hurt you for the world.' He didn't know what else to say, or how.

'That's another consequence of your drinking – that was all I needed, you landing me with a dog,' Katy said. 'Three children, and another before the end of the year, and a pup as well, Please God for the child.'

'Please God,' he echoed her words. 'I'm sorry about the drink and last night. I won't touch another drop, never.'

Till the next time, Katy thought, but said nothing. He had made promises before, she put no faith in them. The children and the dog were under her feet, there wasn't room to move. It made her think of a woman with an earth floor, and a lot of babies, who had dug a shallow hole in it, and confined the children so.

Jamsie, unable to bear her silence, said he'd go up the fields, throw an eye to the potatoes. He went, and while there asked himself what had possessed him, made him strike her? Bad and all as my father was, he told himself, he never did that. While he earthed up the potatoes, he

165

searched for an excuse. – She must have aggravated me in the drink. A man in drink doesn't know what he's doing. But for all that I'm sorry. I'd cut off my hand rather than strike her again. But lately she's been in the divil's own humour. There's no pleasing her. If I look crooked she's up in a minute. Or if I look the other way she's crying. I don't know what's come over her at all. Sure the Lord knows I'm the same man she married. I haven't changed.

He carried on thinking and working along the row of potatoes until he was up close to the hedge that bordered the road. He heard the sound of women's voices and recognized them as Statia's and Mary Doyle's. They stopped by the hedge which was so thick they couldn't see him behind it.

'What do you think of the O'Haras' demesne?' Statia was saying.

And Mary answered, 'I said it at the time – a crying sin to be putting down flowers where a man could grow potatoes.'

'Ah, but sure isn't it a sight to behold,' Statia countered.

'A sight me eye! Isn't the fields and hedges full of flowers for the picking. 'Tis easy to see she knows little about land.'

'And sure how could she, reared in the Lodge without an inch of it? Isn't it more she knew about opening the gates for the gentry,' Statia replied.

– You bloody oul backbiter, it's out on top of you I should jump and give you a red face to match your nose, Jamsie thought as the two women continued to vilify Katy. But if I did they'd brazen it out and tell me a listener never heard good of himself. So he stayed where he was and listened.

'She had the fine ways, all right,' Mary said. 'But wasn't it easy for her, look at the good start she got, too, a grand cottage, and two fields.'

''Twas why Jamsie took her, he feathered his nest well.'

'Musha, Statia, I wouldn't say that. She's a fine girl with a good figure and a yellow poll that shines like spun gold.'

– You're not a bad sort, Mary, Jamsie thought, not moving a foot for the ground was littered with twigs, and a sudden snap would have alerted the women. He was enjoying listening, and wanted to hear how Statia parried the dart about the head of fine hair, for the rub was meant for her with not ten hairs to boast of.

'I'll give you that,' Statia replied, and paused before adding, 'Not like some I could mention with arses like the back of a cab.'

Mary knew well it was to her own daughters, big heavy women, that Statia referred, and being no match at the repartee, the conversation, and the two women, moved on.

He went back to the house. It was a great excuse to relate the gossip to Katy, take her out of her sulks.

'Did you hear that, Statia and Mary say I only took you for the two fields.'

'Maybe it was so,' Katy replied coolly, but he sensed a thaw.

'Aye, maybe so. Only you didn't have them in the beginning.'

'I had more than I have now. I had shoes on me feet.'

'You did too, and a lovely blue cloak.'

'So you remember.'

'I remember it all.'

She let him kiss her then, and tell her he loved her, and was sorry. And for a while after that she thought little of Peader. For as long as a month Jamsie didn't go to the public house, then lapsed, but instead of becoming sullen, brooding or castigating him she sought escape again in fantasies of Peader. Maybe one day he would come back. He had promised to love her always. Maybe at this very minute he was thinking about her, wishing she was his wife, that he had never left Kilgoran.

More and more she indulged in her fantasies, not only in the dark after Jamsie fell asleep, but in the daytime, too. Sometimes she met Michael, Peader's father, after Mass, or walking with his crony Dinny Crowley. Whatever animosity Michael felt when she jilted Peader was gone this long time. He gave her news of Peader, that he was well, had a good job, was still single. And always finished the conversation with the same remark, 'Be God you'd think it was to America he went and not Dublin at all. Sure he could be home in no time, and yet not once in four years has he set foot near.'

Katy knew the reason Peader never came home. It was to do with her. He couldn't face seeing her another man's wife. He loved her still, of that she had no doubt. Wasn't it plain to see, or else he'd have married by now. Hadn't he sworn he'd love her till he died? This knowledge gave her strength to surmount the bad days and nights. Peader would never cease to love her. One day he would come back, and declare again his love. She thought no further ahead than that, it was enough.

In the four years he had been in Dublin Peader changed jobs and lodging houses many times. But wherever he went he took with him his love of Katy and longing for Kilgoran. He read a great deal, buying second-hand books, papers and pamphlets, and followed with interest the career of Daniel O'Connell. He was overjoyed when O'Connell became the first Catholic Lord Mayor of Dublin. For Father Matthew, preaching total abstinence and exhorting people to take 'the pledge', he had admiration, but was unable to follow his principles. For often of an evening he sought and found solace for his loneliness and yearning for Katy in a glass or two of porter.

He began attending the meetings O'Connell was holding to support his efforts to repeal the Union, watched with admiration the tall broad-shouldered figure. Here was a man, he thought, who could right the wrongs of Ireland. Who could unite the people, the peasants and the clergy, the rich and the poor. A clever, handsome man, a politician and a lawyer. One who could use the letter of the law to wrest from England what she wrongfully held. He had done it before, at the Clare Election, in getting Catholic Emancipation. He strained forward to hear every word O'Connell spoke; cheered with the crowd, laughed with them, and when O'Connell finished speaking, clapped until his palms tingled.

Walking back to his lodgings after the meeting his mind was filled with the Liberator's speech. He lay in bed still thinking about it. Marvelling that such a man existed, a man who would one day lead the nation out of bondage without the spilling of a drop of blood. It was a thrilling prospect that he thought much about. One morning after attending a meeting the previous night he woke and realized that for several days Katy had not been in his mind. The lapse of time between memories of her increased, and eventually the day came when he could recall her with affection and no more. Gone was the burning love, the yearning that had made his days and nights miserable. He was whole again.

The heart was being lowered into the grave, it hung suspended, blood pumping from it in a bright red stream so fast it quickly filled the hole, spilled over the sides and came in a thick red wave washing towards Charlotte's feet. She screamed, her own heart pounding, and woke up. Then quickly closed her eyes to shut out the blackness of the room. Desperately she hoped that someone would come, that Papa or a servant had heard the scream. Please let someone come, she whispered, but no one did.

No one ever did, never. Though the dream returned frequently, ever since she heard Hannah tell Katy how Mama had died. She forced herself to breathe slowly, deeply, until her heart slowed. Telling herself it had only been a horrid nightmare. A very bad dream, that is all, she said aloud. And the scream happened in the nightmare. That is why no one heard – why Papa never came to comfort her.

Gradually her heart stilled its pounding, the terror diminished, she opened her eyes, and the darkness seemed no longer so black. Soon she was able to distinguish the shape of familiar objects – the press, a chair, the screen. Morning was coming, she thought, the sun would shine, everything would be all right. By the lake, in the fields, or in her favourite place – a fold between two hills, a little wood, where silver birch grew, wild flowers, and big, silky, purple thistles, the sun would be shining.

She would go there: there she never felt frightened. Even the loneliness, which came when Catherine married, was never so bad in the wood. And if Papa remembered that today was her birthday, and had ordered from Dublin the drawing materials she had asked for, she would try to capture on paper the birds that came to rest on the trees, the flowers and the thistles.

As the first fingers of dawn penetrated the room she thought about her father, and in turn her sisters and brother. Of her grief when Catherine went, the eagerness with which she looked forward to her return at Christmas. She remembered her joy when Papa told her she was a good clever girl bringing the priest's plight to his attention, even though he had tempered his praise with a reminder that she must not listen to the servants' gossip. How proud and important she had felt then. And with what eagerness she had counted the days until Olivia got married, and Charles left home. For then she was sure she and Papa would be very close. No more scenes between him and Charles. How she had hated those loud angry voices coming from the library, Charles' always louder than Papa's. But once he and Olivia went, there would only be herself and Papa. He would invite her into the library, perhaps read to her. Show her on the globe of the world places he had travelled to, tracing with his finger the route his ship had taken.

But all that was before she heard Hannah tell Katy how Mama had died, how his heart had gone down into the grave with her. Then she knew Papa could never love her, never had. The dream began then. It was her punishment for disobeying Papa, for listening at doors to the servants gossiping. Hardly a day had passed since that conversation that did not trouble her. Sometimes she imagined she heard the screams of her mother echoing through the upstairs wing, or saw the men straining to lift the bed, placing blocks of wood beneath its end. But mostly she imagined her father's heart being buried in the grave and grieved for the suffering her life had caused him. So that she tried to trouble him seldom. Sat silent at meal-times unless he spoke, never disturbed him in the library.

'Good morning, Miss Charlotte.' The maid's entrance dispelled her thoughts. She put down the tray and drew back the curtains, sunshine flooded the room. 'Look at that now, wouldn't you think the weather knew it was your birthday! Fourteen years of age, doesn't the time fly? Sit up now and have a sup of tea.' The servant put the tray before her, and a pillow behind, then moved about the room, talking and picking up discarded clothes, telling Charlotte not to let on, but that Hannah was making a lovely cake for her. That maybe she had better get up for the Master had been in the dining-room this long time.

Lord Kilgoran rose from the table when Charlotte entered and came forward to her. 'Happy birthday, darling,' he said, and led her to her place where a large parcel was waiting. 'I hope it's right, is what you wanted.' He stood by while she undid the package, thinking what a lovely girl she had grown into. – How beautiful are her large brown eyes. She is like Catherine, the same sweet gravity about her, though smaller and more fragile in stature. Such a shy, timid creature. I wish I knew how to talk to her; I seem to startle her into silence when I attempt to converse with her.

'Oh Papa! how wonderful,' Charlotte exclaimed as she unwrapped the pencils, sketch book and box of water colours. 'Oh thank you, thank you.' She almost kissed him, he almost did the same, then the moment passed, was lost. He returned to his chair, and they ate their breakfast in silence.

Katy went into labour the day Jamsie lifted the potatoes. According to her reckoning she was not due for another month, but when the signs became unmistakable she sent for Statia, saying when she arrived, 'It must be the relief and excitement that the crop was good started me.'

'Whatever it was it's done the trick anyway,' Statia confirmed, and told Jamsie to tell Katy's mother.

'I'll not leave you this time. The fourth has a way of coming quicker. And don't be making them faces and noises, sure this one will fall out.'

As the labour progressed, Katy, her mother and Statia gossiped about births and deaths, how people in Kilgoran were lucky to have sound potatoes. There were places in the land less fortunate. This year of '41 would go down as another bad year. The women recalled times when there wasn't a potato to be had in the length and breadth of Munster, how people starved and died of fever. But that God seldom sent two poor harvests without a good one in between.

And Eileen O'Donnell, looking at her daughter pacing the kitchen, sometimes bent by her pains, wished Katy could have been spared such a precarious living. Three mouths to feed, and before morning another one. God help her, if it wasn't for Hannah's scraps and the bit I give her, where would she be? Then Eileen told herself – what's done is done, my wishing won't make it otherwise, fitter for me to put the children to bed.

By the time they were sleeping, Katy's pains were bad enough for her to lay down. Statia told Jamsie it was no place for a man, to make himself scarce.

'Spend the night with Padraig,' Katy, in between contractions, called to him. Not, she knew, that he would pay the slightest heed, and up to Johnny's he would go. Him being with Johnny worried her, she feared he might inveigle Jamsie into joining a Secret Society. Why, she wondered, couldn't Johnny and Jamsie be more like their brother Padraig – a decent, sober man who was gathering every penny to take himself and his family to America. She wished that for everyone's sake Johnny and his no good wife would go far away. Her thoughts were cut short by a speeding up of her pains, and in less than half an hour she delivered a girl. 'You were right,' she said, grinning at Statia, unable to understand the look of consternation on her face, 'it fell out.'

'Then please God that the next one will as well,' Statia said, as Katy's grin became a grimace and labour commenced again.

'What ails me? What's happening, this isn't the pain of the afterbirth. Oh, Holy Mary take pity on me ...'

'Whisht now, astoir,' her mother said. 'Be patient for a minute and it'll be all over, there's another child.'

'Another child! But ...' Speech deserted her, as seemingly without cease she was engulfed by pains. Through the haze of them she saw her mother's anxious face, and heard as if from a great distance Statia's voice. 'The second child's the wrong way round, 'tis often so with twins, and maybe it's dead.'

Katy didn't care. She cared about nothing, not that the child was dead, that she should die herself: death would be a welcome release. She would endure no more, do no more. Then Statia was commanding her to push. She disregarded the instruction. Her strength was gone, she did not have the energy to lift a hand never mind force a child into the world.

'You have to. Come on now. You can do it. You have to!' Statia commanded.

'I can't, oh don't. Leave me, I can't.'

'You can so and you will. Lift up that child, Eileen, show it to her. Look at it. Do you want to leave it motherless and the others 'ithin? Let me have no more nonsense out of you – now push.'

'Oh God! Oh Jesus! Mother! Mother! Mother!'

'Another little girl. There now it's all over. It's all done.'

Katy lay back exhausted. She closed her eyes. 'Don't you want to see them?' It was Statia's voice again. 'They're beautiful, two little red-headed girls, and born with cauls. They'll be the lucky children – grown up to be beauties and never meet their death by drowning. Them born with a caul never do.'

Reluctantly she opened her eyes for she wanted nothing but to sleep, to escape from the deadly weariness. She saw her mother kneeling by the foot of the bed, the Holy water bottle in her hand, shaking out drops, making the Sign of the Cross. Immediately she was alert. 'What are you doing? Why are you christening them?'

'Only because they came before their time,' Statia said. 'They look fine and healthy, but they're small and you'd never know. Let her see them, Eileen.' Her mother brought them, she looked, and at once felt a fierce protective love for the sandy-haired snub-nosed babies with wide-open eyes staring as if they knew at what they were looking. Two identical, pert faces, like inquiring birds. 'Don't let them die,' she prayed aloud. 'Please God spare them. I didn't want them, I'm sorry. Don't take their life away now. Don't punish them because of me.'

'Whisht now, and trust in God,' her mother said.

Statia found a basket and packed it with rags. 'I'll want something warm to cover them. They were dragged out of the nest too soon.'

Eileen took off her shawl. 'Take this, I've another at home.' Statia arranged it over the babies, and carried the basket to the corner by the fire.

'We'll keep them there night and day and please God in a month they'll be as right as rain.'

Jamsie was mesmerized by the sight of them. 'It's uncanny. No matter which way I look at them there's not a ha'porth of difference.' But Katy believed she could already tell one from the other.

'The first one, the one I'll call Peg, has a nose that's longer than Nora's.'

'May God bless your eyesight,' Jamsie replied. 'In a thousand years I couldn't see it.'

The babies stayed in their basket by the fire, only being handled for feeding and cleaning. Statia came daily to inspect them. Neighbours visited and brought their children to see the twins that so far no one but Katy could tell apart. They were marvelled at, praised, and their luck at being born with cauls commented on. Statia had stretched the cauls over two basins to dry, asking Katy at the time where they were to be put for safe keeping. And she had replied, 'In the box under the bed with my wedding dress where I keep my treasures.'

After a month the babies began to thrive. Their sandy red hair had a curl to it. Jamsie reverted to his old ways, and whenever he could went to Carey's. Alone by the fire Katy thought about Peader: how different her life would have been married to him. Lost in her dreaming the time flew until Prince cocked his ears and scratched at the door to go out. And Katy put aside her dreams and let him go to meet Jamsie who was coming down the boreen.

In he would come, smiling all over his face, expecting a welcome like Prince lavished on him. Not asking, nor caring how she had spent the hours, whether the children had woken. Wanting to kiss her, get his hands on her. Often before he arrived she planned to refuse him, sin or no sin. But if he was sober enough to persist he had his way, for no matter what her mind dictated, her body said otherwise.

After their love-making she would rise from the pallet and go to pass water.

'Why do that?' she had asked when six weeks after the twins' birth Statia said she must.

'It might delay your next child.'

'How so?'

'Don't ask so many questions, do it, that's all,' Statia had insisted.

'Then why didn't you tell me before, after Bridget for instance?'

'Wouldn't I be putting myself out of business? Anyway you were well able for children then, but twins is hard.'

Then Katy had asked was it a sin. And Statia laughed and asked how could passing water be a sin, wouldn't you burst if you didn't. Satisfied with that for an answer Katy did what she was advised, and was delighted with the results. Here were Peg and Nora going on two and no sign of another child.

When she was not overtired or worrying about food the children delighted her. In Bridget she could see herself, the same yellow hair and brown eyes, see her mannerisms enacted by her daughter as she stood hands on hips scolding her brother. And Thomas paid as much attention as his father did to Katy, using his blue eyes, his smile and charm to wheedle his way. She saw that Mary Kate lacked lustre compared to Thomas and Bridget, her hair didn't shine, nor her eyes sparkle. She was dawny and quiet, easily ignored, and Katy's love for her was tinged with pity – an emotion the twins never evoked in her. They made her laugh, sometimes cry or scream at them from exhaustion or exasperation. At every opportunity they were out through the door. When she wasn't pursuing them up the boreen she was separating them when they ganged against Mary Kate, grabbing her food and playthings. They got more slaps than the others, more hugs and kisses. – They are so gorgeous I could eat them, Katy frequently thought. And though I know I shouldn't, I love them the best. After such thoughts she would be consumed with guilt and make much of the others, telling herself she would stop favouring Peg and Nora, all her children were lovely, and thank God for them.

Chapter Eight

Five years after her wedding Catherine was still childless. Morning and night she prayed that God would bless her union and Edward's with a baby. As each month passed with its proof that her prayers were unanswered, her despair deepened, was tinged with bitterness. She became envious of Olivia, who had two children and expected a third; envious of the burgeoning bellies of wives in the regiment; of Katy surrounded by children, when she returned to Kilgoran.

'Why them, and not me?' she often asked herself. 'Why am I denied this one thing I want so much, for myself, but for Edward too.' Dear Edward was as loving and attentive as the day she married him. If he also felt disappointment, he never made her aware of it. What a wonderful father he would be. What a failure she was. God had singled her out, and each month her womb wept for its barrenness.

One afternoon, giving way to her despair she lay on the bed and cried. There Edward discovered her. Alarmed, he went to her. He sat on the bed and bent over her, stroked her hot flushed face. 'Tell me what's wrong?' Tears poured from her eyes, her body was convulsed with sobs.

Edward raised her, held her close, comforting her as one would a child. When at last she was able to speak she told him of her sorrow for failing him. 'I wanted so much to give you a child and I've failed. I'm useless – a barren woman.'

'Oh my precious love, don't talk so. You mustn't say such things. I love you.' He kissed her face, and gently blotted her tears. 'I love you for yourself. I never think like that.'

'Oh, but I am. I know how deeply I've disappointed you, though never once have you reproached me.'

'Now, Catherine, listen to me.' He made her regard him, his voice became firmer. 'I've watched your grief these past years, and known its reason. You never spoke of it, and foolishly neither did I. Maybe you interpreted my silence as reproachful, but it was never meant so. You must believe that. I love you. I always will. These five years have been the happiest of my life. A child would be an added delight. But you must not think I dwell on that, or love you one bit less because God hasn't seen fit to send a baby.' He stroked her hair. Her body shuddered with the end of her sobbing.

'Oh Edward, I love you too. And I've never felt you reproached me. Maybe I'm selfish, maybe my grief is more concerned with myself than I thought. I dwell on it every day. I pray too, and every month I think it will happen, that this time God will answer my prayers. You've no idea how I suffer. I keep telling myself everything is His will, but doesn't it sometimes seem unfair?'

'Yes, if you dwell on it – it does. If you rail against it, and look for explanations then it seems unfair. You mustn't do that, it leads to bitterness, makes you envious of others. Don't do that, my darling. Your nature is too noble, don't allow it to be corroded with envy and bitterness. Pray instead that God will grant you acceptance of His will. And remember that I love only you. And if we never have a child will love you more not less. Promise.'

'I promise. I feel better already having spoken to you.'

'Good girl. Now, rest for a while. I'll send your maid along later with some tea.' He made her lie back, and kissed her tenderly.

After that day Catherine continued to pray for a child, but remembering Edward's words she also prayed for acceptance of God's will. Gradually the bitterness diminished, though her longing for a baby was as great as ever. On her next visit to London where Olivia had a town house she arranged to see a doctor specializing in women's complaints. He assured her she was in perfect health, advised plenty of fresh air, rest, and moderate exercise. She followed his advice, and to keep her mind fully occupied became involved with societies for the welfare of soldiers' wives. Aghast at the conditions in which they lived, she visited the cellars and verminous rooms, appalled when she saw the accommodation allocated to those few allowed to live in barracks, the inadequately screened corner of the barrack room sleeping thirty soldiers, and the four or six married families behind their partition. Husbands and wives, babies, boys and girls. What courage they had, she thought, how much they must love each other to undergo such privation in order not to be separated. But no matter how exhausted she was physically or emotionally by the sights she witnessed, at some time during every day her mind returned to her own longing for a child. And she resolved that when next she went to Kilgoran she would talk with Statia. Statia knew things, what exactly she wasn't sure, but she recalled the servants' gossip. 'There's many a woman thought herself barren until she went to Statia.' Of course such things were nonsense, she told herself, but she had tried everything else. There was nothing to lose, she would ask Statia.

Katy's mother and father died within a month of each other; Eileen collapsing one day as she opened the Lodge Gates, clutching at the spot on her chest where for years she had worn Statia's medal. Paudeen came running to the cottage to tell Katy, but her mother was already cold before she got there. She could not believe it, could not believe that never again would she hear the familiar voice scold or praise her. That the hands which had held hers during her labour, had sewed clothes for the children, altered her wedding dress, embroidered the wool cushions staring her in the face, were still for ever. – All the things they could do, she thought looking at her mother's hands, and they'll do no more.

She linked her father to the graveyard, thinking how suddenly he was like an old man, his step faltering, the hand resting on her arm so frail, and she had a premonition that he wouldn't be long after her mother.

'It was his chest,' Statia said the night he died, but Katy knew otherwise. It was grief. And she pondered how strange was the thing between men and women. No one seeing her mother and father together would have thought they loved each other.

There was a new coachman waiting to move into the

Lodge cottage, so after the funeral Katy packed her parents' possessions. She was surprised at how little had belonged to them – the furniture, even the bed, was the property of the House. She took the few clothes, cut down they would come for the children, the embroidered cushions, a rosary and a mirror from above the fireplace. Wrapping the looking glass in a skirt of her mother's, she remembered her mother telling her how long ago in Tipperary it was bought from an Italian pedlar, a man by the name of Bianconi who sold statues and mirrors. How the same man now had horses and cars running the roads of Ireland and had made his fortune. The mirror would be handy, Katy thought, and each time she gazed in it, would remember her mother telling the story.

She grieved for both parents, but it was her mother she missed most. It was of her she thought when she passed the Lodge Gates and saw the new woman, for her she cried in the night, and of her she dreamed. She was wracked by guilt for the trouble she had caused her mother, the unkind things she had said of late in Jamsie's defence. Laying awake in the dark with him sleeping soundly she would recall the night of the fight when she chose him above Peader, how that must have been a terrible shock to her mother, the shame it caused her. Then her mind which had been free of Peader for many months would centre on him: he would understand her grief if he was laying beside her. She could talk to him about it. Jamsie paid no heed. He was sorry at the time, did what had to be done, the same as he had when his own parents died, but that was that. As he said, 'It comes to us all, what's the use of thinking about it, life is for the living.' Peader would have spoken differently. Ah, if only, she would think longingly before falling asleep.

In the spring of 1843 a letter came to Peader from his father, who wrote:

Every time I put pen to paper or get word from you, I say thanks be to God for the penny post. Did you ever know the likes for speed and convenience? Well son, how are you? The weather here is grand, the potatoes and grain in, and thriving. We've had enough rain so I'd say the hay will be good.

'Tis many the long day now since I've seen you, and it does be very lonely sometimes. I'm not as young as I used to be, and it's a sad thing to know that I could go tomorrow, and my only son living up in Dublin. Would you never think of coming home? If anything happened to me, Kilgoran would be sure to renew the lease, never fear, he's a decent man, and mightn't raise it either.

Jamsie O'Hara and the crowd at Carey's are always asking for you. You're missed sorely at the hurling matches, there was never another like you. Wouldn't it be grand if you were here for making the hay?

Your loving father.

Peader thought about the letter for a long time before answering it. His father he reckoned must be well over seventy, and the farm too much for him.

God knows, he had missed Kilgoran all right, every-thing about it. Missed the look of it, the smell of it, the men in Carey's, running with the hurling stick, meeting the ball, beating everyone to it, sending it in a spin to the other end of the field. He had missed it all. There was never a summer when he didn't think of the May fly rising, how word of it went round as if passed by magic. How when the mackerel were running he'd push out the boat beyond the headland and fish for them. He missed it all, but he had learned to live without it, found other interests, even other friends. Dublin wasn't such a bad place when you got to know it, and now with him following O'Connell it was where everything was happening.

But he could not leave his father to get old alone. He would return, follow O'Connell from there, his meetings were going round the country, he would go to them. When he did answer the letter he told his father he was coming, though he would not be in time for making the hay, he would be there to help with the harvest.

Katy dreamed she was married to Peader, living in the farmhouse. Jamsie was dead, but not yet buried. She was aware of this, but did not care. Thomas, Bridget, and Mary Kate were living in the cottage with the corpse, the twins were with her in the farmhouse. Every now and then Jamsie got up out of his coffin and appeared at the bed where she lay, looking down at her and Peader, laughing at the two of them. She saw that his habit was too short for him and thought his legs looked nice. Then, though she never moved from Peader's side, she saw Jamsie's brothers come to take him to the graveyard. But they didn't take the coffin, only the body carried on their shoulders. She watched it from the bed until they got to the cemetery gate, then she screamed and screamed. She woke up and Jamsie did as well.

'What ails you?' he asked.

She was so relieved to find him alive beside her, she forgot they had fallen out before going to bed, wound her arms round his neck, told him she loved him, and never to die on her.

'Why would I do such a thing,' he said before covering her mouth with his.

Katy went to confession. On the way she was tormented at the thought of telling all to Father Bolger. What would he think of her? And though never outside the confessional would he mention the subject, he'd know what a sinful woman she was. For although confession was between you and God, wasn't the priest listening? Wouldn't he know well who was speaking? And wasn't it bound to cross his mind when he saw her?

The alcove was curtained, and inside it another curtain separated priest and penitent. Katy entered, knelt and made the Sign of the Cross.

'Bless me, Father, for I have sinned, it's three months since my last confession.' She said no more for a minute, and the priest prompted her to go on.

'I had this dream, Father, about a man, not my husband. In it, do you see, he was dead, my husband that is, and God forgive me I was glad.'

'And apart from that what sort of dream was it? Did you commit an impure act in it?'

'I did not. We were only laying on the bed.'

'Tell me now, the man in the dream, do you see him about you? Is he a neighbour?'

'He is, but I don't. He's been gone this long time.'

'Are you given to thinking about him when you're awake?'

She did not answer directly. 'Well, the way it is, Father,

my husband drinks, and then I do be wishing I'd never married him.'

'Would I be right in thinking at those times you wished you'd married the other man?'

'You would, Father.' Her voice was no more than a whisper.

'Every time you do that you're committing a mortal sin. If you want to be married to another man, you're wanting all that marriage means. Isn't that so?'

'I wouldn't do it at all if it wasn't for the drink.'

'Don't make excuses for yourself. You've come here to make a good confession. If you tell lies to yourself or me, you might as well go home. The drink is many a good man's fault, and no excuse for you at all. Now put these sinful thoughts out of your head. And with the help of God they won't intrude on your dreams. You've more to be doing with your time than wasting it on foolish sinful thoughts. I want you to promise never to indulge in them again.'

'I will, Father, and I won't, never again.'

'For your penance say a decade of the Rosary. Now make a good act of contrition.'

Katy began the prayer, the priest to pray in Latin. He was still praying when she finished hers. She waited until he stopped and through the thin material saw him make the Sign of the Cross and heard him absolve her. She left the confessional and went far up the church to say her penance. Holy Mary Mother of God, she prayed when her Rosary was finished, don't let me ever think such things again. Never let anything happen to Jamsie. Spare him to me, and I'll never sin again. I'll be a good wife and bear with him. I'll say an extra round of my beads night and morning, and never let a bad thought cross my mind again.

She continued praying until she heard the church door close and knew Father Bolger had returned to his house. Then she rose and felt as free and light as air, for her sin that had weighed like a stone round her neck was lifted, cast away.

Dano's desire to increase his grazing land grew yearly, and as it did so the picture of Hell painted by Father Bolger faded until it was no more than a faint image in the distant future which could be ignored for the time being. And so he sent another notice to the tenants on the bog that their rents from 1 May 1843 would be increased. This time Johnny O'Hara did not inform Father Bolger. Instead he went that night to a public house in the next village and got into what appeared to be a casual conversation with a man at the counter.

The next evening they met away from the public house, Johnny as prearranged catching up with the man who was sauntering along the road. They exchanged greetings, remarked on the weather as two strangers might.

'Walk along with me now as if we were talking about nothing in particular, and going nowhere in particular,' the man said. They continued for a couple of miles by which time darkness concealed them. Yet before turning into a field the man looked this way and that, making sure they were not observed. Across two fields they went, then over rough, rising ground to where a mountain rose. Down its slope fell a stream in a froth of white like shaken silk, its brightness visible in the dark. By its side they climbed to the top, over the mountain and clambered down the other side until they reached a narrow ledge. Carefully they edged along until it broadened into a platform and entrance to a cave.

'The way the rock folds it can't be seen from below. 'Twas here in the Penal Days Mass was said,' the man informed Johnny as they entered the cave. It was pitch black inside. The man went ahead calling back, 'Keep behind me, close to the wall. There's gaps in the ground with a fierce drop below.'

Inch by inch Johnny moved, his hands groping the wall. It was so quiet in the cave he heard his laboured breath and that of the man in front. He made himself not think of the fierce drop, and concentrated on going forward. Once he found no purchase for his foot, and shuddering as if drenched with icy water brought it back.

'Take a bigger step,' came the word from in front.

He stretched his leg and found ground. On and on in this fashion for what seemed hours he progressed until at last he saw a faint light ahead and heard the whisper of voices.

The stranger called back, 'You can let go of the wall now – the ground's firm from here on. A stranger day or night entering the cave would be long gone to their death.'

Johnny was trembling when he let go the wall, his heart thudding, his breath laboured. He stood still for a minute until the fear and excitement went. The passage was wider from here on opening in front into a chamber lit by a rush light. He could make out the forms of men, six or seven, one much taller and bigger than the rest.

'Wait here for a minute,' his guide said, and went forward to talk in whispers to the others. Then a voice boomed within the cavern walls, and echoed, 'O'Hara, commere.' He approached the group; the light was too poor to distinguish features. The big man stepped out a little way from his followers. 'So you want to join us?'

'I do,' Johnny said firmly.

'You took your time making up your mind,' the other said.

'It was my intention this long time. But between one thing and another I put it off.'

'Tell me then what caused your decision this time?'

He told them about Driscoll wanting the fields. How last time the priest had held him off. About this time. How he wanted no more favours, hadn't asked the priest to plead. The men listened, and when he finished his story the big one quizzed him about his family, his parents. Fastening on the fact that Jamsie was a tenant of Kilgoran's. Asking if Johnny had told of his intention to join the Society to his brother beholding to Kilgoran.

'I have not. Not mentioned it to no one, not even my wife.'

'And Driscoll now, do you know the lie of his land?'

'I do, every foot of it.'

'Has he a dog?'

'He has, a big brown one. Your man here knows all about him,' Johnny said turning his head slightly to nod towards the man who had brought him.

'I worked for Dano before moving to the next village. The dog'd eat out of my hand,' the man confirmed.

The big man then returned to his companions; they

huddled together and spoke to each other quietly so Johnny could not hear what was said.

'They are deciding now,' the stranger said, coming close to him. 'You're in or you're dead – pitched down through the floor back there. But sure you knew that before you came. No one who comes is let leave if he's not in. 'Twouldn't be wise at all.'

The decision seemed to be taking a long time, Johnny thought, maybe it wasn't going in his favour. He began to sweat although it was cool in the cave, and his heart battered. There was a weakness in his legs and a dryness in his mouth so that he had to keep swallowing. Then the big man turned from the others. 'You'll take the oath, you're in.'

Unable to speak for the moment, Johnny nodded; the strength returned to his legs, his heart slowed, and the saliva wet his mouth.

'Repeat this after me,' the big man said, and slowly and solemnly began to recite the oath. '*I swear by God, by His Holy Mother, by Ireland and Saint Patrick that tonight I join with true heart the Men of Munster. To them I pledge my word, my strength, my life. With them I will seek out those who bleed the people of Ireland white. With them I will destroy the stock, property, even the lives if necessary of those men who take from the people what is rightfully theirs. That I will seek out the wrongdoers, be they English, Irish, Catholic, or Protestant, stranger or friend, even my own flesh and blood, anyone guilty of such deeds. I swear that I will lay down my own life, rather than betray by word or deed my fellow members of the Society, and that I will take the life of another who would divulge such information. All this I swear in the name of Almighty God.*'

After the oath-taking the big man shook Johnny's hands; in turn the others stepped forward and did likewise.

'We'll give Driscoll a warning first. Pin a note to his door, and see what his response is. A month tonight we'll meet here again. Away you go now, good night and God go with you,' the leader said.

Johnny and his escort went back through the narrow passage. He felt sure-footed and unafraid. They parted at the foot of the mountain, and each went a different way to that which they had come. Padraig brought news of the rent increase to Father Bolger.

'I was half expecting it. I'm surprised he's held back this long,' the priest said.

'Do you know, Father, we were just getting on our feet. Without the rise by next year I'd say there'd have been money for a passage to America. It was too good to be true. I'll pay it this time, otherwise we'll be on the road, but what about after, and maybe Johnny's word is right, and he'll evict us anyway? 'Twas for that very reason I wanted to go to America.'

Here was a man, the priest thought, who deserved a chance. A man who walked the feet off himself going from one hiring fair to the next, who went to England and worked, digging the railways, who hadn't let drink nor tobacco pass his lips for years. And all his effort would go for nothing, swallowed by Driscoll's greed. 'I'll do my best, Padraig, but I don't hold out much hope. Go home now to your wife and children and I'll have a word with Dano,' Father Bolger said.

Dano was outside his house, Mrs Driscoll in the gig about to drive off, and one of her daughters holding the reins. They all saluted the priest but no one asked him in.

'Well, Father?' Dano said, making it clear whatever business there was would be conducted out of doors.

'You held your hand for a long time, I'm asking you to do the same again.'

'Then you're wasting your time, I've lost a fortune through you.'

'Dano, you'll lose more than a fortune, you'll lose your eternal soul.'

'I'm prepared to take a chance on that.'

'If you go ahead with this I'll refuse you absolution,' Father Bolger threatened.

'I'll find a priest who won't,' Dano replied, his pale eyes glaring defiance, his big head lowered.

– A bull if ever there was one, he'll not budge an inch. He's not worth the courtesy of a 'good day'. So thinking, the priest turned and hobbled back to the pony and trap.

– There's one chance left, he thought as he drove away. I'll have a word with Lord Kilgoran, ask him if he can use his influence. He turned the pony's head to Kilgoran House. Going up the drive he passed Charlotte who waved to him as she walked by. The poor child, he said to himself, she has the lonely life nowadays. There's not much doing in the House, none of the great parties and balls. He recalled that Mary Doyle had told him Miss Charlotte spent every fine minute, and some that weren't fine, out rambling the fields, sketching and drawing, and had added that if it wasn't for the interest Hannah took, half the time she'd have no one to talk to. A lovely girl, too, who should have company, the priest concluded as he pulled up outside the House.

'If you'd step into the library,' the maid said, 'I'll tell the Master you're here.'

He looked round the room at the shelves from floor to ceiling filled with red, blue, green, and brown leather-bound, gold-tooled books, at the wealth of knowledge contained in one place. His glance moved to the framed maps, and sets of hunting prints. So much on which to feast the eye and mind. He was about to examine the globe of the world, give it a twirl, see the brightly painted countries and oceans go spinning round, when Lord Kilgoran came in.

'Ah, good to see you, Father. Sit down, sit down. The pony behaving?'

'He is, your Lordship, he's a little beauty.'

'Good, well done.' Lord Kilgoran sat opposite the priest. 'And the rheumatics, not troubling you I hope?'

'Not too bad at all. I hope it's not inconvenient calling without notice, but the matter's urgent. Maybe you would help.'

Father Bolger explained about Dano and the increase. The hardship it would involve, the people's fear of eviction. He said nothing of his own fear that desperate men like Johnny O'Hara might take the law into their own hands.

Lord Kilgoran listened attentively. When the priest concluded he asked, 'You're aware of course that I own no part of that land.'

'Indeed I am, your Lordship, more's the pity you don't own every bit of it, then I wouldn't be on this errand. But I was thinking that you would know who employs the agent that Dano leases the land from.'

'I'm afraid I don't. I knew his grandfather. Used to see him years ago in Dublin, before the Union. More than forty years ago, we were young men then. Didn't know him awfully well. His family had a house in Dublin, never lived in the country, though. Came here sometimes, did a bit of fishing and shooting. Only time they ever saw their land, don't you know. Lots of families like that. I doubt if the young fellow's ever seen the sky over Ireland. Not interested in things like the welfare of his tenants, so long as the rents keep coming. Suits his purpose to have a less than fair fellow running the place. And in turn suits the agent to have chaps like Driscoll – all rack-renters – the tenant pays the price.'

Father Bolger thanked him, and bade him goodbye. When he was gone Lord Kilgoran returned to his chair, and thought how he had blamed the young man's lack of interest on never having seen the sky over Ireland. Sadly he reflected how that was not always so. Look at Charles – he cared not a fig for Ireland, nor the estate. He was setting out to ruin it. By every post came demands for money to pay his debts. And like a fool he sent it, though he knew every penny was gambled. But one day Charles would drive him too far. Force him to change his will. It was the only way to save Kilgoran, painful though such a step would be.

In the meantime he must economize himself, economize more. Refuse invitations. He couldn't afford to return the hospitality. It was monstrously unfair on Charlotte. Poor child, where was she to meet people of her own age? Still, it couldn't be helped, economies had to be made. And if things didn't improve the dairy herd, the prize cattle, must go. Have to cut back on staff, too. Sometimes, he thought before rising to go and change for dinner, life and its problems seemed too hard to bear.

Dano tore down the notice warning him against the rent increase. Since his stand against the priest he felt a new man, possessed by twice the strength. Neither clergy nor Secret Societies would oppose him. He would show them. From now on let them beware, they were dealing with Dano Driscoll, he was a force to be reckoned with.

Padraig was the only one living on the bog with enough money to meet the rise. From the thatch where the money was secreted he took the majority of it, knowing as he did so that the chance of a new life in America was now as far distant as the stars.

That night Johnny visited the cave on the mountain and reported how Dano had received the note, and that the increase had gone ahead.

'He's the brave man, the same Dano,' the big man said, then asked, 'How many met it?'

'Only me eejit of a brother.'

'In that case Dano will move again, wouldn't you say?'

'He will all right.'

'Let me know the minute he does. We'll pay him another visit and this time leave more than our calling card.'

Charlotte watched the rain. It was, she thought, down for the day. Leaden skies, not a break anywhere – her plans to spend the morning sketching, doomed. What a bore that was, now she would be confined to the house. Then coming up the drive she saw two shawled figures –

Katy and Statia, they would be going to the kitchen to gossip with Hannah. She would go down and join them.

Before she left the window there was a knock on the bedroom door and a young housemaid came in. 'I found this, Miss, behind the head of the bed,' she said, holding her palm, on which lay a small object, towards Charlotte.

'What is it?'

''Tis a medal, a holy medal. It wants a rub,' the maid said, and hawed it with her breath, then rubbed it on her skirt before offering it again for inspection.

'Why, I'd forgotten all about it. Now I remember – Katy gave it to me. Fancy it turning up after all this time. Thank you, thank you very much.'

– It was supposed to keep me safe in the dark, Charlotte remembered as she looked at the silver disc. Katy promised something to guard me the day Catherine was married, and later gave me the medal. Perhaps, she thought, if I hadn't lost it I might not have had the horrid nightmares, who knows? Maybe it wasn't too late, there was probably a prayer to go with it. She would ask Katy. She put the saint's emblem in her pocket and went down to the kitchen.

'Miss Charlotte, why you're more like Miss Catherine every day. The same beautiful hair, God bless it,' Katy greeted her.

'Beautiful,' Statia repeated. 'You'll break someone's heart yet, Miss.'

Charlotte blushed. She was never completely comfortable in Statia's presence. Her praise was always too lavish, and she never sure how to take it.

'I wouldn't be at all surprised to hear tell one of these

days you were engaged to be married,' Statia continued. 'I'd say the men will be fighting for your hand.'

'For the Lord's sake, Statia, don't be blathering so much,' Hannah said crossly. 'Miss Charlotte could have all the young men she wants. She doesn't need you to tell her that. But she's in no hurry.'

– Dear kind Hannah, Charlotte thought, defending me. I've never had a beau and am not likely to for I go nowhere, and no one comes here.

'I only opened my mouth and you jumped down it. Well I can see where I'm not wanted,' Statia said and got up, wrapping her shawl round her. 'Rain or no rain I'm going home.'

They often quarrelled so, Hannah and Statia, Charlotte knew. It must suit Statia to leave, for often she had known her stay when Hannah had been far more cross with her.

Charlotte asked about Katy's children, and inquired especially about the twins. Katy related some of their escapades which made Charlotte laugh. Hannah made tea and cut sweet cake and the three of them stayed round the fire for an hour or more. Then Charlotte took out the medal and asked Katy if she remembered it.

'Indeed I do, Miss. It was to stop you being frightened in the dark. That was a long time ago, sure you're a young woman now, you wouldn't be frightened in the dark any more.'

'No,' Charlotte said, in the face of such an assumption unable to confess fear.

'Do you know what,' Katy said, 'that medal got me Jamsie.' Charlotte listened avidly. 'Statia gave it to me. Well I asked her for it, for you, Miss Charlotte, it was

199

intended at the time. But when she handed it over, she thought it was for me. It was the day before Miss Catherine's wedding. And at the time everyone thought I was to marry Peader. There was only the banns to be arranged. I remember how Statia said, "Sleep with that under your pillow and you'll get your heart's desire," meaning Peader of course. Well, I said nothing, but decided I'd hold on to it for a while, like. And do you know it was no sooner in my possession than I met Jamsie.'

'Go way!' Hannah said, and her eyes were as bright and expectant as Charlotte's.

'Honest to God,' Katy said, then she laughed and turned to the girl. 'You do the same.' Charlotte blushed again, and looked discomfited. 'Ah, go on,' Katy coaxed, 'sure where's the harm in it. Just slip it under your pillow and by this time next year you'll have your heart's desire.'

'I don't even know what it is,' Charlotte said.

'Well try it anyway, love, sure you've nothing to lose,' Hannah said. They looked at each other and then began to laugh.

Katy was no sooner back home when Statia arrived, out of breath from running. 'Wait'll you hear the latest. On the way back from the House I met Michael, and you'll never believe it.' She stopped talking and sat down to catch her breath.

'Believe what? You've got me dying of curiosity. Tell me,' Katy urged.

'Peader's coming home. His father read me the letter in the spills of rain. He's coming home for good – after six years.'

First Katy felt faint, then so joyful she wanted to dance round the room. All her promises to the priest forgotten. *He was coming back.* She would see him again. In front of Statia she remained cool. 'That's grand for Michael,' she said. 'When is Peader arriving?'

'In time for the harvest. It'll be like old times.'

– Three weeks, Katy thought, he'll be here in three weeks. I'll see him then.

'You're in great humour,' Jamsie commented several times during the following days when Katy never got cranky with the children, let Prince come and go as he pleased, and sang as she went about her work.

'Why wouldn't I be, isn't the weather beautiful, the crops thriving, and everyone in their health,' she would reply, and return to her thoughts of Peader.

One evening, Jamsie slipped an arm round her waist and said, 'I was thinking, won't it be grand to have Peader back. I missed him.'

'You never said. I don't think you mentioned him, not since before we married.'

'Sure what was the use? I never thought he'd be back. I was wondering if maybe he's thinking of marrying. Maybe there's a girl above in Dublin, that after he's acquainted Michael of his intentions he'll be bringing her down.'

'He is not! There's no girl!' Katy's raised voice was definite in its denial.

'And how would you know?'

Realizing she had shown too much interest, she quickly lied. 'Statia saw the letter to his father. There was no mention of a girl. Statia wouldn't be mistaken over a thing like that.'

201

'No, she would not,' Jamsie agreed. 'Still, all the same I'd say he won't be long about finding a wife. The mothers for miles round must be dancing for joy, counting the shillings and engaging the matchmaker.'

Katy wanted to shout contradictions. Tell Jamsie the mothers could scratch for dowries how they liked. It was for none of their gold or silver, cows or land, nor their daughters neither, that Peader was coming. It was back to her he was journeying. He loved her still, he always would.

Another letter came to Michael with details of Peader's arrival. In his delight that at long last his son was coming home, the old man went from house to house telling his neighbours, and stood outside the chapel on Sunday to catch any he had missed. Everyone crowded round him, shaking his hand, clapping him on the back. It was the best news they had heard for a long time, they said. He beamed with pleasure, and invited all to come to the bit of a night he was throwing in Peader's honour.

The day before Peader's arrival Katy took down her mother's mirror, and began scrutinizing her face, her fingers tracing her features, touching her skin. How rough and flaky it had become, she thought, there were lines at the corners of her mouth, and not the same gloss to her hair. 'A sight, that's what I am,' she said ruefully, 'looking old before my time.' Then she smiled at herself for her vanity, and the downward lines disappeared. 'You!' she said aloud. ''Tis the sour puss, that's all, nothing to do with age. Stop looking at yourself for you'll see oul Nick.'

She put away the mirror and washed her hair, then sat on one of the two big stones by the door to let the sun dry it. The children ran up and down the boreen playing a game, the dog running after them. After a while Katy brought out a basin of water and soaked her feet. Jamsie came down from the field and sat on the other stone.

– If only I had a pair of shoes, Katy thought. What will Peader think of me barefooted? She was grieved and ashamed that he should see her so. Jamsie watched her through half-closed eyelids. The sight of her hair loose, and glimpses of calf as she lifted a foot from the water made him want her. He closed his eyes to block out the disturbing images, telling himself that wanting his wife in the afternoon was like wanting the moon. Once it was the old woman, now it was the children who could come in on top of them.

'You'll go to the Cross to meet him?' Katy asked as she dried her feet.

'Pull down your skirt you brazen strap, or I'll be forgetting what time of day it is. I will, I'll meet him.'

'I might do the same,' she said.

'How could you? Aren't you above in the House sewing?'

'On the way I might.' – I will too, she thought, I'll not let everyone else in the parish see him before I do.

Chapter Nine

It rained the next day, a rain so fine you could not see it fall, yet it drenched the ground, dripped from the trees and the overhanging thatch of the cottage and prevented Katy's children from going out to play. This morning of all mornings, she thought, when I wanted them from under my feet. She stopped thinking long enough to say a silent prayer that the rain would stop, then continued to fret inwardly. – I'll get nothing done, and me having to go to the House, wanting to see Peader arrive, and tidy the place first.

The children ran round the little kitchen making a lot of noise, shouting, laughing, bumping into each other, quarrelling and tormenting the dog. Katy said another prayer for patience, then erupted. 'You're very bold children, sitting like angels till you father took off, and look at you now! The minute he's out the door you're as bold as brass.'

Thomas and Bridget stopped what they were doing, looked at each other, then at Katy. Peg and Nora gave up their attempt to ride the dog, and stared too; only Mary Kate looked suitably impressed. Then as if a joke passed secretly between them the twins and the older two burst out laughing. Katy's face creased into lines of annoyance, her eyes narrowed and she shouted, 'I'm warning you, that laughing will end in crying.'

Momentarily startled by the loudness of her voice the children attempted to stifle their giggling. But seeing the suppressed merriment in their eyes, and maybe because her prayer for patience was granted, Katy said to herself, 'I'm a disgrace of a mother, screaming and roaring like a tinker because I've myself worked up about Peader. I'll not get good of them this way. Mightn't I as well sit and take my ease, tell them a story while I'm doing it, and maybe the rain will cease. And sure if it doesn't who's to notice the floor isn't swept, or the ashes lifted.'

She sat down and announced her intention. Immediately the children gathered round her, each clamouring for their favourite story, making nearly as much noise as before, so that she had to say, 'Whisht, or I'll not begin at all.' They were silent and she began with a tale of the *bean sidhe*, Peg and Nora's favourite. She imitated the wailing noise the fairy woman made while she combed her long grey hair, and warned them that if ever they came upon the creature not to go close for fear she threw the comb. If she did, the one it hit was sure to die before the year was out. The twins moved closer to each other, their bright eyes widening with delighted fear. Thomas pretended nonchalance, and told Katy to hurry up with the old story and tell the one about the Battle of Kinsale. But Bridget protested, 'It's my turn, the girls first. Tell about the child taken away in the night.' So Katy related how a poor mother and father woke one morning to find their beautiful baby son gone and a wizened fairy child in its cradle. Elaborating their sorrow when they saw the changeling, until Bridget's brown, gentle-expressioned eyes filled with tears, moving Katy to hurry to a happy ending before Bridget was overcome with inconsolable grief.

The girls lost interest when it came to Thomas' turn, and Katy was beginning to do the same, for she had noticed that the kitchen was suddenly brighter. The day was taking up, she could tidy the room, and still be in time to see Peader. She sent Nora to look out the door while she hurriedly told the tale of the long-ago battle. 'It's stopped,' Nora called. They could go out to play, Katy decided.

'Kinsale would be the grand place to see,' Thomas said, as the story concluded. 'Could you take us there one day?'

Katy, now eager to get rid of them, made an idle promise for Kinsale was ten miles away and it was unlikely they would ever go so far. But Thomas was only four and surely he'd forget, she thought as she rose, and began shooing the children like a flock of hens towards the open door.

'You won't forget about Kinsale, sure you won't?' Thomas said, hanging back. 'You're always promising things.'

'I will not. Out you go now. Away up the Hazel Grove and take the dog with you. Go on now this minute, or it's the broom I'll take to you.'

They went, and she watched them racing up the boreen, the dog bounding from one to the other barking excitedly. The sun came out and shone on her face so that when she went back into the kitchen it seemed darker than usual. Only the turf fire burning well shed light, for the one small deeply set window admitted little.

Her mind as she began to tidy the room was full of the thought of Peader. Very soon the coach would come to

Carey's bringing him. There was a feverish excitement in her as she anticipated their first meeting, it lent her a false energy so she moved quickly round the room brushing the floor. Strands of her golden hair escaped from its knot as she bent and searched with the heather broom beneath the table for bits of grass, twigs all the children walked in, and black and white hairs from Prince's plumey tail. Collecting the dust and debris in a pile she pushed it across the floor and with a flourish of the brush out through the doorway.

There she paused to look at the fields sloping up to the road and beyond that to the low hills dotted with white-washed cottages like her own, at the pale columns of smoke ascending into a sky now clearing of clouds, at the little fields planted with potatoes and grain. Today the familiar scene took on a dazzling beauty, the potato blossom was snowier, its pink centre rose-hued, the grain burnished, the sky's blue brilliant, everything enhanced by the joy that filled her because Peader was coming. Soon she would see him, their eyes would meet, regard each other shyly at first, then the love that was theirs would burn brightly, flare, so that each would know time had not extinguished it.

She returned to the house, took down the mirror and arranged her hair, spat on a finger and smoothed her eyebrows. Looking down ruefully at her feet, soiled already despite how carefully she had washed them the day before, she rubbed at her dusty toes with the hem of her petticoat, and told herself she'd have to do.

Before leaving she took a look round the kitchen, altered the arrangement of the three stools before the fire, thinking as she did so that Peader might drop in sometime today, and she'd want it nice. She pushed the table nearer the window, moved the settle in line with it and plumped up her mother's cushions, then stood back to admire the effect. It was to her liking – except the brown stain over the chimney breast ingrained by years of smoking turf. But she consoled herself that everyone's chimney piece was so, no matter how many coats of lime you dashed on it the stain came through. Peader wouldn't notice that at all. Wasn't it there when she came to the cottage and would be there long after she was gone?

But she was satisfied with everything else. With the pieces of delft and the few utensils neatly arranged on the shelf, the holy pictures bright against the whitewashed walls, the tidy way the dark, well-burning sods of turf were arranged in the corner. Not that, she told herself, Peader would have an eye for anything except herself. But for all that she wouldn't want him thinking she was a streel of a woman because she went barefooted and wore a shawl.

She left the cottage and hurried towards the Cross, her heart in her mouth as she neared it. They were all there. Peader's father, Dinny Crowley, Tim Coffey with the horse and cart, Jamsie and his brothers. All in a crowd outside the door, and well-oiled by the look of them. The women who had come stood away from the men. Katy joined them.

'He's coming back not a minute too soon, poor Michael's failing,' a woman beside her said. Katy scarcely heard what was said for the coach was coming, stopping, Peader's father moving forward. Then he was down, she could see him. He was gorgeous. He hadn't changed, except for the lovely city clothes. His hair was the same red gold, her heart hammered, and she wanted to run from the women, push aside his father, and say I'm here, I've waited. I love you.

She had to wait longer, while he embraced his father, while the men came up and shook his hand, while Jamsie approached him and they threw their arms round each other, stood back to look at one another, laughed with delight, and embraced again. Then Peader looked to the women and saw her. He came over, but not directly to her. Stopping to talk to this one and that, the young girls looking at him with admiration, girls who were children when he went away. Brazen hussies, Katy thought, all hoping. Well, their hopes were in vain, he had come back to her.

'Katy,' he said, 'Katy O'Donnell, it's good to see you again.' She was tongue-tied, but it didn't matter for she was looking into his eyes and they were telling her what she wanted to hear. 'You look grand, Katy.' He held her hand. She was sure he squeezed it. – If only, she thought, everyone else would vanish, and leave us to say what we want to.

'It's great to see you too, Peader.' Before she could say more he was claimed by the men, taken into Carey's, for they said he must have a terrible thirst after the journey. He was gone before she knew it. Jamsie hung back to tell her he'd go home in a minute to keep an eye on the children. Then only the straggle of women were left, and one by one they went away from the Cross and Katy set out for the House.

Light-footed, and carefree she went along. He was back.

He was hers. He had held her hand, looked into her eyes. He loved her. Tonight she would be in his company. The thought that Jamsie would be there, and half the neighbourhood as well, she quickly stifled. Nothing should spoil this wonderful moment. It was enough just to know that she was in love, and that her love was returned.

It was good to be back. To sit in his father's house surrounded by friends. To talk again with Jamsie. To see Katy, he had forgotten how beautiful she was. Peader looked across the room to where she was sitting listening to Statia. She's like a rose, he thought, a golden rose set down in a garden of lesser flowers. For a moment he let his mind journey to the time he courted her, dreamed she would be his, then he dismissed the thought as he had earlier in the day before the coach arrived at Carey's Cross. For a while then he had wondered what his reaction would be when he stepped down and saw her. Not certain if the cure he believed accomplished in Dublin would stand the test. But quickly he realized, as he greeted her, held her hand, and looked at her lovely face, that he was indeed whole again. She was beautiful, he felt great affection for her, but love thankfully was gone.

The neighbours told him about Dano and the rent increase, about the notice, and how he had torn it down. 'The days of men like him are numbered,' he replied. 'O'Connell will see to that. Nothing will stop him in his fight to repeal the Union. And when we have our own parliament, a man can call his soul, and his hearth his own.'

Father Bolger dropped in and stayed for an hour. He

was delighted, he said, to have Peader back. The parish wanted young men. It wasn't a bit of use everyone being in the cities. There was a need for the likes of Peader, men who would go out and come back with news of O'Connell, follow his Monster Meetings, let the people know.

'You'll be going I take it to the one in Tara next week?'

'I will surely, Father.'

'Good man yourself.'

'Padraig here's been telling me about Dano Driscoll, what do you think his next move will be?'

'I'd put nothing past him,' the priest replied. 'To tell you the truth I'm surprised he hasn't acted before.'

'Thanks be to God, we're all right. We paid the increase,' Padraig's wife said.

'With a man like Driscoll that means nothing,' Johnny O'Hara said. And the priest, not wanting to dash the poor woman's hopes, made signs to him to say no more.

At every available opportunity Katy gazed across the room at Peader, quickly averting her eyes at the slightest indication that he was about to turn in her direction. Once when Jamsie was standing by him she compared them. Jamsie was looking eejity, and no wonder for he had stayed in Carey's until long after she was back from the House. She hated him when he was like this. Waving his hands about, laughing all the time the way a fool would, and the signs of having slept in his clothes for the last hours before they came to Peader's. The cut of him!

Father Bolger said he would be going, and let them have a good night. He knew listening to politics, however important, wasn't their only reason for being here. After he left, things got going, the talk became general. There was dancing and singing, and drinking of poteen and porter, but all nice and easy for there was a lifetime ahead to enjoy Peader, no need for intensity like wakes or farewells to one off across the sea to America.

For Katy, being in Peader's presence was like a dream come true; after all the years they were together again. She could hear his voice, now and then he smiled at her from across the room, and when they danced he touched and spoke to her. Each look, gesture and word of his she interpreted to her liking, every one proof of his love.

Then, more than halfway through the evening, Jamsie came to stand by her, bent and in a low voice said, 'Get up and come home now.'

'Now! Why? I won't. I'm enjoying myself.'

He bent lower, his voice an insistent threatening whisper. 'I've been watching you, that's why – making a holy show of yourself.'

'I don't know what you're talking about,' Katy replied.

'Come out and I'll tell you – if you don't I'll streel you by the hair.'

– My God! he means it too, she thought, looking at his face that had a mad expression on it. He's not drunk enough, that's the trouble. In that half-cut state when he loses his reason. Sure I've done nothing. 'All right,' she said, 'but how'll we explain our leaving?'

'Say you're worried about the children – anything you like, but get up, and come out. I won't tell you again.'

There were protests from the company when she said they were going and gave her reason.

'What harm could come to the children?' Statia asked. 'Who in Kilgoran would touch a hair of their head?'

'Ah, don't go yet,' Michael coaxed, 'sure the night's still young.'

'It's the fire I do be afraid of. The twins are meddlesome, if they woke they might touch it.'

The excuse was accepted. They began saying their goodnights. Michael said, 'You'll come back, Jamsie, won't you? Sure once you've seen Katy home what's to keep you?' And Jamsie said he would. Peader suggested that the next time they would gather in Katy's. 'It's central, and no worry about the children.'

Once they were outside Katy stopped on the road and demanded to know Jamsie's reason for dragging her away. 'I was enjoying myself,' she said, 'and you spoiled it.'

'No mistake about it – you were. Making a show of yourself. Throwing yourself at Peader. Letting no one get a word in with you prating for all you were worth, looking at him like a sick cow.'

'You're losing your mind,' she said, positive she hadn't in the slightest given herself away.

'Losing my mind, is it? Well, I'm not losing my eyesight. I saw the glance you gave him, all longing. The way you held on to his hand when the dance was finished.'

She walked on quickly trying to think of an answer. He followed her. They were well away from the house, cross-ing a field, a short cut to the cottage, a rough unplanted field where the Hazel Grove was. She stopped by the trees, her answer to hand. Her laughter rang out in the night's silence. 'Look at that now! I married a jealous man.'

He stood close to her, towering over her. 'You'll not do it again.'

'Do what? I did nothing. It's jealousy making you see things. And anyway – you only married me – you don't own me. From you I got them words, and they're true enough. You don't own me. I can look at who I like.'

Jamsie caught hold of her, held her arm, was hurting it. 'You're mine – you'll do as I say. I'll kill you if you don't. I'll take your life if you ever look longingly at another . . . Do you hear me?'

She wrenched her arm free, turned from him. His voice continued. 'Was it his fine city ways, and the fine city clothes that caught your fancy? Or were you hankering for him all the time? Is that it? Did you only take me because he cleared out? Was I the second choice, and all your words lies?'

Still she said nothing, though thought, *no not then. Then it was true, every word. I loved you then.*

The moon went behind a cloud, the night became dark. 'You've nothing to say to that, have you Katy? Well don't. Never open your mouth again if that's what you want, think your thoughts. But you're mine, mine, remember that.'

He forced her face round to his, tried to kiss her. She struggled, turning her mouth from him. He tightened his hold, imprisoning then lifting her. She kicked against him uselessly. 'Scream if you like,' he said as he bore her into the trees, and still holding her securely bent and laid her on the ground. He knelt over her. 'Will you kiss me now?'

'I won't. Let me up. You've gone mad. I'm your wife. Let me go.'

'My little wife,' his voice mocked. 'And I'm going to take you here on the flat of your back under the stars. I'll make you forget there's a man in the world except me. Go on now, scream all you like.'

She wanted him, but he would not take her by force. Not throw her to the ground like an animal for branding. To scream was no use. They were far from the farmhouse, and everyone from the cottages was there. Anyway, what explanation could she give if anyone came running? But still she wouldn't make it easy for him. She began to struggle, he held her tighter, she became intensely excited. In the dark she couldn't see his face. He straddled her. She felt the cool air on her skin as he disarranged her clothes. From habit she closed her eyes. Then deliberately put her arms round him, as deliberately as she avoided touching his hair, calculatedly keeping her face turned to avoid his lips. By the feel of his curls, the taste of his mouth she would know it was Jamsie. Her revenge was to receive him telling herself it was Peader penetrating her body. The love-making went on for a long time, and soon she had no thoughts, only sensations and ecstasy. And when she opened her eyes the stars were bright, the cloud gone from the face of the moon, and she thought it was the sweetest loving there ever was. Not able to decide if it was so because she believed it was Peader laying above her, or the novelty of making love in a star-bright night.

Jamsie gave her his hand to stand up, but said not a word. They walked the rest of the way home in silence.

After that night Katy was discreet to the point of coolness with Peader who came frequently to the cottage. Sometimes he brought newspapers and journals with word of O'Connell's continuing struggle for Repeal, and details of the next Monster Meeting at Clontarf. Surreptitiously, while he read aloud to Jamsie, she watched his face, the expressions playing over it, his mouth and the gleam of his teeth.

When he had been fishing he brought mackerel with blue and mauve-hued glistening skin, and silvery pollack which stretched the food sent down by Hannah. He smiled often at her, and once when they were walking up the boreen with Jamsie and the children in front his hand rested for a minute on her back while he explained something.

All the while in his company her manner was outwardly cool, but inwardly she glowed, her belief in his love reinforced by the attentions and kindness. And was content with this, for what else could there be? She was married, she had a family. They couldn't be cast aside, even if she had considered leaving Jamsie.

She was convinced the choice was hers, that she only needed to indicate her willingness to flee and Peader would fly with her. It was a great comfort to know this, and enabled her to surmount her worries and troubles. It was exciting and satisfying to know two men loved her so deeply. There was a stillness and contentment about her when she contemplated it.

Jamsie noticed the change, and was delighted. He believed he was responsible for it; he had mastered her the night in the Hazel Grove, and though initially he felt shame for the way he had taken her, came to see that it was all for the best. She was happy, and he was happy for her. There was a bloom to her. He told her so, and frequently made love to her. Sometimes it crossed his mind how Katy's well-being coincided with Peader's return, but he never allowed his mind to linger long on that subject.

Peader woke before daylight. For a moment not knowing where he was he lay perplexed until his mind cleared and he recognized his whereabouts – he was at the Hill of Tara. Despite being cold, cramped and thirsty a thrill of excitement went through him. He was here! Daniel O'Connell was coming, and so were tens of thousands from all over Ireland, coming to Tara to hear the voice of their Liberator speak to them from the seat of the ancient kings.

He rose and surveyed the morning. Dawn was breaking, the rising sun a fuzzed orange behind the mist. Around him at the base of Tara's Hill others had also slept, he saw them stretch and shiver, and look about them. – Like me, he thought, they've come early for a good position. He drank water from the bottle he had brought, and then poured some in his cupped hands with which he splashed his face. Refreshed and revived, he settled down to watch for sight of the Liberator arriving.

The mist rose from the lush grassy plains surrounding the hill, and dispersed – the routes became visible. After hours of waiting Peader saw in the distance a mass darkening his view. For a long time it seemed to come no nearer nor to lose its solidity, then gradually he discerned movement, saw people individually, banners fluttering, flags held high waving.

A man watching beside him spoke. 'There's millions of them, look. They're coming every way.'

And Peader saw that it was so, all the ways leading to Tara were thronged.

They were near enough now for the sounds of voices to be heard. It was like the noise of the incoming tide, Peader thought, then a new note was added, came floating towards the hill – music. Nearer came the people, and he saw the sun shine on musical instruments, and the bandsmen in uniforms of green and white, and women's bonnets, summery dresses, black shawls, red petticoats, holiday finery and the garb of the poor, the old, the young, men and women.

There were men on horseback, one rode to Peader and the ones beside him with orders for them to move further down from the hill. 'This space will be for the bands, forty of them. Go along now.'

Though disappointed they had lost their vantage, Peader and the others moved without argument. In and round him the crowd flooded, until soon he was surrounded. He looked about him, it was the same everywhere. He could feel the heat of those next to him, see the sweat on their faces. He sweated profusely himself, yet there was not room to move, to take off his jacket.

The bands played and the people sang. Peader joined in. The mood was gay, good-natured. He stood on tiptoe and craned his neck, for in front of him a man had raised a child shoulder high, obscuring his view of where Daniel would stand to deliver his speech. Desperately he manoeuvred himself into a seeing position. Almost immediately a cheer went up, not great to begin with so that voices could be heard shouting, 'May he live forever!' 'Long live the Liberator!' 'God bless our Counsellor!' Then as realization dawned that Daniel O'Connell had arrived the cheer became tumultuous.

In front of Peader more children were hoisted to see the Liberator. Hats, bonnets and kerchiefs ascended before his eyes and floated back. But through them all, he could see the portly figure clad in brown surtout, hands to his neck loosening his cravat, the broad-browed face with its crown of curls, the crooked smile. Saw the hand raised, those standing round him become silent, and the silence spread until it reached all the corners of the area where the ecstatic multitude were gathered, so that the only sound was that of a lark soaring into the noon sky. Then Daniel spoke.

'We are at Tara of the Kings from where all the laws of the land came. A fitting place for this meeting – the biggest of them all to be held. A sight no government can afford to ignore. Thousands of Irish men and women peaceably assembled. Step by step we are approaching Repeal of the Union. It cannot be refused. No government will ignore the will and wishes of an entire people.' He paused and the crowd roared deliriously. 'And the entire Catholic people united for the first time in history is what now exists. Here! Standing before me – you – the people!' He paused and the crowd roared again. He raised a hand, and silence fell. 'The sight of such a people is not only grand, it is appalling – capable of exciting fear.'

The sun at its zenith shone fiercely down. Peader noticed that O'Connell's face was brick-red, that he dabbed at it with his kerchief, felt for his discomfort, and though crushed on every side by bodies, soaked with sweat, and wry-necked from his awkward position, so enthralled was he by sight and sound of the Liberator he was unaware of his own feelings. He listened spellbound as Daniel O'Connell explained how the appalling presence could be used to advantage. 'Step by step you are approaching the great goal – Repeal of the Union. But – it is with strides of a giant. And in October that giant will enter the capital – take up its position at Contarf. Stand in its might where Brian Boru defied and defeated another invader.'

Nothing stirred when he finished speaking, not a wind, not a pennant nor flag, even the breath of the people seemed stilled. Then their joy exploded, the air was rent with the great cheer that went up, and on and on. The message of the Liberator passed back by word of mouth through the ranks, the plain become a tossing sea of green and white waving flags, and into the sky the cries of exultation continued to ascend.

The neighbours were coming to Katy's to hear Peader's news from Tara. Hannah was the first to arrive. 'A griddle cake with currants, and tea as well!' Katy exclaimed with delight when Hannah displayed her gifts.

'More I'd have brought, but things are getting tight in the House, and Mrs Cummings watching every stir, you'd think it was out of her pocket the money was coming.' Hannah wore her best black dress and a string of jet beads. Katy admired the necklace. 'A present for my birthday from Miss Charlotte,' Hannah said.

'Isn't she very kind, and grows more beautiful every day. Sit down on the settle. Jamsie's gone to meet Peader, they won't be long, nor the others either.'

Mary Doyle came next bringing a small jar of poteen; she sat on the bench with Hannah. The children were outside playing. Now and then the twins ran in asking for the bread they knew Hannah had brought. Katy refused, telling them it was for later, and if there was any more careering they'd go to bed. The women talked about the weather that was glorious, and bound to be good for the potatoes. Hannah said you wouldn't feel the time now until Christmas. That the House would be full, for the girls would be home, their husbands, Miss Olivia's children, and Master Charles.

'What's the latest on him?' Mary Doyle inquired.

'The same as ever – in debt and danger. 'Tis a pity he doesn't stay where he is, all he's good for is trouble.'

Then they talked about Dano, Hannah wondering had he turned over a new leaf.

'Three months now since he put up the rents, everyone except Padraig in arrears and Dano hasn't moved.'

'A new leaf, my eye!' Mary Doyle said, 'He's hatching something.'

As Katy remarked that Statia was late, the twins came in to announce that Dinny Crowley and Michael were coming.

'God bless all here,' the two men said when they came in.

'Sit up to the fire and make yourselves comfortable,' said Katy. The men sat and Dinny relit his pipe, puffing hard at it until it was going well. Michael said he couldn't wait to hear all the news from Tara. And Katy thanked him for letting them gather in her place. 'It's very kind of you, and I'm grateful.'

'Not at all. Isn't it better than you having to leave in the middle of the evening to see to the children.'

And Katy thought – if you only knew the truth of that evening, and felt herself blushing.

While they waited for the others the talk centred on O'Connell. Dinny recalled the time Dan stood against Vesey Fitzgerald in the Clare election. 'Be God!' he said, 'that was a day for Ireland all right. I do laugh every time I think of it. The great Vesey, a sitting member for ten years, having to stand again for he was up for the cabinet. And along comes Dan and opposes him, and what's more beats him.' He started to laugh, took the pipe from his mouth. Laughing and clapping his thighs the more he thought about it, forgetting the smouldering pipe until sparks fell into his lap and a smell of scorching was noticed. He was busy putting them out when Statia arrived.

'Leave it alone, Dinny boy. Them things cause terrible trouble.'

Dinny became embarrassed and didn't know where to look. Everyone else laughed except Hannah who blushed and nervously fingered her beads.

'What kept you?' Katy asked.

'The child I was bringing into the world.'

'I forgot. What did God send?'

'A big lump of a boy.'

'Did his mother have good health?' Hannah inquired delicately.

'The best, dropped it like a young cow. Saving your presence, Hannah, I do forget you're a single woman,' Statia apologized, and winked at Katy. 'I have a terrible thirst on me,' she said as she sat on the end of the settle, making her fat self comfortable so Hannah and Mary had to move up.

Katy knew she had seen the poteen, and was hinting. – Let her, she thought, it's not being touched till the men arrive.

Talk again turned to the crops, and then a contention began between Michael and Dinny as to where the first potatoes were grown in Ireland. Dinny being sure it was Kerry, and Michael adamant that it was in Youghal, that Raleigh after bringing them from Virginia grew them in the garden. 'Youghal it was, he was Governor at the time.'

'Thank God for them anyway, wouldn't we be in the sorry state without them,' Katy said.

'I don't know,' Michael replied contemplatively. 'Sometimes I think 'twould be better not to be depending on something with all their vagaries. For wouldn't the people be in a sorry state if they ever failed completely.'

'God between us and all harm!' the women said in unison, and made the Sign of the Cross.

'All that'll change when Dan succeeds,' Dinny proclaimed. 'When we have our own parliament things will be different. Men will have money to buy their wants. They won't live at the whim of a landlord, or depend for their life on potatoes.'

'They do be giving the men terrible urges. There's more people now in Ireland than ever there was. Terrible urges, isn't that a fact, Dinny?'

Dinny's face went red, but he ignored Statia's gibe and continued extolling the benefits O'Connell would bring. All the changes there would be.

'It's not a lot our plight will change,' Statia said cynically.

'That's a terrible thing to say,' Hannah exclaimed, aghast at the statement.

''Tis true for all that. Sure the same Dan's no better than many an English landlord, as quick to evict as the next. And for all his talk of not shedding blood, didn't he take the life of a man in a duel one time in Dublin. That's Dan for you.' She folded her arms across her breasts and looked defiantly at Dinny.

'You bloody oul divil, you've done nothing but aggravate me since you came. Passing remarks on an innocent doing was one thing. But slandering the name of O'Connell, I'll not stand for. I won't stay a minute longer in your unlucky company,' Dinny said, and got up to go.

Hannah, Mary and Katy said soothing words, and Michael told him not to mind Statia, that she never meant the half of it.

'I did so, every word,' Statia shouted. Dinny went puce, and in the middle of it all Peader and Jamsie arrived. At once the arguing ceased as all eyes were turned to them, and questions came from everywhere about Tara and O'Connell. Katy poured out the poteen for the men, and a small amount for Statia. Jamsie tossed his down, and she wondered how the gullet wasn't burned out of him. She busied herself making tea and cutting up the griddle cake, looking quickly and then away from Peader to Jamsie. Thinking what a handsome pair they were. How Peader's citified look was gone, his face brown, his hair bleached more gold than red by the sun. And Jamsie – she felt a pang of guilt for he was her husband, the father of her children, and she loved him too.

While she handed round the cake her mind fantasized

that she was given leave to choose between them, and decided she could not. For she liked this about one, and that about the other. In her mind's eye she rearranged them, swapping features, picturing Peader with blue eyes, Jamsie grown slimmer. She imagined Peader with more of Jamsie's forcefulness, and him with a measure of Peader's gentleness. Then they'd be perfect men, and maybe I could take my pick. She glanced covertly to where Peader was sitting answering Dinny and Michael's endless questions about Tara. At the same moment he looked in her direction and smiled and her indecisiveness was resolved – she would chose Peader every time. The love for me is shining out of his eyes. Quickly she bent her head, no one must witness such a thing. No one but a fool could mistake it for what it was.

All the unspoken love was there. A great sadness welled in her as she considered it. Thought of the long years ahead, them growing old, denied their love. And denied she knew it must be – for she was Jamsie's wife, would be until the day she died. That's all there was to it, and she would have to make the best of what she had. Think about Peader, dream about him, but never again pretend when Jamsie made love to her that it was Peader in her arms. That was a mortal sin, she might just as well go out in the field and lay with him, in the eyes of God the sin was the same. And if she was to die in her sleep after such thoughts heaven would be denied her.

The children came in clamouring for food, putting an end to her thoughts. She gave them bread, told them to bid the neighbours goodnight, and that she'd be in to say their prayers in a minute. Then she sat down and had a legitimate excuse for watching Peader as he related about O'Connell, repeating his speech. Hope shone out of the face of the listeners as they considered the bright future that was coming.

When it was time for the people to leave, Katy and Jamsie stood in the doorway calling farewells and watching the shadowy figures go up the boreen until they were gone from view. Jamsie was no sooner in bed than he slept. Katy thought about Peader, though she knew it was a sin and tried to dismiss the thoughts. But they persisted. And she wondered what happened to a woman who married twice; after she died and went to heaven – which husband would she sleep with?

Chapter Ten

The days were drawing in, and though the sun shone the heat was gone from it so that the evenings had a chill to them, and the grass in the morning was wet. The bracken was brown and twisted, and the brambles black with berries – the twins' hands and lips purpled from eating them.

Katy sat by the door watching her children. Peg and Nora gorging the fruit, Bridget, Thomas and Mary Kate chasing each other, bumping into cobwebs stretched between the bushes, clawing the invisible silken threads from the faces. – Thanks be to God, she thought, they are healthy and happy, and I am myself. The potatoes are in, stored in the pit, we got a good price for the barley so the half-year's rent is secure. I've even got a few shillings in the thatch towards the pig I'll have one day.

Out of the corner of her eye she saw Jamsie come up from the field where he had been stacking the discarded potato haulms. He had a sulky face on him, and she knew why. He wanted to go with Peader to O'Connell's Monster Meeting at Clontarf. Well, he could sulk as much as he liked, he wasn't having her savings for the fare to Dublin.

Yet she wished the situation had not arisen. Things were going well between them until the trip was men-

tioned. But since her refusal he had a sour puss on him.
– Look at him now, she said to herself, like Thomas when
he's been deprived of something. You wouldn't think he
was a grown man. She continued to talk to herself.
Shouldn't he know robbing the thatch is for no one's good.
Wouldn't a little bonham be better any day of the week
than a trip to Dublin. Wasn't that soon forgotten, and
would put no food in your belly. He definitely wasn't
having it, not if he kept a face like a fiddle till the cows
came home.

But as the day of the meeting came nearer she began
to waver. He desperately wanted to hear O'Connell. He
had walked the feet off himself looking for a day's work
to get the fare, but got nothing. He hadn't had a drink for
a week. Then one morning Hannah came down to the
cottage and made up Katy's mind for her.

'Well,' she said, 'you'd never credit what's after happening.'

'What?' asked Katy. 'I hope 'tis nothing bad, you look
awful white.'

'It's bad enough. Miss Charlotte's maid, Maura, and all
the footmen are to go. The poor Master had tears in his eyes
when he told them. I don't know what the world's coming
to. I tell you, all the changes will be the cause of killing
him. And what's to become of the House with only a
handful left to run it? God forgive Master Charles, fleecing
his father that's what he's doing. I tell you the place is being
destroyed. Before long I'll be having to send to Driscolls for
a jug of milk for there's hardly a cow left. Mind you it's
an ill wind that blows nobody good, you'll now be sure of
a bit of work at Christmas when they all come home.'

When Hannah was gone, Katy looked out through the window. Jamsie was bending down pretending interest in the garden, but she was certain his mind was on Dublin.

'Commere,' she said going to him, taking him by the arm and leading him to where her coins were hidden. 'There,' she said, pointing to the spot, 'reach in your hand.' He did so and uncovered them.

'Take them,' she said, 'and the sour puss off you as well, you can go to Dublin.'

'I couldn't,' Jamsie protested half-heartedly, 'don't you want the pig?'

'It can wait – take them now before I change my mind.'

His hands were already groping, his eyes delighted as he fingered the money and put it in his pocket. Then he caught hold of her, kissed the tip of her nose, twirled her round, put her down and went running to tell Peader he'd be with him.

He talked about nothing else for days. Telling Katy how he had never been further than Cork city in his life. 'You're lucky,' she replied, 'I've never been beyond Bandon.' He and Peader, he said would catch the Bianconi, the Bians made great time. They did eight or nine miles an hour, and the fare was only three ha'pence a mile. Three or four horses pulled them. 'Peader says they're like big outside cars. Aren't they the marvellous things, all the same, and little the poor would see of their native land, if it wasn't for Bianconi.'

As the Bian drove into Dublin, Peader pointed out the sights to Jamsie. 'That's the Phoenix Park,' he said, 'it runs for miles. There's soldiers, look.' Jamsie looked: through the trees ablaze with autumn leaves he saw the scarlet tunics, gold-laced, helmets bobbing, the sun glinting on them, chestnut, black and brown horses. The car left the Park behind and drove along the quays. Peader commented on the smell and told Jamsie it was from the brewery. 'Guinness's, it's over there, and them's the long narrow boats that take the porter down the country.'

'A glass or two would go down a treat,' Jamsie said, and asked what the building ahead was.

'The Four Courts, and to your right is Christ Church, where Cromwell stabled his horses, and Strongbow is buried. But after today we'll have no more of that. Today'll be the beginning of an Ireland without conquerors.'

'That'll be the day,' Jamsie agreed, though he was more interested in looking about him than listening to Peader, and the sight and smell of the brewery had given him a terrible longing for a drink. He suggested one to Peader when they dismounted and were walking northwards in the city. But Peader said, no, there wasn't time, they must get to Clontarf early.

The streets were thronged with people heading the same way. Jamsie and Peader joined them, were pushed and jostled, and entreated by hawkers to buy favours. Everyone seemed in good humour, dressed in their holiday best, and an air of expectancy emanated from them all.

'This'll be a day to remember,' Peader said as they neared the Bridge.

'It'll go down in history. You'll be able to tell the children you were there.'

Then they saw the soldiers blocking their way, and O'Connell's marshals spread out, shouting explanations to the press of people prevented from crossing the Liffey. The good humour was evaporating, angry shouts taking its place.

'What in the name of Jasus is happening?' a voice called out.

'The Meeting's proclaimed. It's banned. O'Connell's had to call it off. Turn round and go home.'

Stunned silence followed the announcement, followed by a roar of frustrated rage. The crowd began to push forwards, Jamsie and Peader borne with it. There were cries of, 'Oul Peel, oul Orange Peel. The bloody get, the bloody oul bastard, 'tis his doing. The curse of God on him.'

'Go no further now, boys,' a marshal entreated, his hands raised in supplication. 'It's Dan's wish that you should disperse in peace. He wants no heads broken, no blood spilt. 'Twould be useless anyway to try. There'll be no meeting. You'd never cross the Liffey. Look around you, them's not hurley sticks in the soldiers' hands. You wouldn't get a yard forward, and if you did, the guns of Pigeon House fort are aimed over the bay on Clontarf.'

Eventually he persuaded them to turn about, dejectedly they returned the way they had come, Peader and Jamsie with them. 'Our hope is gone now,' Peader said, 'nothing will ever be the same again. They'll crucify O'Connell for he brought the giant too near for their liking. There'll be nothing in front of the people now except America. There'll be no living here.'

Late in the evening of the same day Tim Coffey on his way back from the town called at the cottage. Katy knew immediately by his face that something was up. For Tim had a face that seldom moved, and could relate news of

231

a wake or wedding without joy or sorrow crossing it. But now it was working with an angry excitement as he shouted, 'The Meeting's been proclaimed.'

'Sure it couldn't, Jamsie and Peader went to it.'

'I'm telling you it is. I saw the notice that came post-haste, signed by O'Connell himself. The government put a stop to it – the hoors!'

'Ah, Tim, they're only chancing their arm. Sure there's thousands going. How could they turn them back?'

'Slaughter them if they had to, and think nothing of it.'

He left her to a sleepless night, for if he was right, she might never see Jamsie nor Peader again. They could be killed. She prayed as fervently for one as the other to come home safely. She wanted them both alive, wanted her life to go on as before.

Father Bolger also had trouble sleeping, wondering how the people gathered for the Meeting had reacted to the news of its banning. He hoped Dan had been able to hold them, that there had been no violence. Nothing would have played more into the hands of the English government than a bloody battle. Proved that the Irish could not be trusted, that peaceable protest was not in their composition. Reaffirmed their view that a hand pointing a gun was all they understood. An eruption of violence in Dublin would have been into their barrow.

'My poor unfortunate people, I hope today you weren't driven beyond your endurance. Footsore and weary you'd come miles to hear the Liberator, to protest in peace. And who could blame you if met by the might of England you didn't turn the other cheek. But may God grant that you did, that another battle was not fought at Clontarf.'

From the altar next morning he spoke quietly to his parishioners. Sympathizing with the disappointment he shared with them. Urging them not to lose hope. The banning of the Meeting was only a temporary setback. They had lived through many such. The Repeal Association would continue. Daniel had shown them how to unite. It was easy to break a single stick, but tied together the strongest man could not break a bundle. They would survive, and one day succeed. Then he asked them to pray that no one had been harmed in Dublin, that all who had set out would return safely.

Katy was overjoyed when Jamsie and Peader came back. She hugged Jamsie and smiled at Peader, hoping she conveyed some of what she was feeling for him. He thought how beautiful she looked, that marriage had made her more so. That she and Jamsie were meant for each other, and it was the wise decision she made the night she gave him up. His admiration for her showed on his face, but Katy saw the expression as further proof of his love.

News came to the village that Daniel O'Connell was arrested, and for a time there was anger, followed by despair, then gradually events of everyday life took precedence. The women coming from the well talked of births and deaths, dreams they considered unlucky, or ones of good portent. The men cutting turf, their slanes digging long channels, lifting the sods, footing them in such a way the wind could pass through to dry them, talked about forthcoming hurleying matches, whose chance they fancied, and where they might find a day's work before Christmas.

The men from the bog who had been labouring in England came home. There was unaccustomed money in their pockets, and Carey the publican did good business. Padraig O'Hara put by the rent with the increase included. Johnny laughed at him. 'You're an eejit. You're the only one who's paid the extra. That notice frightened the life out of Dano for all that he tore it up. That was all show. He hasn't lifted a finger and won't.'

'Maybe so,' Padraig replied, 'but I feel more secure and the wife can sleep easy.'

From the chimneys of the cottages, through holes in the thatch of cabins, or where there were no holes, under the door, turf smoke rose and swirled, and everyone was thankful that if they had little else there was no scarcity of firing for winter was nearly on top of them.

Charlotte getting ready for bed thought about Christmas, and counted the days until Catherine, Olivia and the children arrived. It would be good to have them home, to have their company at meals. To hear voices and laughter – no doubt there would be quarrels once Charles came, but even that was better than gloom and silence.

She began to undress, struggling to undo the frock which fastened down the back, and wished there was someone to help, or that her arms were longer. It was a nuisance since so many maids were dismissed. Hannah would come willingly, but the kitchen was so far, it wouldn't be fair to ring for her. Her room got into a dreadful mess, clothes never put away, the mirrors tarnished, dust everywhere. When finally she was out of the dress she resolved as she did many times that she must learn to do all the things once performed by the servants. Beginning this minute, she told herself, and put the frock on a hanger. For a while she worked to restore order to the room, then, tiring of the task, sat on the bed and took from around her neck Katy's medal.

She put it beneath the pillow and got into bed. Her thoughts returned to Christmas. She hoped Catherine and Olivia would like the water colours she had done for them. And she must finish the one for Papa, he loved holly. – Poor Papa, he's so miserable these days. Everything seems to go against him. He misses Tara and Toby dreadfully. How awful it must have been putting them down himself. That was how much he loved them, wouldn't trust anyone else to do it. Her eyes closed, she was very sleepy. Pleasant thoughts came to her. One day she would meet a man and fall in love. He would be her heart's desire; her fingers felt under the pillow and touched the medal.

They came to the bog early on a bright cold morning, five men on horseback, three walking, carrying crowbars. Only the hens were stirring, scratching the dirt. In the mud cabins people still half asleep huddled close to smoky fires. Johnny O'Hara was in bed, his wife kneeling on the hearth raking the ashes. Padraig was wide awake, and hearing the horses whinny looked out of the door, saw Dano, the soldiers, police and men with crowbars. 'Jesus!' he exclaimed and called to his wife. 'They've come. Someone's going to be evicted.'

'Thank God it won't be us,' she said, joining him by the door.

'It could be anyone. I hope it's not Johnny.'

'No, they've passed his place. They've gone on to the next lot of cabins.' More people came to their doors, the women and children half dressed, and watched, no one saying anything, staring fearfully until their cabins were passed.

'Go and call your Uncle Johnny,' Padraig told one of his children.

'Is that wise?' his wife asked as the child ran off. 'Mightn't he cause more trouble?'

'He'll not,' Padraig assured her.

One by one the families left their doorways and headed after Dano and his retinue. They stood on the edge of the field where the huddle of cabins were and watched Dano get down from his big black stallion, and the police dismount. Dano went from house to house, six of them, called through doors, banged on those not open. Terrified women appeared, children ran out crying, the men emerging sullen and silent.

'He's putting out the lot of them,' Padraig whispered to his wife. 'Jesus! look at that, he's evicting every one of them.' The women screamed abuse, clung on to the doors attempting to bar entrance.

'Give us a chance, Driscoll, the winter's coming, we've young children, sick, old people,' a man pleaded.

Dano stood flanked by the constables, the mounted soldiers behind while the three men with crowbars went from house to house. 'You've had all the chance you're having. Take your sick and yourselves to the workhouse,'

Dano shouted, then turning to the crowd on the edge of the field, bellowed, 'Don't forget it's your turn next, six at a time, that's the way I'll run you out.'

Johnny came running to stand by Padraig. 'The bastard,' he said, 'the misbegotten, bandy bastard,' he said as he watched a woman dragged screaming from her doorway, followed by her husband and bewildered children.

'Wouldn't it suit him fine for the man to try defending his cabin, give him an excuse to turn the polis and soldiers on him.'

'Shouldn't somebody run for the priest?' Padraig suggested.

'What could he do, except pray?' Johnny replied.

The crowd watched in hostile silence the police prise fingers that clung to doors, the bedding, pots and straw pallets being flung out. Heard the demented cries of the women, the whimpering of terrified children, and Dano's voice exhorting the men with crowbars to hurry up with the tumbling. It took no time to dismantle the mud walls and sod roofs, down they fell and lay in piles from which trickles of smoke swirled upwards.

Dano, the police and soldiers rode away, and the crowbar men took to their heels. The crowd moved in and helped to carry their neighbours' possessions to the ditches where they would shelter.

'God's curse on him,' Statia said to Katy when she related news of the eviction.

'May he die roaring and roast in Hell,' Katy added. 'I wonder what will happen now, do you think the Society might move?'

'I'd say they would, and could you blame them?'

'The poor unfortunate people, what will become of them, thrown out of their homes?'

'They'll walk the roads and beg. There's thousands before them, and nothing but the workhouse in front of them. Men and women dragged from each other, the little children too, all parted.'

'May God save and protect us from such an end,' Katy said.

They separated before reaching Dano's land, Johnny going with the man he had met in the public house, the remainder led by the big man taking a path that would lead to the cattle. Johnny and his companion got down in the grass and wriggled on their bellies across a field.

'Have you the rope and bit of meat?'

'I have.' Johnny answered the whisper with another. He felt a tickle at the back of his throat, a desire to cough, he swallowed his spittle to suppress it.

'One yelp out of the dog and we're done for. I hope to God he remembers me.'

'He will surely,' Johnny reassured.

They were nearing the edge of the field, the farm buildings and house taking shape. The man gave a low whistle that might have been the call of a bird. The dog came silently, searching, sniffing the edge of the grass. It got a familiar scent.

'Give me the meat.'

Johnny handed over the scrap. 'Here boy, here Bran,' the man's voice coaxed, holding out his palm. As the dog ate the meat he collared him by the scruff of the neck, talking all the while. 'There now. You're a good boy,' soothing, reinforcing his bond with the animal.

'The rope.' Johnny gave it to him and he slipped the noose over the animal's neck, easing up the knot till it fitted comfortably. 'There's a grand fellow, sure aren't you very good.' He stood up and told Johnny to do likewise. 'That tree there. You do the throwing and hoisting.' Bran led the way, the rope trailing between his neck and the man's hand. While they walked him and Johnny kept an eye to the house, there was no stir, nor light.

When they were under the tree the man sat down in the grass and the dog did the same moving close to him, licking his hands. He let go the rope, and fondled Bran's head, keeping him near and calm. Johnny picked up the rope and climbed into the tree and arranged the cord; the end dangled, he got down.

'Move him over a bit,' Johnny said. 'Right, that's it,' he said as his hands went up the hempen strands, and he had it taut. He jerked hard and the dog was lifted, dangled, the noose tightened, but not enough. The dog attempted a bark that came out in a thin desperate choking yelp.

The man joined Johnny, his hands on the rope, they pulled together, the dog's legs danced in the air, his tongue lolled from his gasping mouth, his thick neck hair impeding the way of the rope, prolonging the agony. Then the frenetic leg movements ceased, the breath no longer rasped, the only sound a stream of water falling into the grass.

'Let's go, 'tis done.'

Their hands released the rope, the dog fell with a thud. 'Run for it now,' the man said, and went. Before Johnny could do the same a shout came. 'Bran! Where are you? Commere, Bran.'

An oblong of light appeared where the door was, and Johnny saw Driscoll framed in it. Saw him step out of the light and come towards the tree. He hugged close to its trunk and waited. Dano was running. Johnny undid the cudgel from his belt, held it ready.

'Bran! Where the bloody hell are you? I'll give it to you, where are you?'

He stumbled over the dog's body. 'My Christ, what ...' Johnny hit him on the side of the head. Dano staggered, turned, his hands up protectively. He saw Johnny, went for him. 'I know you, you're an O'Hara, you're from ...' The cudgel swung, crashed on his skull. Dano sagged. Johnny kicked his legs from under him. He fell beside the dog. Johnny bent and struck the stick across his face, against his nose, then he spat on him and ran the way the other man had gone.

'Get up you hoors!' The men went round the cattle hitting them on the rumps, raising them, herding them, driving them out of the enclosure on to the cliff path.

'Get that one in the front moving.' A knotted stick landed hard on the leading bullock making it run, the others followed their leader. Up the cliff path they went, more sticks encouraging the laggards, up, and then down with the slope of the track, the gradient impelling them forward. Headlong down the path they thundered, their hooves throwing up dust that blinded the men and made them cough. They jumped out of the way of the animals caught up in their flight to death. Over the cliff they went, the roar of the incoming tide drowning any sound they might have made, any noise of shattering bones as their carcasses landed on the jagged rocks at the foot of the cliffs. Two beasts, who all the way had to be urged on, slowed, attempted to escape, their hooves scrabbling at the steep-sided verges. They were beaten back on to the path. The men gathered round them.

'There's only the two, is it worth bothering?' a man asked.

'Think of the acres they need to graze – it's worth bothering all right. Get them going,' the big man commanded. As if sensing that to their death they were going the bullocks still resisted, impervious to the blows on their backs, heads and faces. The men separated, four of them round each beast, and by pushing and pulling they inched them up to the edge of the cliff and heaved them over.

'Is he dead, Father?' Mrs Driscoll asked. 'Are you in time to give him absolution? Don't tell me he's dead without the Grace of God.'

'He's alive, but only just I'd say. He needs help.'

'Sure you'll help him, Father. Give him the Last Sacrament. The doctor might not be here till morning. Anoint him, Father, I wouldn't want him in Hell for eternity.'

'I will of course, isn't that why I'm here,' Father Bolger said, looking down at the unconscious face of Dano, at the flattened nose, the broken stumps of teeth visible through the open mouth, and prepared to administer Extreme Unction. Dano should be absolved of his sins, venial or mortal, he would not be denied God's mercy. At this moment it was not for him to pass judgment on him,

Father Bolger thought, undoing the vial of Blessed olive oil. The family knelt round the bed. The priest dipped his thumb in the oil and, making a small Sign of the Cross with it on Dano's forehead, prayed. 'Through this holy anointing, and His most tender mercy may the Lord forgive you whatever sins you have committed by the sins of sight,' he crossed Dano's eyes, repeating the words, anointed his ears, 'by hearing', blessed with his thumb the bruised lips, 'taste and speech', lightly touched the broken nose, 'by smell', moved on to his hands, 'by touch'. Mrs Driscoll rose and turned back the bedclothes exposing Dano's feet, the priest crossed the soles of them, and concluded the prayer, 'And steps. Amen.'

'With the help of God he may pull through,' he consoled the woman before he left. 'But he's very sick, you know that.'

'I do, Father.'

'What happened, where was he?'

'In the bed asleep. Then he woke me, thought he heard the dog, and went out. We found him there. He knows who did it. He came round for a minute, and tried to tell us, but sure then he was gone again.'

Father Bolger bid her goodnight, asking God as he went that if Dano was to die, let him die without regaining consciousness and naming names, causing a hanging. – And what if he lives? he asked himself. Whoever he names will be transported, but that's better than hanging. Nobody deserved to die for the likes of Dano.

Chapter Eleven

Statia ran to the cottage with the news. 'Katy! Jamsie! Are you up?' she called.

'We are this long time. Come in,' Katy called back.

'Dano's been killed, his cattle clifted, and the dog hanged.'

'The poor oul dog. Sit down and tell us all,' Katy said.

Statia related what she had heard, then added that she wasn't sure if Dano was dead, or only nearly. 'But listen to this. He saw who done it.'

'Sacred Heart! He didn't!' Katy was aghast.

'Who was it?' Jamsie asked.

'Now that I don't know. Dano passed out before mentioning a name.'

'Thanks be to God, that he may stay passed out,' Katy replied, and wondered what part Johnny had played in the business. She hoped no one was caught for no one deserved to swing for Dano, and not one in Kilgoran would have sympathy for him. Johnny's part in the raid would be suspected, but his name pass no one's lips.

'What'll happen now, I wonder, do you think . . .' Before she finished the sentence a shadow fell across the threshold. It was Peader. She turned her back to the company and busied herself with the fire that needed attention.

243

Avoiding looking at Peader helped her in the fight she was waging to overcome what she believed was her love for him. It was what the priest had bid her do, put the other man out of her mind. She didn't always succeed, but tried, which was what mattered. The night in the Hazel Grove was a sin, letting on it was him and not Jamsie. But she found excuses for that – Jamsie had to be punished for taking her so, what else could she have done? She thought all these things as the poker raked ash and highered sods of turf, she heard his voice and longed to turn round, see his lovely face, watch the smile play round his mouth. But she wouldn't again deliberately feast her eyes on him. Maybe that way he would stop haunting her. Maybe that way she would succeed in forgetting that she loved him. Not looking at him was a beginning anyway. Statia was saying: 'You'll be above in the House from tomorrow. Hannah tells me the family will be over at the weekend.'

'That's right, they will. And before you know it there'll be Christmas. Thank God, though the Master's short of money we'll still have the goose.'

'Wouldn't it be a poor Christmas without the fine fat goose?' Statia said.

'Do you fancy a ramble, Jamsie?' Peader asked.

'Where?'

'I thought I'd go up to the little wood above in the fold of the hills. There's great berries on the holly. We could pick an armful.'

'I'll leave it till through the week. Maybe another day I'll take the children.'

'All right so, I'll be off then.'

'Pick a bit for me while you're at it,' Statia called after him, and only then did Katy rise from by the fire.

The thicket was ablaze with scarlet berries, in front of it, reaching up, Peader saw a girl he did not recognize. Hearing his footsteps, she turned and smiled. 'Good morning, Miss,' he said, still none the wiser, though he knew she was gentry, and resembled the Kilgorans, the oldest daughter who got married before he went to Dublin. But it couldn't be her, that was six years ago – this girl with brown hair tumbling round her, cheeks as red as the berries, and eyes smiling hesitantly at him was young – sixteen, maybe seventeen years.

'I'm Charlotte, Charlotte Kilgoran,' she said.

He tipped his cap. 'It's a fine day, Miss Charlotte, though cold. Good day to you.' So that's who it was, he said to himself as he left the wood. The youngest of Lord Kilgoran's daughters – no wonder he didn't recognize her, she was a child the last time he saw her. He walked on thinking about the girl, how lovely she was.

During the following days he continued to think of Charlotte. Recalling her face, how pretty it was, the cloud of hair brown as a robin's wing, how startled her eyes were when she turned and saw him, like those of a young doe. He wondered what brought her to the wood on such a cold morning. It was a long way to walk for a look at holly when it grew in abundance near the House. Then he remembered something else, there had been a book, maybe a large pad near her feet – a sketch book, that was it – she had come to draw the holly. In the little wood many things grew. After Christmas came the snowdrops, violets, a host of lovely things to sketch. He might, he thought, go there another day.

Charlotte had no difficulty recognizing who the man was. He was Peader Daly – one of her father's tenants. Peter, Hannah once told her the name was in English. Once before he went to Dublin he had taken her and Olivia out in his boat to fish for mackerel. She had thought how nice and kind he was then, and was sad when she overheard the servants say Katy broke his heart. Wasn't it strange that he had come into her secret place, she said to herself, and wondered if he would again.

Day and night someone sat by Dano in case he regained consciousness and spoke the name of the culprit. Early one morning his wife thought she heard him speak. In a flash she was up, bending over him. He opened his eyes, stared blankly at her.

'An O'Hara, one of them from the bog,' he said, and passed out again.

'Quick, quick!' Mrs O'Driscoll's shouts woke the house. 'Get down to the barracks, your father has spoken.' Her sons and daughters and the servant came running. 'Go back and mind the fire,' she ordered the maid, then lowering her voice to a whisper, gave the information, and sent one of her sons to the police barracks.

The police sergeant was so excited with the news he forgot to mention that the two horses had gone lame. Driscoll's son was gone before the thought struck him to ask for the loan of Dano's stallion.

'What'll I do?' he asked the constable. 'Word'll have to go immediately into the town.'

'The only other horse near at hand is Michael Daly's mare, but I doubt if he'd lend it. Your best bet is the House. Go up and acquaint Lord Kilgoran with the news, and you'll have a mount in no time.'

'You're right,' said the sergeant. 'Daly would suspect something and not lend the mare.' He looked at the clock. ''Tis early to call at the House, I'll wait an hour or so, and break my fast in the meantime.'

Charles was in the library with his father when the sergeant came, pretending interest in the lecture Lord Kilgoran was delivering about his debts. The policeman apologized for the early hour, told his news, and asked for the loan of a horse.

'Which O'Hara?' Charles asked.

'That I don't know for sure, Sir. I'm on my way now to talk to Driscoll.'

Lord Kilgoran thanked the sergeant for informing him, and told him to go to the stables, a horse would be provided. When he left, Charles said, 'Johnny O'Hara I'd put my money on, wouldn't you, Papa?'

'Don't jump to conclusions, Driscoll might have been raving.'

'It had to be someone from round here. Johnny, I'd say, with an accomplice who knew the dog. Not Padraig or Paudeen, whatever they call the elder brother, definitely not the type. And somehow I don't think Jamsie; might have before he married O'Donnell's daughter, not now, I'd say she's broken him in.'

'Look here, Charles, you haven't a shred of evidence for what you're saying. Guesswork, that's all it is; leave it to the law, there's a good fellow. Now to come back to the business we were discussing earlier, you are forcing me to consider changing my will. God knows it's not something I want to do. Are you listening, Charles?'

'Yes, Papa,' Charles replied and looked suitably penitent. He launched into a list of excuses for his recent debts, promising that he intended to mend his ways. The lies slipped easily off his tongue, while at the same time his mind contemplated Johnny O'Hara's wife. Yesterday he had seen her when he rode up on the bog. Had spoken to her, reminded her of the two golden guineas. 'Three then,' he had said when she refused. She shook her head, and smiled. She had become more slatternly, fat, dirty, yet she fascinated him, her refusals making him want her more. Well, now perhaps he had found her price.

'I'm glad to hear it. I knew you would see sense eventually. In time you'll be pleasantly surprised how satisfying managing the estate ...'

'What will the sergeant do – go straight from Driscoll's and arrest O'Hara?' Charles interrupted.

'Arrest?' Lord Kilgoran looked puzzled. 'O'Hara, what has he to do with our conversation? Were you really giving me your attention, Charles?'

'Of course I was, the thought just crossed my mind, that's all.'

'I see. No, I shouldn't think so. Not immediately. He'll have to have assistance. Call for more police, the military. I wouldn't think an arrest will be made before tomorrow.

It would be foolhardy for the sergeant and one constable to attempt anything like that up on the bog.'

'Mmm . . . sorry for having interrupted you, go on with what you were saying about the estate.'

Lord Kilgoran returned to outlining the benefits to be derived from running the estate, Charles to his plan. Tonight he would tip off Johnny O'Hara, then bed his woman. Kill two birds with one stone; he'd enjoy seeing the law made a fool of, floundering in the bog for a fish that had got away.

That evening at dinner Charles looked round the table at his family. – What a censorious-looking lot they are, he thought, well all except Olivia, she's a good sport, might even laugh if I told her my plan for later. Catherine would be horrified, and that husband of hers – typical soldier, straight-backed, pompous, talks to you as if you were one of his men on parade. And Peter, Olivia's husband, what did she ever see in the fellow apart from his money? What a dreary lot they are. Charlotte, who used to be rather nice, changed into a mixture of Catherine's saintliness and the servants' superstitious ways.

God, he could scream. And what a draughty hole the House was. He cast his eyes round the room, wavering candle lights, tongues of flame dancing round the logs in the grate as the wind blew down the chimney, billows of smoke. What did he care if he never inherited it? Who in their right mind would want it? Catherine perhaps. She'd enjoy that, being the lady of the Manor, riding out on errands of mercy. Was doing something of the sort in Aldershot. He finished his wine, and asked for more.

'What do you think, Charles?'

'About what, Edward?' What boring topic was the fool raising now, Charles thought, looking at his brother-in-law. Why can't the fellow get on with his dinner, and let me go about my business.

'We were talking about O'Connell, wondering what sentence he's likely to get.'

'Damned agitator, should be hanged,' Charles replied. He decided to liven things up. If he did sufficiently his father might order him from the table. 'Never should have got Emancipation, only one thing the Irish understand, brute force. Hang him.'

'I say,' Peter spoke. 'Isn't that a bit drastic, he hasn't done anything that warrants such drastic measures.'

Charles could see the indignant expression on his father's face, Catherine going puce with anger. A little bit longer, a few more well-chosen comments and he would be asked to go. From the top of the table would come his father's voice. 'If you cannot behave like a gentleman you will not sit at my table.' Two or three derogatory remarks should do it.

'Drastic, nothing's too drastic for Ireland or the Irish. Foul swamp. Priest-ridden peasants.'

'Hush, Charles.' Olivia sitting next to him reached out and touched his hand. 'You'll upset Papa, you'll be sent from the table. Behave yourself.' He pretended anger, shrugged off her hand. He was really into the part now, enjoying his role.

'O'Connell was thrown into gaol where he belongs.' He raised his voice. 'The fellow's a charlatan. Why are you all defending him? What is he to us? Hypocrites, all of you.

Gone native. And you, Papa,' he stood up and pointed to his father, 'you are the worst of any. Full of compassion for O'Connell, for your drunken, lazy tenants, while I'm constantly castigated for my peccadilloes.'

'Sit down, Charles. Behave like a gentleman or I shall ask you to leave the table,' Lord Kilgoran said.

Charles nearly laughed aloud at how predictable they all were. His father looking as if he had been struck, Charlotte like a startled rabbit, Edward horrified at such behaviour in front of the ladies, and Peter, open-mouthed like a cod. One last parting shot to make his action appear more genuine, to ensure he was ordered from the table. 'I retract nothing,' he shouted defiantly.

'Go,' his father ordered, and he went.

Johnny answered his knock on the cabin door. 'Yes,' he said, not very civil.

Charles told him about Dano and the police, the accusation against an O'Hara.

'I know nothing about it. Why did you come here? It's no concern of mine. Driscoll's only my landlord, I'm sorry the man was hurt.'

'No, well, my mistake, thought you might be interested,' Charles said. In the smoky room he saw the girl, some children and an old woman, her mother he supposed. The girl stared at him. 'Just thought I'd mention it, that's all. Goodnight then.'

'Goodnight,' Johnny said and closed the door.

Charles mounted and rode off, reining in the horse when he came to a small copse, he got down, smacked it lightly and it trotted into the trees. He waited, watching the road; not long afterward he saw Johnny flee. 'No concern of yours, eh?' he said aloud, going to where the horse was and tethering it, then he returned on foot to the cabin.

'Oh! It's you again,' the girl said. 'Come in.'

She stood close to him, he could smell drink on her breath, and the musky odour of her body. 'Get rid of them.' He nodded in the direction of her mother and the children.

She spoke in Irish to the old woman sitting in the ashes smoking a clay pipe. The woman took the pipe from her mouth, stared with a mocking look at Charles before cackling.

'Filthy old witch,' he said under his breath, then louder, 'Get rid of her.' Taking her time about it the grandmother collected the children and left.

It was stifling in the room, smoke stung his eyes. He looked at the bed of straw – his skin crawled, he stifled a desire to scratch.

'You'll not tell on him, Sir,' Johnny's wife said undoing her skirt. 'You'll say nothing, sure you won't.' She stepped out of the skirt and pulled the bodice over her head. She wore no petticoat, no drawers, no shift. 'You won't, will you, Sir. Lay down here by the fire, sure you must be tired from all the riding.' She took his hand and brought him to the pallet.

Catherine, Charlotte and Olivia left the men to their port and cigars and went to the drawing-room.

'Wasn't that a dreadful scene?' Catherine said, sitting on the pink damask sofa, Charlotte beside her.

'Typical Charles, he'll never grow up. Remember his

252

performances when we were small, almost always sent from the table. I don't think he means a word of it, he should have been an actor.'

'Don't make excuses for him, Olivia, he's no longer a child. Look at the effect it had on Papa, I thought he would have a seizure. What made matters worse was that earlier Charles had given his word to mend his ways. Papa told me before dinner. This morning he took Charles to task about issuing post-obits, threatened to disinherit him. Charles was very contrite and convinced Papa of his good intentions.'

'What's post-obits?' Charlotte asked.

'Never you mind,' Olivia answered shortly.

'Olivia! Don't dismiss Charlotte like that – she's not a child. She has a right to know what's happening. It affects her future.'

Olivia said nothing, and went to look into the over-mantel, touching her hair, patting her face. Catherine explained. 'Well, you know about Charles borrowing from money-lenders. For a long time Papa paid back the loans, now he finds it difficult to do so. But that doesn't stop Charles, now in return for the money he issues notes promising to repay when he inherits Kilgoran.'

'You mean when Papa dies!' Charlotte said, and looked horrified.

'Yes, when Papa dies, and if there's enough of these notes oustanding everything could be seized.'

'The estate could be lost?'

'It could, and will unless there's a miracle.'

'But that won't happen. It can't. Papa isn't old, he'll live for years,' Charlotte said hopefully.

'I hope he does, I pray that he will. But the only solution is for Papa to disinherit Charles.'

'He wouldn't do that. How could he anyway, the estate's held entail male – son to son,' Olivia said, turning from the mirror.

'It's not, unfortunately.'

'But I thought all estates had this entail, some in favour of the male, but all of them protected from debtors seizing them.'

'Unfortunately Kilgoran is one of the exceptions, it's held in fee simple. Papa can leave it to anyone belonging to him, but, and this is the worrying thing at the moment, Charles is the heir, and on the head of that he can borrow enormous sums. That's what he is doing, that's what I was explaining to Charlotte about post-obits.'

'Well – why hasn't someone ever made this clear to us? I bet you Charles doesn't understand it. Did Papa make it clear to him this morning?' Olivia asked.

'I'm afraid it didn't get that far. Charles promised to improve, Papa believed him . . .'

'Then Charles won't even attempt to change. He thinks the estate is his no matter what. But I still think you're exaggerating. Lots of young men get into debt, it doesn't mean the family fortune will be lost.'

'Most young men have some interest in their future. Charles hasn't. He doesn't like Ireland, Kilgoran, not in the slightest.'

'Oh, for heaven's sake don't keep on about it. So he doesn't love Ireland, neither do I. Not everyone is like you and Papa, besotted by the place and the natives.'

'Aren't we natives, too? We were all born here,' Charlotte said.

'Why don't you go to bed?' Olivia snapped. 'Of course we were born here, that doesn't make us natives like Hannah and Statia and Katy – going to confess, believing in fairies, not ploughing a good field because there's a rath in the middle – that sort of thing.'

'What a horrid person you are. I hate you. You and Charles. I wish you hadn't come,' Charlotte said, and began to cry.

'You're both impossible. I knew this was how it would end. I'm going to bed.'

Catherine comforted Charlotte and made excuses for Olivia. 'You mustn't mind all she says. She is really very kind, and loves you and Papa dearly.'

'I don't think she does. I don't think she loves anyone but herself.'

'Oh, but she does. You don't know what she suffers to come and see you. She's a bad sailor, gets violently sick. She loves you greatly to go through such an ordeal. Don't think too badly of her. And now we should go to bed, the men might be ages yet.'

Katy looked out through the cottage door, and saw the frozen ground, the puddles coated with milky-looking ice, the grass like short sharp spears. She went back in and bound her feet with rags before setting out for the House. Hannah told her about the row the previous night, and how she had heard Master Charles coming home late. She made her a cup of tea and Katy sat to the fire putting her feet close to the range.

'Not that near,' Hannah said, 'let them thaw a bit first or you'll get chilblains. Isn't it a pity with all the fine shoes about the place, there isn't a pair to fit you. God love you, sure you must be perished with the cold of them.'

'Am I in the nursery this morning?' Katy asked.

'Where else?' Hannah replied, 'and I don't envy you the chore. That nurse Miss Olivia brought with her has tall orders – wanting her tea this way, and her bread and butter the other. You'd better go up now or she'll be complaining.'

The nurse was waiting and gave Katy her instructions. With sweet smelling soap she washed the children, and smoothed fine dusting powder into the creases of their limbs. Thinking how it was well for them with all their comfort. The older two were near in age to Thomas, and sometimes their clothes were given to Katy. She dressed the baby in cream flannel, put on layers of muslin and lace, and swathed it in fine woollen shawls. Then she made the beds and washed the children's soiled clothes. All the while the nurse sat by the fire issuing orders and toasting her feet.

The baby got cranky and Katy picked him up, he was sleepy. 'Put him down. Crying is good for his lungs. Handling will spoil him,' the nurse by the fire ordered.

'You hard hearted oul jinnet, 'tis a pity someone didn't handle you,' Katy said under her breath. 'I'd have him asleep in a minute with love and a song.' She put the child in his crib and said nothing, for the children and the nurseries were the nurse's business.

When it was time to go Hannah gave her a parcel of food, the remains of the last night's dinner. Wrapping up pieces of venison, the leg of a fowl, bread, sweet cake and a bowl of dripping that had thick brown jelly congealed on the bottom of the fat, Hannah said, 'The Master may be in debt and danger, but he still keeps the best table in the county.'

Halfway home, Bridget, Thomas and the twins met her. 'What did you bring us, Mammy?' the twins chorused.

'Oh wait till you see. Wait till you taste it,' Katy answered. Peg and Nora weren't content to wait, wanted a sight and a share there and then. She threatened to box their ears if they persisted. They did and she slapped them and they roared all the way home.

The food was devoured, the bread spread with dripping, the meat with mouthfuls of potatoes, the chicken bones chewed, the last morsels of flesh and gristle sucked off while Prince went demented with hunger and impatience. After the meal so sated were the children with unaccustomed food, and the heat from the fire, they fell asleep while Jamsie was giving out the Rosary, and were carried into bed.

'I didn't want to say anything in front of them,' Jamsie said when he and Katy were alone. 'Our Johnny's gone.'

'Gone, where and why?'

'God knows, but he has, last night. Dano came to for a minute and said it was an O'Hara. Someone got word to him.'

'Sacred Heart of Jesus! You'll all be suspected, you and Padraig.'

'Sure how could we, what had we to do with it? Anyway the police and soldiers were up the bog already. They asked for Johnny, and went when they couldn't find him.'

'That means nothing. They'll be back. Mark my words they'll be back. I knew it, something's been hanging over me all day. I knew there was trouble afoot.'

All Jamsie's efforts to reassure her were in vain. Something terrible was going to happen, she could feel it, like a stone inside her. A heavy weight pulling at her heart. Jamsie would be lifted, blamed for something he had no part in. The police wouldn't rest until they had someone for assaulting Dano. They would come for Jamsie, and it was all her fault. God was punishing her for her sins. For loving another man, for not trying hard enough to put him out of her mind. Her lovely husband would be dragged from her side, her children left fatherless because she wouldn't listen to the priest. Fooling herself that not looking in Peader's direction would blind God. God that could see everything.

'I'm telling you,' Jamsie said, 'you're worrying about nothing. Johnny's gone and that'll be an end to it.'

'I only hope you're right,' Katy said, looking at his face filled with concern for her, 'but I doubt that you are. What would become of Johnny if they caught him?' she asked, picturing Jamsie in his place.

'That would depend on what happens to Dano – if he dies, they'd hang Johnny – if he lives, Johnny would be transported no less. But amn't I telling you they'll never get him, and there'll be no more about it.'

She cried for most of the night cradled in Jamsie's arms, and when she wasn't crying prayed that Dano wouldn't die. 'Please let him live. Please Holy Mother of God intercede with your Son for me. Don't let Dano die. I don't want Jamsie transported, but better that than to hang. Please make Dano well. If you'll only do that I'll never commit another sin. I'll never scream at the children again, and if I have fifty more children I'll welcome them. Don't let my husband be taken from me. Please God. I'll never give Peader another thought.'

Jamsie rocked and soothed her, stroked her hair, and rubbed her back, kissed her eyes wet with tears, and then her lips. Told her he loved her, as his hand sought her breast, and for a while she forgot her fears.

The village buzzed with the news that the soldiers and extra police were back and that Dano though still in danger of death was fully conscious. Unable to communicate her fears to anyone, Katy went to work and performed her duties in a daze. She was almost sick with relief when she arrived home and saw Jamsie there. The fact that Peader was there, too, for once had no effect on her. They were talking about Driscoll, how the police had been up at his farm all day. That though he was conscious he was very weak and had said no more about his attacker.

'What more is there for him to say? Didn't he mention a name. And didn't you say that was an end to it now the bird has flown,' she said rounding on Jamsie, her worry and fear finding an outlet in anger.

'I was wrong by the look of things,' he admitted. 'Maybe they're hoping Dano saw someone else, too.'

To take her mind off it she took the children to pick the holly that Jamsie had forgotten to get. 'If we leave it a minute longer the birds will have every berry eaten, and what good would that be?' she said in a tone of forced jollity. They were passing the Four Fields of Red Clover.

In the centre of each was a raised mound of earth. – Dano's fields, Katy thought, it must go between him and his rest that the raths prevented him making good use of them. The greedy, grasping man that he is, but even he wouldn't defy the little people. Becoming aware of her uncharitable thinking, she asked God to forgive her breaking another promise she had so recently made.

The wind blew from the north-east, stinging the children's cheeks. They ran on ahead, and Katy chased after them. Casting aside for a while the lead weight that bore down her heart, her hair came undone and streamed like a yellow pennant in the wind. They talked to her about Christmas while she reached down the glossy green branches heavy with ripe red fruit, and broke them, piling their arms high, pushing fearful thoughts deep inside her as she watched their happy faces glowing from the cold as brightly as the berries.

On the way back, she told them how on Christmas Day they would all walk with her into Connolly's and she would buy them sweets. Wasn't Connolly's the grand shop, she asked them? It was, they chorused. She made a game of it to keep the bad thoughts of despair from her mind, asking them questions.

'Tell me now, do you remember all that's in it?'

'Hams and fancy shawls hanging from the ceiling,' Bridget said.

'Barrels of porter and sacks of meal, and stuff on the shelves, rolls of it,' Thomas said. 'And that queer big sheet of fish all white from the salt, that I licked once.'

'What else, come on now, sure that's only the half of it.' And they searched their memories of last year's visit. 'Peg and Nora, you've said nothing.'

'Sweets and tobacco for Daddy,' the twins said when they were nearly home.

Peader was gone. Katy asked if any of the neighbours had come with more news of Dano. 'Ne'er a one,' Jamsie replied. And she said to herself, let him be sitting by the fire safe and sound on Christmas Day. Before the children went to bed she told them the Christmas Story, blowing on their hands the way the cattle did to warm the baby Jesus with their breath, and regaled them with descriptions of how the goose would be stuffed and cooked for their dinner. Paudeen would be bringing it down from the House tomorrow, Christmas Eve.

'Beef tea,' Mrs Driscoll said.

'But Ma'am, it's Christmas Eve, 'tis a day of abstinence.'

'Not for them near death's door it's not, warm it up now like a good girl. Try a mouthful, love,' she coaxed, bending over her husband, ''twill give you strength.'

Dano sipped at the spoon, and the sergeant bent closer, watching, listening as he had for several days. – In the name of Jasus would the man never talk, he thought. Was he to be here forever, and tomorrow Christmas Day? This time if Dano mentioned a name there would be an arrest. But the name had to come from his lips. It wasn't a bit of use his wife going on that she had distinctly heard him say O'Hara. The word had to come from him himself.

Dano waved the spoon away, appeared to go to sleep and the sergeant cursed. Then to his delight he heard the voice, low and slurred because of the state of his teeth, the words hissing through the gaps. 'O'Hara.'

'Are you sure?'

Dano nodded his head.

'Which one, the one in the cottage – Jamsie O'Hara?'

'No,' Dano whispered, opening his eyes, 'the one living on the bog – my tenant – up on the bog.'

'Thank Christ!' the sergeant exclaimed and made for the door, ignoring Mrs Driscoll's admonition that he should be ashamed of his language.

'Get down to the barracks, get the military up, and the warrant signed by the magistrate.'

'What name will I tell him?'

'O'Hara – the Christian name can go in later.'

Padraig was in bed when they came pounding on the door, kicking it in, shouting, 'Get up, O'Hara.' They dragged him out as he was, without trousers. He resisted. 'Bring two of the soldiers,' the sergeant shouted. The police and soldiers took a limb each, and frog-marched him, his face inches from the ground, sometimes scraping it. His nose became clogged with earth and he had difficulty breathing, but he heard all right the screams of his wife ringing out in the Christmas morning.

Holding an arm and a leg apiece police and soldiers carried him to the gaol. In the cell he was beaten, and questioned. He protested his innocence. 'I didn't do it. I never went near the place.'

'Driscoll says you did. Where were you that night? Who else was there?'

'I never left my wife's side. I don't know. I didn't do it.'

When he fell from the blows, they dragged him to his

feet, threw cold water over him. When he could stand no longer, they kicked him. 'I didn't do it,' he gasped before becoming unconscious.

His wife ran after the soldiers and police frog-marching him, screaming. 'What are you taking my husband for? He's done nothing, nothing, do you hear me!' The distance between her and the men lengthened, she collapsed on the ground and lay pounding it with her fists saying over and over, 'Oh Padraig, what'll they do to you, you that never harmed no one.' She lay in the dark, in the cold, crying for her husband, cursing the police, the soldiers and her brother-in-law Johnny. Then she got up and walked across the bog to the road, and then on to the priest's house, banging on his door until he heard and opened it.

'They've taken Padraig. What'll I do, Father? Tell me what to do.' She was demented with grief, half-dressed, blue with cold.

Father Bolger brought her in and put a coat round her shoulders. 'Tell me what to do, Father. It wasn't Padraig, you know that. You know he's never been mixed up in anything.'

'I know it well. Sit down and drink this to keep off the chill.' He poured a glass of whiskey. 'Go on take it, it's medicine.'

'You know who it was, you've got to tell them. Tell them it wasn't Padraig. Tell them he never left my side the night Dano's cattle were clifted.'

'Child, it would do no good, they'd never believe a word of it. Dano told them, and they'll take his word.'

'But don't you see how it was? They were the image of

each other, like twins, like two peas from a pod. Explain that – they'll have to let him go.'

'They won't. They want someone for that happening. Dano, if he lives to go to court, will swear it was Padraig he saw, he'll be believed. I can speak for his character, but my word will mean nothing. May God comfort you.'

'Then I'll tell them myself. I know who it was. I know where he went of an evening. He didn't think I did, but I did. I know someone from that village. I know about the fellow he met in the public house there.' She put away the glass of whiskey untouched. 'I'll tell them. I'll tell them where to find the other culprits, and say the name of my brother-in-law.'

'You won't do that. You'll say nothing. Not even if Johnny was here where hands could be put on him. First you'd achieve nothing. Oh, they'd pick him up all right, but they wouldn't let Padraig go. They know there was more than one man that night at Driscoll's, and why couldn't it be Padraig? What more natural than that he was with his brother? Didn't he have a grievance against Dano? No, Padraig would stay where he was.

'And if you tell about the next village, the man in the public house, you'll be branded for the rest of your life, and your children too, as informers. Your neighbours won't care that you did it to save your husband. Oh, they might for a minute, but in the long run all they'd see is the men being brought to trial, transported, hanged maybe because you talked. You'd have no living in the place, and Padraig would still not be freed. Whatever sentence the others got so would he. You'd be hounded out, if one night you weren't killed by a member of the Society. So we'll

264

pray that Dano recovers, that the judge is merciful, and you'll say nothing.'

'I'll say nothing,' the woman said, her face woebegone, her eyes glazed, her voice no more than a whisper.

It was still dark when Katy set out for Mass. In cottage windows Christmas candles flickered, nearing their end, having shown the way all night to the Mother and Child. In the sky the stars too flickered, grew pale and went out.

In the chapel yard Katy saw people gathered in groups, and knew something was wrong. No one stood out in the yard on Christmas morning before Mass, there was the crib to see at the foot of the altar. As she came nearer she could hear their voices, then they noticed her and fell silent. Statia detached herself from a huddle of women and came to her. 'They came for Padraig,' she said. 'They took him not an hour since. He's blamed for the trouble at Driscoll's.'

Relief flooded through Katy. Padraig, thank God, not Jamsie, she thought. Then, that they were only starting, and would come still for Jamsie. Then she thought of gentle, kind Padraig that never hurt anything, and of his wife and children.

Through Christmas Day and beyond Katy waited for the police to come. Every footfall made her heart jump. The goose on her plate was tasteless, and the promised walk to Connolly's not taken. 'I'm too tired,' she lied when the children reminded her of her promise. Not able to tell the truth. Not able to say she wouldn't stir from the cottage, lest while she was away they came for Jamsie.

The twins cried and stamped their feet, and said it

wasn't fair, then after a while came to stand by her, put their arms round her and kissed her.

On the day after Saint Stephen's she went to work, fearfully looking back at Jamsie when she left, convinced he would not be there when she returned. Nothing could lift her spirits, not the money she would earn while Catherine and Olivia were still at home, not the near certainty that with it she could buy the pig. For, as she said to herself, what good was any of it if Jamsie was in gaol?

In the kitchen she listened uninterestedly to Hannah gossiping about the family. How Charles had gone back to England sooner than expected, that Charlotte was already grieving at the thought of Catherine returning and that wasn't it a pity that for the first time in living memory the hunt didn't take place on Saint Stephen's Day because the Master could no longer afford the expense.

She went about her tasks expecting any minute to hear someone call her, tell her to go home, that Jamsie was arrested. Some evenings when she arrived home Peader was there talking about Padraig, how he had been shifted to a prison in the next town, but not charged yet. Telling Jamsie when he asked, 'Why the delay?' that they were waiting to see whether or not Dano died. Katy listened and prayed for the thing to come to a head, believing that not until Padraig was tried and sentenced would Jamsie be safe.

Prayers were offered at all Masses for Dano's recovery. People came from far and near to pray fervently for an outcome that meant the difference between hanging and transportation. Johnny O'Hara's wife and her mother were shunned by their neighbours. Father Bolger drove

266

out to their cabin, stood outside the shut door pleading for admission, wanting to offer comfort, fearing for their souls, suggesting confession, but the door remained closed in his face.

Peader's mind was so preoccupied with thoughts of Padraig, and the trial of Daniel O'Connell fixed for February, he never went as he had intended to the little wood where he had met Charlotte. Neither did she, for the last days with Catherine were precious, must not be wasted.

On the day before Catherine was due to return she made Charlotte promise to come to England. 'You really must come, darling. Papa will take you. Spend part of the time with Olivia – see London. That would be lovely for you, you've never been.' Charlotte made a face. 'You'd like it – well for a little while anyway, then come down to me. Edward is away a lot during the summer at camps. We'll have a marvellous time.'

'Just the two of us?'

'Just the two of us,' Catherine promised. 'You'll be so happy.'

Olivia came in while they were finalizing their plans. She thought the visit to London was a wonderful idea, and enthusiastically promised parties, outings and lots of young men. Then Catherine said she was going out to say goodbye to some of the tenants, and Olivia rolled her eyes heavenwards.

'Shall I come too?' Charlotte asked.

Catherine searched her mind for an excuse – if Charlotte accompanied her she could not ask Statia's advice, which was the purpose of her visit, calling on the other tenants only a way of making the visiting seem usual.

'No, on second thoughts I won't if you don't mind.'

Relieved, Catherine said, 'No, of course not,' and went to the kitchen where she asked Hannah to call Paudeen.

'Good morning, Ma'am,' he said when he came. – The last time I noticed him, he was a child, Catherine thought, looking at the tall young man.

'I want apples, Paudeen. We have some?'

'Tons, ma'am. A basket, is it?'

'Yes, please, a big one, and a small one for Statia. Then I'll need you to drive me.'

Paudeen went on the errand, and Hannah said, 'I don't know what we'd do without him, he sees to everything.'

'Yes, he seems to,' Catherine replied, and felt sad for all the changes that had occurred in the House. The servants were gone, the grooms, gardeners, maids and footmen. Only Hannah, Mrs Cummings, a couple of girls, Nan in the dairy, her father's man, and the coach driver remaining from the numerous servants that once ran the place.

The smell of apples preceded Paudeen into the kitchen. 'Look at that now,' he said, as he entered carrying the big basket close to his chest, the smaller one balanced on top. 'Aren't they beauties?'

'Beautiful,' Catherine agreed, lifting a fruit, holding it to her face, inhaling the sweet smell that took her back to childhood, to orchards, the trees clustered with apples, the feel of windfalls underfoot, the angry whirr of disturbed wasps. 'Beautiful,' she said again, then told Paudeen she was ready to go.

She left Statia's visit until last, told Paudeen she would carry the apples herself, and for him to call back in half an hour. Immediately she began walking down the path, doubts as to the wisdom of consulting Statia on her child-lessness assailed her. She was a fool, she told herself – a superstitious fool. What could Statia possibly know that the London doctor wasn't aware of? Why would Catholic prayers be heard more readily than those she sent up night and morning? How Olivia would scoff if she knew. Yet so desperate was her longing to have a child, she cast away her doubts, and proceeded to the cottage.

'Miss Catherine, come in, come in, and more than wel-come. Sit down.' Statia knocked the cat off the stool, pulled up her skirt and gave a quick rub to its surface. 'There you are, Miss, make yourself comfortable,' she said, and won-dered if there was something else to the visit besides the apples which Catherine pressed her to take.

'The blessings of God on you, they're beauties,' she replied, speculating what would she do with them. Not eat them for sure. Apples the few times she had eaten them never agreed with her. 'Don't mind me inquiring,' she said when Catherine was seated, 'but are you keeping well?'

'Yes, very well indeed, Statia, thank you.'

'I'm glad to hear that, you look it too,' Statia said, though she doubted the truth of Catherine's reply. She looked far from well. Not sick, but something ailed her, and she had an idea what it might be. Wasn't the poor child married this long time and no sign of a child. Nothing took the bloom off a young woman quicker than believing she was barren.

Before Statia's penetrating gaze Catherine lowered her eyes, pretended interest in the cat, making inane remarks about its size and colour, not knowing how to frame the question uppermost in her mind. Then she decided upon a lie. She would pretend the inquiry was for a friend – Statia would know it was herself she was talking about, but go along with the deception – it would be less embarrassing for both of them.

'I have a friend in England,' she said and paused, before she could think of how to proceed further.

Statia smiled encouragement and said, 'Sure where would you be without one. I hope your friend enjoys good health.'

'Oh yes,' Catherine replied hastily, 'her health is excellent except for one thing.'

'The poor creature, what ails her, and may she soon be well.'

'She has no family, though she has been married many years.' Catherine felt the blood stain her face and a fine perspiration bead her lip from the unaccustomed effort of lying.

'That's a terrible misfortune. But sure a few years is nothing. Nothing at all. I've known them that were married twenty years before God blessed them with a child.'

'Really?' Catherine exclaimed, her voice full of hope, wishing for enough courage to inquire outright what, if anything, one could do to help bring about such a miracle.

'Oh, yes, indeed, many a one. Now if your friend lived in Ireland and was a Catholic there's saints she could pray to, and a well beyond in Kerry where she could go. I don't suppose she's a Catholic, your friend?'

'No, she's not,' Catherine admitted.

'I didn't think so,' Statia said. 'Then the prayers mightn't be any good. I don't know if that's because God wouldn't be listening, or that maybe the one praying wouldn't believe He was – prayer's the queer thing. But there's another thing she could try.'

Catherine leaned forward eagerly, 'You mean something where religion wouldn't matter?'

'I'd say no, I'd say it wouldn't matter a bit.'

'What is it, what need she do?'

'Get a friend or relation who's had a baby to bring it to her – the very first time the child is taken out, to your friend's house it must be brought. Then let her hold it, and wish for her own child.'

'Oh,' Catherine said, unable to hide the disappointment she felt. She had no idea what she had expected to hear, but somehow it wasn't that. It seemed too simple, no magic about it, and she knew she had been foolish to come.

'Well thank you anyway, Statia, I'll tell my friend,' she said rising. 'I think I hear the gig, half an hour I told Paudeen.'

Statia went with her up the path, racking her brains to think of some other advice suitable for Miss Catherine, not able to make light of it as she could to one of the neighbours by suggesting that maybe what she needed was a different man for the night.

They stood at the top of the track waiting for Paudeen whom they could see approaching. Then just before he came Statia remembered something, and lowering her voice she said, 'Saving your presence, ma'am, for talking about such things, but, you could tell your friend to lie still in the bed after her husband has had his way – lie still for a long time. They do say that's very good all right.'

Catherine blushed again, and thanked Statia, glad that at that moment Paudeen arrived, sorry she had come, sorry for making a fool of herself, yet already going over in her mind who she could ask to visit her with their new baby.

Not long after Christmas Katy went down to Statia's. 'It didn't work,' she said as soon as she entered the room.

Statia was tearing a strip from a flannel petticoat. 'What didn't?' she asked, putting down the garment.

'What you told me to do, passing water after I'd been with Jamsie.'

'Well weren't you lucky it worked for so long. How many have you missed?'

'Only the one,' Katy said.

'One is nothing, it could be the cold weather. If not it'll be September when the child is born, please God.'

Chapter Twelve

For more than a week beginning on Candlemas Day there was a false spring. The sun shone, the air was warm, the birds active and snowdrops thrust up through the earth. Katy saw primroses by the well, her spirits rose at the sight of the flowers, the feel of the sun on her face. Life was good, she was carrying a child she welcomed, her children had come through the winter, and sight or sound of Peader no longer disturbed her. She had put him from her mind – Jamsie was her only love. They would live happily in the cottage for the rest of their lives, and at the next fair she would buy her little pig, the money was put by for it.

During the premature spring, Dano's life was declared out of danger. Father Bolger said prayers of thanksgiving that he had been spared; that now Padraig would not be charged with murder. Prayers were also offered for Daniel O'Connell whose trial was impending.

One morning while Jamsie and Peader speculated as to what sentence he might get, unbidden into Peader's mind came a vision of Charlotte as he had seen her turning from the holly bush, smiling and introducing herself. Suddenly he became overwhelmed by a desire to see her again. On such a fine day, he thought, she might visit the little wood, he felt compelled to go. And much to Jamsie's amazement bid him goodbye and left.

On the same day Charlotte when she went out of doors felt the pull of spring, and thought of the wood where the silver birches grew. There would be snowdrops, primroses perhaps, buds breaking through branches, she must go there.

Arriving she set up her easel and stool, and wondered if Peader had ever returned here. She supposed not, and felt a sadness that never again, except in passing, might she see him. Never speak to him unless to say 'good day'. And she pondered how strange it was that someone she scarcely knew should occupy so much of her thoughts. How since meeting him before Christmas, each night when she placed Katy's medal beneath her pillow, she said his name and believed he was her heart's desire.

She began to paint, became absorbed in trying to capture on canvas the drift of snowdrops, and did not hear Peader's footfalls, not becoming aware of him until a shadow fell across the easel. Then she turned and saw him. He came slowly towards her. She saw his hair shine in the sun, he was smiling. She thought – I love you, her heart beat uncomfortably fast, and she knew her face was becoming red, and hoped he wouldn't notice.

'Can I see?' he asked, pointing to the picture. He bent to look, his sleeve brushed against her. She could smell the wool of his short coat, feel his breath soft on her face.

'It's not finished. It's not very good,' she said in confusion.

'It's good all right.'

'Do you think so really?' Her agitation increased so that

274

the paint brush fell from her hand. They bent at the same time to retrieve it. He picked it up. As he straightened his eyes were on a level with hers. She saw how green they were. He remained half-crouched looking at her. She couldn't look away.

'The flowers are beautiful,' he said, and she thought she imagined what he said next. 'Like you.' He gave back the brush and stood up. His hand touched her shoulder and he let it remain.

'Peader,' she spoke his name shyly. 'I didn't think you'd remember me. I hoped you would, but I thought we might not see each other, not alone, you know.'

'I know,' he said. 'I thought the same thing, I was always thinking about you.'

'I was too,' she confessed, and got up from the stool. His hand that was on her shoulder moved down her back, he drew her close. He was looking into her eyes.

'I'd like to see you again, do you think you could come?' He thought she was beautiful. He wanted to hold her very close, to kiss her lips, but hesitated, she might take fright.

'Oh, yes. I could see you, every day I'll come here. No one will know.'

Then he kissed her and she wasn't in the least frightened, so he kissed her again.

While the weather remained fine he came each day. Sometimes he arrived first and fretted while he waited that she would not come, that she was ill or prevented in some way. But so distracted was he with love for her, he gave no thought to the most likely thing that would prevent her coming. He dwelt on her being suddenly sick, or an unexpected event occurring, but never that her father might find out and forbid her to come. He thought only of her as the woman he loved, and he a man who loved her equally, never that she was Lord Kilgoran's daughter and he her father's tenant. Until a morning when the sky was overcast, when cold rain fell, winter returned, and two other things occurred. Padraig was charged with felonious assault and committed for trial at the next Assizes, and word came from Dublin that Daniel O'Connell had been sentenced to a year's imprisonment and a fine of two thousand pounds.

He walked down to Katy's cottage in the driving rain, knowing that today there would be no meeting in the little wood. Aware of the gulf that separated him and Charlotte – a gulf that had nothing to do with weather, but was one of class and religion, and he despaired. He loved Charlotte more than anything in the world. He would lay down his life for her. Yet he could not walk through the gates of Kilgoran Lodge, go up to the House and ask to speak with her. Tell her the weather was too cold, too wet, that he would visit her instead at home. He seethed with rage at the injustice of things – at Padraig's wrongful imprisonment, at O'Connell's vicious sentence, at the subterfuge he would have to employ to continue seeing Charlotte.

Statia was in the cottage railing against what had happened to Daniel O'Connell. 'Poor oul Dan, sure the year in gaol'll finish him altogether. Convicted by a hand-picked jury – not a Catholic amongst them, nor a Repealer neither. A packed jury! Poor Dan – our Liberator – the only man who ever did anything for us.'

– That wasn't what you said about him the night

Peader came back from Tara, Katy thought, you didn't have a good word for him then. And she smiled at the fickleness of Statia.

She was given much to smiling these days as her resolve not to imagine she loved Peader instead of Jamsie grew stronger, just as the child she carried grew stronger, increased in size, her contentment keeping pace with it.

Peader, she noticed, seemed in bad humour, no doubt, she assumed, it was to do with the savageness of O'Connell's sentence. He and Jamsie began to discuss it, and she listened.

'I doubt that we'll ever get Repeal of the Union now, or not for many a long day,' Jamsie said.

'We will not. Ireland's finished. If it wasn't for my father I'd go to America. It's the only place where a man can have freedom, where who you are doesn't matter. It's where everyone that's young should head for.'

'And what about the likes of me, Peader – the old, are we all to be left? If the sons and daughters go who'll give me anything for straightening the limbs of the dead, taking the grimace of death off the faces? How will I live with no children to bring into the world? And what sort of a land would it be with the fields silent, doors hanging from their hinges, the thatch grown over; nothing left but the brown-stained chimney breast to show that a fire ever burnt on the hearth? Answer me that now.'

'For the love of God, Statia, will you shut up,' Katy said. 'Isn't Peader only talking. Sure why would he want to go no more than yourself? What could make him or one of us shift?'

Peader thought of Charlotte above in the House, not

able to meet him because of the weather, not able to get word to him, nor he to her. No one should have to endure such a thing and if it wasn't for his father nothing would stop him going to America and taking Charlotte with him.

Up on the bog Johnny O'Hara's wife took her mother's advice and stopped going to the well for water. 'Let it be thought you're afraid of the women since Padraig was taken,' the old woman counselled. 'I'll do what needs doing, then no one'll know there's a child on the way.' So Johnny's wife stayed close to the fire, sometimes wondering if he was dead or alive; sometimes whether the child was his or the young Master's for she had enjoyed them both on the same day. Well and good if it was Johnny's, but if it was a Kilgoran, and Johnny walked the face of the earth, he would come back and take her life. So she stayed out of the neighbours' sight, and bided her time.

The weather got worse, rain turned to sleet, then a heavy frost set in. Charlotte, unable to go to the wood and not hearing from Peader, decided Hannah had to be taken into her confidence; she could not endure another day without word of him. Hannah could take messages by way of Katy's – Peader was always there.

She went down to the kitchen and approached Hannah in a roundabout way. 'Anything strange?' she asked, sitting up to the range where Hannah was skimming broth.

'Only poor Michael, God help him, fell last night and broke his hip. Statia was here just now and told me. She thinks he mightn't last.'

'Michael – you mean Peader's father?' Charlotte asked.

'What other Michael is there?'

'Of course,' Charlotte replied, and decided to postpone for the time being trying to contact Peader – she would wait until the old man was better, or at least for a few more days.

She inquired again the following day about Michael, and asked if Peader was upset.

'Upset is not the word for it,' Hannah replied. 'Far more than you'd have thought considering Michael's a good age, not in pain, and doesn't something have to come for everyone's end. But Peader's been queer this while back, not like himself – if I didn't know to the differ I'd think he was in love.'

'Maybe he is,' Charlotte said, overjoyed to hear that, for what else was it? Peader was missing her.

'Sure who would he be in love with?'

'Anyone,' Charlotte said, 'you'd never know.'

Hannah smiled affectionately at her, and told her to go away out of that.

On the day Charlotte heard Michael died she told Hannah of her love for Peader and implored her help. 'Don't you see,' she pleaded, 'I must get word to him now. Even if the weather improved he won't be able to see me for a while. He'll be doubly heart-broken, please Hannah, tell Katy, and ask her to help us.'

'Miss Charlotte, you don't know what you're asking – you don't know what you've started. God knows Peader is a lovely man, a great catch, but not for you. Sure you're the Master's daughter. I can't have hand nor part in it.

279

Nor won't drag Katy into it, it could be the cause of terrible trouble for everyone if your father found out.'

'Oh please, Hannah, you have to. I love him. I've never had anyone love me for myself alone. I'll die if you won't help, if I can't get word to him.' She went to Hannah and put her arms round her. 'You have to help me, no one else would, there's only you, say you will, Hannah.'

Hannah shushed her, the way she had when Charlotte was a little girl. – God look down on her, she thought, she's still only a child, what am I to do? Maybe it would be wise to do what she asks, given its head for a while it might peter out.

'All right, astoir, I can't refuse you anything. I'll tell Katy, and we'll fix something up. Go you now and write your letter, and I'll take it to the wake tonight. Katy will see that he gets it.'

Katy walked home from the fair with the pig under her arm. – I got him at last, she kept thinking with satisfaction, and for a good price too. Now we won't know ourselves with the comfort. He'll eat the skins and weeshy potatoes and grow into a big fat animal. Next year if all goes well I might buy another. Her mind planned happily ahead.

– I might even get a cow, and in no time we'd have money to lease another bit of land. With the cow we'd have milk, and the money I'd get for the calf would buy a churn. I'd make butter to sell at the market. I might even get an ass and cart, and sure what would a few hens cost? On she walked, her head full of dreams, the pig peeping out from under her shawl.

The twin ran round the pig squealing as loudly as it did,

wanting to make a plaything of it till Katy stopped them. Jamsie said it looked healthy enough. Katy asked him to make a shelter for it.

''Tis as well we have Kilgoran for a landlord,' Jamsie said.

'Why so?' Katy asked.

'Anyone else would put up the rent for an improvement.'

'So they would – imagine calling a pig-sty an improvement.'

'Isn't it easy to see you had the different rearing, weren't used to sleeping by the side of an oul sow. It wasn't from choice my mother or her likes did it. I'll find a few branches for a shelter.'

While they were deciding the best place to erect it, Statia came with news Michael was dead . . .

'The Lord have mercy on him,' Katy said, and blessed herself. 'Poor Michael, he was a good man.' And for the first time for ages she thought about Peader, remembering the night of the fight and how Michael had hurried him away home.

'Will you help, there's not a soul of a woman belonging to the Dalys,' Statia asked.

'I will to be sure,' Katy agreed.

At the farmhouse she sympathized with Peader. 'I'm sorry for your trouble.'

'I know that, Katy,' he put out a hand and touched her. 'My father was fond of you, there's no one he'd rather see to him.'

His grief, she thought, made him more handsome, he had the sort of face that didn't need smiles to enhance it.

– He's taking his loss very hard, sorrow is written all over him. Maybe, too, the realization that now he's all alone has brought back memories of how I might have been by his side. She felt a twinge of regret that she wasn't.

Peader watched Katy and Statia go in to the room where his father lay, seeing and not seeing them for his mind was wondering if Charlotte had yet heard the news, and would she understand why he had neglected her? Guilt for thinking such things and his father not cold gnawed at him, but try as he might he could not banish them.

Statia and Katy knelt by the bed and said a prayer for the soul of Michael, and afterwards began preparations for laying him out. They washed and bound him, straightened his limbs, arranged his face, closing his eyes, tying up his chin so his mouth didn't gape. Peader was sent to order a habit, coffin, whiskey, snuff, tobacco and a supply of short clay pipes, and told to get word to the keeners. Before he left Statia asked him, 'Is it the bed or table for waking?'

'The bed I suppose, it's where my mother was waked.'

'All right so, though there's them that like the table.'

'Not from choice surely,' Katy said. 'Isn't it only them that hasn't the accommodation use the table?'

As she went about the house taking sheets from the press, candlesticks and bowls from a cupboard, her mind toyed with the notion that this was her own home. This was her linen, the brass candle-holders and comfortable beds, her belongings. She looked into Peader's room and thought of him spending long lonely nights there. Nights

282

when he would think of her, wish she was by his side. She forgot all her promises to Father Bolger and indulged her fancy. She stood so long lost in her dream world that Statia came looking for her, asking if she had forgotten the man in there, Lord have mercy on him, stiffening?

Michael was put into his habit, laid on a clean sheet, another drawn up to below his joined hands in the fingers of which his Rosary beads were entwined. Katy pinned sheets round the wall, and covered the mirror so the face of death was not reflected: the candles were lit, Holy water and snuff placed on a bedside table.

'There now, doesn't he look grand? All ready to meet his Maker. May I have as good a send-off when my time comes,' Statia said.

The neighbours came, young and old, men and women, babies in shawls, children by the hand. The women who owned shoes carried them to save wear on the soles, slipping them on before entering the house.

They sympathized with Peader, went to look at the body, blessed it with Holy water, said he was a lovely corpse, only gone a step before them, knelt and prayed, those of them who snuffed taking a pinch before returning to the kitchen.

Then the keeners arrived, tall thin women shrouded in mourning, resembling gaunt black birds. They set up the keen, a thin high wail of desolation, an ear-piercing protest against man's mortality. An unearthly sound, anguished and demented, striking terror into the hearts of the mourners, reminding them of their inevitable end, of the yawning grave. Then the pitch of sound altered, became recognizable as human. Michael's virtues were litanized, the loss he would be to his son, to all who had known him.

Grief was drawn out, catharsis accomplished: tears spilled, Heaven and the promise of Eternal life remembered. Then the keen died away, the keeners were plied with whiskey, slipped money by Peader, went, and the wake began.

The old men and women filled the duideens with shag and lit them. Tea was made, porter and spirits passed round. Mary Doyle brought news that Father Bolger was still away on a sick call, but she had left word for him. Hannah arrived, her face blue with cold, shivering and pinched-looking.

'God bless us, the frost is cruel, the ground's like a rock,' Dinny Crowley on his way in to sit with the corpse said. 'That it may thaw before the funeral. I remember a wake years ago when the frost was that fierce a spade couldn't be got into the ground.'

'What happened so, Dinny?' someone said.

'Instead of lasting two nights the wake went on for seven. Like Michael 'ithin,' he inclined his head to the door of the room, 'the man was being waked on the bed, and I needn't tell you the family was cranky for lack of sleep – and him stretched out in comfort.'

'God between us and all harm!' Hannah said and blessed herself, 'I hope the same thing doesn't happen again. Will you join me in a prayer I learned long ago in Connemara. I'll say it slow for you to say after me. It never fails.' Anyone who could find room knelt, the others bowed their heads, and Hannah prayed.

'Oh, Christ that was crucified on Friday, who pourest

284

Thy share of blood to forgive and free us, the grace of the Holy Spirit be in our heart and in our mind; every petition that we may ask the Son of God – make it easy for us.'

Line by line it was repeated after her, and afterwards a petition was sent up for God to grant the grave-digger power to open the ground. When the praying was finished Hannah sat beside Katy who any time Jamsie wasn't looking in her direction gazed fondly at Peader, falling in love with him again.

'I want to talk to you on your own,' Hannah said, and Katy saw that she was very agitated.

'You're not still worrying about the ground – it'll thaw before morning,' she said reassuringly, placing a hand over one of Hannah's.

'I am not, it's the living that's troubling me. Come in now to see the corpse, and I'll tell you, no one else must know.'

'Dinny's there.'

'Dinny's hard of hearing betimes, anyway let on we're saying the Rosary.'

Katy followed Hannah into the room, they knelt at the foot of the bed as far as they could from Dinny. Taking out their beads they raised the crosses to their lips, kissed them, and Hannah commenced 'The Five Sorrowful Mysteries', loud enough for anyone to hear, then lowering her voice to a whisper and using a rhythm that could have been praying, she intoned, 'Miss Charlotte has notions of Peader, and he of her. I said I'd help, and you'd do the same. You will, won't you?'

'Sacred Heart of Jesus!' Katy responded, and felt her blood run cold. Hannah fingered her beads and continued

285

whispering, ' 'Tis maybe only a passing thing – what else could it be? – but while it lasts it must be secret in case the Master heard tell. You'll pass notes, and Jamsie on times when they meet see that the road is clear. You won't refuse for I did the same for you. I said you'd help.'

Katy stared at the corpse, and inside her head screamed, *It's not true. He's mine. I won't help. I won't lift a finger to further Miss Charlotte's fling.* But to Hannah, she said, 'All right,' for she could do nothing else. To refuse she would have to give reasons, let it be known how she felt for Peader. Let Jamsie know that his suspicions the night Peader came back from Dublin were true.

'I knew you wouldn't let me down,' Hannah said, and then, because Dinny was looking in her direction, said loudly an 'Our Father'. When his gaze returned to Michael she carried on talking to Katy. 'I've a letter from Charlotte, you'll see that he gets it. Amen,' she concluded for someone else was entering the room. They returned to the kitchen. The faces of the men and women swam before Katy's eyes, she felt sick, needed to escape, to run away and lick her wound, to be alone with her sorrow. While she contemplated leaving, someone passed her a plate of food. 'Give that out,' they said. She went round the people, when she came to Peader he smiled at her, and she wanted to catch hold of him, make him tell her it was a lie, every word Hannah had spoken – a lie, but she said nothing, and moved on.

More whiskey and tea was drunk; stories of other wakes related, deeds of Michael's, how once upon a time there wasn't a man in the parish could run with the speed of him. Then a voice began to lilt a plaintive air, others joined in. From a niche above the fireplace Peader took down his father's fiddle and accompanied the singers. Katy watched his long slender hands on the instrument and saw them stroke the brown hair of Charlotte, and felt the first stirring of hate for the girl who had taken her place.

To Peader's accompaniment more songs of love and loss were sung, each word seeming to Katy specially written to express her grief, so that she cried openly. Hannah sitting beside her said, 'Don't be fretting, sure Michael had a good life, and is in Heaven, please God. Don't cry for him, child.'

The songs finished and Peader played 'The Blackbird', feet began to tap out the rhythm of a hornpipe.

'If there was room I'd dance it,' a farmer's wife, short and fat, announced.

'Don't let that stop you, girl,' her neighbour encouraged, 'we'll move back.'

Stools were stacked one on top of the other and pushed to the wall, chairs put outside and a space cleared for the dancer. The woman began to dance. Through the mist of her tears Katy watched the intricate steps performed, and heard the staccato taps on the flag floor like the sound of nails being driven into her broken heart.

Faster Peader played, and the woman matched her pace to his playing until the music stopped, and breathless amid clapping, and cries of *aris, aris*, she collapsed on to the lap of the only man seated. He squeezed her and she squealed. Everyone was now in high spirits except Katy. Peader played a jig, and the farmer's wife dragged up the man to dance, other couples joined in. Jamsie coaxed Katy to dance. 'I'm too tired,' she refused. He accepted her excuse.

'Rest then,' he looked at the dancers. 'All the same,' he said, 'doesn't a good wake take some beating.'

Before they went home Hannah slipped the letter to Katy. 'Give it to him now while there's no one looking.'

– Into the heart of the fire I should throw it, Katy thought as she took and concealed the note in her pocket. Every time she moved the sound of the paper whispered the proof of what Hannah had told her.

Peader went with them to the door. Katy's hand was on the letter, yet she was unable to take it out, to give it to him. She could tell Hannah she forgot, pretend it got lost. He should not have it. Dawn was breaking as she and Jamsie began walking away from the farmhouse, the air warmer than the previous day, the ground softening.

'It looks as if God is answering Hannah's prayers – the funeral won't be delayed.'

'Yes,' Katy replied absent-mindedly, for she was still deciding about the letter.

'We might get an hour's sleep before the children waken – what's that you have there?' Jamsie asked, looking at the envelope Katy was holding towards him.

'A letter from Miss Charlotte for Peader, I forgot to give it to him.'

'Miss Charlotte! What in the name of God would she be writing to Peader for – has he come up in the world without me knowing?'

'Maybe he's hoping to,' she said bitterly, then quickly changed her tone lest she betrayed her feelings, and making a joke of it told him that they had notions of each other. That Hannah was sure it wouldn't last, and would he go back now, call out Peader and give him the letter.

288

She watched Jamsie hand over the note and saw Peader's face take on the radiance of the morning, and felt her heart break. In the days that followed it seemed as if a vital part of her had died, been removed, leaving an aching emptiness that nothing could fill. Not the sight of her children, the sound of their laughter, nor the affection which the twins lavished upon her, their pert cheeky faces filled with concern when she sat listlessly by the fire. They brought her drinks of water, stroked her cheeks, and said, maybe she should lie down.

When she woke in the mornings she wished she had not, did not want to rise. When night came she found no solace in sleep, nor in Jamsie's arms where she lay as though paralysed.

On the day of the funeral Statia remarked, 'You're looking terrible drawn, mind yourself.'

'I'm tired, that's all,' Katy said, and longed to tell some-one the truth. Cry out that her heart was broken – that Charlotte Kilgoran had taken her man – that at this minute she wouldn't care if it was herself being shoul-dered to the grave for she was already dead.

Letters came down to the cottage cancelling or altering meetings between the lovers. Katy saw with what eager-ness Peader handled them, how quickly he left to be alone reading them. On afternoons when meetings were ar-ranged in the little wood, Jamsie would see that the road was clear for Peader, whistle the tune arranged as a signal. Returning to the cottage he made jokes about his part in the business, laughing and telling Katy how he and Peader were like a pair of children, and didn't love make you do the queer things. Katy listened and looked at him, not seeing his face, unaware of her surroundings, as in her mind she followed the lovers into their trysting place.

Then one morning on her way to the well she met Charlotte, the first time she had seen her since discovering about the affair.

'Oh Katy! I'm delighted to see you,' Charlotte said. 'I've been wanting to thank you. I don't know what we'd have done without your help.'

Rage flared in Katy, jealousy consumed her.

Eagerly Charlotte went on, 'Without it I could never get word to Peader. Can you believe it – me and Peader? It must have been the medal. You said it would grant my heart's desire. I'm convinced it was that. It worked for you too, didn't it?'

Katy wanted to claw at the smiling face, wanted to wind her hands in the brown hair and pull until Charlotte begged for mercy, promised never to see Peader again, never to breathe his name. Peader was hers, would always be hers.

Instead she replied, 'Yes, Miss, no doubt it was,' and studied the smiling face, searching it for flaws, blemishes. All the while asking herself, what could Peader see in it? How could he not but compare it with hers? How was it possible to love this dawny thing with big moon-like eyes – eyes of a sucking calf? A puny creature with neither breasts nor hips. All she had was her hair to commend her.

Charlotte continued to enthuse about Peader, how lucky she was to have found him, his handsomeness and cleverness, and Katy to regard her with loathing. Gazing at the face which once she had admired, stroked, wiped tears from, and kissed.

'Oh, Peader, Peader,' she said to herself, 'aren't you the fool for all you're the fine scholar. Can you not see she'll use you as a plaything until her father finds her a man, then you'll be thrown aside. She'd never marry the likes of you. You're nothing in her eyes. Oh the fool that you are, and me waiting for you.'

Jealousy drove all thought of Jamsie from her mind, all knowledge that she was a married woman with five children and another expected. Now the only thing that stood between her and Peader, she was convinced, was Charlotte Kilgoran. For a wild moment she considered throwing her into the mud surrounding the well, daubing it on her face, matting her hair with it. Unsuspectingly Charlotte looked on as Katy filled her wooden buckets, then said she must go, and bid her goodbye.

Katy walked home faster than she usually did when carrying the buckets, not caring that she spilled much of the water, bent on destroying if not Charlotte, then something of hers. She put the pails down and went into the bedroom and dragged out the box with her treasures. On the top of her blue wedding dress, beside the twins' cauls, lay the tiny handkerchief given to her by Charlotte. Snatching it up she went to the kitchen and tore it into shreds, then threw the scraps of cambric and lace into the heart of the fire.

Padraig was brought from the prison cell, up a dark flight of narrow stone steps, into the light which hurt his eyes after his long confinement. He had grown thin, his face had a greenish pallor, and his hair, long and matted, itched from the lice infesting it. His wrists were manacled, rubbed raw from the chafing iron fetters. A warder on each side of him guided him along a corridor, then he was in the court and a sea of faces swam before him. He searched them for a glimpse of his wife, for any familiar face, and saw none, only heads and features all blurring into the other.

He was moved about like a puppet, placed in the dock, and from very far away heard himself being charged, noticing only that he was called by the English of his name – Patrick O'Hara, and thought it sounded strange, no one had ever called him so before, except his father once or twice for a cod.

Gradually, as the trial proceeded, the fever that burned him cooled, his head and vision cleared, the faces that before were indistinguishable took shape, and he saw his wife, and beside her Father Bolger. She was crying quietly, and he cried quietly too, the tears running down his face caught up in the straggly beard. – I'll never take you now to America, nor lay beside you, never see the faces of my children, nor the bog red in the evening with the myrtle.

He saw Dano get up on the stand, watched and listened as if it didn't concern him – from a far distance, for the fever was clouding his brain again.

'Is this the man you saw strike you?' Dano turned his broken-nosed face to look at him, then looked back at the judge.

'It is, your Honour, the same man.'

'You are absolutely sure?'

'No doubt at all – O'Hara, I saw him as plain as I'm seeing you, that's him.'

Padraig heard his wife scream again and again, saw Father Bolger taking her from the court, and was glad she was gone. Glad that she wouldn't hear his sentence pronounced – let the priest break it to her gently. Sometimes he had to be prompted to answer questions asked of him. He heard the flurry of sound and saw a body of men leave the room, saw them come back again, and none of it seemed to matter, for none of it was real.

'Fourteen years transportation to Van Diemen's Land,' the judge said, and he wondered in what direction across the sea that was, was it anywhere maybe near America.

Chapter Thirteen

Charlotte and Peader were far into the wood, lying beneath the trees, saying farewell, for tomorrow she was going to England. Above them the branches were interlaced, the sunlight filtering through, pale, falling on Charlotte's face, making her seem ethereally beautiful, exquisitely fragile. Peader gazing at her felt a fierce protective love – she was so young, so innocent, so in need of looking after; trusting everyone, believing no obstacles stood in the way of their love, convinced her father would welcome him as a husband.

His fingers traced the outline of her face. Like a little heart, he thought, and despair filled him for he knew the reality of their situation was far from what Charlotte envisaged. One whisper of their meetings reaching Lord Kilgoran and, far from welcoming him as a husband, her father could have him run out. For the time being their secret was safe with Katy, Jamsie and Hannah, but what of the future? The rest of their lives couldn't be spent meeting in the wood. He knew the alternative – to have her for his wife he must take her away, put an ocean between her and Kilgoran. America was their only hope. It was an awful sacrifice to ask of her, make her leave her father, endure three months in the hold of a ship, eating weevil-speckled biscuits, putrid meat, packed into the dark bottom of the ship with all the hundreds of people – she who had never known what discomfort was.

'You've gone very quiet, is it the thought of me leaving tomorrow making you sad?' Charlotte asked, catching hold of his hand and bringing it to her lips.

'Aye,' he said, 'the thought of being without you it is. The birds will stop singing when you go, the flowers will wilt, and I'll die for loss of my love.'

'Don't say such things – you mustn't, not even in jest. Don't ever talk of dying.'

'Ah don't cry on me, sure I was only letting on.' He held her close. 'I don't want you going away, not even for a minute, but I know you have to say goodbye to your sister before she goes to India. Hush now.'

'If it was anyone else but Catherine I wouldn't leave you – you believe that, don't you?'

'I know you wouldn't.'

'You and Papa and Catherine I love. I wish we could all be together. I wish you were coming with me. I wish you would write to me while I'm gone.'

'Oh Charlotte love, I've told you why I can't. How would you explain letters arriving from Kilgoran?'

'I could pretend they were from Hannah.'

'You know well, and so does your father and sisters, that Hannah can't write her name, never mind a letter. Leave it as it is, you write to me, and please God the time will soon pass.'

'I will, every day. I'll write from Olivia's in London, and from Catherine's as well. And I'll think of you each day.

Oh, Peader, I don't want to go, I don't want to leave you, I'll miss ...'

'Hush now, my little brown bird.' He stroked her hair and kissed the tears, making a joke, telling her how salt they were, so she smiled.

On the day the first letter came for Peader, Katy watched his face as he handled it, saw joy suffuse it, his eyes and mouth smile, and noticed how quickly he made an excuse to leave, to be by himself and read it, she knew.

'Isn't it easy to see that fella's in love,' Jamsie said when he went. And Katy wanted to go running up the boreen after Peader, catch hold of him, plead with him to say it wasn't so. Hear him say she was his love – Charlotte only a passing fancy that meant nothing.

'I wonder what'll come of the affair?' Jamsie said. Katy made no reply. 'Ah well,' Jamsie said, 'time plays queer tricks. Who'd ever have thought Peader Daly would fall for the Master's daughter and her for him?'

''Tis a passing thing, that's all,' Katy said to reassure herself.

'I don't know about that – it's a long time passing. I'm going down to Dinny's, he does be lonely since Michael went.'

When he was gone Katy took down her mother's mirror and studied her face. She didn't like what she saw – discontent in her eyes, lines at each side of her mouth, brown stains splotched on her neck, brow and cheeks. She hated herself. Blamed her appearance on the child she was carrying, and on Peader's desertion. How could anyone love her? she asked herself, replacing the glass.

Her body felt gross and ungainly. Who could admire or desire it? – you'd as soon rave about a cow due to calve. She looked at her two bare feet, broken-nailed and dirty, like a pair of cruibeens – she should wash them, but didn't have the heart. Who was to notice them anyway? Certainly not Peader who nowadays scarcely glanced at her face, never mind her feet – and Jamsie – she was convinced that if every hair on her head fell out, and her teeth too, he wouldn't see the difference. Would still reach for her in bed, caress her mound of belly, and say, 'You're beautiful.' 'Making children, that's all he wants you for,' she remembered her mother's words. To believe them suited her wretchedness, and the jealousy which blinded her to her own attractiveness, and the love Jamsie felt for her.

She slumped despondently by the fire, too uninterested even to throw a sod of turf on, though it was burning low, gazing into its dying heart and tormenting her own with remembrance of Peader's face when he saw Charlotte's letter.

'Mammy, we're hungry,' the twins coming into the kitchen said. Lost in her thoughts Katy didn't hear them. Peg went to her, touched her shoulder.

'Mammy,' she repeated, 'me and Nora is terrible hungry.'

Shaken out of her reverie by the little hand insistently nudging, the voice asking for food, Katy said, 'Are you now, well I'm sorry for you, love, but sure isn't everyone hungry, and will be till the new potatoes are lifted. Maybe later on Hannah will bring down something.'

'You said that yesterday, and she never came,' Peg complained.

'You're right, she did not. Poor Hannah – when there's nothing to bring she feels ashamed. Commere now, and I'll tell you what to do.' The two little girls moved close to her, each one resting a sandy red head against her.

'Dip the mug in the bucket and drink the water slow, 'twill fill you for a bit, and when your father comes in I'll boil the bit of meal, won't that do?'

'I hate meal,' Nora complained, and Peg said the same. And they asked in turn, were there no potatoes?

'Don't you know well there isn't, and won't be till the crop is dug.'

The children looked uncomprehendingly at her, their blank gazes reminding her they were only three years old – what did they know or care that June, July and August were hungry months, except that their bellies were often empty. – God love them, she thought, they have to get used to it the same as everyone else, coddling them wasn't a bit of good, a little hunger never killed anyone. So putting them from her she said, 'Go now and drink the water.' They moved away, pouted and scowled. 'Now this minute, and take the puss off you.' They defied her, standing, beginning to complain again, till she got up, and made to run at them, then they scurried out.

Peader hurried home and read Charlotte's letter.

London June 1844

My Darling,
Such a long time I'll be away, and can only think of the hours I'll be separated from you. I cried as the ship left Ireland and I watched the coastline fade, knowing that you were there and I being borne from you. Again on the long journey by coach to

Chester where we stayed overnight, the horses' hooves seemed to be saying, 'He's far away, he's far away'. It was a horrid journey.

Everything is horrid, London and Olivia. Do you know what she said on the evening I arrived – that I looked like a tinker with my bird's-nest hair and sun-burned hands and face. Darling I don't, do I?

But there are some good things about London – like Olivia's French chef who cooks the most delicious things, such pastries, and mouth-watering sorbets. I'll never be able to eat Hannah's puddings again.

She is so bossy, you wouldn't believe it, and is determined to make me what she calls presentable. First my skin has to be seen to. So each night Olivia makes me rub on a concoction prepared by her maid. Actually it tastes rather good – eggs, almonds and sweet oil – that's for my hands, and I have to wear gloves to bed. On my face I spread the juice of crushed strawberries – to blanch my sun-tanned skin. The juice dribbles down and I lick it – Olivia says I'm disgusting. I shall come back to you all pale and languid – hope you'll love me that way.

Do you miss me very much? I miss you all the time. Olivia talks about me meeting suitable young men, and is arranging a dance for me. I laugh silently while she talks and hug my secret. I wonder what she would say if I suddenly announced, 'Don't bother – I have the most suitable of young men. The most gorgeous man in the world.' Can you imagine her face!

Because of the dance, and parties she is planning I am to have new clothes. According to my horrid sister my clothes too are a disgrace, and not fit to be seen. So next week I'm to be measured, pinned and tucked. What a frightful bore. How much rather I'd spend the time with you, my love, in our little wood.

I forgot to say I'm writing this in bed – by candlelight just in case a servant should notice the lamp and inquire if I was ill or something. I stole some stamps from Olivia's writing desk. I hope some poor servant doesn't get blamed, but otherwise I wouldn't have been able to send the letters.

Olivia lives in Berkeley Square. The house isn't as old as Kilgoran, but quite old, from the time of Queen Anne, that's a long time ago isn't it? There are plane trees in the square, their bark prettily dappled, but not as pretty as our silver birches. I watch the birds fly in and out and think of you and long to be home again.

There are gasoliers in the main rooms, they hiss and smell peculiar. According to Olivia they cast unkind shadows on ladies' faces, and if there is a guest she doesn't particularly like she seats them under the gasolier. I tell you she is horrid.

The house is very elegant, nothing old or shabby like some of our furniture at home – one is almost afraid to sit. The guests who come to dine are very fashionable, but I'm quite bewildered by their conversation. They speak so knowledgeably about everything – opera singers in London and Europe. I had never heard of Jenny Lind before coming here, nor Tambourinin, what an ignoramus I am. They talk about politics, too, of which I also know nothing. Though last night I did pay attention when I heard Ireland mentioned. Daniel O'Connell was being discussed. Not everyone, darling, at least not here, likes him as much as you do. One of the guests talked about a man called Trevelyan. Have you heard of him? He doesn't like the Irish, doesn't like our turn of mind, whatever that means. Olivia's guests laughed about him. They said even while courting his wife, he talked non-stop about his pet subjects, steam navigation, and the education of the natives. Can you imagine! The poor woman. I'm glad you're not like that. Apparently he's one of those dreadful people who always thinks they are right. Papa said people like that are dangerous. He works at the Treasury.

How I chatter on about such rubbish. I must buy a present for Katy, she is so kind to receive my letters. Perhaps when I go to see Catherine I'll tell her about us, then she might help, allow me to have letters from you. What do you think?

Before I came to bed I looked through the window and saw a beautiful moon. I wondered if you might be going home from Katy's and look up at the sky. Maybe at the very moment I was looking. When I finish this letter I will slip out of bed and peep through the window in case you are late leaving Katy's and only looked just then. So goodnight, my love. If only I could kiss you how sweetly would I sleep. Soon, though, soon.

Charlotte

Peader read the letter a second time and was filled with a sense of despondency. – What a gulf separates us, he thought. What an innocent child she is not to see it. Then he began to wonder if London would open her eyes to it. Would the grand houses and fashionable people, the young men invited to her dance make her aware of his own shortcomings in the eyes of people like the Kilgorans? He fumed at the injustice of not being considered good enough to have her for his wife. That he who was a Daly, a descendant of poets and scholars, could not claim the woman he loved. That he who could write as fine a hand as anyone could not sit down and pen a letter to her, telling of his love, of the emptiness in his heart since she went. Could not warn her that to mention his name to Catherine might be their undoing.

He put away the letter and began pacing the room thinking, then talking aloud to himself. 'I'll take you far away. No one will come between us. You'll be my wife. No one shall hinder us. I'll take you to America. In America it won't matter who our fathers were, or the homes we came from. I'll work for you, and cherish you and love you more than a man ever loved a woman.'

He stopped talking and walking, sat down and considered what he had decided. He could foresee no obstacles so long as the secret of their love was kept. Charlotte would be willing, but he wouldn't ask her to leave until she was eighteen. Give her a year and a few months more with her father. If he had his way they should go as soon as she returned but, much as she loved him, he felt instinctively she would be loath to desert her father so soon. So he would wait, and please God the secret would be kept.

Through June and July he waited for her letters, when they arrived read them eagerly, and counted the days until her return. Always he read the letters more than once, afterwards tormenting himself that at one of the dances or parties she described, a man considered suitable by Olivia or Catherine would replace him in her heart. He imagined her in the arms of such a man, dancing in the finery with which she had been fitted out; saw his rival smile upon her, and she regard him with adoring eyes. The man his imagination conjured up was effete, an officer in ceremonial uniform, all that he despised in men. From such a vision he was able to find a bitter consolation, laughing at himself, at Peader Daly the patriot, the despiser of the English and the landed classes falling in love with the girl from the Big House. Asking himself, 'Sure what did you think could come of it, but what did?'

And so he spent his time, his moods oscillating between hope and despair, waiting for letters, waiting for the end of July and Charlotte's return. After her final letter arrived, with news in it of the date she was leaving England and word that she never after all told Catherine her secret, all his fears were banished, and so great was his relief and joy he took the letter to Katy's that evening.

'She'll be back next week, you'll see the way to the wood is clear, Jamsie?'

'I will indeed,' Jamsie said, smiling tolerantly at him.

'Listen to this, Katy, it's about Miss Catherine, you know she's off to India. Charlotte's heartbroken.'

'With God's help it'll mend: she's you to assist with the healing,' Katy said, but the irony was lost on Peader who began to read.

Catherine sails next week. I've cried my eyes out every night at the thought of us being parted for so long. I'm sure she doesn't want to go, but as she says, a wife's place is by her husband.

Staying here has been much nicer than London. Catherine and I talk often about Kilgoran, and mention Katy, Hannah, Statia and everyone. I told her Katy is having another baby. Isn't it a shame Catherine hasn't had one. She loves them so. There are always babies being brought to the house, she even invites the wives of Edward's men to tea after they've had new babies.

'And then it just goes on about other things,' Peader said, folding the letter and putting it back in his pocket. Then he and Jamsie talked about O'Connell, wondering if his appeal would be successful. Katy thought about Catherine and how sad it was that God hadn't blessed her with a child.

Her own baby was bunched in a ball under her ribs, hurting her every time she drew breath. She pressed on her belly, rubbing her hand to and fro to ease the discomfort. Statia had told her the child was upside down, that it was his head pressing that made her ache, but not to worry there was time enough yet for it to turn. So preoccupied did she become with her sore ribs there wasn't room in her mind to feel jealous over Peader's obvious delight in Charlotte's letter.

Peader knelt by the side of the road pretending interest in a beetle manoeuvring a fragment of leaf, waiting for Jamsie's whistle to tell him the road was clear. Nobody passed while he waited, – and sure if they do, he thought, they'll only think I have more time than sense.

Charlotte, waiting, heard the prearranged signal. Soon he would be here, take her in his arms, kiss away the aching loneliness of all the days and nights she had been away. Looking down at the folds of her green velvet day dress she fretted that Peader might not like it, nor the silver-grey mantle either. He had never seen her dressed so before.

He was almost here, she could sense his presence. Her heart beat faster, the green velvet gown felt restricting and much too warm. Maybe he wouldn't like it, and she wanted so to please him. He certainly wouldn't like the bonnet that held captive her hair. Quickly with fingers sweating and clumsy she undid the ribbons, took it off and tossed it on the grass.

Then he was here, coming towards her. She saw his beloved face, and ran to meet him. 'My love,' he said, 'my little love, my little bird.'

In September the Law Lords reversed the sentence passed on Daniel O'Connell; he was released. On the same day Katy gave birth to a son. ' 'Twould be fitting to call him after the Liberator,' Jamsie said when he saw the baby, 'and we'll ask Peader to be his Godfather.' He smiled fondly at Katy. 'Two sons we have now,' he reached and touched the infant's head close to its mother's breast, 'there's riches for you, a man with two sons could do anything.'

'He could indeed,' she replied returning his smile, remembering how it was long ago when he was the only man in her world, and wishing it was so again.

Late in the night of the day Katy's child was born, Johnny O'Hara's wife went into labour. Attended by her mother she gave birth easily.

'What is it?' she asked when she heard the infant cry.

'A boy – the spitten image of its father.'

'What father?'

'Look for yourself.' The old woman held up the baby.

'Bring him close, it's dark, I can't see.'

Her mother came near. 'Did you ever see such a likeness? Wouldn't you think it was the young gentleman himself.'

'Take it away. Get it out of here quick!'

'I will, now, in a minute. There's cloud coming up, it'll cover the moon. I'll go then.'

The child, unwashed, lay in its covering of slime and blood, kicking and crying vigorously. Its mother turned over in the bed and slept. The clouds covered the moon, the old woman wrapped it in a rag and set out on her journey.

It rained heavily during the night: the next morning a ghillie beating the river saw the infant washed up in the weir, its limbs tangled in twigs, swirling leaves and debris thrown up by the yellow-stained tumultuous waters.

*

Because Statia delivered the majority of babies in Kilgoran it was to her the police went asking questions as to who had recently given birth. And she went with them to view the child. Afterwards she hurried to tell Katy the news. Mary Doyle and Hannah were there, having come to see Katy's new baby.

'It was a boy, God bless him, perfect, except he was stone dead, like a drowned rat, and drowned he was,' Statia announced.

'You don't mean ...' Katy said aghast.

'I do so, and said the same to the constable. Tell me sez he, whose is it? That I couldn't, I told him. The mother of him didn't advertise she was carrying. 'Twas a well-kept secret. And what's more that child was alive and kicking when it went into the water. That's what I told him, the same as I'm telling you.'

'God between us and all harm sure you wouldn't do that to a dog,' Hannah said, and blessed herself.

'Are you trying to tell me someone threw the child in the river?'

'Well it didn't walk, nor fall in, and had well taken its first breath. So somebody drowned it.'

'I wonder who the mother was? As far I know there wasn't one expecting the same time as myself,' Katy said.

'Who the mother was I wouldn't like to say, but I know the father for sure.'

'Who?' the three women asked Statia in unison.

'Master Charles, the look of him stamped on the child. I saw it with my own two eyes.'

'In that case I've no doubt who the mother was,' Mary Doyle said, and made preparations to leave.

'Keep it to yourself then,' Hannah advised.

'Oh, don't worry, I've a silent tongue, I won't breathe a word of it.'

On her way to the chapel house Mary met two women, one from the village, the other from up on the bog; she told both of them about the child and who the parents were. 'Mind you,' she concluded, 'I don't believe a word of it – God forgive the scandal-giver.'

Father Bolger was on his knees praying. Asking God to cast doubts and hatreds from his mind. Blind him to sight of Dano thriving while Padraig's wife and children were destitute, nothing before them but the workhouse. Pleading for cease to his bitterness against those who had wrongfully imprisoned O'Connell, made him into an old, sick man.

'Dear Heavenly Father,' he prayed, 'sometimes I don't understand You at all. You know I want to, but You make it hard. Dan's out of gaol, but he'll never be the same, the Repeal Movement is done for, there's voices in it crying for violence. Why, oh Lord, do You let it happen? Why do You send me pains like red-hot needles to pierce my bones? Do You have to make life so hard? Forgive me for doubting You, don't let me despair. Don't let me lose my faith. Grant me patience and love for my flock. Never let me forget my mission is to save men's souls from hell. Grant me that, Lord Jesus, and the perseverance to go out again and try bringing salvation to Johnny O'Hara's wife and that mother of hers.'

He struggled up from his knees, telling himself as he made his way to the house, that some time this week he would try again for admittance to the O'Haras' cabin, confront that oul faggot of a mother if she opened the door, and if she didn't, bang on the door till she did if it took all day and night.

Mary was in the kitchen making his dinner, putting down in the pot of milk a small hake, laying the table with salt and butter, and a brown griddle cake. She talked while she worked, telling him about the child in the river, who the mother and father were. He listened without interruption, having long ago given up attempting to curb Mary's scandal-giving.

'Is that so, Mary, isn't that a terrible thing,' he remarked when she finished; it was his stock reply to whatever she told him, and seemed to satisfy her, for she continued with the dinner in silence.

While he ate the meal he decided there was no time like the present, he'd make his visit to the bog after dinner. There were two souls in need of salvation, more so now than ever, if Mary was to be believed.

The woman from the bog to whom Mary had also told the news hurried home and soon passed the story to her neighbours.

'The hoor!' they said, one to another. 'A murderer amongst us – taking the life of an innocent child, fornicating with the Master's son. We'll run her and her mother out of it – years ago we should have done it.'

With words and gestures they fed their anger till it grew to enormous proportions, becoming a force which propelled them in the direction of the O'Haras' cabin. The young girls and small boys went with them. The husbands and sons watched them go, saw the waving arms, shaking fists, heard the curses and threats. ''Tis the women's business,' their smiles and silence implied, 'let them settle it.'

The old woman heard the commotion and looked out through the door. She saw the women and knew why they came. 'Get up quick,' she called to her daughter, 'they're coming to run us out, we haven't a minute.'

They went, the two children running with them. 'Quick, quick, they're catching us up,' the girl called back to her mother. The crowd closed the gap between them. The old woman fell, and hands reached at her, tearing her hair, scratching her face. 'Jesus! you'll kill me,' she screamed.

'We will so, like you did the child.'

Further up the field the young girls and boys brought down Johnny's wife, shrieking with frenzied delight as they began tearing at her clothes.

'*Leave them alone! Get from them! Do you hear me!*' The voice of Father Bolger thundered across the bog. 'Do you hear me. I'll be down there in a minute to take the whip to you. Go on now, back to your homes – you lotta savages.'

Reluctantly hands let go holds on hair and cloth, slowly the crowd backed away. Johnny's wife moved to her mother, her children followed her and huddled by the old woman, watching the priest hobble over the sedge, his soutane flapping, a whip in his hand.

'Away you go now, home this minute,' he shouted to the hovering crowd.

'But Father, we were going ...' a woman began to explain.

'I know well what you were going to do. Go home I tell you.'

Muttering amongst themselves, they began to move, looking back now and then at the priest approaching the two women; stopping when they considered a safe distance had been put between them and their clergy.

'Cover yourself,' the priest commanded Johnny's wife whose breasts were exposed through the reefed bodice. Defiantly she stared at him, though her hands dragged the torn stuff across her chest.

He bent to help up the old woman. She knocked away his hand. 'God's curse on you and them,' she said, and spat.

'Get up. Get back to the cabin the two of you. Collect what you can and go wherever you were going. I'll stay for as long as it takes and lift you part of the way. I can't stand on guard for ever, and the minute I leave, they'll be back.' He nodded his head in the direction of the waiting, watchful crowd.

'He's right, mother, do what he says. They'll be back.'

He waited outside the cabin door. Across the field the women stood poised, ready to descend on their prey if he deserted them, waiting to pounce, flush them out, kill them even.

'Where will you head for?' he asked when the mother and daughter left the cabin clutching their bundles.

Neither answered nor looked in his direction. 'Get up in the trap.' He held open the door. The girl helped in her mother, lifted in the children. When they drove off the waiting crowd sent up a jeering cheer. After driving many miles Father Bolger set down his passengers by a crossroads. They remained silent, their expressions hostile. 'May God Bless you,' he made the Sign of the Cross in their direction. They turned and walked away. He took two silver coins from his pocket and dropped them on the road. Johnny's wife heard the clink of money, ran back and pocketed them.

Father Bolger watched until they went from view. 'You're safe at least from neighbours. God send you may repent before it's too late, all I can do now is pray for you,' he said to himself as he turned the pony's head and began the drive back, thinking as he went about the frailty of man, himself included. His failure to have got through to Johnny's wife; it was long ago he should have sought her out.

Then there was Katy O'Hara, something was amiss there. Something to do with Peader. She concealed it well enough, but he wasn't fooled. Of the fact that it was all in her mind he had no doubt, and was equally convinced that Peader was unaware of Katy's thoughts. But she had a hankering for him, it was plain to see, never more so than the night he came from Dublin.

Sinful thoughts could put her soul in jeopardy. They could also affect Jamsie's life with her. Poor Jamsie, whose only fault was a liking for the drink which he readily confessed. What could he do about it, he asked himself? In confession he prompted Katy to confess past sins, inquired if anything troubled her mind. But apart from the once, a while ago now, she never referred to another man. He couldn't force her to speak, confession to be of any use had to be freely made.

He shouldn't, he reminded himself, be dwelling on particular sins, identifying confessors with them. Everything he heard in the confessional should be cast from his mind. But it was easier said than done. However, it had to be strived for. The seal of the confessional was inviolate; without it what man would kneel before another, even if the other was acting as an intermediary for God, and tell him their innermost secrets. No one.

Never by word, deed or gesture could a priest use knowledge gained in the sanctity of the box, never, unless the penitent gave his permission for such use. So he could stop tormenting himself with what was going on in Katy's mind. To reinforce his decision he asked himself would he have harboured such suspicion of her had she not confessed to hankering after another man? He considered it long and honestly, admitting finally that he would not. But because it wasn't in his power to control completely the workings of his mind, concluded that his preoccupation with politics could well be responsible for his lack of perception. That was something he must guard against. Politics wasn't why God called him to be a priest. He was a priest to save people's souls; to point the way to Eternal salvation. He had been neglecting that.

Too much of his energy went into the rights and wrongs of Ireland. Children were being conceived outside marriage, murder had taken place while he pondered the injustices done to O'Connell. Railed against how Dan's once loyal followers were reneging on him. It was not why God had ordained him. And it was time he remedied his way of thinking. It was time he hauled his parishioners over the coals; time to remind them what was the point of existing.

*

Two Sundays afterwards, by which time Katy was churched and her son Daniel baptized, the dead child buried and the constabulary no longer asking questions, Father Bolger preached his sermon.

'One after the other you are committing deadly sins. Three weeks ago a child was washed up in the weir. A child conceived and born out of wedlock – the fruit of lust. A child without benefit of baptism – gone to spend Eternity in Limbo – denied forever sight of the face of God.'

He paused for breath, his face angry and righteous, his crippled hands clenched one in the other. 'There are men and women in this parish, men and women sitting before me today surrendering their will to the demon drink. Father Matthew pointed out the error of your ways. The power and curse of drink, warned you of its consequences – the child in the river was one of them. Drink and lust go hand in hand. Drink is the curse of the country.

'Any form of over-indulgence is a sin. Over-indulgence in food or drink is the sin of gluttony. The man or woman who drinks too much poteen, or gorges themselves on potatoes is as guilty as the man feasting on rare beef and drinking claret.

'The man who covets his neighbour's wife, his cow, pig or land is paving his way to Hell as surely as if he bent to lay one stone in front of the other. The woman who looks at a man not her husband will dance for the Devil. The woman who stands all day gossiping or sits roasting her legs in the ashes will roast in a fire fiercer than any she can kindle on her own hearth.'

The congregation shifted uneasily, a few attempting to stifle coughs. Katy's eyes strayed from the priest to the

313

front seat and the figures of Dano Driscoll and Connolly, then quickly her eyes turned to regard the golden head of Peader, and back again to gaze at the priest winding up his sermon, thundering his warning.

'I'm warning you that unless you mend your ways, repent and ask God's forgiveness a terrible malediction will fall on you. Put Satan and his ways behind you before the Almighty shows His face in anger. In the name of the Father, and of the Son, and of the Holy Ghost, Amen.'

Walking home with Katy after Mass, Statia said, 'God bless him, isn't he God's Holy anointed, but I wonder where he gets his information – gluttony how are you! And did you notice he said nothing about the likes of Dano?'

'You're a terrible scandal-giver, Statia, and into the bargain don't listen, for he did so mention the likes of Dano. Wasn't that the bit about coveting things. He has to pull us up after a thing like that happening to the child. And he was right about the drink, there's many a one too fond of a drop . . .'

'There is, I know that,' Statia hastily agreed.

'Well sure that's all it was, just reminding us to mend our ways. And as for the gorging, that's only so we never give in when the hunger's bad and eat the seed.'

'Aren't you right, every word out of your mouth the truth,' Statia said. Katy felt pleased with herself, Statia was heeding her, as she herself would heed the message in the sermon and think not of Peader.

'Of course I am,' she said with a touch of smugness which lasted until they came to the spot where they would part, and Statia said, 'All the same he's sitting down now to hake boiled in milk, or a piece of fat bacon and butter swimming his potatoes. I know you're having the same, so I'll not delay you.'

There's no getting good of her, Katy thought affectionately, watching Statia waddling down to her cottage. No getting good of her at all.

Lord Kilgoran read to the end of the page, realized he had not taken in one word and put down the book. – I loved reading, he thought, but I can't concentrate. He took off his spectacles, closed his eyes and rubbed them. It did nothing to relieve their tiredness, no more than the fresh air or exercise did for his constant headaches. He opened his eyes and looked round the blue morning-room. It was a pleasant place to come after breakfast when the weather was bad, small enough to be cosy. It had been his wife's favourite room. He thought about her a lot these days, about her and the past. Finding in the long-ago memories a respite from his worry over Charles, the decision he was trying to reach – should he disinherit him?

Anyone in their right senses would not hesitate. Charles had not set foot in Ireland since last Christmas, almost twelve months now. He deserved to be disowned. But it was easier said than done. It went against the grain. Never in the history of Kilgorans had such a thing happened. From the time his first soldier ancestor was granted the land a male issue was the heir.

And supposing he could bring himself to break with tradition, to whom would he leave the estate? Catherine seemed the natural choice. But would that not cause dissent? All their lives his daughters had taken it for granted that the property would come to Charles. Altering his will might alter that. Not that Olivia would want it, though that was no guarantee she would welcome Catherine inheriting. Charlotte was only a child, probably show no interest, but you could never tell. He had seen many families split over such matters.

All the thinking made his headache worse, his mind was confused, so much to decide. He had thought Catherine was the right choice. Now he wasn't sure. There was Edward to consider. He might not be keen on the idea. He was still a young man with many years before him in the army. Of course he could send in his papers, resign his commission.

It was all too difficult. He needed to talk it over with Catherine. But that would have to wait, pointless writing to her while she was still at sea. He would wait, there was no immediate hurry. And who was to say that things might not improve?

Chapter Fourteen

Charlotte talked, Peader listened, looking down from where he sat beside her, at her face animated with hope and happiness, outlining their plans for going to America.

'We'll go before sailing stops for the winter. Just imagine – only four more months and we'll be gone.' She smiled up at him, stretched and made herself more comfortable in the grass, putting her hands behind her head so her breasts were thrust up in the silky stuff of her blouse.

'You'll sell the potatoes – there'll be lots to sell for you won't be here to eat them, and there'll be the money from the grain, and I have a little saved. We'll be quite well off.'

'We will,' Peader said, his eyes looking at her breasts, moving down to gaze on the line of her thighs moulded where her skirt clung to them, thinking – let our secret be safe. Let us go. Let her be my wife and lay every night by the side of me.

'I'll write a long letter to Papa, and Hannah will give it to him when we've gone. Poor Papa, I wish it didn't have to be this way. It's awful leaving him all alone.' Her eyes darkened, the radiance leaving them.

Peader bent and kissed her, then said: 'Don't start grieving – you know there's no other way. We mustn't wait any longer – you mustn't change your mind, we're lost if you do. Every minute we stay there's a chance we'll be found out. Anyone could ramble into the wood, it's not private, anyone could come, your father maybe. Don't change your mind on me Charlotte – I couldn't bear it.'

She twined her arms round his neck. 'You silly, silly thing, as if I would. Of course I won't change my mind, nothing could make me. One day Papa will understand, I'm sure he will, might even come to America to see us. Wouldn't that be lovely? And stop that frowning, no one will ever come into our little wood.'

The hungry months came round again, hungrier than ever this year for a week had passed without Hannah bringing food from the House. Then when she did arrive she was apologetic for the paltriness of what she brought, and explained how tight things were. 'Katy child, I don't know what the outcome will be. The poor Master must be demented with the worry of it all, there's money for nothing, and now talk of Mrs Cummings leaving.'

'She'll be no great loss,' Katy replied, 'hunger's mother!'

'She won't, but all the same the disgrace for the Master not having a housekeeper. She says she won't stay in a place with such a small staff. Isn't it terrible all the same. Everything in that beautiful mansion going to wrack and ruin. And after September when Miss Charlotte goes I'm afraid to think what will happen to the poor man, he'll take it very hard.'

'It's all arranged so?'

'More's the pity it is, and amn't I to blame for encouraging it in the first place. But didn't I think it was but a passing fancy, and look at the consequences.'

'You weren't to know,' Katy said.

Since the priest's sermon she had tried to put Peader from her mind. Now the mention of Charlotte's name revived her feelings, her love for him, and jealousy of her. While Hannah continued to lament her part in the affair Katy sought and found what she believed was a way of stopping the lovers eloping. She would tell the priest. And by the time Hannah left, Katy had convinced herself that her motive was inspired by concern for Peader. A word from Father Bolger would prevent him making a terrible mistake.

She picked a day to visit the priest when Mary Doyle wouldn't be there, for though she wanted Father Bolger to intervene, she wanted the knowledge to go no further, didn't want Mary with her ear to the door.

'I don't know who's the biggest fool – you, Jamsie or Hannah,' the priest said when she finished her story. 'Don't you know it could mean the loss of your habitation if Lord Kilgoran finds out?'

'That's what I was thinking,' Katy lied.

'It took you long enough to think so. And as for Hannah – she must be in her dotage.' He got up from his chair and paced the room. 'I don't know,' he said, 'I'm supposed to have my finger on the pulse of the parish, and I never heard a murmur. Are you sure it's still going on? Isn't it a wonder Mary didn't hear tell of it?'

'Oh, going on right enough, isn't that what I'm telling you, Father. Aren't they off to America.'

'I'll soon put a stop to that. Right then, Katy, leave it with me. Nothing could come of an affair like that but trouble – you did a wise thing coming.'

319

So light was her step on the return journey her feet barely touched the ground, and her heart sang with joy for if she couldn't have Peader neither would Miss Charlotte – Father Bolger would see to that.

Every day she waited for news that the priest had spoken, that the romance was finished. She heard nothing, but consoled herself it would come, Father Bolger was biding his time.

Her humour was great as she contemplated Charlotte being thwarted, and Peader hers once more. It made her eyes bright, and her skin glow. One morning Jamsie commented on how well she looked, put an arm round her waist, sneaking a hand up to her breast, and suggested she send the children up the Hazel Grove to play.

Playfully she slapped away the hand, told him he should be ashamed of himself in broad daylight, and got round him to take the children for a walk instead. As they were leaving Thomas hung back and reminded her of the promised trip to Kinsale. 'You never took us and you said you would.' He looked accusingly at her.

'You're right, I did too promise. Isn't it you that has the grand memory. 'Twas a long time ago – two years since it was mentioned. You'll be the grand scholar yet.'

'Will you take us so?'

'Oh I will to be sure.'

'When will it be?' Thomas was not allowing himself to be easily fobbed off, and stood his ground.

'One day soon. Maybe after we've lifted the potatoes. And I'll tell you what – we'll make a day of it. We'll bring food, wouldn't that be grand?'

Thomas nodded his head eagerly. And Katy, caught up

in the make-believe, and calling on memories of picnic baskets packed long ago in the Big House, began to describe what food she would take. 'We'll have brown and white bread cut thin and buttered. Salmon, pale pink slices of salmon with a lovely silvery skin. And cold chicken. Pies and sweet things. Fruit, maybe apples and pears. I'll bring a can of new milk and cordials. There'll be so much food you'll have a belly like a pup.'

Thomas' eyes widened with delight and his tongue ran over his lips. 'When will it be? Say the day, do.' And Katy, recalled to reality, answered cautiously. 'The day I couldn't name, that would be the hard thing now knowing when we'll lift or what the weather will be. But one day we'll go to Kinsale. Now run after your father or I'll change my mind,' she said, pretending sternness, and he ran.

She went into the kitchen and put on an amount of potatoes to cook, consciously avoiding to count them, for that was unlucky. When the pot came to the boil, she laid the mugs on the table, grateful that today she had buttermilk given in exchange by a woman for a bit of sewing. She drank from the jug, relishing the thin sharp tang that cleaned her palate of the bad taste always there when she had not eaten since the previous night.

– Buttermilk has the grand flavour, she thought, but wouldn't a sup of new be lovely, the smooth feel of it on your tongue, the sweetness, and the satisfying weight of it in your stomach. All the churns there used to be in the dairy, milk and cream in abundance – all gone now. All gone, she recalled, to pay off Master Charles's debts that came in faster than the waves on the shore.

When the potatoes were cooked she teemed the water into the pig's bucket, returned the pot to the fire, shaking it till the skins were about to split, pulled it from the heat and covered them with a clean cloth. The dinner was ready, the child asleep, she would sit in the sun till Jamsie and the children came back.

She sat on one of the smooth stones by the door. The sun was very hot, it beat down on her face. The air was fragrant with the scent of honeysuckle, spicy pinks and turf smoke. She closed her eyes, patterns danced behind her lids. It was lovely taking her ease, no one demanding her attention, she might doze for a while. Yet after a minute she became restless with the unaccustomed leisure, opened her eyes and listened in case the baby woke. Then began fretting at how long her family were away – the potatoes would be ruined. Her mind, she mused, was tormented with potatoes. If she wasn't worrying how they fared in the ground it was worrying how they fared in the pot.

In the field the pink-eyed blossoms on tall haulms moved in a breeze that had just risen. Katy watching them sway in the little wind continued thinking about potatoes. Wondering what people ate before they came. Anticipating the lifting of them, the spade turning over bushels of them, pale skinned, dozens hanging from one root. Enough for everyone, please God, and plenty for the pig. It would be grand then; a child not looking up in your face with hunger in its eyes.

The little wind grew stronger making her shiver as if someone walked on her grave. The potato stalks bent their heads, she shivered again and felt fearful for no reason she could think of. – Wasn't everything in the world grand for her today, she asked herself? What was there to fear? Weren't there all the signs of a good crop? You could see them growing in front of your eyes. Wasn't the weather right for them, but inside her head a voice said, 'Like the weather you can't depend on them.' She shut her ears to the voice, and concentrated on all the benefits of potatoes. The ease with which they grew, a bit of ground and a spade was all you wanted – a child could grow them. And look at the return, four to six times the amount in weight coming out of a field that wouldn't yield quarter that much in oats or barley. How easy they were on the palate, anyone could stomach them, even a child coming off the breast. A man like Jamsie could eat a stone in a day. They were a gift from God, and with His help they'd never fail entirely.

Danny's crying broke into her thoughts. She brought him from the house and sat him on her lap. 'Whisht now,' she hushed him, 'there's Dada coming down the path, and Bridget and Thomas.' The child stood up on her lap and danced for joy, his hands outstretched to the twins who came racing towards him, calling his name.

'You just got back in time,' Katy said as the sky darkened. 'I think there's a change in the weather.' They went inside and began the meal.

'A sun shower, that's all it is,' Jamsie said watching through the open door rain hopping off the ground. 'It's too heavy to last.'

'Oh, it's you, Father! What brought you out on such a terrible day? Come in, sit down.'

323

'I haven't been here since your father's funeral, Lord have mercy on him.'

'You have not,' Peader replied, looking quizzical, wondering what brought the priest now.

'No, well then ... I thought it was time we had a talk.'

'That's grand. Was there anything in particular you wanted to talk about?'

'Yourself and Miss Charlotte.'

Peader's quizzical expression was replaced by one of surprise, then anger. 'Who told you? Who else knows?'

'Not her father, if that's what's worrying you, and it should.'

'It would.'

'That's something anyway – the man has enough troubles without you adding to them.'

''Twasn't that I meant. If he knew, Charlotte would be sent away.'

'The further the better for everyone's sake. You'll put an end to the business, Peader.'

'I will not. I can't. I love her.'

'Love indeed! Get sense will you. You don't think Lord Kilgoran would sanction your affair? How could he?'

Peader got up from his seat, went close to the priest, stood over him. 'Listen, Father, this is none of your concern.'

Unruffled by Peader's threatening stance or raised voice, the priest replied calmly, 'Ah, that's where you're wrong. Everything in the parish is my concern, all the more so when it means trouble. And trouble is what you're bringing, for his Lordship, for the girl, and the fools who help you. And don't tell me it doesn't matter because you're taking her to America, there's many a slip twixt the cup and the lip. And if you succeed in running off what do you think'll happen after her father learns the truth? Do you want to see an old woman like Hannah packed off to the workhouse – Katy and Jamsie without a roof over their heads – that's what you could be the cause of.'

'They're all excuses, every one. It's religion that's brought you here. Religion that has you talking to me as if I was a child.'

'You're acting like one, getting indignant that I'm concerned with your faith – I'm your priest, of course religion brought me here – you didn't think I'd clap you on the back for taking up with a Protestant.'

'I knew it, behind all your talk of concern for Lord Kilgoran, and Katy and Jamsie – it's my soul you're after.'

'I am, it's my business, but you do me an injustice, Peader and well you know it, if you think my concern stops there. Tell me now, what would you propose doing if for some reason the journey to America fell through?'

'There's no fear of that. To America we're going, to a land where how you worship doesn't matter. Religion's the curse of this country, if it wasn't for it we could stay where we are.'

Father Bolger laughed derisively. 'God help your sense if you think being a Catholic is the only objection Kilgoran would raise. If you believe that you're either vain or foolish, and I thought you were neither.' He waited for a response from Peader and when none came continued, 'Do you think if you were a Protestant small farmer you'd be in? Are you codding yourself that Daniel O'Connell would welcome a dairy-maid for a daughter-in-law? Well, he wouldn't no more than your mother, so I'm told, would have welcomed Katy O'Hara as your wife. 'Tis the ways of the world, religion makes it worse, that's all. And you'll solve nothing pacing the floor like a caged creature, come here and sit down.'

Peader stopped pacing, but remained standing, glaring at the priest.

'Thank God looks can't kill,' he said lightly, attempting to ease the atmosphere of hostility radiating from Peader. He failed, and let his own annoyance take command of his voice. 'You never answered my question: What are you proposing to do if America falls through – court the girl in secrecy till she's an old woman? Or were you thinking, maybe you'd disgrace her, and force her father's hand that way – is that it?'

'If you weren't a priest I'd hit you for that. Another man I'd knock through the door. Go now in the name of God before I forget your cloth.'

'I'm sorry, Peader, I shouldn't have put it like that, you left me little choice. I'm trying to bring you to your senses. You're not the first to fall for a girl at the Big House – it never works.'

'It will for us. I'll make it work. We're going to America, and you nor anyone else will stop us.'

To himself Father Bolger admitted defeat. For the time being there was no use pursuing it. All he could do was pray that Peader came to his senses before too much harm was done.

'I'll go then, and leave you to ponder what I've said. You're a stubborn proud man, they're good qualities in the right circumstances, but ...'

'No more now, Father, good day to you.' Peader held the door for the priest.

As soon as he went, without bothering to put on cap or coat, Peader hurried to Katy's. Water dripped from him as he pushed to the door and announced, 'Someone told the priest.'

Katy felt the blood rush up her neck, stain her cheeks, and averted her head lest Jamsie or Peader notice and guess she was the culprit.

'Who could have done that, sure no one knows, only us. Katy, you didn't tell Mary Doyle by any chance, or Statia?' Jamsie asked.

'God forgive you for even suggesting such a thing.' She put on a show of indignation. 'Look at the colour you've made me go mentioning it.' Her blushes accounted for, she turned to face them. 'You must have nearly died, Peader. He forbid you, I suppose?'

She waited for his reply, knew what it would be. Peader was God-fearing, he'd be led by the priest.

'Forbid me he did.'

'And so?' Jamsie asked.

'I told him it was none of his business. I told him I loved Charlotte, and no one would stand between us.'

She heard Jamsie congratulate him. Tell him he was his own man, more power to him. The priests did too much interfering, the people were led and said by them, and she felt her heart break. He was lost to her now. Charlotte who had everything, had him, too, and in a little while would take him far over the sea. He who was the light in her darkness, her solace when weariness and hunger wore out her spirit. He was beautiful and demanded nothing of

327

her, not her time, nor attention, not her body. He just was. Like the sun in the morning he just was.

– Make something happen to stop him going, she wished. Let the boat go without him. Let the Master find out. Let her be thwarted, anything befall her, anything that prevents him leaving, marrying her.

Peader and Jamsie were speculating as to how the priest found out. She joined in, suggesting this and that. Agreed with Peader that extra care must be taken between now and the time they sailed, all the while willing that it should not happen. Telling herself she could bear the thought of their secret meetings for ever, would pass all the messages and letters, so long as Peader remained in Kilgoran.

In the morning she woke with a headache, and without putting a foot outside the door knew a storm was brewing. Knew by the pressure within her skull, the unease in her stomach and an irritability which increased as the day wore on. She scolded the children, and screamed at the dog for being under her feet when he was doing no more than passing. So great was her physical discomfort and sense of foreboding all thought of Peader and Charlotte was far from her mind.

Unconsciously she communicated her fear to the children so they huddled close together – eyes fearful – waiting for they knew not what. Katy's apprehension grew worse when Jamsie left to dig a pit in which Statia could store her potatoes once they were lifted. The rain which had been falling stopped, the heat became oppressive, there was an unnatural stillness, an eerie silence, no bird called, no breath of wind sighed. Katy's head felt as though a band was round it, being tightened, pressing in through her hair, through the skin of her scalp, crushing her skull, constricting her brain. She sought relief from the tension by screaming again at Prince, 'Shut up that whingeing and whining,' dragging him by the scruff of the neck towards the door. As terrified as she was of the coming storm, he resisted, so she had to drag him all the way. Hurriedly she pushed him outside from where he yelped frantically.

The heat became worse, the silence threatening. Then a breeze rose which quickly became a strong wind, whirling down the boreen, tugging at the hedges, bending young trees, lashing the flowers, blowing leaves in front of it, rattling anything unsecured. Then, as if exhausted by its whirlwind tactics, and pausing for breath, the wind grew quiet. Katy held hers waiting for the next onslaught. The sky grew black as night.

She made the Sign of the Cross, saying the words aloud. The children imitated her. 'God between us and all harm, and protect ...' Before the prayer was completed the thunder exploded, a blinding flash rent and lit the sky, its brilliance illuminating the kitchen, Katy and her children fallen to their knees, praying. 'Holy Mary Mother of God bring us through this hour of peril, we beseech you.' Interrupting her prayers to warn the children, 'Shut your eyes or it will blind you.' Peal after peal of thunder rumbled over the roof, simultaneously lightning flashed. In the minute pauses between claps of awesome noise, Prince's piteous cries, and frantic scratching at the door were heard. With a hand shielding her eyes Katy opened it and let him in, scuttling back to kneel and pray, 'Sacred Heart of Jesus save us, spare Jamsie out in it.'

329

The rain began again, it turned to hail and rattled down. With the discharge of the storm the tension in Katy's head eased, her head no longer ached, now only a nameless dread remained. A fear of the appalling noise, the blinding streaks of light. A fear that this storm such as she had never before witnessed was a portent of evil, a manifestation of Hell – of blackness and heat and searing light.

After what seemed like an eternity the sound of the thunder diminished, the pauses between the lightning grew longer. Prince inched out on his belly from beneath the settle, the twins crawled to him, stroked his still-quivering body, kissed him and said, 'Don't be afraid, sure Mammy says it's going away.' Katy rose from her knees, opened the door, saw the clouds part, the sun shine, and the world as it was. 'Blessed be to God,' she gave praise. Peg and Nora ran out with the dog, Thomas, Bridget and Mary Kate following them. Water dripped from the thatch, puddles brimmed every hollow, the children splashed in them, the pig wallowed in the morass his sty had become. Jamsie returned, not even damp, having sheltered in a cottage. He and Katy agreed it was the worst storm they had known. But it was over. It had cleared the air, the fine weather would return.

But the expected fine weather did not come, and for weeks it rained. Soft fine rain alternating with heavy downpours, sheets of sleet, showers of hail. Without cease in whatever form water fell from a pall of grey cloud that robbed the atmosphere of light, shrouded the hills and hovered wraith-like above the trees. The world was weeping for her sorrow, Katy fancifully imagined, as daily,

Hannah, Jamsie or Peader himself discussed how soon he was going with Charlotte to America, wondered still who had told the priest, and worried about the hardships Charlotte must endure on the journey. – That she may, Katy hoped.

The rain still fell, and sometimes a wind rose shrieking like keening women, blowing down the chimney, scattering the ashes from the grate, sending swirls of water beneath the badly-fitting door. On other days when the wind rested, the fire would not draw, and all Katy's efforts on bended knees, fanning with her breath, could not coax a spark. The turf smouldered, sending out smoke that made the children cough. Their clothes were permanently damp, and from each journey outside they returned drenched, their feet and legs caked with mud.

Then when it seemed as if forever they were condemned to live beneath overcast skies, one morning the sun rose, the clouds blew away, and it shone. The hearts of everyone lifted when they saw its light and felt the heat. Bodies tense from cold and damp relaxed, people smiled and laughed aloud. Life was good after all. Flowers that had drooped beneath the weight of water lifted their heads, turned their faces to the sun's restorative rays. The heat after such rain caused luxuriant growth to burst forth. Ivy and wild woodbine sent out new tendrils grasping for a hold, reaching and entwining all within their grasp. In Katy's garden, flowers bloomed for a second time, and in the fields pink-eyed potato blossom, ears of corn and beards of barley bent under their own weight. Everywhere there was rejoicing, that despite the worst summer weather anyone could remember the potatoes were thriving.

Tim Coffey was let into the lovers' secret, and for a price agreed to take them late at night to the port. One afternoon soon after making the arrangement he came to Katy's. She was about to wash her feet, but at the sight of Tim pushed the pail to one side, thinking hopefully that Tim might have backed out of the deal. She bid Tim welcome, eager to hear what he had to say.

'Where's himself?' he asked, sitting down.

'Gone to the strand with the children. Peader's out in the boat fishing, if he gets anything we'll have a grand feed. You're welcome to a bit.'

She had given him the opportunity now to say what brought him. Tim was slow, she knew, to begin a conversation, so she waited.

'Thanks all the same, but I won't stay. 'Twas to tell Jamsie I heard a strange thing today, but I'll see him again. Sure it might be nothing anyway.'

'What was the strange thing you heard?' Katy inquired. If he had nothing to say about Peader and Charlotte, she might as well hear the latest.

'A disease come upon the potatoes, the like of which has never been seen. Fallen out of the sky, maybe.'

'God between us and all harm! Could such a thing be so?'

'It's what's being said. Though said very quiet like. People wanting you to know, but afraid to say it loud – the way you would about something terrible.'

Katy watching Tim while he talked noticed how he was

332

ageing, how thin he had become, the shanks fleshless through the legs of his trousers. He was failing fast, going soft in the head, too. Why else would he say such queer things about the potatoes that ten minutes ago she'd seen in the field, and never beheld a finer looking lot?

'Wisha then, Tim,' she said after a while, 'I'd say 'tis talk, that's all.'

'It's talk I never heard before.' He stood up. 'Tell himself when he comes in.' He bid her goodbye.

'Poor Tim,' she said looking after him, 'it comes to us all if we live long enough. But for all that you disappointed me. News to gladden my heart I thought you were bringing.' She dismissed him from her mind, brought the bucket and sat soaking her feet, thinking of how in a few days the potatoes would be in, a grand day spent in the fields, a night with the neighbours gathered in the kitchen. Even the knowledge that soon afterwards Peader would be gone not spoiling her pleasure. – And anyway, she told herself, something could still happen to prevent him.

Jamsie and the children came back from the beach, bringing two fine pollack. While they were eating she told him what Tim had said. 'That's not like Tim, the age must be catching up with him,' Jamsie said dismissively. And Katy was relieved, for now and then while she prepared the food and sat to eat it, Tim's words troubled her.

After the dinner Hannah came bringing a bacon bone and a lump of cold lamb. 'Have it, and you'll get it,' she said, surveying the remains of the fish.

'Isn't it always the way. Never mind, we'll be glad of the food tomorrow. How are things above?' Katy asked.

'Ah,' Hannah sighed. 'I wish I'd had no part in it. She's beside herself with excitement. In one way Peader's been the making of her – she thrives on the love. But when I think that in a week she'll be on the high seas, with God knows what in front of her, and what'll happen when the Master finds she's gone, I wish I'd never meddled in the first place.'

'Do you think the Master will suspect we had knowledge of the goings on?'

'Wouldn't he be a fool if he didn't?'

'I hope he's not too hard on us. Wasn't it a pity Father Bolger didn't succeed in putting a stop to it.'

'It was and it wasn't. For us and the Master it was, but Miss Charlotte would have died of a broken heart.'

'That was a queer business all the same,' Jamsie commented. 'Not one but the three of us knowing anything about the affair, yet someone was able to tell the priest.'

'I've puzzled my brains thinking about it,' Hannah said, 'and the only conclusion I can reach is that Father Bolger made a shrewd guess. He does be about a lot in the pony and trap. He might have seen you Jamsie, heard your whistle, maybe caught a glimpse of Peader or Miss Charlotte on the same road and put two and two together.'

Katy, not knowing which way to look, changed the conversation, asking Hannah if any news had come from Miss Catherine.

'There was a letter posted on the way to India, don't ask me where for I couldn't get my tongue round the name. The Master was delighted. Now that the maids are few I bring him the cup of tea myself, and I swear to God if I saw him read the letter once, I saw him half a dozen times.'

'Miss Catherine was the lovely girl. Never caused her father a minute's worry,' Katy said.

'A perfect lady,' Hannah replied.

'Do you remember the day she got married?' Katy looked wistful.

'And the night?' Jamsie interjected.

'Oh indeed I do. There was me and your mother, God be good to her, admiring you and Peader, and in a minute there was ructions,' Hannah said.

Katy looked at Jamsie, he smiled at her. She saw him again as if for the first time. He winked at her. 'We've had the grand nights,' he said. Hannah readily agreed they had. Katy smiled back at him, she knew it was only to her he was talking.

'I hear someone coming,' Jamsie said and looked out through the window. 'Oh, it's them two, Statia and Mary Doyle. I'm making myself scarce. I'll be by the door.'

Down the boreen they came, Statia's shawl loose about her, puffing and panting with the heat, Mary light and spry like a small rodent darting ahead.

'It's well for you with nothing to do,' Statia said.

'You're killed too with the work,' Jamsie teased back.

'Commere,' Statia said when she was abreast of him. 'Is there any truth, do you think, in what Tim's saying about the potatoes?'

'Divil a bit I'd say,' he replied, and the women went in to Katy.

A bee flew past his head, landed in the flower garden and began working the spiky lemon and blue lupins, burrowing into the foxgloves, emerging backwards, legs coated with pollen; idly he watched it, and heard the

335

women's voices drift from the kitchen. Statia complaining about the heat, and the thirst on her. –An oul rip if ever there was one – after the poteen. Herself and Mary were the right pair. He smiled wryly, remembering the day he'd heard them talking about the garden, and how he'd only taken Katy because of it. It was one of them two who got word to the priest about Peader, nothing surer.

Now he could hear only the one voice – Statia's relating the story of the Four Fields of Red Clover – she'd have them going now – her and her piseogs. The bee left the flowers, he watched it fly to the potato patch and come to rest on a pink-eyed snowy blossom. – Poor oul Tim, he thought, I wonder where you got that story from, were you drunk, or beginning to ramble? He got up from the seat and went up the field.

In the kitchen Katy sat on the settle, elbows on the table, small hands cupping her face, listening spellbound to Statia relating the story of the fairies in the Four Fields of Red Clover.

'A cousin of mine that's dead this long time told me. And he'd had it from the man it happened to, God rest them both. Well anyway this man was coming home one night with a good sup taken, passing the fields, and he saw them. The night was bright as day with the moon shining, and there they were dancing. Such dancing it was, like feathers blowing in the wind, them all dressed in colours of the rainbow, and the sweetest music you ever heard. But no sooner did the man stop when so did the playing, and out of the crowd hops this little bit of a thing with a cranky puss on him. Over he comes, and the man watching felt the power drain out of him, not able to put one foot before the other.'

All of a sudden Statia stopped talking, coughed, and began clearing her throat.

'What happened then, Statia?' Hannah asked, when the pause and throat clearing continued.

'I don't know at all, it's gone astray on me.' She put a hand to her head, running her fingers through her sparse grey hair, looking distressed. 'I've had a lightness, and it knocked the tale astray.'

– And you won't find it, Katy thought, if I don't produce the bottle. Jamsie'll kill me for parting with the last drop, but without it she won't finish the story.

'Hold on a minute then till I see if there's anything for the lightness,' she said, getting up and going out to the place where the poteen was hidden.

'May God bless you, now where was I?' Statia inquired when the spirit had revived her.

'Where the man was paralysed with the fright,' Mary Doyle prompted.

'He was so, rooted to the ground. Then the queer little thing with the cranky puss spoke. "What are you doing here at this hour of the night?" I needn't tell you the man wasn't able to open his mouth, his throat and tongue petrified. "Go from here this minute, and if you breathe a word to a living soul ill luck will attend you and yours." With that the little fella leapt into the middle of the field, the man got back the power of his legs and took to his heels as if all the divils in hell were after him, with the screeching and laughing of them in the fields ringing in his ears. A terrible unnatural sound he said it was.

337

'His wife was waiting for him. Wanting to know where he'd been, and why, and with who? A sharp-tongued woman she was, and before it he forgot the warning of the queer creature, and told her everything. The minute he did the screeching that had tormented him all the way home got worse. Then, and ever after he heard it, day and night it sawed through his brain. Two months to the time he saw the dancing, God took him out of his suffering, and two weeks to the day he went into the clay his crop failed, and everyone else's in the vicinity. And that's the gospel truth.'

Statia, having concluded her story, folded her arms across her breasts, sat back and with a look of satisfaction regarded the mesmerized women.

After a moment Katy let out her breath. 'Aren't people terrible foolish, look at the affliction that man brought on himself and others.'

'That he may be in Heaven interceding that the like never happens again,' Hannah said.

Jamsie, back by the door after inspecting the potatoes, heard the end of the story, and smiled at the foolishness of the women. He listened to them talk of other things, to Katy telling them how long ago her grandmother had a parchment describing the pedigree of the O'Donnells, how they were once kings in the north, and she herself belonging to them.

He hoped they'd hurry up and finish, he was tired standing by the door. When they left and he went in he reminded Katy how he'd only taken her for the cottage and fields, how sometimes when she gossiped all day he regretted it. She laughed and remembered the other times when he confessed his love, and told her he'd have slept on the side of a road to be near her.

Later when they were getting ready for bed she told him the story of the Four Fields.

'Aren't you the foolish woman – you and your stories,' he said affectionately. 'And isn't Statia the great liar. The man was drunk when he passed the fields, stocious, and seeing things. Footless drunk, heard the wind, and saw the grass swaying, that's all that it was.'

'Listen to that now,' Katy said while he brought the pallet out. 'Isn't it grand to know everything, and believe nothing.' She knelt to sweep in the hearth, shovelling hot ash on the turf to keep in the fire until the morning.

'I heard you telling your own story – Kings of Ulster – how are you?' Jamsie laughed, and shook down the pallet.

'Was it nothing better you had to do with your time than stand by the door listening to the women – you're killed with the work.' She picked up a pillow and threw it at him. He caught it and aimed it back. 'Ah, don't,' she laughingly pleaded, 'you'll wake the child.' He put it down, turned away and began to undress.

'But it's true all the same – I am an O'Donnell.' He looked round.

'Did I ever deny it?' He was teasing her, she liked it, and responded, pretending annoyance, indignation, playing his game.

'It's true I tell you,' she said.

He laughed out loud, turned his back and continued undressing. She ran to him, pulled him round. 'Long ago there were things to prove it – parchments and the like, stolen by the begrudgers.' Her hands closed into fists, reached out to pummel him. He captured them, drew her close.

'Your eyes dance when you're annoyed.' She struggled in his hold. 'I love you when you're raging.' He drew her to him. 'A ghille, a ghillie mo croidhe,' he said bending to kiss her, 'hasn't everyone in Ireland a story of a parchment lost or stolen long ago.' He kissed her, let go her wrists and put his arms around her. 'Do you know,' he said when the kiss was finished, 'Ireland must have been the queer place all right in them days.'

'What days?' she asked dreamily and innocently, for she believed the game was done.

'When the O'Donnells were kings, and everyone in the land a poet, or hard hero, every man and woman with a gift for one thing or another. Mustn't it have been the rare times living with all the poetry, the singing and fighting, and no man to do a day's work.'

'There was so,' Katy said wriggling out of his arms and jumping into the bed, 'for there were plenty of O'Haras.'

'Is it nothing at all we were then?' he asked in pretended sorrow.

'Nothing at all only labouring men. Pull the cradle close to the bed and blow out the light.'

'You're teasing,' he said, slipping in beside her.

'I am not. It's true. As true as I'm an O'Donnell. Look at these and this.' She shrugged off his arm and held up her small, fine-boned hands, kicked off the quilt and pointed a high arched foot, sat up and fingered the long column of her throat. 'It's all there, that's breeding, it shows.'

''Tis a pity then I can't see them – a dark night's a bad

time to be showing your signs of pedigree.' He pulled her down beside him and held aloft a tress of her golden hair. 'Is that another one of the signs? And these?' He kissed shut her eyes, then raised his face and said, 'Sure I always thought O'Donnell was a red-haired giant of a man with blue eyes. What happened to that part of the breed?'

''Twas a long time ago,' she murmured, and nestled closer to him.

Chapter Fifteen

All her wishes had been in vain, nothing had happened to prevent Peader and Charlotte leaving – now nothing would – in days they would be gone, so thought Katy as she set out on a walk with the twins.

'Which way will we go?' asked Peg.

'Let's go to the lake,' Nora said.

Katy replied, 'All right, the lake,' not caring where the walk took them for her mind was occupied, trying to make sense of what sort of woman she was – last night giving herself to Jamsie, twining him to her, thrilled to the core of her being, and this morning grieving over another man.

What madness had possessed her, made her love him more than Jamsie, made her loathe Miss Charlotte for stealing him, sent her running to inform the priest? She could find no answers, knew only that when he went part of her would go with him, that her life would never be the same again.

On she walked, attempting to clear her mind, to pay attention to the children, answer their questions. They came to the path by the river, and walked along its spongy banks, water seeped up through the sedge, tufts of white bog cotton flecked it. Now and then Peg and Nora bent to pull at the silky strands.

Midges danced round Katy's head, colliding with her face, irritating her skin. Horseflies landed on her arms and ankles, the brown bodies settling so easily and gently the bite was in before she knew it. The twins ran ahead, occasionally stooping to pick lumps of turf and throw them in the river. The air was hot and still, the water's placid surface disturbed only by the landing clumps or a rising fish.

Katy called Peg and Nora back, warning them to be careful. Explaining how they must never come here alone.

They crossed stepping stones and went on a little way to the lake, going round to the far side where she and Jamsie had done their courting. She remembered how it was then, and wished it was still so, that her heart was whole, that more than half of it didn't hanker for Peader.

She sat on an outcrop of rock near the water's edge, noticing how the trees were changing colour, the green golden, the rowan scarlet-berried. Saw Peg and Nora pick up handfuls of leaves already fallen, throw them above their heads, laughing as they cascaded down about them, and thought what a lively, good-humoured pair they were. Never still for a minute, able to find amusement anywhere in anything, they'd grow up to take the world lightly.

Soon they tired of the game with the leaves, and ventured to the water's edge. Dipping feet in the little waves washing in from the slaty blue lake. Squealing at the cold of it, becoming more daring, holding up their ragged petticoats, wading in. Katy watched until she judged they had gone far enough, any further and cauls or not they'd find a watery grave. She called them. They pretended not to hear, so hitching up her skirt she followed. Nearing them she reached a hand for each and her skirt fell down. 'Now look what you've been the cause of, I'm wringing wet.' Once out of the water she slapped them. 'You pair of whipsters, it's the last time I'll take you anywhere.' While she squeezed water from the hem of her skirt they ran ahead, out of her sight, and then she heard them call for her to come quick.

They were kneeling by a dead rabbit. 'Look at him,' they chorused – 'the poor thing's dead.'

'He is.'

'Can we bury him?'

'You can not. He's been dead for days, and is crawling with maggots.'

'Will he go to Heaven?' Peg asked.

'Maybe he will – to a Heaven for rabbits and the like.'

'Not to the same Heaven as us?'

'Ah no, sure rabbits don't have souls.'

'Is it nice in Heaven?' asked Nora.

'Oh it is, a grand place, all the angels and saints around God forever.'

'Why can't we go there then?' the twins spoke in one voice.

'We will one day. Please God we all will – but not for a long time, you do have to wait for room. But one day when we're very old we'll go to Heaven. Now don't be moidering me with any more questions, run on home.' They raced away, laughing and calling to each other.

They were out of her sight when Peader came into it, a long way off, walking towards her. What was he doing up this way, she wondered. Maybe, her fancy told her, he's

344

come looking for you, to say farewell. She quickened her step and her heart kept pace with it. The distance between them lessened. – How beautiful he is. How his hair shines, the neatness of him for a big man. I wish he were mine. I have to stop him leaving. He is mine. Charlotte will not have him for a husband. He's mine, mine. I love you. I'll die if you go.

Peader spoke before her. 'I saw Peg and Nora, in a state they were about the rabbit.'

– Don't smile at me, don't look at me that way, I can't bear it when you do, she thought. She made a remark about the rabbit, said it was stinking. Then a voice she didn't will to speak said imploringly, 'Don't go, Peader. I love you. I know you love me, you told me, remember you said it – the night of the wedding.'

She heard the voice as if it was someone else's, not coming out of her mouth, but from a distance, and couldn't silence it. 'You promised to love me always. Miss Charlotte's not for you, she's not your kind. Don't go on me, don't leave me.'

The voice stopped. She saw Peader change colour, his cheeks flush with embarrassment, then pale, saw the look of sorrow come and be replaced by one of pity. Heard him plead, 'Don't say any more, Katy, sure you don't know what you're saying. You're Jamsie's wife, you love him. You always did. Don't say another word now – it's only some queer oul humour that's come over you, making you say foolish things that in a minute you'll regret.'

She wanted to run away, hide her shame, douse her burning face with cool water, say no more, as he advised. But she could not move, and the voice was answering for

345

her. 'What's foolish about the truth? Wouldn't you be less of a fool if you listened and remembered. Admitted it's me you love, not her. It was me you were promised to. Remember the promises – you haven't forgotten – you couldn't.'

She was outside of herself now, hearing the voice, watching herself go to him, catch hold of him, attempt to embrace him, imploring, 'Say you never forgot, that it's me you love, me you want.' The self that stood back and saw pity leave his face, and revulsion replace it, witnessed his hands ward off those that reached for him, step back out of their reach. She saw it all, the expression come and go, the revulsion, confusion, then the clear green eyes cloud with concern, and heard him speak, his tone soothing. 'You're sick, Katy, not well, let me take you home, let me help you,' coaxing, wheedling, the way you would with a child, a simpleton.

Then she hated him, stepped back into herself and ran and ran until her breath was gone, and a stitch clamped her side. Collapsing face down on the grass she lay gasping, crying when her breath came back, 'Oh Sacred Heart of Jesus pity me. What have I done, what came over me? How can I ever raise my head again?'

Peader followed her, and stood looking down at her body convulsed by sobbing. – Poor lovely Katy, what has come over you, he thought. He wanted to lift her from the ground, take her home to Jamsie, see her safe. He bent and reached out to touch her, then drew back. He was the last one she would want to see now. He remembered the night she had chosen Jamsie instead of himself, his sense of rejection, the shame he had experienced, how all he had wanted was to run away and hide. If Katy had meant a word of what she said just now, then she would be suffering the same torture. What made her say such things? They couldn't be true. Her poor mind had become deranged for a moment. She loved Jamsie. A moment of madness, that's all it was. With the help of God she would forget it had ever happened. And not a word of it would ever pass his lips.

Quietly he moved away from her, far enough not to hear what she was crying out. He crouched behind a bush from where he would watch to see that eventually she went home.

Katy stopped crying and calling on God to pity her. Then her sense of shame was followed by one of fear. Fear that Peader had run for Jamsie, told him, then anger swept through her – Charlotte had won. She had seen it for herself in the way Peader scorned her love. At this very minute he could be laughing at her, mocking her, regaling the neighbours. Dejection claimed her and she called again to Heaven for help. 'Oh God, let me die, don't ask me to face any more.'

The sun slid down the sky, the air cooled, blew on her flushed cheeks, cooling her, drying the tears. – Let night come, and me fall asleep, never to waken, never to see Jamsie's anger, don't make me live with my shame, don't ask me to endure the scorn and ridicule in people's eyes. She became silent and lay quiet, her eyes closed.

'Mammy, Mammy! Where are you? Were you hiding on us?' The twins found her, bent over her, she opened her eyes and saw the delight in theirs, thinking she was playing a game with them.

'Will we run now and hide, and call out when we're hid?' Peg asked.

'In a place where you'll never find us,' Nora added.

'I wasn't hiding – I fell asleep, just sat down and fell asleep.'

'Maybe you were tired,' Peg consoled.

'That's what it was – I was very tired, we'll go home now.' She stretched out her hands, they took one each, and she let them think they pulled her up. Their chattering restored her sanity. She didn't want to die – what was done was done. Thanking God that the madness hadn't possessed her sooner – Peader would be gone in a few days, she could avoid him until then. And as she neared the cottage, she knew she had done him an injustice; he would not tell Jamsie, nor anyone else, she knew him better than that.

'That's the third time this week the constable's been nosing around, wouldn't you say it's peculiar?' Statia remarked when she met Katy coming from the well.

'I said the self same thing when I saw him. Could it be poteen he's after?'

'It's something, though he let on he was just passing, admired the potatoes without saying, "God Bless them", so I told him not to be passing remarks like that, maybe inviting ill luck.'

'You did right, there's been far too much talk since Tim started the rumour.'

'There has indeed,' Statia agreed. They filled their buckets and walked home, Statia asking before they parted, 'Anything else strange?'

'Not a thing,' Katy replied, and imagined Statia's face if she told her the strangest thing of all.

The day was bright and sunny, but not too hot, and she hoped it would hold, it was ideal weather for lifting. There was no one in when she got back, only Danny asleep on the bed. The children she supposed were down on the strand, they'd come back with tossed hair, their pockets full of shells and sand, their skin when she kissed them tasting of salt; and they'd be starving, looking for food, there was nothing like the strand for giving you an appetite. – God love them, she thought, their bellies will have to stay far back for a day or two yet. But next week – next week the potatoes will be in, the pit full, and for a day or two we'll make gluttons of ourselves. She let herself dwell on the taste of them, fresh out of the earth, boiled, dipped in salt, a feast fit for a king.

She wondered where Jamsie was, if he had gone down to Carey's or up to see Peader? To see Peader probably. – Thank God, she said to herself, he's steered clear of here since I lost my reason for the while, though I suppose I'll have to face him before he leaves for America. How I'll do it I don't know. It's up to see him Jamsie's gone, for he can't understand why he hasn't showed up, though I keep telling him it's all he has to do, making arrangements to sell the boat and his crops, he's gone now to find out for himself.

The sound of the twins calling broke in on her thoughts. She went to the door, and saw them running from a thicket up near the potato field. They came flying down the track. 'You didn't go to the shore,' she called seeing their mouths stained purple, long scratches down their arms. 'You've been picking berries.' She smiled, the twins found ways of filling their bellies, even if not for long, not bothering whether the fruit was ripe; in an hour they'd be griped and running out to the bushes.

'Oh, mammy there's a terrible smell,' they chorused. 'Like the dead rabbit only worse. Will you come and see what it is.'

They took hold of her hands, pulling her along the path. She stopped, sniffed the air and could smell nothing. 'I hope you're not making a fool of me,' she said.

'We're not, honest to God!' Peg said, and Nora added, ''Tis by the potatoes.'

Katy allowed herself to be led past the flower garden and up the track to the edge of the field. Then she got the smell. 'God bless us!' she exclaimed, clapping a hand over her nose and mouth, fighting the desire to retch for the stench was vile. In a muffled voice, she told the twins to run back to the house, thinking as she did so that whatever was causing the smell was more than a dead rabbit.

It crossed her mind that maybe it was a body – the body of a poor man who tramped the roads. That perhaps he had come in the dark, weak with hunger or sick, wandered in among the plants, collapsed and died, been there for days. But as the thought clarified she was already dismissing it – if a man had fallen the haulms would be crushed and broken; Prince would have barked, drawn attention to anything laying there.

Keeping her nose and mouth covered until she reached the cottage where the twins waited by the door, she said, 'Whatever it is I don't know, but keep from there. I'll get

350

your father to look when he comes.' She went into the kitchen and found Danny awake, down from the bed, reaching for the fire. Slapping his hand, picking him up, and at the same time telling herself she was a foolish woman out sniffing the air like a dog and the child nearly burnt alive.

While waiting for Jamsie to come home, she tried to dismiss her fear that something, what she couldn't imagine, lay among the plants. But the smell which seemed to have entered her brain, a smell more foul than anything she had ever known, was a constant reminder. And as soon as Jamsie came in she sent him to investigate it. Returning after a while, he said there was nothing to account for it, but agreed it was terrible.

'Could it be anything to do with the potatoes, do you think?'

'Yerra, how could it? What has a stench to do with potatoes?'

His reply wasn't reassuring, for now that the thought had occurred, others followed it. Memories of what Tim said about a strange disease, rumours repeated by Statia and Mary Doyle, someone mentioning a bad odour, they all flooded back. She tried to dam her mind against them, forcing herself to think of other things, but they swamped every other thought, until she abandoned her attempts and said to Jamsie, 'Would you not take a look to be sure, dig up a root?'

'You're a terrible woman,' he said, bending to slip on the brogues he had taken off, 'but if it'll ease your mind, all right so.'

Danny had fallen asleep again, she put him in the bed

and followed Jamsie out. He shouldered the spade and the two of them walked towards the field. The children coming back from the strand saw them, and came running, whooping with joy at the prospect of new potatoes for their supper. Peg and Nora tagged on.

The smell was worse than earlier, the air laden with it, thick, tangible almost. Katy thought she could taste it, and again felt the desire to vomit.

Jamsie put the spade into the earth, placed his foot on it, aligned himself for the thrust and lift. The sun was bright on Katy and the watching children, the birds singing. Only the smell marred the day, that and the unease which weighted her heart. 'But now, in a minute,' she told herself, it would lighten, her fear was foolishness, 'the potatoes will come up, pale and wholesome. Beauties!' She would carry home a lapful.

The spade rose, and the haulm bent sideways. There was no sign of a potato, not even the tiniest ones that clustered round the roots at other times. Nothing at all. Only thick black slime oozing over the spade, hanging in globules that dripped back into the earth, and over all the terrible stench.

'Sweet Mother of Jesus! Oh, Sweet Mother of God what has befallen us!' she cried.

Jamsie was down on his hands and knees scrabbling with his fingers, clawing the earth for the potatoes that must be hidden. They had to be there! They couldn't have vanished! Then he was up again, grasping the spade, his hands covered with the foul substance, digging along the row, turning over always the black slime. ''Tis maybe only this row,' he said again and again until the words ran one

352

into the other and sounded meaningless. Without stopping he dug for an hour. The sun shone down on him: sweat dripped from him mingling with the filth in the opened ground. Katy followed him from row to row, her eyes wild with desperation. The children looked on silently from the edge of the field, the twins sucking their thumbs, Bridget with an arm round Mary Kate, Thomas making circles with a lock of his hair on his forehead the way he did when something troubled him.

The cries of Danny unattended in the cottage became louder until his screams at last penetrated Katy's anguished mind, made her turn, and Bridget go running back, Katy stumbling after her.

The smell of putrefaction went with them, clinging to their hair, to their clothes, but so distracted was Katy it no longer troubled her. Danny, out of bed for the second time that day, had fallen, was wedged between the table and settle, still screaming when she arrived. Katy moved the table and picked him up. She nursed and rocked him, her hand patting his back, but said not a word of comfort, her actions mechanical, her eyes not once regarding him, staring blankly into space.

The twins and Mary Kate followed down from the field and came in. Mary Kate began to cry for her mother's attention. Katy ignored her, too. The twins, disturbed by Katy's unusual behaviour, leant against each other and held hands. Bridget attempted to comfort her small sister who refused it and clung to her mother's skirt. After a while Peg and Nora feigning indifference turned their backs and stood in the doorway watching Jamsie still digging, and Thomas moving along the rows behind him, his eyes searching the ground as if he might find the vanished potatoes.

'Take him,' Katy said as if talking to herself, but out loud, when Danny refused to be pacified, holding him at arm's length towards Bridget. Then with Mary Kate still clinging to her skirt she sat down and one by one unfastened the child's fingers, and pushed her away. Mary Kate screamed. Katy pulled her apron up in front of her face so it covered her head and began to cry, crying from deep within her, hiccuping sounds that jerked her back and shoulders.

Bridget walked the floor trying to quieten Danny, Mary Kate now clinging to her petticoat, the kitchen reverberated with the crying children and the weeping woman.

At last Danny fell asleep, his head lolling on Bridget's shoulder. She was staggering under his weight but afraid to lay him down for fear he woke. Mary Kate stopped sobbing, wiped her eyes with filthy hands leaving her pale face streaked with dirt. The twins came back from the door – looked in bewilderment at their mother, approached and gently touched her. She did not respond, they backed away and crept under the table to lay with the dog.

The light was beginning to fade, and the fire almost out when Statia arrived. Going up to Katy she put her arms round her and pulled her close.

'Child I'm sorry, may God comfort you.' Katy ignored the proffered sympathy, continuing to cry, to keep her face covered by the apron. Statia bore with her, offered comfort for a while longer, but when the while lasted too long she pulled the apron from Katy's face. 'Come on now, you've had your cry. Let that be enough. There's no one dead, not

354

himself, nor one of your children. Get up and see to them. They're dirty and hungry. Cold too for the spark's nearly gone from the fire, and half demented with fear. And no wonder with you keening as if everyone in the world was dead and buried. Get up, Katy O'Hara, do you hear me?'

Katy raised her head and stared dazedly round the room, wiping her eyes with the corner of her apron, long sighs shuddering through her body.

'Look at them!' Statia commanded. 'Look at them, girl!'

She saw Bridget weary with the weight of the child, Mary Kate fastened leech-like at her petticoat, the twins peering from under the table. 'Ah I'm sorry, I'm so sorry. Give me the baby, Bridget, sure he's too heavy for you. Commere to me, all of you,' she held open her arms. They came to her. She took Daniel, Bridget standing by her, putting an arm round her shoulders, the twins knelt before her, Mary Kate burrowed between them finding a place for her head on her mother's lap. Katy was crying quietly now, tears falling down her face, Peg and Nora reaching to wipe them, to kiss her.

Statia let the kissing and crying go on for a few moments. 'That's enough now,' she said brusquely. 'Away out and find a few twigs, we'll want a good fire, you'll want something to eat, and your father a wash.'

'There's nothing, only a handful of meal,' Katy said when they'd gone for the firewood.

'I brought another bit, and a drain of milk. It's on the table. Put down that lump of a child and make stirabout. You'll manage, it's not the end of the world. Crops have been lost before, maybe I'll lose mine tomorrow. Crying won't alter anything. Make the porridge.'

It was dark when Thomas and Jamsie came in from the field. 'Every one,' he said, 'every one,' he repeated quietly as though the room was empty and he talking to himself, 'all rotten, not sign, nor shape of a potato. Nothing, only the slime, the thick black slime.'

'Whisht now, Jamsie boy, 'tis God's will whatever it is. Fill the bucket for him, Katy, to stoup his feet, and throw them shoes to air.'

While Jamsie washed, Katy stirred the oatmeal. Ruefully he said, 'And there we were thinking Tim was wandering, and it the truth.'

'To think we knew and did nothing,' said Katy.

'The government must have known, too. That's what the constable was after, and not poteen, isn't it plain to see,' Statia remarked, and then wondered how her crop and those of the neighbours would fare. 'With God's help let it only be yours affected and between us we'll make up the difference,' she said before going home.

'I'm that troubled in my mind I won't close my eyes,' Katy forecast as she bid her goodnight.

But despite her uneasy mind and heavy heart she was no sooner in bed than she slept. Then it was morning, for an instant on wakening she forgot the previous day, till the smell pervading the cottage brought memory and with it fear, but also the beginning of resignation, for though the potatoes might be destroyed, the fire had to be re-kindled, Jamsie and the children seen to, the remains of the stirabout warmed.

She got up, pulled on her bodice and skirt, went out and up behind the bushes, deliberately not looking in the direction of the ruined field. Returning the dog followed her into the kitchen, making a fuss, licking her bare feet. She revived the fire, raking away the white ash, feeding in small bits of twigs and turf till it lived again.

Kneeling by the end of the settle she said her morning prayers. Thanking God for bringing her safely through the night, asking for His grace to help her through the day, and for all the potatoes not yet lifted to be spared. Rising, she went back to the door, able now to face sight of the devastated field. Again she repeated her prayer that the neighbours might be spared, not wanting harm to befall them, knowing that in the coming months her family's hope of surviving lay in the salvation of their potatoes.

She put the porridge to warm, then called Jamsie and the children. Bridget and Thomas came out of the room looking tidy, the twins had their clothes half on and half off, Mary Kate in her shift, following them into the kitchen. Katy brought out Danny, his face rosy and crumpled from sleep, the rag with which she bound him at night hanging down, soaking. She held him close, loving him, the smell of him.

She gave Jamsie the first helping of meal, and thinned the remainder. She shared with Danny the few mouthfuls put for herself, then put him to the breast.

The day was fine like the previous one, a day, she thought, when it should have been a pleasure to be lifting. A day when in other years Jamsie would have gone to Statia's with a light step, whistling as he went. When he and Peader would have made short work of the task, when the children would have followed along the rows throwing the discarded stalks to one side, the women gathered gossiping, giving thanks as the potatoes came up. Celebrated the new crop by boiling more than enough for the evening meal, and spent the evening in one of the other cottages rejoicing, telling stories, singing, if the humour took them, dancing to the fiddle, and if there was no fiddle to the mouth music.

Now it was all different, silence reigning as Jamsie and Peader began to dig Statia's field while she and Katy looked fearfully on.

''Twas brave words I spoke yesterday,' Statia said; 'they're easy enough to find for someone else's loss.'

The spade came out of the ground, black slime dripped from it. 'Oh Sacred Heart of Jesus, pity us,' she screamed. From surrounding fields came the wailing of other women as the state of their crop was revealed, cries of desolation and abandonment floating on the calm air.

That evening the neighbours gathered in Katy's. Hannah reminded them of Father Bolger's sermon the previous year. The women quickly crossed themselves, terror clutching their hearts as they recalled the priest's words, believing God had singled them out – made an example of them. Each remembering occasions when they had offended Him. Statia bringing to mind ridiculing Father Bolger on the very day he had warned them. Mary sorry for her loose tongue, and Katy plagued with guilt for letting thoughts of love for a man not her husband, hatred and jealousy of Miss Charlotte dwell in her heart. And all the while God had been watching them, knowing their secrets, biding His time.

And yet, terrified though she was at maybe having brought down the wrath of God, Katy could not completely banish from her mind thoughts of Peader. How this very minute he was above at the farm raising his crop, how all his arrangements for leaving were made – a price already agreed for his potatoes if they were sound. And what matter if they weren't, neither him nor Miss Charlotte would suffer. In America they'd have plenty and each other. 'Let me not think of them,' she silently prayed. 'Let me not offend You again, dear God. Haven't I enough torment thinking of my family in want. Let them go and be gone. Put an end to the shame that sweeps over me whenever I think of what I did, make my heart whole again.'

'Glory be to God they're safe and sound, every one of them. Growing in the field next to mine, and there's not a blemish on them.' Dinny, back from Peader's field, was beside himself with joy and wonder. Soon after him came Jamsie and Peader.

'Could you believe it?' Dinny kept saying. 'How could such a thing happen?'

The next morning Peader came to the cottage early. 'I'll not sell,' he announced. 'I'll share them according to everyone's needs – you'll get the most because of the children,' he addressed himself to Katy. She couldn't raise her eyes to look him in the face, shame and gratitude filling her, making it impossible to give her thanks. This was the first time since her confession of love she had been in his presence, and she didn't know what to do, but knew she couldn't sit silent before such a generous gesture. Then, before she was forced to say anything, Hannah arrived.

'Peader, it's bad news I'm afraid. I've a note from Miss Charlotte.'

'What's up?' His voice alarmed. 'What ails her, she's not sick?'

'She's not, here, read it, she'll explain it all.'

Katy watched the letter change hands, saw Peader tear the envelope, the colour drain from his face as he read, heard the break in his voice. 'She isn't coming! She's not coming to America – she can't leave her father.'

'Why not, what's changed her mind?' Jamsie asked.

'You wouldn't ask if you saw the Master, the poor man's heartbroken over the loss of everyone's potatoes,' Hannah replied.

'Oh my God!' Katy thought, as the realization dawned on her of what had happened, 'I wished for them not to go – willed for something to happen. But not this, not for my wish to be granted in such a way. I didn't mean for an affliction to be brought on everyone. That wasn't my doing. Surely I didn't make this happen?'

Peader folded up the letter, put it in his pocket and said he'd have to be going. All the joy he had experienced when unearthing his potatoes, his pleasure at being able to help his neighbours, vanished from his mind as he hurried home to read again Charlotte's letter.

Darling Love,

I've lain awake all night thinking what to do. And now, though it breaks my heart to tell you, I've decided I can't leave – not yet, not while Papa is like this.

If only you could see him, you'd know I can do nothing else but stay. You wouldn't believe the change in him – he's become old overnight and I fear for his sanity. He's convinced the tenants will die, and that it's his fault, for he has no money to help them.

Tomorrow I'll meet you, but I had to send word immediately.

I love you too much to have let you go on believing for even one more minute that everything was all right. I love you so much.

Charlotte

Alone, sitting in his room, stripped of what few personal adornments until last week it had held, Peader put his head in his hands and cried. He had lost her, he was convinced – she would never come now. Her father would get worse, day after day she would postpone leaving him. Now she would never be his wife, lay beside him in the night. There was nothing in front of them, only secret meetings in a wood. Walking along a road waiting for a whistle to tell him the way was clear. His little brown bird that he loved more than his life was lost to him.

In their meeting place he held her close, this time she cried, and he dried her tears. 'All right, all right, there now, don't cry, we'll put up with it for the time being, sure it can't be helped.'

'Oh Peader, if you could only see him, you wouldn't believe it's the same man. I couldn't leave him, he'd die, I know he would. If only Catherine was here, she'd know what to do, she would help him.'

'Maybe he'll mend, we'll wait. Maybe,' he said, though he didn't believe it, 'help will come from England, from Dublin, relief or something. We could go then. In the springtime when the boats sail again, by then something will turn up.'

Eagerly she clutched at the straw. 'Yes, that's what we'll do, Papa will get better, everyone's bound to help. It'll be all right, in the springtime it will all be better.'

*

361

Gathering in each other's houses of an evening gradually the story of the failure was being pieced together from word brought by travellers stopping off at Carey's, news that Tim heard in the town, and items which Peader read from papers and penny journals. All over the land some had lost their crops, while others, like Peader, had been spared. The women found a little comfort knowing that Kilgoran wasn't the only place afflicted. Maybe, after all, it wasn't the wrath of God, but something different altogether.

But *what*, they and the men wondered? And where did it come from? Did it fall out of the sky, or rise from the bowels of the earth? Was it the unnatural weather further back, or the frost early in the year? Jamsie suggested it was the new manure, birds' droppings brought in from foreign parts that caused it, until reminded no one in the vicinity used it.

Dinny believed he had the answer. 'Too much interference with nature,' he proclaimed. 'Men thinking they'd mastered God's secrets! Pulling light from the sky to make electricity! Putting iron roads across the land for carriages without horses to run on.'

Tim was adamant that if his warning had been heeded and the potatoes dug early, all would have been saved.

'Pity then you didn't heed it yourself,' Dinny retorted, and an argument developed between the two of them until Peader said whether they'd dug early or not made no difference, for some that had been sound when dug, in days or even hours developed running sores and rotted in the pit. They learned to call the strange malady by many names, a cholera of potatoes, a dysentery, a murrain, a

362

blight, got used to it, even to the smell which lingered, and hope remained. Help would come from somewhere when the small stock of potatoes given by Peader was gone, when anything they could sell was sold; and next year please God the crop would be sound, plenty always followed scarcity.

Peader shared none of their optimism. No one would help, he told them. Lord Kilgoran might have, had he the means, but they all knew his situation.

'If you've any sense hold back the November rent, sell whatever you can and get out – go to America.'

Katy watched his face while he spoke, saw the bitterness in it, and knew his concern was not wholly for them. From Hannah, who got it from Miss Charlotte, she knew how he railed against a system which forced him to keep secret his love affair, the fear that consumed him at the prospect of it being discovered and Charlotte forbidden ever to see him again. She felt grief for him, and love still, he didn't deserve such a thing to happen to him, he was proud and open, shouldn't be forced to practise deception.

'No one will lift a finger to help, and shall I tell you why?' Peader paused, everyone waited for him to tell them. 'It's against the Government policy – what they call "laissez faire" – interfering with the economy they'd be if they gave free food, or cheaper food, going against what all of them believe in. All them with money – the landowners, shipowners, merchants, even down to the little shop-keepers, every one of them supports the policy. That's why there'll be no free food, no cheap food – for who'd buy if they got for nothing, or next to nothing; business everywhere would be ruined. That's how they think, that's why there'll be no interference, that's why we'll starve.'

'Musha then, Peader, isn't that a queer way for the Government to think?' Jamsie said. 'Sure we haven't any money to buy cheap or dear, we never had. There isn't one in the kitchen tonight who earns a wage except Hannah there.'

'Isn't that my point? Isn't that what I'm telling you? Why, if you don't hold back rent, and go as soon as sailing starts again you're done for. You'll all starve.'

'God spoke before you, Peader – it's all in His hands,' Hannah said, and the women eager to find consolation agreed with her. 'And anyway I'd say you're exaggerating about everything. Nobody's starved yet, and they won't, you're adding to things, and that's not like you,' Hannah reproved gently.

'Exaggerating! Is that what you think?' Peader raised his voice. 'Well isn't that the queer thing to say and you living in the middle of it. Then there's no minding them in London and Dublin who are saying the same thing.' He picked up a journal, hitting it with the flat of his hand for emphasis. 'It's in here. An exaggeration – that's what the failure is. The Irish always exaggerate. Never use one word where three will do. That's how they think of us. We're great characters, easily dismissed. And sure who's to blame them if you, Hannah, think the same.'

Katy saw Hannah's face crumple before Peader's tirade, her hands move agitatedly in her lap, and knew if the conversation wasn't changed her kind gentle Hannah would be made to cry. 'Do you know?' she said, making it up as she went along, 'a woman I met above on the road,

364

a stranger, told me how in Macroom last week, there was a calf born with two heads.' The topic was taken up, some denying the possibility of such a thing, others recalling similar happenings, and the remainder of the evening passed with no more talk of the failure or government.

Chapter Sixteen

To spare the potatoes given by Peader, Katy ate very little, filling herself instead with water so that her hollow belly swelled. At mealtimes she gave Jamsie the largest helping, sharing the remainder according to each child's size. The twins, voracious eaters when food was plentiful, constantly complained about their meagre portions.

Sometimes Katy only scolded them, reminding them they were lucky to have anything. Other times she slapped them, and was sorry afterwards for she knew that like everyone they were constantly hungry but, unlike herself and Jamsie, even Bridget and Thomas were unable to understand the calamity which had befallen them.

Hannah continued to bring scraps when they were available, Peader sometimes gave a fish, and Statia, if given part of a rabbit poached by a grateful new father, shared that. It all helped, but soon Katy knew no matter how carefully she eked out the potatoes something would have to be sold, or starvation would look them in the face. She considered what she had. There was the pig – he was a good size, and it might be as well to let him go, he was hard to feed. Sometimes at night she woke and lay afraid in the dark, wondering if Peader was right, were things as bad as he said, would they get worse? Should they not pay the rent and keep the money for a passage to America – it wouldn't be enough, but might be with what she got for the pig, that was if she held on until he was the right size for bacon. Round and round in her mind went her troubles, filling it, so she scarcely thought of Peader and Charlotte. She was grateful for the warmth and comfort of Jamsie in the bed beside her, and often reached for him, and he took her while still half asleep.

Then one morning Statia told her Connolly was buying things.

'What sort of things?'

'Like Dano before him, whatever he thinks he'll make a penny on,' Statia said, and when Katy was alone she went into the bedroom and pulled from under the bed the box with her treasures. She lifted them out one by one and laid them on the quilt, the cups and saucers from the Lodge, a tablecloth of her mother's, yellowed along its folded lines from lack of use, the twins' cauls wrapped in a piece of rag, and the peacock blue dress she had worn to her wedding. She shook out the gown and held it up to her, keeping it in place by bending her chin, her hands smoothing out the creases, her fingers caressing the silk. The scent of Miss Catherine was still about it. Katy inhaled it, the perfume evoking memories of the day she had received it, the day she wore it to be married. – Isn't it the queer thing about smell, how it brings everything back as if you were looking at it, she thought, and saw her mother altering, pinning and tucking the dress about her. Saw herself on the morning she first wore it, remembered seeing herself in the glass and thinking she was beautiful; then her disappointment when after Bridget the dress

367

didn't fit her, and how she put it away with her treasures, saving it for some lovely time in the future.

– Now it would have to go, it and the cloth, the cups and saucers too. It wasn't a bit of good thinking about the past – there'd be no lovely times for a while, certainly not until next year and the new crop, please God. She wrapped the dress round the china, and the cloth round them all, and set off for the shop.

Connolly's was six miles distant. Katy had not been there since the previous Christmas and was surprised by the changes. The shop had been partitioned, but in such a way you could see the two parts from the door. One half still held the groceries, the hams and shawls hanging from the ceiling, everything squeezed up and packed closer together, the two chairs Katy saw were still there for well-to-do customers to rest on while their orders were taken. The smell of smoked bacon, cheese and currants wafting out made her feel weak with hunger.

She could see that the other side of the shop was now no more than a narrow passage, that the counter wasn't altered, but the shelves which had once held bales of stuff were jammed with used bedding, clothes and spades, boots and shoes, holy pictures and mirrors, and that the narrow passage was crowded with women, bundles under their arms, pots and kettles still black with soot in their hands. Beside one of the laden women Katy noticed a little girl with a heavy bucket dragging her arm trying to keep close to her mother.

She entered and moved along in the crowd till she got to where Connolly's young son was doing business, casting a quick discerning eye over the offerings, and stating a price. There was no bargaining; the women accepted, grumbling and calling down the malediction of God on the son and his robber of a father as they pushed their way back through the throng.

Katy got four shillings for her bundle, went round the partition and bought a stone of meal. 'Three shillings,' Connolly said. She asked for a piece of soap, then saw the Christmas candles, and asked for one. 'That'll be three and eightpence,' Connolly told her. She knew the candle was an extravagance, but sure what did it matter, wasn't she robbed anyway with meal three shillings a stone. All hope of making the money last was gone, and what would Christmas be without a light burning through the Holy Night? Didn't you have to have something more than just food? Connolly had surely robbed her – he had her treasures and the money back as well she thought, picking up the fourpence change and her purchases. 'Well, may all my bad luck go with them, and God forgive him and his likes for afflicting people in their terrible want,' she said to herself as she began the journey back.

The Mass was almost over, Father Bolger kneeling at the foot of the altar saying the concluding prayers. There was a stir in the congregation, shawls were adjusted, rosaries slipped into pockets, men's hands reached for their caps. Then instead of when he rose from praying returning to the sacristy, the priest turned to the people and addressed them.

'There's an announcement I have to make concerning the failure.' A fit of coughing seized him and while he cleared his chest the men and women strained forward eager for him to continue his speech, hope evident on their faces, waiting to hear tell of a miracle.

'As you know,' Father Bolger continued, 'there's men above in Dublin looking into things, educated men, men of science that came over from England for that purpose. They've been studying the disease and have suggestions. Not to raise your hopes, I'll tell you how they seem to know as much about it as I do about sailing the seven seas. But that doesn't stop them giving advice. There's leaflets been sent down to all parishes – thirty copies per parish. So I'd ask those of you that have English to take one apiece and read it to your neighbours. It'll give you a laugh if nothing else. God Bless you now.'

Jamsie and Peader went round to the priest's house to collect the leaflet, Statia, Katy and the children going on ahead. 'Isn't it well for the gentlemen in Dublin with nothing to do but give advice,' Statia remarked on the way home.

'Indeed,' Katy agreed, and when they arrived at Statia's told her to come to the cottage. 'The men won't be long after us, come, do, we might as well hear what's to be said.'

While they waited Statia sat up to the fire, and Katy put on the pot of meal that had been steeping overnight, stirring and talking at the same time.

Jamsie and Peader came soon and Dinny Crowley with them. They were laughing when they came in. 'Tell us so, what did the men in Dublin have to say?' Katy asked. The pot boiled and she moved it up from the heat, and sat down.

'Oh, wait till you hear, it's grand advice,' Jamsie replied

and she recognized the mockery in his voice for all that
he smiled. Statia got up from the stool to let the men close
to the fire and sat by Katy on the settle.

'Go on then, Peader, read it to us, we're dying with
curiosity,' Katy urged.

'Tell me first have you such a thing as a grater?' Peader
inquired, his face serious and voice earnest.

'I have not.'

'Or a fine hair sieve?'

'No, and well you know it, why?'

Then with a straight face still he informed her gravely,
'In that case I'd be wasting my breath reading the leaflet.'
Jamsie and Dinny laughed aloud.

'Ah, give over and read the thing for the Lord's sake,'
Statia said impatiently, 'haven't we been killed waiting.'

Peader then began to read instructions for making
partly diseased potatoes into bread. The sound flesh was
to be grated, sieved into a tub, the pulp washed, squeezed
and dried on a griddle over a slack fire. If a fine sieve was
not available fine linen could be used instead. The water
in which the pulp had been washed would now contain
starch. If meal, or flour, and the dried pulp was added to
it a wholesome bread could be made from the mixture.

Katy and Statia looked more amazed by the minute, and
when Peader paused in the reading, Statia asked, 'Are they
amadhauns or what, the same men! Fine hair sieves,
graters and linen! Did you ever hear the like! And even if
we had such things, where's the money coming from for
flour and meal? And if we had the money who'd be killing
themselves rasping and grating.'

'Not to mention,' said Katy, 'that the smell, never mind

the taste of partly diseased potatoes would poison you.'

'The men in Dublin have thought of all your objections – the obstacles in your way. They know the work and worry it will be, and that at first you mightn't succeed. They're very considerate, God bless them,' Peader said with bitter irony. 'They're understanding sort of men, and what's more have faith in us. Let me see now for a minute how they put it.' He glanced down at the leaflet. 'Ah yes, listen to this, it's great encouragement. "Never let it be said that a true Irishman wouldn't exert himself, wouldn't have the courage to meet difficulties other nations are overcoming." Now, what do you think of that? Doesn't it give you great heart?'

'The curse of God on them, and all the eejits like them,' Dinny spat into the fire.

'I didn't know the blight was anywhere else as bad,' Jamsie said.

'Well, if it is I'll tell you this, nowhere else where it might be are the people depending on potatoes for their life – nowhere else in the world except Ireland.'

The October weather stayed fine, cool, but the days were bright and crisp. Everywhere an autumnal beauty garbed the land, leaves of oak, elm and beech golden and russet, bright red berries, bracken curling, the grain fields pale stubbled, everything in accordance with its season. Only the potato patches stood out like an eyesore, the earth upturned like giant mole hills, the discarded stalks rotten, littering the ground, for few had had heart to clear them.

Every time Katy looked at them fear clutched her heart,

the memory of the day they lifted returned, the evilness of the smell, and she asked herself, what if it should happen again? Like everyone else when not confronted with the evidence of the blight, she said and wanted to believe that plenty always followed scarcity, that God wouldn't let the same thing happen twice, but doubts came – in the small hours – in the bright October days while looking at the stricken fields.

Then a day came when Katy knew the pig would have to go. She told Jamsie of her decision, and he agreed to take it to market.

'Get a good price now,' she called after him on the morning he set off. It was a fine morning and Jamsie was enjoying the walk. Now and then he stopped to pass the time of day with a neighbour. Sometimes he had to make way on the narrow road for carts taking strong farmers' wives and their produce to market. – Plenty of food, he thought, eggs and butter wrapped in cabbage leaves, fowls and the like for them with money. He met others like himself on the way, poor men driving the one cow or pig, forced to sell or starve.

The fair was thronged, the narrow streets packed with people and cattle, inches deep in dung, pools of water, stained bright yellow. The public houses were packed, noise, laughter and the smell of porter spilling out. Jamsie passing thought how well a jar would slake his thirst, walked on and saw women with baskets of potatoes, offering them for sale, urging people to buy, and knew they were eager to get rid of them in case the little running sores appeared and they dissolved in corruption.

He guided the pig in and out of the crowd to where the selling was.

'Be Jasus, they're a robbing lot of hoors!' a raw-boned, red-headed man barring his way said. 'The finest bonham you ever saw – one that last year I'd have got my price for. Today I got nothing. Look at that!' He held out his hand with a few shillings in it. 'I've a good mind to go back and throw it in your man's face – the hoor, and take my pig home. The wife will kill me.' He looked again ruefully at the money in his palm, shook his head, laughed and turned into the nearest public house.

– The wife will surely kill you now, Jamsie thought, like mine will if I don't get a decent price. He noticed when he arrived at the pen an atmosphere not as usual. No clapping of backs, or spitting on hands when money was exchanged, and no bargaining. Only the buyer stating his price in a take it or leave it way – the sellers looking dejected, accepting. 'Five shillings,' the dealer said.

'In the name of Jasus, are you having me on – I gave that when I bought it – I've been feeding it since – look at the size of it.'

'Five shillings,' the man repeated, and Jamsie knew he had to take it. He walked back through the fair, past the public house into which the red-headed man had gone, and was sorely tempted. Stood for a minute on the step, listening to the laughter, and drunken voices singing, thinking it would be grand to go in, vent his feelings at the way he'd been robbed with others in the same predicament. He remembered Katy, and turned to go, then said aloud, 'Ah to hell with it all,' and went in.

Katy watched the sun, knew by its descent Jamsie

374

would soon be home. The next time she looked it was almost gone and no sign of him. She didn't have a doubt as to what he was doing, but wasn't sure where – he could be in Carey's or not have left the town. – If I could be sure it was Carey's I'd risk making a show of myself and go down, maybe I could stop him spending every penny.

She kept listening and watching by the door for sight or sound of him, and went running up the boreen when she heard the sound of footsteps above on the road. She nearly died when she saw it was Peader. 'Katy,' he said, 'are you looking for someone?'

'For Jamsie – I thought you were him. Was he below?'

'No, I haven't laid eyes on him all day.'

– How would you, she thought, and you no doubt wrapped up in the arms of Miss Charlotte above in the woods.

'He went in to sell the pig, he's late,' she explained.

'Will I walk back a bit of the way and see if he's coming?'

'No, don't,' she replied quickly, knowing the state Jamsie would be in, that Peader would escort him, come into the cottage – she couldn't bear to see the two of them together. Couldn't be faced with a drunken husband – a waster who has spent what she was depending on for food, and the man she might have married. 'Go you home now, he'll be along soon.'

'Goodnight then, Katy.'

'Goodnight,' she said, and went back to the cottage and waited. Jamsie came soon afterwards. She looked to the door as he entered, saw him sway, clutch the wall for support. – That's what I married, she thought contemptuously, and wanted to scream with rage, to fling herself at him, hurt him, somehow make him realize the enormity of what he had done. But she restrained herself, remained seated, looking at him.

'What ails you, aghra, you're very quiet?' He sat down opposite her.

– Don't even open your mouth to him, don't answer him – he's stocious, footless. Leave it till morning, she told herself. But anger got the better of her. 'Where's the money from the pig?' she screamed. 'What have you done with it – the money to take the hunger off your children. Where is it?'

She watched him make an effort to understand what she was saying, an effort he couldn't sustain, his eyelids drooped, he began to snore.

'Where is it?' Her voice was frenzied. She got up from the stool, ran to him, caught hold of his shirt with both hands shaking him, her rage lending her strength, so she raised his chest and shoulders and shook him like a terrier worrying a rat. Her screaming woke the children, Bridget and Thomas came from the bedroom, the twins following them, stood cowering, watching Katy rock Jamsie back and forth hitting his head against the wall.

'You're hurting him, Mammy, stop it, you're banging his head, you'll hurt him, stop, Mammy, stop!' Thomas was beside her, pulling at her arms.

'I'll kill him. I'll kill him – he sold the pig and spent the money, all that I had in the world.'

Jamsie stood up, pushed away her grasping hands, swayed as if he would fall, steadied himself, and went out the back.

'Listen to that, listen, do you hear?' she commanded the

children. 'That's him vomiting up the money. That's your father for you. Listen to that. That's the price of the pig, what would have kept you from starving.'

She recognized the accusation in Thomas' and Bridget's eyes before first one, then the other said, 'Daddy's only sick. He's very sick,' and they made to go after him. Katy called them back.

Peg and Nora came to Katy, their faces perplexed with fright at having to take sides, but they had chosen, had sensed that she was the one in need, she the one sick in heart and mind. They clung to her, saying nothing, just holding on to her. She drew comfort from them, calmness, so her rage abated, her reason returned, felt sorrow that all of them had witnessed such a terrible scene.

'Your father's better now, listen, he's stopped being sick. Go on into bed. It'll be all right now, everything'll be all right in the morning. Go on in now, I'm sorry I woke you.' The four of them went into the room. After a while Katy looked out through the door and saw Jamsie sprawled on the ground. For a minute she got a fright thinking he was injured, had fallen, struck his head. She went to see, he was sleeping, she left him.

'May God forgive you,' she said the next morning, 'for I never will.' He began to explain, make excuses about the fair, how he was disappointed at not getting enough for the pig.

'I want to hear none of it. You took the bit out of your children's mouths – you've left them to starve, and I'll do the same to you. From now on what comes into the place you'll get no share of. The flesh can melt from your bones, and if pity touches me I'll remind myself of last night. You can die before my eyes and I won't care.'

She denied him food, feeding what small amounts were available to the children when he wasn't in, hardening her heart not to put by a portion for him; in the same way she denied him her body, sleeping as far from him as the pallet would allow, wakening instantly if his hand reached for her in the night, pushing it away. Once she dreamed he forced her, as he had the night years ago when Peader came back from Dublin, and in the dream she rejoiced that he had, and woke to the reality of their separateness.

Never in her life had she known such misery; the meal and potatoes were finished, they existed on the scraps Hannah gave, berries, and an occasional fish brought by Peader when he came to collect or leave Charlotte's messages. In the presence of the neighbours Jamsie acted as if all was well between them but, when they were alone, never spoke to her, never complained about not getting a share of the food. She longed to give in, it scalded her heart to know he must be twice as hungry as she was, starving, for a week had passed since the night he came in drunk, and the flesh was melting from him. Surreptitiously she regarded his face, saw the hollow cheeks, his pallor, and cried inwardly for what had happened between them. Sometimes she believed it was all a punishment from God – the failure of the crop, the silent bitterness she and Jamsie showed to each other, it was God's displeasure that she had wanted a man not her husband. His commandments were not to be mocked. He had shown His hand, and signs on it she was paying the price for her sins; for

378

her jealousy of Miss Charlotte. Wasn't it plain to see? – Peader's crop had thrived, he and Miss Charlotte were together, loving each other – off to America in the spring. All her scheming, wishing and wanting had been in vain. All the suffering her children were enduring was her doing.

One day when such despair claimed her she knelt down on the floor by the settle and prayed. Asking God's forgiveness. Promising to amend her faults, to banish jealousy from her heart, to share what she had with Jamsie, attempting to block from her mind the memory of what he had done with the money. Kneeling with her arms on the corner of the settle, her head bent upon them, so intent was she on asking for help and forgiveness, she did not hear Statia come into the kitchen.

Statia stood and waited until Katy raised her head. 'Oh, it's you,' she said, looking round. 'I didn't hear anyone. I was saying a prayer.'

'Well, maybe it's answered. There's great news. Daniel O'Connell and the Dublin Corporation are going to the Lord Lieutenant, no less, to demand food for the people.'

'Thanks be to God!'

'Sure I never doubted that Dan would stand by and see us starve. He'll soon tell them in Dublin what's what.'

'Oh, he will, and he'll succeed, I can feel it here inside me.' Katy's hand hovered near her heart. 'The end of our suffering's in sight, all our prayers are answered.'

She felt happiness well up within her – the bad times were at an end – today Jamsie would have his share of the food, the silence would be banished, all be as it was, and next year there'd be so many potatoes a regiment couldn't lift them.

There was a small yellow turnip for the dinner, not more than a spoonful each when it was boiled. 'Eat that,' she said, offering it to Jamsie.

He looked from her to the vegetable, then back again. 'I don't want it.'

'But you'll have to eat, you'll starve.'

'So I have for a week – the way you said I would.'

'Oh for the Lord's sake, Jamsie,' she said impatiently, 'eat it will you!'

'I won't.'

'Then turn your arse to it!'

She went out of the room before her temper got the better of her. Later when she returned the turnip was gone. – He drew in his horns, she thought, but if he thinks everything's back to normal he has another one coming – and at night she continued to move away from him in the bed.

On a raw damp morning Daniel O'Connell left his house in Merrion Square for the journey to Dublin Castle where, with other prominent citizens, he would put to the Lord Lieutenant proposals to avert the calamity facing the poor of Ireland.

Before descending the flight of granite steps, he paused on the top one and looked up the street for sight of the mountains. Today the mist obscured them, and today more than ever he needed sight of them. They weren't as grand or glorious as those of his native Kerry, but mountains all the same. Immutable as so little in life was. He could raise his eyes to them, draw strength and hope from them. They reminded him of his youth. Such a long time ago. The life that was in him then, the joy, the hopes he had held. All gone. And going so gradually, a day, a minute, a second at a time, that you never noticed until one day you were an old man. A tired old man. Others saw it too. He was finished, they said, old, worn out. The charitable ones blamed it on his imprisonment.

He stood for a moment longer staring in the direction of where the mountains hid behind the mist, longing for a glimpse of them. Then, as if in response to his will, the mist shifted, the sun appeared and they were visible. His face became transfused with joy, and he stared oblivious of all else.

At the kerb the waiting coachman stamped his feet, and swung round his arms clapping them against his back to keep warm. The horse's breath seemed solid on the freezing air. The sun went, the mist closed over the mountains. Daniel shivered, and wrapped tightly round him his great frieze cloak. Had he glimpsed them, he wondered, or was his mind like his strength also deserting him? Turning away, he quickly descended the steps. The coachman tipped his hat, and opened the carriage door. 'It's a bad day, Sir. No sign of it lifting.'

Daniel nodded, got in and leant back against the black leather, buttoned upholstery. – A bad day, aye, that's what it will turn out to be, he thought, as the carriage moved off. But he would do his best, a man could do no more than that. Along the Square the coach went, the horses' hooves clattering on the cobbles, turned the corner towards Saint Stephen's Green while Daniel pursued his thoughts.

Uppermost in his mind a presentiment that the cause he intended pleading was already doomed: that preconceived notions existed, notions not admitting the reality of the potato failure, the plight of the people. If he was right the poor of Ireland would die in their thousands, those who had flocked to his meetings, placing their pennies, their hopes in his hands.

The carriage turned down Grafton Street, slowly proceeding, for the narrow winding street was choked with vehicles, conveyances, Daniel saw, of the rich, of elegant women browsing or buying in the fashionable shops. At College Green traffic brought his coach to a halt. Looking through the window he surveyed the scene; people going about their business, students from Trinity College, and the beggars. Always the students and the beggars, he thought, watching the limbless, blind, faces eaten by sores, every describable malady, there they were appealing for alms, the genuine and the mountebanks. But no more than usual. No sign yet of the destitute hordes starving because of the rotten potatoes. But come they would, leaving cottages and cabins, deserting villages, swarming alarming hordes of them, fleeing starvation, attempting to evade death.

In and out of Trinity strolled the students while Daniel mused on the plight of the people, and watched the young men of fine cut – the privileged Protestants. So once long ago must Swift, and Goldsmith, Burke and Wolf Tone have strolled, men who became poets and patriots, clergymen and politicians, Protestants, too, but good men with the interest of justice at heart.

Would the carriage never move forward? Was he to arrive late? He fumed while he waited, his anger casting away presentiments, visions of the future, the past. They were another side of his nature, they must be dismissed. He was a lawyer, facts were his business, facts he must consider.

Peel, the Prime Minister, knew in August blight had crossed the Atlantic, knew there wasn't a sound potato in Covent Garden, that the disease was rampant in Belgium. And what had been done? Nothing! Not a hand lifted when everyone knew that once the disease reached Ireland starvation would follow as surely as night followed day. Nothing but useless advice, how to make bread from stinking potatoes, suggestions to heat them to temperatures for which you'd need a furnace not a turf fire, and some fool of a Duke recommending curry powder as a means of satisfying hunger. Curry powder, someone had queried? 'Why not,' replied the Duke, 'the natives of India thrive on it.'

At last there was movement, the carriage went on up Dame Street and began to ascend Cork Hill. Food was what was needed, the ports thrown open to let it in. Distilling and brewing of grain stopped. Corn stopped from leaving the country. Work provided so people could buy the food.

The coach turned into the Castle yard, drew up behind others of the deputation. While he waited to alight, his mind slipped back to previous years, to the day at Tara. How certain he had been then that his methods were the right ones, that they would succeed. But were they, he pondered? Or should he have heeded those in the Movement who urged the unleashing of the giant he held before Clontarf? Could it have wrested power from this place he was about to enter? And if it had, what of the present situation? Blight would still have crossed the Atlantic. But the consequences would have been different – dealt with more humanely. Yes, of that he was sure. More efficiently – who could tell? They were imponderables.

Of only one thing was he positive – violence was abominable. It blinded men to their original grievance, and solved nothing permanently. Bitterness was nurtured and long hatreds grew longer; down the years the savage gained reverence, became a hero. No, he thought, as a footman opened the carriage door and helped him alight, he wasn't sorry he had spurned violence, even if by so doing he had for the time being deprived Ireland of what was rightfully hers.

The Lord Lieutenant awaited the deputation, imposing, splendidly uniformed, surrounded within this ancient fortress by the panoply of state. He gave to the delegation a cold reception, denied them the opportunity of pleading their case by reading a prepared reply.

'Reports on the potato crop varied widely – contradicting each other. Therefore, it was still not possible to form an accurate opinion until digging was complete. The deputation's proposals would be placed before the Government. They must all be maturely weighed, and before the majority of them could be implemented new legislation would be required.' The Lord Lieutenant concluded, wished the deputation good day, and bowed them out.

On the return journey Daniel O'Connell slumped despondently in the carriage. The mist which earlier had obscured the mountains worsened, hovering wraith-like round street lamps, fogging entrances to narrow courts, seeping in through the coach's doors and windows. Daniel shivered and longed for the warmth of his home, longed for sleep to blot out the failure of his mission, his resentment at Lord Heytesbury's reception. The carriage jolted over the cobblestones, keeping him alert, his mind working. A reply ready to hand – there was no one like them for taking the ground from under you. Past masters at the art of dismissing; their iciness cooling your courage. It was something about them, an indefinable thing present in their countenance. Whatever their features, whether coarse or chiselled, they all had it – a coldness – an hauteur. Bred in them from years of conquest, those not born to it soon acquiring a degree once they rubbed shoulders with them that were. They appeared to lack heart and give. And both, he sadly reflected, were needed in abundance if the starving millions were to be saved.

In Dublin and throughout the country people waited hopefully for news of Lord Heytesbury's answer to the deputation. One man who had gathered with the crowd outside the Castle was sure the mission had succeeded.

'You could tell by Dan's face. By the way he waved.' The rumour spread from person to person. To a group waiting outside the Hibernian Hotel for the Bianconi, went with them into the country. At other staging posts it was repeated so that by the following day men and women everywhere believed they were to be showered with free food. The Queen was sending money. The making of whiskey for England was to stop, and be made instead for the poor, and given for nothing.

Those who believed, squandered what little they had. Boiling three or four days' supply of potatoes for one meal. Spending precious coppers for a taste of the whiskey that soon would flow through the land. Others were moved to generosity and parted with food to those less fortunate.

In Kilgoran Katy and her neighbours waited too. They also heard the rumours, but had no reserves into which they might dip, and had the warning voice of Peader telling them rumour was all it was. Dan would leave the Castle the way he went in – empty-handed.

The neighbours who had gathered in Katy's to hear Peader's news after the meeting in Tara did so once more, waiting for him to bring word of what O'Connell's visit to the Viceroy had achieved. Katy looking round at the company thought what a different scene it was tonight. None of the gaiety, Statia not tormenting Dinny Crowley with her jokes, Michael's vacant stool, the look of want and hunger on everyone's face, the bit of hope they had vanishing as Peader arrived and read from the *Freeman's Journal*.

'"They may starve! Such in spirit if not in words was the reply given yesterday by the English Viceroy to the deputation which prayed that the food of this Kingdom be preserved, lest the people thereof perish."'

'They couldn't do that, they wouldn't let us starve!' Katy said incredulously when Peader finished reading.

'They could and would. Food will keep going out of the country, grain be made into whiskey, and not a hand lifted to help the afflicted,' Peader said.

'God's curse on them! May they die roaring like a jack-ass and roast in Hell. May the grain they're robbing us of stick in their gullets and choke them, and the insides of the animals they're sending over the water swell with corruption and poison them deaf to the cries of hunger.' Dinny was breathless and purple in the face with the effort of such a long and vehement speech.

'It's to America we should have gone, and if there's no improvement I'll go with the daughter and son-in-law,' Mary Doyle declared.

'Everyone should head for it – Ireland's finished. You'll consider it, Jamsie?'

'On what?' asked Katy, irritation at Peader getting the better of her. Jealousy flaring at the thought of the ease with which he and Miss Charlotte could up and go. 'With what would we pay our way – talk is cheap.'

The curtness of her voice was not lost on Peader, he looked discomfited and said no more about America.

– Men! Katy fumed inwardly. Two that I thought I loved, and what have either of them done for me? One I made a fool of myself over, and the other a fool of me. All over me for his wants, and nothing else. Not an ounce of reliance in him, a fine chance there'd be of him foraging for a bit of food, never mind the means to go to America. And by any chance if he laid hands on the price of a fare, he'd drink it before I saw the colour of it. Look at him now, grinning all over his face at something Tim Coffey was saying – the only one in the room that appears not to have a care in the world. Handsome all right, but handsome is as handsome does.

In bed Jamsie reached for her. She shifted further from

him. He came after her, raising himself, bending above her.

'Don't touch me – take your hands off me.'

'Come on, Katy,' he coaxed, attempting to kiss her. She averted her mouth. 'Don't be like that now.' His voice was playful. 'I can touch you if I want, take you if I want.'

'You could indeed. You did once. Threw me to the ground like an animal. Took me against my will.' A part of her longed for him to do so again. She felt excitement mounting. Above her his face was shadowed, darkness hiding the hollows and haggardness that hunger had etched on it. She wanted to caress it, take him to her, cradle his head against her breast, let him suckle her. But whereas in times past her body had always triumphed, made her forget his faults, now that wasn't so. In her mind bitterness burned brightly, consuming all other feelings. Love him again she never would. He had failed her.

He moved from her, lay down and began to speak. 'You had a softness once to you, but it's been gone this long time. I've watched it go. Now there's nothing but bitterness left.'

'Is it any wonder with you for a husband, and me half mad with worry, not knowing where the next bit's coming from, watching the children fade before my eyes.'

'The change was in you this long time, it's not all the fault of the failure.' His voice was very quiet, and sad. 'I could see it happening, something eating into you. I puzzled my brains as to its cause. It wasn't only my drinking – I knew that, there was no other reason I could see. The once – the night you said I took you like an animal, I'm sorry for that, I thought you had a notion of

388

Peader, I was inflamed with jealousy. But for all that I threw you to the ground I never thought of you as an animal. I loved you. I've pleaded with you many a night since I sold the pig, I'll plead no more, nor force you neither. You've become a hard bitter woman, Katy, the girl I married is gone.'

He turned away in the bed. She lay still, silently crying, guilt surging through her, thinking of the sins she committed every time she compared Jamsie unfavourably with Peader. Hell was waiting for such a sinful woman. She must amend her life.

Jamsie shifted restlessly. Her feelings of remorse increased. She was about to turn to him, ask his forgiveness, tell him she was sorry. Then the shifting ceased, he breathed easily and evenly, she knew he slept. Her contrition evaporated. – What should I say I'm sorry for, for raising my voice when you squandered the money, for letting you know the taste of hunger? Is it down on my knees you'd like to see me, asking your pardon, you that this minute for all your broken heart is sleeping like a baby? Well I will not. The fault isn't all mine, and if you never lay a finger on me again I'll cry no tears, and what's more, thanks be to God, have no more children.

Peader clasped Charlotte to him, raining kisses on her face. 'I've missed you so much,' he said in between kissing. 'I thought I'd never see you again. Is your father better? Hannah told me he'd had a bad turn.'

'Oh, darling, darling, darling Peader! I love you. But now you must let go of me and hear the marvellous news. Papa is quite better, better from the chill he had last week, but best of all quite recovered in himself from the depression that came with the failure.'

'Thanks be to God, if that's gone then there's nothing to stop us going to America in the spring. What brought about the cure?'

'A letter from Olivia. She says great things are afoot in London to relieve the distress here. Olivia knows everyone. Remember I told you of the important people who dine there, well one of them talked about a Relief Commission being organized, and straight away she wrote with the news to Papa. Isn't that wonderful, no one is to starve, no one will die after all. You're such an old pessimist.' She reached and kissed him, then continued, 'Of course it's all very secret, especially this part – Olivia says the Prime Minister is sending in tons and tons of Indian Corn, even though it's making him unpopular with the Government. Apparently there's ructions about it. Papa was so relieved when he got the news, he got better at once. Though he's a bit of a pessimist, too. Already he's worrying in case Trevelyan, I told you about him, the one who always thinks he's right, should be in charge of supplies.

'Anyway our worries are over. By the springtime Papa will be well enough for me to leave. Imagine, only a few more months and we'll be together for always.'

Chapter Seventeen

From the Relief Commission in Dublin, letters were sent to every landowner in the country. When Lord Kilgoran's arrived, Hannah took it to the library, knocked, and waited to be called in. She noticed her Master's disappointed expression as he handled the letter and knew he had believed it was one from Miss Catherine. 'I could have told him it wasn't, there was a different feel to the paper, and the stamp wasn't the same,' she talked to herself.

– The place is in a terrible state, she thought, noticing the dust thick on the wainscoting. While I'm up here I'll give it a rub. And lifting up the hem of her skirt she began dusting the oak panelling.

Lord Kilgoran scrutinized the envelope, turning it this way and that, as if by so doing the sender's identity would be revealed. 'Not from India,' he talked to himself. 'From Dublin – official seal.' Once more he turned over the envelope before slitting it, removing the letter and beginning to read. Exclaiming when he finished, 'Absolutely ridiculous! The thing's a circular, dispatched without account taken of to whom it was sent.' He threw the letter on the desk, took off his spectacles and with finger and thumb massaged the bridge of his nose. Then rose, began pacing the floor, and began again to talk out loud, commenting on the contents of the letter.

'Organize a committee of prominent citizens, magistrates and clergymen! Don't they realize the prominent citizens have long since left Kilgoran, and with them the magistrates and clergymen. Surely Connolly and Driscoll wouldn't be considered prominent – the fellows are a pair of rogues. Connolly would want the rights to sell the Indian Corn for the highest penny, and Driscoll, if Public Works were established, claim priority for his road and ditches.

'There's no one suitable except myself and Father Bolger – a committee of two! The priest would certainly have the interest of his flock at heart. But interest's not enough. Massive funds are needed, and his experience of fund-raising is limited to collecting pennies. The damned fellows in Dublin know nothing.'

He walked to the library window and looked out over the sweep of park, saw the trees stark in the bright cold January light, and thought how it hadn't been so cold for years, not since he was a boy. The wind was vicious, it was cold enough for snow. He remembered how once long ago it had snowed. The novelty that was. Novel and beautiful. Wakening in the morning to find the world transformed, snow everywhere, white, dazzling, the prints of birds traced on it, the shapes of trees and bushes altered.

How the tenants had marvelled. He could still recall the wonder on their faces. The young men and women, the children gambolling in it; the exhilaration of riding on such a morning. It hadn't lasted. The wind changed, blew from the west as it usually did, the brilliant white blanket dissolved, disappeared.

But all that was a long time ago, a different time. Not when the potatoes had failed, not when for months people were near the point of starvation. And he was an old fool reminiscing, distracting himself from the real issue – the letter, what was he to do about that?

Returning to the desk he put on his glasses and read it again.

'The success of the venture depended upon the cooperation and contribution of the landowner. The Government will award through the Relief Commission two thirds of monies collected by local committees. At a later date the Government will award equal amounts of money.'

Despairingly Lord Kilgoran shook his head. He could not form a committee, could not contribute anything. He began to talk aloud to himself. 'They might as well ask for the moon! Don't they realize half the November rents are outstanding? Without the rents I haven't enough to pay the servants' wages, the few that remain. How can I contribute anything?'

A timorous tap on the door interrupted his soliloquy. The door opened and the anxious face of Hannah looked round it.

'You rang, Sir?'

'I didn't.'

'There's nothing you want then, Sir?'

'No, nothing at all, thank you, Hannah.'

She closed the door, and Lord Kilgoran, unaware that the sound of him talking to himself had alarmed her and made her invent hearing the bell, continued to speak aloud. 'I haven't the money, that's all there is about it. No shame in that. Must be others in the same predicament – half the country, fortunes squandered keeping up appearances, on horses, hounds, parties, spendthrift owners and sons.'

He became silent, the little confidence he had drummed up deserting him. – What a deplorable situation to be in, he thought. How can I admit openly I'm insolvent, plead poverty for not being able to help my own tenants? I can't do it. But I'll have to find some way of helping, I can't sit by and see them starve. Something must be attempted, and soon. Not wait for committees to sit, papers to be processed. People could be dead and buried; it's now they need food, and seed potatoes, or come September they'll starve again.

The horses would have to go – he'd start his own relief scheme. Catherine's mare, the stallion belonging to Charles, he'd never miss it, never came any more. The children's ponies, Olivia didn't come either. He would sell them, have to keep his own, a couple for the coach, and one for about the place. It was heartbreaking, like losing old friends. Not a bit of good grieving, drastic measures were required. Food was the thing, and seed. – There'll be enough left to pay the servants' wages. The rest of them'll have to go too. Not Hannah, of course, nor Paudeen, and the fellow by the gate. I keep forgetting he's not O'Donnell, never remember his name.

His spirits revived as the plan to raise money took shape. He began to talk out loud again. 'Should have done it sooner. Wasted too much time. See to the tenants myself, and write to those damn fellows in Dublin. Tell them I want no part in their scheme.' He reached for pen and ink.

Jamsie made good his threat never again to lay a finger on Katy, never by word or gesture showed any desire for her. Surprised at first, for idle threats and promises were part of his nature, eventually she decided she did not care. Telling herself she didn't love him, probably never had, and anyway, wasn't it as well he left her alone – the last thing she wanted was another mouth to feed.

As it was she didn't know how to feed them she had. Help was coming from nowhere. Oh, there was plenty of talk! Relief being organized, money sent by the Queen, by charitable societies and fine ladies in India – a pity none of it reached Kilgoran.

'What is to become of us?' she asked herself one bitter cold morning when Hannah had brought nothing for several days, and all they'd eaten was a couple of eggs Jamsie stole from a nest. What were they to do with no seed potatoes – how could plenty follow scarcity if no seed was planted?

They were doomed, she believed, unless a miracle happened. Unless someone suddenly showered them with food, or she found a crock of gold to take them to America. The flesh was melting from her children – hollows at their temples, in their cheeks, eyes too big for their little faces, the look of their childhood gone too soon.

Everything that could be, sold, the second pot, the spare bucket, her mother's quilt, even the mirror. Thomas not able to go to school, and him the promising scholar, for even if the coppers were available there wasn't a rag to bind his feet on frosty mornings.

Even the weather had turned against them, falls of snow and icy winds, like the one blowing today, finding its way into the room. She shivered as it knifed through her ragged clothes. If Jamsie thought his lack of attention was worrying her, he was as far out as the wind that blew his first shirt, she had more on her mind than love.

Father Bolger sat down to his dinner of salt cod and four potatoes sent up by a comfortable farmer's wife. He propped the newspaper against the milk jug and read while he ate, the details of Famine Relief. When he had finished the last mouthful of fish, the last morsel of potato and drunk a mug of milk, he laid down the paper and thought about what he had read. Peel had at least done his duty ordering Indian Corn. It was better than nothing providing there was enough of it, and that the people had money with which to buy it. The Public Works were supposed to take care of that, roads to be built, piers erected, and fields drained; wages earned.

He sighed. – That might be all very well in other parts of the country, but not in Kilgoran. There'd be no Public Works here. The road such as it was was long since built, the bog reclaimed years ago, and where could a pier stand on Kilgoran strand?

No, he thought, his parishioners would have a long way to go looking for a ticket to work. And even then, he doubted if they'd get one, for there'd be ten men to every job. That's if the scheme got going in the first place, for by the time applications for grants from grabbers wanting improvements to their own holdings were sifted, the surveyors came down and went back to Dublin, the people could have perished.

His thoughts returned to the Indian Corn. Yalla male, the people called it, and weren't partial to the stuff. He didn't blame them, having tasted it himself during another scarcity years ago. The colour was enough to destroy the appetite, no wonder someone had nicknamed it Peel's Brimstone. But hunger was a good sauce, it would keep the life in them so long as it was given out, not left to grow mouldy in corn stores and provide a feast for the rats.

After the horses were sold, Lord Kilgoran sent for Paudeen. 'I want you to do something for me,' he said when Paudeen arrived.

'Yes, Sir.'

'It's to be a secret. No one must know anything about it, you understand?' His voice was high and eager as a child's, his eyes shining with excitement.

'I do, Sir, I'll not breathe a word.'

'Good boy. This is what we'll do.' He lowered his voice, reached in the desk drawer, brought out a chamois bag and handed it across to Paudeen. 'There's twenty sovereigns. Take it and the cart into Bandon and buy potatoes. Some for seed, the others to eat. Make sure they're sound. Take plenty of sacks to cover them. And remember no one's to know. It's to be a surprise.'

'I will, Sir, and then what'll I do with them?'

'Bring them back here of course. We'll sort them in the carriage house, no one goes there now.' For a moment a look of sadness crossed his face. 'Nor to the stables, not any more.' Then the look vanished, and heartily he said,

397

'Right, Paudeen, off you go, get the best money can buy and don't delay.'

'And where are you off to?' Hannah asked when she saw Paudeen yoking the farm horse.

'On business for the Master,' Paudeen replied with an air of importance.

'Oh! is that so? What business might I ask?'

'You might not,' Paudeen said, but smiled to take the sting out of his answer.

'Well, the young pup!' Hannah exclaimed as he drove out.

She was full of curiosity, and at the first opportunity asked Charlotte if she knew anything about Paudeen's mission. 'Not a thing,' she replied.

Throughout the afternoon Hannah stayed by the kitchen window looking up from the basement for sight of the yoke, and had almost given up her vigil when she heard, then saw the yellow wheels trundle into the yard and pass by in the direction of the carriage house. She hurried up the stairs to a window from where she could see the cart properly. It was piled high, but with what she was unable to discern for the load was concealed under sacking.

'Well, I'll find out or die in the attempt,' she said to herself. 'I know a way into the loft of the carriage house.' Back she went to the kitchen where she knew there was a key, collected it, then made her way to the loft and peered down through a gap in the floorboards. She couldn't believe her eyes. There was Lord Kilgoran, his coat off, sleeves rolled up, lining creels in a row. And, glory be! Paudeen unloading the cart of potatoes, tons of them! The excited voices of the two men floated up to her.

'I've a board there, Sir, between the seed and the others. Look at them, aren't they beauties, and every one sound as a bell.'

'Grand, Paudeen, grand. You did a good day's work. When you've unloaded give me a hand to fill the baskets.'

– I declare to God, Hannah thought, the Master's like a little boy. Will you look at the way he's sorting and packing. Singing and whistling, and a spring in his step that hasn't been there this long time. Look at the work he's doing, beating Paudeen at it. As handy as if packing potatoes was a thing he did all his life. May God Bless him.

She saw him rest for a moment, and heard him say, 'Remember, Paudeen, it's to be a surprise. So not a word when you go home, eh?'

'No, Sir, not a word. I won't open my mouth.'

– The good kind creature, so that's why you sold the horses. And again Hannah invoked God's blessing on her Master before she left the loft, thinking as she went – oh wait till I tell Katy. If only I could go this minute she'd sleep with an easy mind. But I'll curb my impatience. After the work he's done that man will want something in his stomach. I'll put up a tray for him in the library, and go to Katy's first thing in the morning.

'You're not supposed to know, so let on to be surprised when Paudeen comes,' Hannah said to Katy, then told her the good news, and how the Master had worked. 'A surprise remember,' she impressed upon her before leaving.

Katy watched for Paudeen, now and then walking up the boreen, peeping through the hedge for sign of him. Then when she saw the cart in the distance ran back to the cottage, hiding close to the window from where she saw him come down the path, smiling all over his face, a basket up on his shoulder. He left it down and went back to the cart.

Katy couldn't resist running out to look at the potatoes. She wanted to kneel before them, to touch, smell, handle them. But he might be back any minute, so she just peeped to make sure they were real, before running inside to the window. There he was again, another basket high on his shoulder.

He knocked and called. She went to the door, pretending to be drying her hands. Paudeen held the basket towards her, blushing with the pleasure of his errand.

'For you from the Master, and the one on the ground's seed potatoes.'

'For me? Are you sure?' Her smile was full of genuine delight, no artifice about it or the joy she felt.

'For you to be sure. Shall I bring them in?'

'Do, do. Isn't that the most marvellous thing? A miracle, that's what it is.'

Paudeen talked while he carried in the baskets. Relating what Hannah had already told Katy. She let on to be amazed, exclaiming incredulously at the account of the Master sorting and packing, singing while he did so. But when Paudeen was ready to go she said with genuine regret, 'I only wish I had something to give you for your trouble.'

'Ah, sure it's no trouble, no trouble at all. I'll be away so. I've the rest to give out.'

'May God bless you and the Master. Tell me now, how is your mother?'

400

'Not well this long time. Not since the brother and sister went to America. But she's improving for they sent the passage money and we'll be soon after them.'

'You too, Paudeen, but haven't you the bit of work above?'

'I have, but how long will it last? You wouldn't know the place.'

'So I believe. Hannah tells me the changes are terrible.'

'Don't be talking,' Paudeen said shaking his head despondently. 'Well, goodbye now.'

When he left she went down on her knees before the baskets, handling the potatoes as carefully as new laid eggs hot from under a hen. She wanted to dance for joy, to tell someone of her good fortune. She longed for Jamsie and the children to come to show them the potatoes.

She filled her apron with them, plenty of them, and carried them to the bucket for washing. Telling herself that just for today she'd be flawhool, make a grand feed. God hadn't deserted them. He had opened a door. And the spring was coming. You could smell it, life was returning to the earth: soon it would be ready to receive the precious seed. And by the time what potatoes the Master had sent were gone, maybe the yellow meal would be given. The worst was over, they would survive.

Her hopes were confirmed when during the week Tim Coffey brought news that soon the Indian Corn was to be sold at a penny a pound, depots set up for its sale, leaflets given out telling how to cook it, and a start made on the Public Works.

'Oh, Tim, isn't that wonderful. We're saved, thanks be to God, we're saved. Did you tell Statia?'

'I thought you'd do that.'

'I will. I will this minute. Come on,' she called to the children, her face transfused with joy, her voice filled with happiness, 'let's run down and tell Statia.'

Her mood was transmitted to them, they danced round her, clapped their hands, and eagerly accompanied her. 'There she is with the bucket, she's been to the well,' Thomas shouted, pointing to the shawl-draped figure that had stopped and put down the heavy pail. For an instant Katy didn't recognize Statia as this old woman, a weary old woman resting from carrying the bucket. – How thin she is, Statia that was the fine, fat woman, and me never noticing until this minute, she thought.

'The wind is fierce,' Statia said when they reached her.

'I didn't even feel it I'm that delighted. Have you heard about the corn? A penny a pound. And work for the men.'

'Yalla meal,' Statia said contemptuously. 'It'll poison us. It did the people in '31. But you wouldn't know anything about that. You were in the Lodge then with plenty.'

'Indeed it won't, it'll keep the life in us.'

'That you may be right,' Statia said, and said no more, not wanting to dishearten Katy who, she thought, in spite of not having a pick on her at the moment, looked not a day older than the children by her side.

Peader hung back in the chapel yard until the last person had taken leave of the priest, then he went to him. 'I wanted to say goodbye, Father, I'll be gone before next Sunday.' He held out a hand.

'Ah, Peader.' Father Bolger clasped it. 'Come round to

402

the house. We parted bad friends the last time, let's not say our goodbyes out here.'

When they were seated in the parlour, he said sadly, 'So you're away – I'll miss you sorely. You know my feelings on the business, I won't go into them again. I'll pray for the two of you, and all concerned. I don't suppose you're sorry to be getting out of what's happening here.'

'I'm not, though I am for them that's left.'

'God help them. Do you know I was looking at their faces while I preached the Gospel. At the hope shining out of their eyes, and eyes are all you can see for the flesh is melted from them. Looking at them and knowing they think their troubles are nearly over. Delighted with their pennyworth's of yellow meal, and that the seed potatoes are planted. Trusting that the crop this year will be healthy. And not one of them with an inkling yet that the Indian Corn they're depending on to keep the life in them between now and lifting, is to be withdrawn.'

'I hadn't an inkling myself. Where did you hear that?'

'From a Dublin priest passing through yesterday on his way to Kerry. It'll be in the papers, them that'll print it, before long.'

'All the work of Trevelyan, I suppose?'

'Oh every bit. All the work of Charles Edward Trevelyan, Assistant Secretary at the Treasury – he's the rock on which Ireland will perish. He hasn't an ounce of compassion, not one. He's blind to everything except pennies and pounds, and balancing books. A man with no doubts, cold and conscientious, who takes duty beyond the bounds of reason, and into the bargain dislikes the Irish. Believes we're all beggars, drunkards and wastrels who take life easy. There was another thing the priest told me, a thing that doesn't bear thinking about.'

'What was that, Father?'

'He told me that on his way here he saw two men catching rats. You might think there's nothing unusual in that. But listen to this, there was no terrier with them. They'd made a kind of trap by the river's bank, and when the rats were cornered they smashed their heads with a stick and made off with them. He was convinced they were for eating.'

'Hunger will drive men to anything. Let's hope it's nothing worse than rats they turn to.'

'What could be worse than them? Do you know the thought of it turned my stomach for a while. I couldn't face the bit of rabbit Mary put in front of me.'

'Men have been known to eat each other in terrible times. There's a record of it in The Black Book of Christ Church. In 1296 it happened. The starving tore down the bodies hanging on gibbets and devoured them.'

'God between us and all harm, that it may never come to that!'

'That it may not,' Peader said, then brought the conversation back again to Trevelyan. 'He's a terrible man all right. Charlotte mentioned him once in a letter from London, and said there were them beyond that thought him the queer cold fish. But tell me now, why is he closing the corn depots?'

'Because by the time they were opened the people were starving and descended like locusts. And that was after only a partial failure. So what, he asked himself, would happen next year if the entire crop failed? Though I don't understand the reasoning behind that, unless he hopes that if enough of them die there'll be less demand. Government funds will be spared, that's all he's concerned with.'

'It's not human, Father.'

'That's where you're wrong, Peader, it's very human. It's the Devil working through man. That's the reason ships leave Ireland laden with food for England, why there's people existing on grass and stinging nettles. It hasn't come to that yet in Kilgoran, but mark my words it will. And the fever, too. That's already in Skull and Skibereen. Out there, so many are dying that quick, the coroner can't hold inquests. Coffins with sliding bottoms are used again and again. Wakes are a thing of the past, and the dead are being thrown into pits. Imagine that, a man's last bit of dignity taken from him.'

'All we can do I suppose is pray this year's crop won't fail.'

'With God's help it won't. Prayer is all we have left, though they're trying to take that from us. The priest from Dublin told me there's Bible Societies making it a condition to renounce your religion before getting the nourishment. Proselytizers! Taking advantage of people's weakness, trading a bowl of soup for a man's soul. Well, Peader, I won't keep you any longer.'

The two men stood up. The priest held out his hand. Peader took it. 'Nine long years it is since the day you came to meet me at Carey's. You were no more than a bit of a boy then. High hopes we all had for the future. Repeal we thought was just round the corner. Your father was hale and hearty.' The priest sighed wearily. 'There's a lot of water gone under the bridge since then.' He shook

Peader's hand. 'I'm sorry to see you go. I'm sorry we had our differences. You won't forget where you came from and send word back. Go now and God go with you.'

'Indeed I won't forget. I only wish things were otherwise, there's nowhere I'd rather spend my life than here. Goodbye and God bless you.'

'It's only the scrapings of the plates,' Hannah apologized as she handed Katy the bowl.

'I'm grateful, without you we'd starve. Sit down, and thanks very much.' She put away the basin, talking while she did so. 'Wasn't it a sin they stopped the yalla male. And there was me thinking I was landed, my worries at an end. Believing everything I heard, work for Jamsie, corn to buy and the money to pay for it.' She sat down opposite Hannah. 'Public works how are you! Not one in the place got a smell of them.'

'And sure them that did in other places never saw the colour of the money for the funds ran out,' Hannah lamented.

'You'll stay for a while,' Katy said. 'Maybe we could talk about the olden days.'

'I would, only I can't. I'm that worried about the Master. I think the poor man's losing himself.'

'Do you tell me? I thought he was well.'

'He was for a while after giving out the potatoes, and while there was still hopes for Relief. Now he's disimproved. The talking he does be doing in library. I declare to God you'd think there was two men there with him answering his own questions. He does be addressing MacNamara, his solicitor, and him not there. Giving the man instructions about his will by the sound of it.'

'May the Lord leave him his senses. I'd say he's bad.'

'He is that. Some days he comes into the kitchen and stands looking around, very confused. My heart goes out to him. If he was anyone else I'd sit him down by the fire and wet a sup of tea. But you couldn't make that free with the Master.'

'You could not,' Katy agreed. 'All the same hasn't he had a hard life? I suppose Master Charles is still careering in London?'

'I'd say so, though there's been no word this long time. But no doubt he's still borrowing on the head of his inheritance.'

'That'll be the bad day for us.'

'A black day for everyone in Kilgoran the day he inherits,' Hannah replied and prepared to go. Then remembering something else spoke again. 'There's another thing worrying me. The Master's started asking about Miss Charlotte. Where she goes and that. Him that never knew from morning to night if she was in or out. I often think that's what drove her into Peader's arms.'

At the mention of Charlotte's name Katy's became tight-lipped, and she made no comment.

'You're not listening to a word I'm telling you,' Hannah complained. 'I was saying that these two days the Master's gone out riding. One time he said to look for Miss Catherine, and yesterday to find her Ladyship.'

'God bless us!' Katy exclaimed, 'the one's in India, and the other in Heaven I hope.'

'He's that confused, the poor creature. For everyone's sake let's hope he doesn't come upon Charlotte and

Peader. I'll go now, say a prayer for him and all concerned.'

The lovers lay in the wood, Charlotte's head in the hollow of Peader's shoulder. Kissing and caressing each other, whispering endearments.

'After tomorrow there'll be no more need for secrecy. On the boat we can be together, our love declared openly,' Peader said.

Charlotte sighed contentedly and nestled closer. 'I wish we were married already, going abroad as man and wife.'

'So do I, the waiting's killing me.'

'We could get married on the boat. Sea captains can perform the ceremony, can't they?'

Peader shifted his arm from beneath her, sat up, and looked down upon her. 'They can, but I doubt if this one would for I doubt we could fight our way through the throng to find him.'

'Will it be that bad, that many people travelling?'

'That many and more. But you'll be all right. I won't leave your side. Maybe I should have spent more on the passage, got you a bit of comfort, but I thought we'd better hold on to the money for when we land.'

She reached for him, pulled him to her. 'I'm not as fragile and helpless as you think. Don't look so worried, my darling. I'll be fine so long as we are together. I could face anything with you beside me. I love you, nothing matters, only that.'

'A gradh mo groidhe,' his voice was hoarse with emotion, 'little love of my heart, my sweet brown bird, I love you, too.' He kissed her, and passionately she responded, twining her fingers in his hair, clasping his head tightly, not allowing his mouth to stray from hers.

His hand stroked her neck, moved to the smooth, round orb of her breast, caressed it, slid from her breast over her waist, down over stomach, gliding on and over the length of her thighs.

In the rapture of their embrace they were lost to the world, blind to the shadow encroaching upon them, to the sound of snapping twigs, the scrunch of leaves. Then an infuriated roar thundered in the silence of the wood, their eyes flew open, Peader looked round and stared in disbelief at the figure of Lord Kilgoran, arm raised, whip held aloft, bearing down on them, shouting, 'O'Hara, get away from my daughter! Get away or I'll flay you alive.'

Peader jumped to his feet, frightened momentarily. Then guilt surged through him, he felt like a small boy caught in a shameful act. Anger cancelled out that feeling. He was a man, there was nothing shameful about his love for Charlotte or the way in which he had been expressing it. But the most powerful emotion was indignation that he had been mistaken for someone else – that being a tenant of this man bearing down on him, whom he had known all his life, he didn't even know his name.

'I'm a Daly, Peader Daly, not an O'Hara.' Behind him he heard Charlotte getting to her feet, felt her hand on him. 'I love your daughter, it's nothing to be ashamed of. She loves me too.'

'Stand away from her.' Lord Kilgoran came nearer still, brandishing the whip. He was close enough now for Peader to see the confusion in his eyes, hear his voice falter.

'The Dalys are decent men, a Daly wouldn't take my daughter in the wood, wouldn't lay with her. You're a scoundrel. I've a good mind to horsewhip you.' But now the sureness was gone from the voice, the arm holding the crop being lowered.

Peader stood very still, not wishing to antagonize the old man. He could see now that's what he was – old and sick. He was sorry to have humiliated him, allowed him to witness what must have appeared sordid. Charlotte was still behind him, she hadn't uttered a sound since the arrival of her father. Now she spoke, pleading, 'Don't let him take me, Peader. Don't let him separate us.'

The sound of her voice had a dramatic effect upon Lord Kilgoran. An expression of cold disdain replaced the one of confusion, his moment of aberration had passed.

'I'm not interested in who you are. Stand away from my daughter. And you!' again he raised the whip, using it to point at the face of Charlotte peering fearfully from behind Peader, 'Come from there at once. My horse is at the edge of the wood. Go and mount. You have disgraced yourself. Go now, immediately.'

She clung to Peader, pleading for him to protect her, not to let her father take her. 'I'll never see you again. I'll be sent to India, don't let him take me, Peader.'

Thoughts of grappling with the old man, knocking him down, absconding with her, flashed through his mind. As quickly as they came he dismissed them. For the time being he was powerless. He could not assault her father. He was an old man, he was her father, he thought he was defending his daughter's honour. There was nothing to do but surrender Charlotte.

He spoke softly to her. 'Go with him. Go for now. I love you. It will be all right. Do what I say, go now. And don't make a scene, leave quietly.'

Slowly she came from behind him. Lord Kilgoran waited, said nothing else. Charlotte began walking away from the place where she and Peader had lain. Her father followed her. She looked back, her face streaked with tears. Her father said something which Peader couldn't hear, and she turned her head, they went on.

Peader waited until he heard the horse ride off, then ran all the way to Katy's, told her what had happened, and pleaded with her to go quick to the House and find out what steps Lord Kilgoran was taking.

'There might still be a chance of us making it to the boat so long as he wouldn't lock her up. He wouldn't do that, would he, Katy?'

His voice was desperate, his face distraught. Katy felt the beginnings of pity stir within her, and for an instant wanted to comfort him. Then something else stirred in her, the memory of how she had confessed her love for him in a moment's madness. How he had scorned her, treated her as if she was a fool. He deserved whatever he was suffering, him and her. Weren't they lucky that all they had to worry about was being found in the wood like a pair of lovesick calves. That they may never see each other again. She would not go to the House.

Yet the sight of Peader's suffering troubled her, almost overcame the bitterness and jealousy that was hardening her heart. Then suddenly she realized the implications of what had happened. Lord Kilgoran knew about Peader and Miss Charlotte, it wouldn't be long before he found out her part and Jamsie's in the affair. 'By tomorrow me and my children could be out on the road, and all because of you. I'll help you no more. I wouldn't set foot near the House. Go home now, Peader, you've caused enough trouble,' she said without compassion.

'Please, Katy. Don't let me down. Look,' he came towards her, his hands outstretched, imploring, 'whether we go or stay the secret's out. Lord Kilgoran will know someone helped us. Don't you see that? And he might be lenient, he was always a fair man. But take the message for me, please, Katy.'

'A fair man, is it?' Katy said. 'Oh, he is that, but we're not talking about rents, leases or evictions now. You're not even talking about courting in the wood, but wanting me to help arrange for you to run away with his daughter. I wonder how fair he'd be when he found that out. I'll have no more to do with it.'

'You can't refuse. He might send her away. If we don't go tonight God knows what will happen, we could be parted for ever. Think if it was you and Jamsie, think how you'd feel. Think what it would be like to be separated from someone you love so much.'

The more he talked, the harder Katy's heart became. The more he showed how much he loved Charlotte, the deeper became her own wound, the pain that love was gone from her life, and the more convinced she was that Charlotte was responsible, for that was a good enough reason for refusing to help, but she had a better one, the genuine fear of incurring Lord Kilgoran's wrath.

'It's no use, Peader. Don't say any more. Not if you got

down on your knees would I go to the House. I won't help you. I can't.' She turned away from him, and remained turned until she heard him go.

Mary Doyle was walking near the Lodge Gates when Lord Kilgoran with Charlotte mounted in front of him, her hair dishevelled, her eyes wild-looking and red from crying, rode in.

'That's the queerest thing I've seen in my life,' Mary said to herself, and without hesitating turned into the drive and scurried up its length. When she arrived in the kitchen there was no sign of Hannah. But from the griddle cake half made she knew Hannah wasn't far. There was, she felt sure, something peculiar going on, and she was determined to know what.

Like everyone else in the parish she had once worked in the House, and so knew her way about. Leaving the kitchen she went along the passage and up the stairs leading to the main part of the House. Carefully she opened the heavy doors, and immediately heard a commotion. Screams and shouts, and the sound of crying. Hannah's voice pleading, 'Don't be too hard on her, Sir.' Lord Kilgoran shouting, 'You will not put a foot outside this door. Not if I have to tie you up. Go with her, Hannah. See to it she gets undressed. Bring out her clothes, every one of them. Empty the press, then lock her in.' And Miss Charlotte's voice screaming, 'No. No.'

– They've gone mad, Mary thought, crouching behind the door, holding an inch of it open. The crying, shouting and pleading grew fainter and she knew they were making their way upstairs. Soon she could hear nothing.

413

But still she crouched, listening, only shifting when there was the sound of footsteps and she guessed that Hannah was returning. She closed the door and hurried back to the kitchen, pretending when Hannah came in that she had just arrived before her.

'Only this minute I walked in. She can't be far, I said to myself, with the soda cake half made. You look terrible, what ails you?'

Hannah guessed Mary was lying, that she had probably heard all that happened. – But what matter now who knows when the Master himself does, she thought, and told Mary all.

Mary was annoyed to discover so much had been going on and she not the wiser. She was tempted to call Hannah a sliveen for her slyness, but bit back the accusation. Hannah looked in no humour to trifle her, and if she didn't order her out, would certainly give no more information. So instead Mary asked concernedly, 'I wonder what'll be the outcome for Jamsie, Katy and yourself for the part you played in the affair?'

'I don't think the poor man's capable of thinking who's to blame. He's been near the edge this long time, and this will tip him over. Not that I wish for harm to come to him, but I wouldn't want Katy and Jamsie in trouble. As for myself I don't care.'

'And them two – Miss Charlotte and Peader. How will they fare?'

'There'll be miles put between them.'

'Would you say so?'

'Oh, nothing surer. The Master has times when he's as

right as ever he was. In one of them he'll get word to Miss Olivia. Then my poor lamb will be sent to London, and on out to India.'

'That's a terrible far away, so I'm told,' Mary said. 'But commere, tell me this. In one of his sane moments mightn't the Master ask who helped the young lovers?'

'Say a prayer that he doesn't, and go home now like a good woman. I've had enough annoyance for one day.'

Chapter Eighteen

Despite the shuttered windows and flapping punkah the heat in the bedroom was stifling. From a hook on the wall folds of mosquito netting fell, tenting the bed on which Catherine lay as though dead. Her skin looked bloodless, her closed eyes were etched with dark half-circles. Only the perspiration beading her forehead, and the almost imperceptible rise and fall of her breasts showed that she lived.

Her hands were outside the sheet, laying on her stomach as if guarding something, a manner she had adopted since first suspecting pregnancy. Now the protective attitude was unnecessary, the child was gone, only pain and an aching void remained in the still slightly convex belly. She heard low voices, her servant's and the doctor's, sensed him entering the nettings, heard the creak of springs as he sat on the bed, yet still she remained motionless, her eyes closed. She could not bear to open them and see the pity in his. Before it she would cry, and if she cried she did not believe she would ever stop.

The doctor raised one of her hands, unobtrusively feeling for her pulse, then held the hand in both of his, trying by touch to communicate his sympathy, his admiration for her stoicism.

'What was it?' Catherine's voice was not more than a whisper.

'A boy.' The doctor looked at the pale face, the eyes ringed with suffering and exhaustion, the recently changed nightgown already soaked with sweat. –God! he thought, India's an abominable place for women.

Briefly Catherine opened her eyes. 'A son,' she said despairingly, and closed them again.

'You were very brave. A brave girl indeed. A miscarriage can be harder than a birth. Edward will be proud of you.' Immediately he regretted his choice of words – the banality of them. Of course a miscarriage was worse than a birth – nothing to show for it. And to talk of Edward being proud of her, that was crass stupidity when now she would be feeling a failure for not carrying the child. It was the heat, it befuddled him, he must go before he uttered more ill-chosen words.

Gently he laid down her hand and rose from the bed. 'I'll leave you to rest. The pills will work shortly, and the ayah has some more for later on.' He parted the mosquito netting and was about to step outside its tent. 'Oh, I almost forgot,' he said, turning back. 'I'll get word to Edward.'

Catherine opened her eyes. He saw the hurt in them, heard the catch in her voice as she said, 'Don't do that. Edward didn't know.'

– Perhaps now she'll cry, it would be better for her, but as the thought registered, the doctor saw her make an effort to control herself, and when she spoke again her voice was normal, her eyes inscrutable.

'I didn't tell him. There had been so many disappointments, this time I wanted to be sure. And I wasn't when

417

he went up to the North–West Frontier. So I pretended nothing was amiss, even that I would go to Simla before the weather became too hot. Which I had no intention of doing because I wanted you to take care of me ... You see, I had it all planned. I imagined his delighted surprise when he returned and saw me. It would have been almost time to have the baby.' Her voice had become barely audible.

'Well of course, if that's what you wish, I'll say nothing, but don't you think he would want to know?'

'Yes, but you mustn't send word. Life on the Khyber's difficult enough without worries from home. It isn't as if he could come, he'll be there for months yet.'

'All right, I'll do as you say. Now you must sleep, sleep's the best medicine. I'll be back later.'

When he had gone, the servant wiped Catherine's face, gave her water, and asked if there was anything else the memsahib wanted. Catherine said no. The woman adjusted the mosquito net before leaving the room, tucking its edges firmly beneath the mattress. Catherine heard the sound of her sandalled feet slapping on the tiled floor as she went to the door, and then it closing.

Only then did she allow herself to cry for her lost son, her lost hopes and for Edward whom she needed now more than ever. Needed him to hold her, weep with her for the child they had created, tell her he loved her, that it wasn't her fault.

She turned on to her side and lay with her knees drawn up, her head bowed. How had her son lain in her womb? she wondered. Was he very small? Was he recognizable as a baby? Did he resemble Edward? Then she wondered where he was, what had the doctor done with him?

The pills took effect and she slept, but only for a short time. She woke and longed for the oblivion of it again. Reached a hand for the bell rope. The ayah would be resting on her mat outside the door, but the effort required was too great and she let her hand fall back on the bed.

She drifted in and out of fitful sleep. In her awake moments she watched two lizards high on the wall. Motionless until flies came into their orbit, then the darting tongues flicked them in. She shuddered, she loathed the little reptiles, the flies, mosquitoes, the snakes. The snakes, oh how she loathed them, even the sight of one paralysed her with fear.

She heard the flip-flap of the punkah overhead redistributing the warm stale air, the half-awake voices of the punkah wallah and his friend drift in from the verandah, and the cry of the muezzin wing its way across the brazen sky calling the faithful to pray. Once she had thrilled at the sound, thought it exotic: once she had thought India exotic. Marvelling at the fabulous sights, the brilliant flowers, the flocks of parakeets, the marble palaces and mosques, and temples. She rejoiced for the endless sunshine, stared in disbelief at enormous moons.

In the bazaar at first she saw only the crowd, the graceful women, bangles glinting on dusky arms; the beautiful eyes of men. All seemed to be movement, vitality. She heard the strange languages, smelled pungent spices, was dazzled by the brightly-hued rolls of silk spilled out for inspection.

But soon the perpetual sunshine became monotonous;

the heat unbearable. The necessary sleep in the afternoon a dread, for you woke not refreshed but dazed, with a parched mouth and aching head.

Now on her visits to the bazaar she saw the stick-like legs of starving children, the swollen bellies, the destroyed eyes, their sockets a haven for flies. She learned of child marriages, and the custom of suttee, declared illegal, but still wives flung themselves on to the funeral pyres of dead husbands. India, she acknowledged, was an alien land in which she would never feel at home.

But Edward did. Edward loved it, so she kept her change of heart to herself, and listened to his plans for the future, his hope that the regiment would stay in India for many years. She attended dinners and invited back the hosts. The men shared Edward's love for the sub-continent, enthused about tiger hunts, polo, pig-sticking, their tours of duty. But the women! What, she wondered, did the women really feel about living in a land thousands of miles from England? Did their retinues of servants, the sight of brilliantly coloured birds, breathtaking perfume of exotic flowers, compensate for all the other things? For separation from their children sent home to England to be educated, and other children dying from cholera, malaria and jungle fevers. What was the truth behind the calm, smiling faces?

Despair overwhelmed her. Tears slid down her face mingling with her sweat on the pillow. Her neck and beneath her breasts itched with prickly heat. She scratched herself and cried aloud, 'Oh, God, how I hate this place. How I hate the regiment and Edward's devotion to it.' She allowed herself to indulge in a fear that usually she kept suppressed. Her dread that Edward would be killed or succumb to a fever, be hurriedly buried because of the appalling climate. Be dead and buried before she had time to grieve for him, lie forever in a land far away from his own.

Far from England and Ireland. How she missed Ireland. She thought of the green fields, of rain falling, gentle, cool rain, and the sweet smell of the earth after it. And she thought about her father, how much she missed him. How she longed to comfort him, convince him his worry over the potato failure wasn't necessary. He could comfort her, too. With him she could become a child again, be surrounded by his protection, forget her failure as a woman.

For a bleak moment she questioned the wisdom of God. Why was her child not allowed to live, when every day in India thousands of babies, millions of babies were born into perpetual want and suffering?

After a while her crying ceased, and she began to seek consolations, to take herself to task. It wasn't God's Will that she should yet have a child. But there was plenty of time. Plenty of time, too, for going to Ireland. Nothing would have changed there, it had always been so, and would be still. Papa's worries about the failure were probably exaggerated, only his concern for the tenants. For apart from his letters all other accounts coming out to India weren't nearly as gloomy.

And Edward wouldn't be killed, nor die of fever. That was just her morbid fears. He would return, and she would make the best of India, there were beautiful things about it, too. In any case she was a soldier's wife, it was her duty to be by his side, to make a home for him, here or any-where else. Just as it was her duty to get well quickly, and next year to have another baby.

A week later she was up and dressed when the doctor called. Smiled disarmingly at his frown of disapproval, and airily dismissed his warning of how she was endangering her health by getting up too soon.

'Oh Richard, don't fuss so. I'm as strong as a horse, and much more comfortable out of bed. Now sit down and we'll have some tea.'

After the tea was served, she asked the question upper-most in her mind. 'The fact I miscarried won't make any difference to me having another child? It won't, will it?' she prompted, when the doctor did not immediately answer the first question.

'Dear Catherine, I hoped that by the time you asked me Edward would have been back. I wish I could make you a different answer, or that there was an easy way to tell the truth. There isn't, so I'll not prevaricate. I don't believe you'll ever carry a child to term.'

'You mean ... never!' Her voice that a moment before had been light-hearted, was now a cry of despair.

'Yes, that's what I mean, never.'

'But that's nonsense.' She shook her head. 'You can't be that positive – you can't.' Her voice had regained confidence, but her eyes were full of fear. 'I did conceive a child. After all these years my prayers were answered. I'm not a barren woman. Why couldn't I have another child?'

Her hand holding the cup shook, tea spilled on to her

cream shantung gown, staining it, soaking into the skin above her rapidly-beating heart. She waved away the doctor's proffered handkerchief, and in a voice losing its certainty, becoming incoherent, pleaded, 'You can't be positive . . . no one can . . . you're not God.'

'No I'm not, but I've been a doctor for thirty years, and have attended countless women like you. It's on that experience I'm drawing. Put the cup down, Catherine, and listen to me. You nearly died, you would have died if medical attention wasn't to hand. If you conceive again it's almost certain that at four months you will miscarry. Do you understand that?'

She nodded her head, and the doctor continued, 'I've seen it happen so often. Women miscarrying year after year, their health ruined, their minds becoming impaired. You must never conceive again. You could lose your life.'

Catherine sat silently, her dark head bowed, her pale hands clasped tightly. The doctor looked with pity at her. – Such a tragedy, he thought. Such a choice to present a young, beautiful woman who loved her husband passionately; chronic ill health, death perhaps, or celibacy. For any woman it was a dreadful blow, for Catherine, alone, Edward miles away, the other wives in the hills, it could be devastating. She must not stay on her own for months. She must go to Simla, at least there the air was cool and she would have company. Of course it was Edward she needed most, but he couldn't be brought back for such a reason.

'Catherine,' he said gently. She raised her head and looked at him in a dazed fashion. 'You mustn't stay here with only the servants. Go to Simla. There'll be company

– the other wives. You love Simla, remember how you enthused about it. It will do you good.'

She shook her head. 'No, I couldn't go there. I couldn't bear the questions. I couldn't face strangers.'

'But they're not strangers, you know so many, they're your neighbours.'

'I'd like to go home, to Ireland.'

'Well, yes, why not. A long sea voyage would do you good. And think of the climate in Ireland, and your family. Yes, that's a good idea.'

Visions of Kilgoran came into Catherine's mind. She saw her father's face, Charlotte's, and the House. And on the way through London she would see Olivia. If she went soon she would be home for the autumn. She thought of riding out in the crisp, cool mornings, the wind in her face, the soft skies. The soft-voiced tenants, the loveliness of it all.

The doctor watched the grave sweet face, saw the strain round Catherine's mouth ease, her eyes almost smile, and guessing her thoughts, urged, 'The best thing for you. Now go and change your gown and then write to Edward and tell him about the baby. Tell him I advised the voyage for your health. Don't mention the other matter. I'll have a word with him when he comes back.'

'When he comes back! ... I won't be here! I can't go. For the moment I was so caught up in the dream of Ireland I forgot about Edward. I can't have him arrive to an empty house. How lonely he would be. He'd think I had deserted him.'

'Nonsense, he'll move into the Mess. He'll be all right, and understand completely that leaving India was vital for your good health.'

424

'No, no, I couldn't do that,' she said agitatedly.

'All right, Catherine, don't distress yourself. I'll tell you what, why not sleep on it? I'll drop in tomorrow and we'll talk again, eh?'

She talked to herself about it throughout the morning. What was she to do? How could she contemplate living with Edward and refuse him her love? But if she disregarded the doctor's advice, what then? She remembered what he had said: 'You could lose your life.' She didn't want to die. But what would life be like denying Edward her body? How could it be endured?

'Memsahib is sick. Afternoon heat very bad. Memsahib must go to bed.'

She waved away the anxious servant and continued to think. Was it possible for a married woman to live without the comfort of her husband's love? Perhaps it was, women were supposed to have more restraint. But for restraint to work, Edward would have to accept the discipline too. Would he? Was it fair to ask him? He was so good, loving and considerate, for her sake he probably would. And then what? Rejected even for such a reason, might he not look elsewhere for consolation?

Like a whirlpool in her mind, thoughts swirled until she felt herself drowning in a sea of misery, and she clutched at her only means of salvation – Kilgoran. In its calm she would be safe. For a while she could rest in its haven, become a child again, throw off the responsibility of making decisions. She would grow strong first, find peace of mind and then come to know how she would live the rest of her life with Edward.

Once her decision was made she wrote to Edward. She

told him about the baby and how sorry she was for losing
their son. She implored his understanding of the fact she
would be away when he returned, but explained that the
miscarriage had debilitated her; that the doctor strongly
advised a change of air, preferably a long sea voyage. She
wrote how much she loved and missed him, how she
prayed daily for God to protect him. But of the thoughts
which had so recently troubled her mind she said nothing.

'Good, good!' the doctor said the following morning
when she told him she would go to Ireland. 'I thought you
might, so on the off-chance I found out about sailing dates.
You can get a ship in two weeks' time. The best thing for
you, you'll come back a new woman.'

'I hope so. There is one thing, Richard.'

'Yes, Catherine?'

'I'd rather you didn't talk to Edward about us, about
what you told me.'

'If that's what you wish of course I'll say nothing. I just
thought it might be easier coming from me.'

'Thank you all the same, but I must be the one to tell
him.'

'Very well. Two weeks, eh. It must be your decision.
Now I expect you'll want to write to Ireland, and your
sister in London, let them know the good news. A fort-
night will see you fit enough to travel. I'll come in every
day until you sail, make sure you are well, and I'll have
a tonic sent up this afternoon. Now I'll leave you to your
letters.'

More than ever before, Peader now spent time in Father
Bolger's company. At first he was hesitant about seeking

out the priest, sure that a lecture would be delivered about his affair with Charlotte and its end. But still he went, for there was nowhere else to go of an evening. In Carey's there would be sidelong glances, words spoken from the sides of mouths, moryah, not meant for his hearing, jokes at his expense. His own home was cheerless, his possessions disposed of when he had contemplated America, and Katy's undisguised hostility when he had run to the cottage pleading for help, prevented him calling often.

So he sought the priest, and to his surprise Father Bolger had not once so far referred to Lord Kilgoran coming upon him and Charlotte in the wood. One day the subject would be raised, of that Peader had no doubt, but in the meantime the priest's kitchen was comfortable and the talk good.

They talked of politics, of Robert Peel's defeat and the new Whig Government. Of Daniel O'Connell's impassioned pleading that help must be given to Ireland. About the fact he was seventy-one and his health failing. 'Poor Dan's finished,' Father Bolger lamented frequently, 'and the Repeal Association too. The Young Irelanders have taken sway, more's the pity for they are men of violence.'

Peader was sceptical of people's faith in the new Government. Whig or Tory, he saw no difference in them, not when a man like Trevelyan held the Treasury in his grip. And they both raged against his decision that this year only in exceptional circumstances would the Indian Corn be imported again.

Then one evening when they had been speculating as to how, if the crop failed a second time, Ireland was finished, in a roundabout way Father Bolger broached the subject of Charlotte.

'Tell me now, Peader, are you still planning on going to America?'

'I am not.'

'Why, and you with all the arrangements made? The boat gone and the farmhouse looking as if no one lived in it.'

'You know well why. Without Charlotte I'll not stir.'

'Oh, I see. All the same isn't that a foolish reason and she being kept a prisoner. Sure how could you take her?'

'I'll find a way. If I have to die in the attempt I'll find a way.'

'That's foolish talk, bravado and well you know it. I hope you wouldn't put it to the test or let hint of it reach her father. Maybe make him exact a vengeance he hasn't so far, thank God.'

Peader looked sullen. The priest was reminded of the first time he had warned him against the affair with Charlotte. – I told you so, but you wouldn't take heed, he thought, but kept the thought to himself. He wouldn't rub salt into the wound, and wounded Peader was. His face for all the brave talk and sullen expression bereft of hope, his body slumped in the chair, the appearance about him of a man who was suffering.

He felt sorry for him, but for all that, there were others to consider. Peader wasn't a bit of a boy, he was a man getting on for thirty, he needed telling.

'I believe Lord Kilgoran isn't well. Hannah says his mind wanders. He's forgetful of everything except keeping Miss Charlotte locked in her room. Isn't that a terrible way for them to be living? Mightn't it be that if you went things would improve?'

'It would make no difference except to break her heart.'

The priest shifted in the chair, he was stiff and his bones ached, he was running out of patience. 'Hearts don't break that easy. But one way or the other wouldn't the girl have her freedom if you went? Which while you're in the parish no matter how forgetful her father is, she'll not get.'

Peader said nothing and Father Bolger continued, 'And besides that there's others to consider. What about Katy, Jamsie and Hannah? Who's to say one day the Master's mind won't clear and it dawn on him that they connived against him. Answer me that now?'

'Don't remind me of that part. You don't think I relish the thought of Jamsie and Katy being thrown out? May God forgive me, do you know what I do?'

'Tell me.'

'I pray that the Master never gets his senses back. Night and day that's the prayer on my lips, that and one that He will show me a way to take Charlotte from here.'

'Well,' Father Bolger said, 'the Lord will decide which if any of your prayers He'll answer. I pray too, night and day, for you to go. That He may answer me first.'

'No doubt He will, you have His ear.'

There was no more to be gained from the talk, Father Bolger decided, he would put an end to it. Besides he was tired, and the pain in his joints gnawed at him. He got up with difficulty from the chair. Peader taking the hint did likewise.

'Go home now,' the priest said, 'and think hard about America. You still have enough to take you, and a bit more for a start. Give the girl and yourself a chance to get over the sorry affair.'

Peader left and set out to walk as he did every night outside the wall of the House, stopping at a place where he could see the lighted window. Thinking of Charlotte inside the room. Of how near she was, and yet oceans might as well have separated them. Raging inside himself at the injustice of what had befallen them. Willing his thoughts to reach her so that she knew he still loved her, and would never rest until she was his.

'You haven't eaten enough for a sparrow!' Hannah said, looking at the tray of food before Charlotte.

'I'm not hungry.'

'Hunger's got nothing to do with it – you'll die if you don't eat.'

'I want to die.'

'Don't you dare say that! Don't you dare fly in the face of God!' Hannah's voice was aghast. 'There's enough dying everywhere, three more families from the bog buried this morning, dead of the fever. So don't let me hear another word about dying. Eat up that food now like a good girl.'

– Was it any wonder the child didn't want to eat, didn't want to live, Hannah asked herself, looking at the thin woebegone face of the girl on the bed. Had her father lost his senses completely, keeping her a prisoner in the room? Not a stitch to wear except a nightdress, him moved into the adjoining room, the door open night and day, only ceasing his watch when she herself brought up the bit of food. Slipping down then to eat his own, and back again before you knew it.

It was a terrible business altogether, and she wished from the bottom of her heart she had never taken part in it. Poor Charlotte's pleasure was short-lived, though for the while she had bloomed like a rose. But look at her now. And Peader like someone demented, a man nearly thirty that you'd think would have more sense, God love him. Pleading with her at every hand's turn to smuggle in letters, and she having to refuse. But what else could she do? Miss Charlotte if she got hold of one wouldn't destroy it. Under her pillow, or down the front of her nightdress it would be pushed. And who was to say the Master mightn't find it? Then the pall that had descended on the poor man's mind after discovering them in the woods, so he seemed blind to anyone else's part in the affair, could lift. If that day dawned it might be the poor lookout for them all.

– Thank God Miss Catherine was on her way home from India. The sooner she came the better. With her in the House the Master would surely stop being a gaoler, his mind would ease knowing she was there and that Miss Charlotte was soon to be taken out of harm's way. Foreign faraway place that India was, it couldn't be worse than the life the child was living now. There with God's help she'd meet a nice young man. She was young, her heart would heal, even if a scar remained.

All the while she had been thinking, Charlotte toyed with the food, but ate none of it. Now Hannah forced herself to be brusque, and scolded her. Reminding her she was lucky to have food when thousands were starving. Averting her eyes from Charlotte's pale, wan face. Pushing down the desire to take her in her arms, rock her like

431

a baby, and say, 'I know, love, you're heartbroken. I know what it's like to love someone and lose him.'

After the scolding she coaxed again, 'Come on now, take a sup of the milk, 'twill give you strength. Only a mouthful, come on now, my little dove.'

Charlotte took the cup in her long thin fingers, like her face they were blanched of colour, weeks of confinement had wiped it away more successfully than all of Olivia's potions.

'That's a good girl,' Hannah said encouragingly as she drank a little of the milk. 'Take another sup.'

'Will you go to Katy's when Papa returns?' Charlotte asked, pausing in the sipping.

'I'd like to if he lets me.'

'If Peader's there give him a message. Tell him I love him. Tell him I'll always love him. Even if they send me to India I'll never forget him. Tell him that. Tell him I'll come back from where I'm sent. One day I will, no matter how long it takes. Tell him to wait. You'll do that, won't you, Hannah?'

She started to cry, sobbing convulsing her so the cup shook in her hand. Hannah took it from her. 'You'll spill it. Ah, don't cry love, sure you have yourself worn out with the crying. I'll tell Peader, of course I will. The minute I see him, I'll tell him every word. Only stop crying now,' she pleaded, wanting to cry herself for the suffering of Charlotte. Afraid that sympathy might overcome her resolve not to aid the lovers. 'Whisht, astoir. Whisht,' she said again, her head inclined towards the door. 'I hear someone coming. 'Tis your father, wipe your eyes now. It's him.'

432

Lord Kilgoran came into the bedroom. – The man's old before his time, Hannah thought looking at him.

'If it's all right with you, Sir, I'll slip out for an hour.'

'Yes, do, Hannah,' Lord Kilgoran replied absent-mindedly. 'The fresh air will do you good.'

– An old broken man, Hannah thought again as she bid him and Charlotte goodnight. She heard the door being locked, the voice asking Charlotte had she eaten, had she had enough, was there anything she wanted? But no word of reply, and knew Charlotte would have turned from him, be laying gazing at the curtained window, as if her eyes might penetrate the heavy hangings, be granted power to see in the dark, see beyond the sweep of park and gardens, be miraculously granted a vision of Peader.

'Goodbye now and God go with you,' Katy called after the two families setting off for America. With Statia and Hannah she stood in the road watching Tim Coffey and his family, Mary Doyle and hers begin the long walk to the port.

'Setting off for the other side of the world with nothing but the clothes they stand in, and a few rags in a bundle,' Hannah said with a catch in her voice.

'And there's the rain,' Katy said, turning her face already wet with tears to look up at the sky, 'they'll be drenched before they get as far as Carey's, sodden to the skin before they reach the port.'

'That's if they ever do.'

'Why wouldn't they, Statia?' Hannah asked as they began walking back to Katy's.

'Haven't you heard tell what's happening to people on the road?' Katy and Hannah said they had not. 'They're being attacked at every hand's turn. Pounced on by men and women like walking skeletons, green round the lips from the grass they've been eating. People gone mad with hunger, robbing anyone passing. A man last week was stripped naked, left the way he came into the world, and his few ha'pence taken as well.'

'God between us and all harm! You wouldn't credit your own would do such things!' Katy exclaimed as they went into the kitchen.

'They'd cut your throat for a crust or the skin of a potato, that's how desperate they are,' Statia said sitting down.

Katy motioned to Statia to say no more for a minute and set about sending the children into the other room. 'And don't,' she called after them, 'be listening at the door to what doesn't concern you.'

Hannah sat by Statia, and Katy knelt to build up the fire. While she put on sods she heard them talk about Charlotte, Hannah saying how she was melting away. Not eating enough for a bird.

Rage surged through her at the thought of Charlotte having the opportunity to refuse food. Her breath blowing the fire gained strength from her fury, her cheeks ballooned, red from anger, and the flames beginning to lick the turf.

'Melting, that's what she is. There's days I don't think she'll last till Miss Catherine comes. Times I want to pick her up in my arms, carry her out of the House and tell Peader to fly with her. But even if I had the strength, there's no chance for the Master seldom leaves her side. Seldom eats either.'

Katy before the fire listened and struggled with her emotion. Furious with the concern Hannah was showing, the sympathetic noises from Statia. Wanting to round on the pair of them, lash out with her tongue. Say wasn't it well for Miss Charlotte, all she had to contend with was a broken heart. Ask what was that compared to six children looking up in your face for food. Day after day having to refuse them. Day after day watching them grow thinner, their lovely limbs wasting, their lips cracked, sores on their skins that had been as smooth as silk.

Ask them, what did Miss Charlotte know about suffering, or love either? Did she know what it was to lay next to a husband as if he and you were strangers? Have a heart grown cold and stubborn, so you couldn't reach out to him?

'You'll have the fire up the chimney if you don't stop puffing and blowing,' Statia said, interrupting Katy's thoughts. She got up from the hearth, and sat with the women who talked for a while longer about Charlotte. And Katy wished for Catherine to come quickly and take her away. And for Peader to be gone too, to anywhere on earth so long as he wasn't with her. Wished for them to be gone their separate ways, deprived of each other. It wouldn't be fair for them to have each other. It wouldn't be fair for God to grant them that.

In an attempt to divert her thoughts she began to talk about all the families that had left for America. 'A quarter of the parish vanished,' she said.

'And that's without counting them that'd died of the

fever,' Statia said. 'Do you know sometimes I wonder if there's a God at all, or if there is then maybe He's blind.'

Hannah gasped, her face paled, then she scolded Statia for being blasphemous.

'What do you know about anything?' Statia retorted. 'You're sheltered from the worst being above in the House. If you saw what I see you might ask the same question. Up on the bog families have died like flies from the sickness, the way Padraig's wife and family did, Lord have mercy on them. And there's Dano getting his field back without having to lift a finger. An oul bastard like that thriving, is it any wonder you'd ask questions.'

'May God forgive you, Statia. Unless you mend your ways you'll never go to Heaven,' Hannah said with genuine concern.

'Well if I go to the other place it's my arse that'll burn and not yours,' Statia snapped.

Hannah, deciding that any more criticism of Statia would result in further blasphemy, steered the talk in what she thought was a safe direction.

'Do you know,' she said, 'I was just thinking about the day the war with France finished. There was a kind of celebration in Clifden, a bit of a parade. I remember it well. My father took me by the hand to see it. I was that excited. I can see it all, as plain as if it was yesterday – the soldiers marching, and the band, and me wearing the big pink ribbon my mother had tied in my hair.' She sat back with a rapturous look upon her face.

Katy said nothing, she had heard the story many times, so had Statia. Before, when Hannah related it, they listened and smiled, afterwards when alone laughing

436

good-naturedly at Hannah's deliberate lapse of memory about her age. But this evening Statia's tolerance had been stretched too far by Hannah's reference to what would happen to her soul. She wasn't letting Hannah get away with it. So with a look of derision on her face and a mocking tone in her voice she said, 'Queer people and queer fashions I'm thinking they had in Clifden.'

'How do you say that, Statia?' Hannah asked innocently.

'Because the war with France finished in 1815. Thirty-one years ago if I'm not mistaken. And it's yourself that would have been long passed wearing big pink ribbons or catching your father's hand at the time.'

Hannah's face went the colour of a beetroot. 'Are you calling me a liar or what? A child I was, by my father's hand,' she blustered. '1815 it was, that's . . .' She began to count on her fingers.

'Thirty-one years ago – you must have been the hairy oul child. A sight all right, wouldn't you say, Katy?'

But Katy wouldn't be drawn. Not for the world would she take sides against kind, gentle Hannah. Not for anything would she assist Statia in exposing her age. God love her, still romantic, maybe still thinking about the boy she had loved, that her mother had put between.

'Leave it for the Lord's sake the pair of you, and let's talk of something else,' she said, and for a while they did. Then Hannah made an excuse to go, and went.

She was no sooner gone when Statia said, 'Bloody oul maids, full of religion, and still hoping for a man! Does she think we don't see the hair sprouting out of her chin. Looking for a man still, and little does she know the comfort of being your own mistress.'

' 'Tis easy for you to talk, you had a man.'

'I did, and thank God I planted him before he put me in an early grave.'

'Didn't you love him?'

'Love how are you? What say did I have in the marriage, wasn't it arranged for me? Though mind you he was a fine man – not bad-looking at all. And for a time I was delighted with myself. In the beginning he was full of plamais and I like butter in his hands. Never denying him his rights. Morning, noon and night he'd be at it. I was young myself and warmed to it. But God bless us after a time it became a terrible chore. For he got stout with all the drink, and wasn't able for the job, falling asleep on top of me. Me laying there thinking the bed was going to collapse under us. Love is right! It went soon enough I can tell you. And I shed no tears when he went. I had the bed to stretch out in, and not be poisoned with the smell of porter.'

– Is that how I'll finish up? Katy wondered when Statia became silent. Will I in the years to come sit by the fire and talk so? Dismiss all the wonder and delight that was love? Mock and make light of what was lost, learn a bitter consolation through the loveless years? Remember only what was crude and foolish about my union with Jamsie?

'You haven't a word to throw to a dog. Is it thinking of America you are, wishing you were off?' Statia said breaking in on Katy's thoughts.

'Yes,' she lied. 'I was.'

'Do you give it much thought?'

'I do and I don't. I say to myself wouldn't I be a fool to do anything hasty like leaving the cottage and two fine fields. Then for that again the fear comes over me, God

438

forbidding all harm, that the potatoes could fail a second time, and then I want to run out of here. But sure thinking is all it does be, for where would we get the passage money?'

'Where indeed,' Statia said and got up from the stool. 'I'll say goodnight so.'

Katy went with her to the door and stood watching her go up the boreen. – Don't let me finish like her, she willed. Let me be weak so that in my weakness I'll become supple and learn to give. Let me find the softness Jamsie says I've lost. Let me have an openness about me so I can tell him my fears. Let me tell him I want his arms around me, my head on his chest, lay secure again in his love. And let him have the same give, let him reach for me, too.

Her mind was full of the longing to put things right between herself and Jamsie, so that when he came soon after Statia leaving, she smiled at him, stood very close to him while relating how Hannah and Statia had had words, even reaching out and touching him. – If he noticed a change in my manner, she thought, he's not letting on. But, she reminded herself, she needed to be patient – what had gone wrong between them couldn't be put right in a minute.

– The divil fire him, for being the stubborn man, she said to herself as she divided the stale bread Hannah had brought, putting one part away for the morning, soaking the rest in hot water and sharing it for the evening meal. Afterwards she put the children to bed, and when she returned to sit by the fire began talking to Jamsie, telling him she knew she was hard to live with nowadays. Looking at his handsome face. It was so thin, the eyes too big for it. She yearned to take it between her hands, to kiss it, to make him know she loved him.

But he gave her no encouragement. She wondered if he was even listening to her – you never knew what went on in anyone's mind, not even them you'd lived with for years. She approached him intending to touch him again, saying before she reached him, 'I don't mean to be short with you, always making digs at you. It's the worry – I'm always that worried about . . .'

'About what?'

'Well, everything.' She stopped where she was, amazed that he'd put such a question, didn't he know she was worried? What else could she be but worried with starvation never far from their door. Resentment stirred in her, her new-found resolution began to waver, and her voice when she spoke had lost the earlier gentle tone.

'I've been living in dread and fear since that pair were found out. Afraid of my life that the Master will come to his senses, know of our part in the affair and evict us.'

Jamsie shrugged his shoulders. 'If he evicts us he will, don't run to meet it.'

'That's great comfort I must say. Great comfort indeed! I hope you'll feel as airy when we're on the road walking to the workhouse.'

'A chance would be a fine thing,' Jamsie said, getting up from the fire, taking his hat from the peg and putting it on. 'In the workhouse you'd be sure of a bit of food. People are clamouring to get in, and the authorities keeping them out. You needn't worry about the workhouse.' He went to the door.

'Where are you off to now?'

'To Carey's.'

'With what might I ask?'

'He's given score again on the promise of the crops.'

'What crops? What are you talking about? We've no crops, only the potatoes, please God. They're for eating, not selling. How will you pay?'

He smiled sardonically. 'I'll worry about that when the time comes,' he said and went out.

'You good-for-nothing waster,' she said to the empty room. 'Me sitting here like an eejit trying to get round you. And you with not a thought bothering you, nothing in your mind only that Carey was giving score.' Bitterly she thought – Isn't Statia right? Wasn't every word she spoke true? What's love, only giving in to the selfishness of a man? She had been a fool to suppose otherwise – love if it had ever existed between herself and Jamsie was a thing of the past. 'And what's more I don't care,' she said to herself. 'Let tonight be a lesson to me. And I'll not sit by the fire waiting for him to come in. I'll drag out the palliasse, and like Statia enjoy the comfort of it, and be asleep before he comes back.'

Some days there was nothing at all to eat, at other times Hannah brought what Charlotte refused and, Katy felt sure, part of her own meals. The children seldom went far from the cottage, not having enough energy. And though Katy found their constant presence sometimes irritating, she consoled herself it was as well for them not to be near strangers passing above on the road, maybe catch the fever from them.

When fear for her family, and sorrow at the bitterness

that ate into her, that made her still unsympathetic to the plight of Charlotte and Peader, not speak to Jamsie if she could help it, became unbearable, she sought comfort by gazing at the hills, looking at the cornfields, the golden grain splashed red where poppies grew, at the potato patches awash with pink blossom, the ditches carpeted with harebells. Taking consolation from things as they should be. A hope rising that soon in her heart, in her home, the same miracle might happen, that all would be as it once was.

One afternoon near the end of August she stood by the cottage drawing hope from the scene she surveyed – the hope alternating with worry, for Jamsie, against her wishes, had taken the children to the strand. Dismissing her protests that they weren't able to walk, and fear that they might meet strangers who were sickening with the fever. 'There's no strangers ever go to the strand, and the walk will strengthen them,' he had said and took them.

Now they were a long time gone, and she worried in case the walking skeletons Statia had described might have come upon and attacked them. Then she heard the dog barking and knew they were returning. He was running on ahead. She wondered where he got his energy from, how he managed to survive. He was that thin, you wouldn't think he had it in him.

'You poor oul thing, where were you all this time? And you didn't bring me a rabbit. A rabbit would have been the fine thing to bring.'

Prince wagged his tail, and Katy continued to talk. 'I'd have made the grand stew. Lovely things they used to do with rabbits years ago in the House. Stuff their bellies with

442

soft white breadcrumbs, herbs and onions, put fat rashers across them to roast. Or sometimes they'd be stewed with young carrots and barley. Dishes to make your mouth water put before the servants.'

The dog, exhausted from hunger and activity, lay down at Katy's feet.

'Ah, don't mind me, Prince, prating about all I could eat. Sure I know there isn't the smell of a rabbit. I do dream about food, all the lovely things I ever ate.'

Then she heard the voices of Jamsie and the children, they were soon at the door, crowding round her, laughing and excited the way they hadn't been for a long time.

'Mammy, Mammy!' the twins chorused as they went into the kitchen, 'wait till you see what we've got for you.'

Thomas glowered at them, and threatened to puck them if they said one more word. Katy entered into the excitement saying she wondered what it could be they had. Thomas, she saw, had something hidden behind his back. 'What is it? Tell me, I can't wait.'

'Shut your eyes,' he said and she did.

'Glory be to God!' she exclaimed in mock terror. 'What is it at all? I think it's an oul frog by the feel of it.'

The children squealed with delight, and told her to open her eyes.

'Two mackerel!' Her voice was filled with wonder. 'Two beautiful shining mackerel! Where did you get them at all?'

'We met Peader on the strand. The mackerel were running, but running the other way for he only got the two,' Jamsie said.

'With the boat he'd have got a shoal. But still wasn't it

kind of him to part with the two.' Katy took the fish that were hanging on a grass loop from Thomas's finger. 'It's a feast we'll have, and Prince have the heads.'

'We've something else,' Bridget said coming forward, holding out her cupped hands. ''Twas Daddy found them, he said they were for you, I only picked them. But they're only weeshy ones,' she said apologetically.

'Sure weeshy wild strawberries are the sweetest things in the world,' Katy assured her. 'Six of them. There'll be one each and the big fella I'll cut three ways for Danny, me and Daddy. A feast is what we'll have.'

In no time the fish was gutted and down in the pot, and the dog devouring the heads Katy had flung outside for him. When the mackerels were cooked she shared them between the family. They ate the cream and brown flesh, the skin, and sucked the bones. The sweet berries they held in their mouths a long time before swallowing them.

'What I wouldn't give now for a cup of tea,' Katy said when the food was finished. 'That's the way it is, an hour ago if someone said I'd have a feed like this, I'd have thought there was nothing else to wish for. And here I am dissatisfied already. That's human nature for you.'

Before long the richness of the unaccustomed food was giving everyone pains in their stomachs. 'They'll pass now in a minute,' Katy told the complaining children. 'Once your belly gets used to having a bit in it again they'll soon go.' And after a while the discomfort went.

Later in the evening Jamsie set out again to drink on score. There was a crowd in Carey's, the biggest he had seen since before last year's failure. Like himself, he knew the majority had no money. But their hopes were high.

The potatoes would be in soon, and God was good, some-where a day's work might be found. You had to live in hope or lay down and die.

– Carey must be giving tobacco as well, he thought, pushing his way through the crowded smoky room. Peader was sitting at an upturned barrel wedged between the wall and counter. 'Be god, that fella's had an early start, he looks three parts cut, not Peader's way at all,' he said to himself.

Peader looked up, saw Jamsie and called him a drink. 'Well?' Jamsie said, sitting down.

'Well what?' Peader asked cantankerously.

'What ails you? Amn't I only making talk.'

'What ails me is annoyance. Annoyance with myself that I didn't get out of here years ago. The night you took Katy from me – that's when I should have gone to America.'

Jamsie felt uncomfortable with how the talk was going. Out for a bit of craic he'd come, not to have Peader looking at him accusingly, referring to something that had never been mentioned before. He was drunk sure enough.

Peader continued to regard him as if it was this minute he had taken Katy, saying nothing, just staring until Jamsie could bear it no longer and asked with impatience and a hint of the anger he was beginning to feel, 'Well what the bloody hell kept you; what stopped you going to America?'

'A thousand things,' Peader said in a slurred voice, his eyes half closed. 'Things you wouldn't give a second thought to. The hills with the clouds on them like a wispy cloth. Smoke going up from chimneys, the smell of the turf

445

burning on the hearth below. The sight of girls dancing here at the Cross, their feet flying in time to the fiddle. The great craic there used to be. My boat rocking on the water. The mackerel running, or the mayfly rising. The madness that took hold of us then with the trout leppin, though they weren't ours to catch. Man, there was a million things. Things here inside me that I wouldn't know how to tell.' He beat at his heart with a closed fist.

The accusatory look was gone from his eyes. He looked like a small boy again, Jamsie thought, like the boy he had sat in the hedge school with, like his lifetime friend. He loved him. He was sorry to see him in such a state.

'Sure you could still do it,' he said.

'Aye, and I will when I find a way to get Charlotte out. Do you know what's happening to her, do you, Jamsie O'Hara?'

Jamsie shook his head.

'Well, I'll tell you. She's starving herself to death. She'll die up there on me. She'll die and be laid in the clay without me ever seeing her face again.'

'She will not. It's only a vagary, it'll last no time, she'll be eating before the week's out,' Jamsie said with all the assurance he could muster.

'She'll die, I tell you, unless I get her out. And how can I? Tell me that?' he shouted, at the same time crashing his fist on the barrel top, making the slops of porter splash his face and Jamsie's. Who, after wiping his hand across his cheek, leant forward and said, 'But commere, what makes you certain she's fasting? I've heard tell she was picking, but not a word about fasting.'

'That's because Hannah thinks Katy has enough to

worry about. But it's the truth. Charlotte hasn't let food pass her lips for a week. Statia told me, she got it from Hannah. And Kilgoran's out of his mind altogether. He was bad enough before, but the starving of her has him raving.'

'God help them all,' Jamsie said. 'Such goings on in the House, it's terrible. But tell me now, isn't the other one, Miss Catherine, due any time? Maybe she'll make the pair of them see sense. You'd never know what could happen. Miss Charlotte could stop the fast, and sure the Master could relent.'

'About me and her? Are you losing your mind, too?' Peader's voice was loud and angry again.

'I didn't mean that. But he might stop locking her up, and you would have a chance. Or Hannah get lenient and take in a letter, bring one out – sure wouldn't that be something.' He reached out a hand to touch Peader.

Peader shrugged it off. 'You!' he said scornfully, 'you always look for the easy answer. Live in hopes, that's you. Isn't that what you're doing this minute? If I wasn't here Carey would be marking up your drinking. You're living in hopes of a good crop, maybe a day's work. You were always the same. The easy answer, the easy way out, that's you, Jamsie. Years ago you should have taken Katy to America. I told you often enough. If I was in your shoes I'd beg, borrow or steal to get my family out. But you ...' Whatever else he intended saying Jamsie never heard for Peader folded his arms on the barrel top, laid down his face and fell asleep.

– Stocious, Jamsie thought. A man that rarely drank unconscious with it. Lashing me with his tongue to ease his own heart. Well, sleep was the best thing for him. Tomorrow, if he remembered, no one would be sorrier than Peader.

Jamsie left him. On the way home he went over in his mind the things Peader had said. He was right. Long ago he should have taken Katy away. Maybe if he had things wouldn't be the way they were between them. It was like living with a stranger. The way she looked at him, her voice cutting him to the quick. All the love and laughter gone out of her. This evening for a minute when he came in with the fish there was glimpse of what she once was, but it didn't last. And when he'd arrive home now, if she wasn't asleep, she'd greet him with silence. If only she'd say something, shout at him in anger like before. If only she didn't most of the time make him feel he didn't exist.

He stopped on the road he was walking. Above in the sky the moon like a globe of silver shone on the little fields sloping to the river. The night was full of sounds, leaves rustling, small animals scurrying in the undergrowth. The air was sweet with the smell of blossom and burning peat.

He looked and listened and breathed in the sweet smells, and thought how he knew every one of the cottages scattered on the hills, in the fields. Knew the name of every man, woman and child within their walls. He could enter any one of the kitchens even at this hour of the night and be welcome. That if God at this minute struck the sight from his eyes, blind, he could still find his way from one end of the parish to the other. And he thought of the empty cottages, Tim Coffey's and Mary Doyle's, and the others. No smoke rising from them. And what a terrible sad thing it was to have to go far across the sea. To leave all this behind. A terrible thing to be a stranger in a strange land. He shuddered and went on.

Katy was on the pallet and appeared to be asleep. He looked at her and remembered other nights. Wanted to kneel down and take her in his arms. Tell her he loved her. Kiss her eyes and her throat, put his hand on her breast, ask her to lift up the shift and let him lay next to her. Feel her skin beneath his hands, her heart beating next to his.

He undressed and got into the bed. She moved away. – Maybe she's awake and doing it deliberately: but, maybe she's asleep and doing it instinctively, he thought with a great feeling of grief and loss.

It rained during the night. Katy heard it when once she rose to comfort Danny who cried that his stomach hurt. She returned to bed and lay for a while listening to the rain before falling asleep. When next she woke it was still dark, but somewhere a cock crowed and she knew it was nearly morning. She got up, put on her bodice and skirt, then knelt before the fire to revive it. Raking the ash, placing bits of twigs on the faint glow that remained, blowing gently again and again until a flame danced round the sticks, feeding it pieces of turf. Then she put on water to boil in a pot.

While she waited for it to heat she went to the window and looked out at the sky. She saw the heavy black clouds parting, a faint light filtering through, the plants stirring in the breeze which was shifting the clouds. She returned to watch the pot, not understanding why there was an uneasiness about her heart. Then she realized what was causing it. Terror seized her. The smell was back, it was here in the room. It was in her mouth like before, she could taste it. 'Oh Jesus, no!' she cried and ran outside.

The smell enveloped her. She saw her flowers bent from the rain, and beyond them the tall potato haulms leant towards the ground. 'They're only like that from the rain. Bent over, that's why I can't see the blossom. And the smell is in my head, imagining it I am. They're not dead, only leaning from the rain. The blossom is there all right, 'tis the light that's poor so I can't see,' she told herself aloud as she pushed through the garden trampling everything beneath her feet in her haste to reach the potato patch.

'Ah no, it's not true. They're all right. They're not dead. They can't be dead.' She walked among the plants that yesterday had been tall and strong covered in a profusion of pink-eyed blossom, touching the withered flowers. The sun rose and she saw by its light that they were blackened, charred as if a fire had swept through them.

'Ah sweet Mother of God pity me,' she cried, falling on her knees among the stricken plants, tears running down her face, dropping on to the sodden earth. 'Ah no, sweet Mother of Jesus!' Then she screamed and screamed until Jamsie and the children came running from the cottage to stare in disbelief at the devastated field.

Chapter Nineteen

Catherine had been on deck since dawn, revelling in the joy of being back in England, holding up her face to the cold wind, delighting in the sight of grey skies threatening rain. As the boat approached Tilbury, eagerly her eyes scanned the waving crowd on the quayside, searching for a glimpse of Olivia. She saw many elegant, fair-haired women who from a distance could have been her sister. But at last she spotted her, there was no mistake, the figure in the exquisite blue mantle with matching bonnet trimmed with silver grey was Olivia. So great was Catherine's delight and excitement, she abandoned her natural reserve, jumped up and down by the ship's rail, frantically waving and shouting: 'Olivia! Look! Here! Olivia!' But her voice was one of many, all competing with a Regimental Band drawn up on the quayside welcoming home its men.

It seemed to take forever before the gangplank was up and disembarkation began. But eventually she was off, clasped by Olivia, their cheeks touching, tears of joy mingling, exclamations of delight, inquiries, more kisses and embraces.

On the journey into London when calm had returned after the rapturous greeting, the sisters began to exchange news. Catherine told of her miscarriage, but did not mention the doctor's warning. Olivia was sympathetic, and assured her there was plenty of time to have babies. Catherine inquired about Olivia's husband, Peter, and the children, asking if they were well.

'Very well. Everyone is well except Papa who seems to be going crazy.'

'Papa! What ails him?' Catherine's voice was alarmed.

'Nothing I suppose, really, except that lately he writes the strangest letters. Keeps urging me to come home. Something about Charlotte being in disgrace. Nothing definite, only hints. The letters start off all right,' Olivia shrugged, 'then they become such a jumble I can't make head or tail of them.'

'But doesn't Charlotte write? Surely if Papa was ill, she would say.'

'Charlotte hasn't written for ages. Do you hear from her?'

'Very seldom, though at one time she was quite a prolific letter writer, but not lately. What on earth could Papa mean – about her being in disgrace? What could she possibly have done, she's only a child.'

'Hardly a child, you forget she's seventeen,' Olivia laughed. 'Perhaps she's found an unsuitable beau, a poor parson, maybe!'

Catherine did not respond to the joke. The smile which had wreathed her face since seeing Olivia on the quayside was now replaced by a grave frown. 'I wonder what can be going on?' she said. 'I know that Papa has been in a state since the potatoes failed last year. He used to write such lovely letters. When they changed I put it down to his worrying over the tenants – he never mentioned trouble with Charlotte.'

452

'That's quite recent, that's only come up in the last few weeks.'

'It couldn't be anything serious. I mean, you don't think Papa is really ill, do you Olivia?'

'Of course not. Probably too much port after lunch. Anyway you'll be there in a few days, see for yourself. Don't look so worried.'

'I am. I'm imagining all sorts of terrible things. I wish now I was going straight home.'

'Well, you're not. You're going to have a lovely time in London, meet your nieces and nephews. We haven't seen each other in ages. Think of all the talking we have to do.'

Catherine looked at the radiant face of her sister, and envied her the ability to take life lightly. She thought, too, of how lucky Olivia was to have a husband from whom she was rarely separated, and four lovely children. She had an impulse to tell Olivia about the doctor's grim warning. Hear her reassurance that it was utter nonsense, and that of course she could have more children. But deciding that this was neither the time nor place for such conversation, stifled her impulse and asked instead, 'Tell me, is there any news of this year's potato crop?'

'Oh that, of course you haven't heard being at sea. It's failed again. All the reports aren't in, but according to Irish sources it's a general failure, unlike last year's which was patchy. But then you know how they exaggerate.'

'Dear God, that's appalling! If it's true that the crop has failed the people are doomed.'

'If it's true, but we don't know that. Anyway don't take on so, you've gone quite pale. Do you want my smelling bottle?'

Catherine indicated that she didn't, and Olivia continued talking. 'You know what they are like, they do exaggerate.' She leant forward and affectionately took hold of Catherine's hand. 'Come on,' she coaxed, 'don't look so gloomy. I've only told you the bad news. Now listen to this. I'm coming to Ireland with you.'

'You are? That's marvellous! I feel better already. Imagine the two of us being back in Kilgoran!'

'Yes, well actually I wasn't planning on quite that. You see there's this ball.'

'What ball?' Catherine asked.

'Clanbrasil's. You know Clanbrasil, he used to come down for the fishing. He's throwing it for famine relief, a charity ball, don't you know. The tickets are frightfully expensive. Everyone's going. That's why I'm so glad you've come. Peter's tied up at the time, and I'd never brave the Irish sea alone.'

'You mean you're going to Ireland, but not going down to see Papa?'

'I might. I don't know. It depends on Peter. He's coming over to fetch me back. It depends on how soon after the ball he comes. There mightn't be time to go to Kilgoran.'

'Olivia!' Catherine's voice was aghast. 'How can you contemplate such a thing?'

'I told you, it's a question of time, anyway Peter and I are planning another visit, we'll go to Kilgoran later on. Now say you'll come with me. Don't forget it's for a good cause.'

'Me? You're not suggesting I come to the ball as well while Papa may be ill.'

'I'm sure he's not ill. You already have him at death's

454

door. He's able to write isn't he? And two nights only you'll be delayed. You can go straight down the morning after the ball. Oh, please say you'll come. I've looked forward to it so much. You and I together again. The Kilgoran girls going to a ball.' She coaxed and pleaded and argued until at last Catherine agreed reluctantly. Then clapped her small white hands. 'Oh I'm so glad. We'll have a wonderful time. I've had the most gorgeous gown made. Wait until you see it.'

'Oh, Acushla, Acushla!' Father Bolger cried, kneeling down beside the stretched body of the pony, running his hand over the silver hide from which the lustre was gone. 'Why did you pick such a time to die on me? This morning of all mornings when there's that many dying of the fever, and them that's not dying, demented with the loss of their crop. Did you not want to see their suffering any more? Could you not face them in this terrible hour that's come upon them? Did you not know that I've every house in the parish to visit, that I've to try and comfort the living, and give grace to the dying?'

Angrily he swatted at the flies settling on the dead pony, shouting at them, 'Go away. Leave him alone.' He laid his face on the rough coat, his tears fell on the little horse. 'I loved you,' he whispered. 'I'll miss you sorely.' With difficulty he got to his feet, the dew had soaked the knees of his trousers and his boots were wet and shiny. One last time he swatted with his hat at the flies. 'God has a purpose for you I suppose, though like a lot of things, 'tis hard to see what or why.'

He got Jamsie to help him bury the pony, and afterwards gave him fourpence. 'Take it,' he said, handing over the coppers, ''tis all I have, but some strong farmer no doubt will want a Mass said, and give me an offering. But bring it to Katy, don't be spending it on drink.'

After Jamsie went, he set out for Driscoll's. It scalded his heart to ask a favour from Dano, but with no horse the dying would die without benefit of the Last Sacrament, his pride was of little consequence beside that.

The Driscolls' house and farm looked more prosperous than ever, the priest thought when he arrived. 'God bless you, Father, come in do. Dano's 'ithin having his dinner,' Mrs Driscoll said when he came to the door. She took him into the kitchen where Dano sat before a plate of potatoes, bacon and cabbage. Father Bolger thought how with his several chins covered in white stubble the jowls on him and his low forehead he looked more like a bull than ever, an old fat bull. 'God forgive me, I hate him,' he said to himself.

'Sit down, Father.' Dano indicated a chair. 'Will you have a bit to eat?'

'No, thanks very much. It's the lend of a horse I'm looking for. I found the pony stretched in the field this morning.'

'Lookit that now! I'd have thought he had a few more years in him yet.'

'So would I,' said the priest, 'but with man nor beast it's something you can't be sure of.'

'Oh that you cannot,' Dano replied, and forked a pile of fat bacon into his mouth.

He was taking his time deliberately, Father Bolger knew, making him sweat for the obligement of a horse.

Well, not if he had to crawl round the parish on his hands and knees would he give Dano that satisfaction, bow down to him, plead. 'Pride,' said the voice of his conscience, 'people dying not in the state of grace.'

Dano continued eating his dinner, and Father Bolger considered the best way to achieve his ends without begging. Dano's vanity – that was the thing – he'd pander that. 'You've a grand family, you can be proud of them. Tell me now, how's the lad doing above in Dublin?'

Dano put down the knife and fork, his chest swelled before the priest's eyes. 'Passing all before him, he'll be qualified next year.' He leant back in his chair, a satisfied smile all over his face. 'What do you think of that now – Dr Seamus Driscoll no less. And the other fellow has a leaning for the law.'

– He's as proud and vain as a peacock, Father Bolger thought. It's his weakness and I'll have to play on it.

'You deserve great credit for the way you've brought them up.' Dano nodded his head in agreement. 'And your eldest daughter, has she notions of doing anything?'

'The wife thinks she has a vocation.'

'Isn't that grand, I'll pray for her. A doctor, a lawyer, and a nun! You must be the proud father. And sure you'd never know one of the young lads might want the priesthood,' Father Bolger said, thinking as the self-satisfied smile grew larger on Dano's face, 'then Dano Driscoll you'd surely have arrived, and believe your way to Heaven was guaranteed.'

'One of them might with the help of God,' Dano said. 'But what am I doing blathering away and you wanting

457

a horse. I have just the one. Come with me now, and I'll show him to you.'

'But what about your dinner?'

'Ah, to hell with my dinner, sure I can't keep you waiting while I eat.'

On the way home after burying the pony Jamsie met Peader hurrying along the road. 'Dinny Crowley's dead. I just found him cold in the bed. I'm going for the priest.'

'Poor Dinny, Lord have mercy on him. It must be terrible to die on your own. I hope he went quick. It was the shock of losing the potatoes I suppose.'

'Maybe, though there was a good age on him.'

'There was. Still, isn't it as well he's dead and won't know the disgrace of having no wake, nor a decent funeral; he'll be buried that quick.'

'And him not dying of the fever for he was well last night.'

'It doesn't matter what takes you, there's no time for doctors or coroners to say. Into the ground quick, and no exceptions . . .'

'I found his burial money, just a few shillings for he'd dipped into it for a bit of food,' Peader said. 'I'll see if it's enough to get him a coffin without the sliding bottom.'

'That you may be lucky. Go you now for the priest and I'll away home and tell Katy.'

Jamsie took the path for home, but halfway there decided his sorrow needed consoling. A man was entitled to a drink at the time of a death. A man needed one. He turned round and went to Carey's.

*

'Not for Saint Peter himself,' said the coffin-maker to Peader.

'But he didn't die of the fever. Couldn't you knock one up quick without the queer bottom? A man shouldn't have to share his coffin with anyone.'

'How else could you manage the numbers that's dying? How could I with the one pair of hands make that many? But I'll tell you what I'll do, seeing that it's Dinny, there's one there that hasn't been used yet. Not a mark on it, not a living soul laid in it. Dinny'll be the first, how'll that suit you?'

'It'll have to do, I suppose,' Peader said.

Katy kept well back from the cart that carried Dinny's coffin and three others to the graveyard. She hadn't wanted to come, was afraid to, but more afraid of admitting her fears to Statia and Hannah. They would have thought her unnatural not to follow Dinny to his long rest. But it was easy for them. They were old, not afraid to die. They had no one to leave, no one to bring the fever home to. She didn't want to go either, in case in the graveyard she stumbled over a grave, that was a certain sign you'd be the next to die, and with the weakness that was in her legs and the lightness in her head she might well stumble.

Peader and Jamsie were at the front, Statia and Hannah behind, and Katy behind them again. No one to mourn those in the other boxes for they were old, their children scattered, their friends dead or too sick to come.

Katy saw Jamsie swaying, his four pennyworth of porter making his gait unsteady. – His belly's full, which is more than can be said for mine or the children. No

459

emotion accompanied her thought, she was tired, too hungry, too spiritless to feel anything. She had no tears to shed for Dinny. No tears for anyone. Everything inside her dried up.

The cart went on, up and over old graves, desecrating them. But it had to be so, there was no one to shoulder the coffins along the narrow paths. Katy turned away her head, she didn't want to see the burials, nor see the empty coffins heaved back on to the cart. She heard the noises, the plank being pulled back, the soft thuds. A feeling returned, a dread, a horror, she didn't want to die, she didn't want her children to die. She was going home, she didn't care what Statia or anyone thought. 'I'm going home, I have to,' she said, and walked away quicker than a moment ago she would have believed possible. She didn't want to be in the path of the returning cart piled with empty coffins going back for the next load. She began to run, clutching her fear close. She was glad of it. It made her know she was alive. She wouldn't die, nor one of hers. She would mind them, eat grass, nettles, anything to keep the life in them. She would live and so would they. They shouldn't stir from outside the door, nowhere, not even to the top of the boreen, nor to the strand. She would defy Jamsie to ever take them again. She would keep them safe.

During the night Jamsie woke with pains in his stomach, in the stillness he could hear the rumblings and gurgling his belly made. Katy moved restlessly, moaned and turned so her face was close to his, her breath that was always sweet as a nut, sour-smelling now. 'Tis the hunger, Jamsie thought, like myself she's starving. Gently so as not to disturb her he laid a hand on her back, through the shift

460

he could feel her bones. Like a feather skimming water his fingers slid over her. He could count her ribs, feel every bone in her spine, where once rounded flesh had been over her hips the joint protruded. 'A ghille,' he whispered, 'you're melting away like snow in the sun. Don't die on me for I couldn't live without you.' Then he removed his hand for fear he would waken her, thinking that while she slept there was ease from the hunger. But morning would come and would come with nothing to break her fast. He had to get food.

An hour before dawn he slipped from the bed, and without making a sound found a small knife with a sharp point, and a can once used to bring milk from the dairy at the House. He left the cottage and went swiftly to a spot near the lake where reeds grew. Kneeling by the water's edge he found one the size he was looking for, broke it and put it in the can. Then quickly went over the fields to arrive at Driscoll's farm before daylight.

He knew the exact spot where the bullocks lay. It was close to some trees and in the shelter of a small rise that gave cover to the animals, and would shield him if the light came early and someone was about at the farm.

On the journey his eyes had grown used to the dark – he could make out the shapes of the beasts, and hear the soft snuffling of their breath as he approached. His bare feet squelched in new cow pats, it was warm, oozing between his toes. The sensation and smell reminded him of another night, another farm, long ago when he had accompanied his father on a similar mission. He hoped he remembered well what to do.

The bullocks were not uneasy when he came close,

none shifted or made a sound. He wanted one standing, and chose one furthest from the others. Putting down the can he slapped the beast's rump, slapping and shoving, encouraging the animal to rise. 'Come on now, get up on your feet, and don't be running away on me.' His hands heaved at the haunches, his fingers gripping the manure-matted hair. 'Get up,' he hissed, pushing, but not too hard in case he alarmed the beast and it bellowed. At last it rose, kneeling on its front legs, then stood on all four.

He rubbed the bullock's back, gentling it, talking softly. 'I won't hurt you. Just a nick, that's all.' He moved up to the neck, still rubbing and caressing. The bullock nuzzled into him. Jamsie reached to the ground for the discarded can and took out the knife, he put it between his teeth. With his free hand he searched for and found a prominent vein between the neck and shoulder of the animal. Between finger and thumb he squeezed the vein to greater prominence. He let go and quickly took the knife from his lips, pushed the point into the vein and cut. He pulled out the knife, let it fall, took the reed from the can, pushed it into the wound and held the can beneath to receive the blood. He judged by weight when the can was sufficiently full, pulled away the pipe, threw it down, and pressed hard with his thumb on the cut vein. The bullock twitched its tail. Jamsie removed his thumb from the wound, the flow had ceased. 'There now, sure it was nothing,' he said, and careful not to spill the can, he squatted down to retrieve the knife, searching the grass until he found it.

From the direction of the sheds he heard the lowing of cows, and imagined their milk-engorged udders. How easily it would flow between his fingers. He wished it was a can of milk he was bringing home to Katy. But the cows were closely guarded, never left loose in the fields.

Katy woke when he came in. 'Where were you at this hour of the morning? And what's that you have there?' she asked nodding at the can.

'The breakfast. Look at that for a feed.' He came to the bed, and held out the can with the blood darkening in it, beginning to thicken.

'God between and all harm!' Katy recoiled at the sight and smell, sickly sweet, yet having a metallic tang. 'What did you kill?'

'Nothing,' he said, and told her what he had done. 'Sure the animal won't miss it. Get up now and I'll show you how to make a fine nourishing cake the way my mother used to.'

'It was a terrible risk you ran,' Katy said as she pulled on her petticoat. 'You could have been killed. They say Dano will shoot anyone on his property.'

'Well thanks be to God he didn't. Watch now.'

He poured blood into the pot covering its base, then held it over the half-dead fire until it set into a flat pale brown cake. The edges curled away from the sides of the pan, but it stuck in the middle, so that Jamsie had to scrape it out.

'I think maybe my mother did something else with it, put reeds or that in the bottom. Taste it. Go on, have a bit, it's good for you.'

Reluctantly Katy accepted and hesitantly chewed a mouthful. It had a strange feel to it, she thought, like the curds in buttermilk only tougher. After another mouthful she forgot her aversion, relished it, and between them she and Jamsie finished the lot. Then she made another of the strange cakes for the children, who ate it ravenously.

Katy was greatly moved by what Jamsie had done, how he had risked his life to bring her food. It showed his concern, there was good in him still. And happily she contemplated his goodness until the too-rich substance she had eaten soured first her stomach and then her mind, and she thought instead, if he hadn't spent what the priest gave him, there'd have been no need to take the risk. With the money she could have bought a couple of ounces of meal, a more natural food altogether. But taking risks, like the drink, Jamsie enjoyed. And he only ever did what he enjoyed. If tomorrow he laid hands on more money the same way it would go. She had to remember that, and not let a brown leathery cake be turning her head.

During the two days after her arrival at Olivia's home Catherine became reacquainted with her brother-in-law, nieces and nephews. The children were pretty, fair and blue-eyed, the girls like their father, and the boys like Olivia. They were adorable and Catherine longed to spend more time with them. But Olivia discouraged that, not allowing her to linger in the nursery, nor the children to stay long when they were brought by their nurse to the drawing-room.

On the night before they were to go to Ireland, Catherine appealed against the children's hasty dismissal. 'Just a little while longer, Olivia, we're going in the morning, it'll be such an age before I see them again.' But Olivia refused and when the nurse had shepherded her charges out, said, 'It's easy to see that you have no children yet, you'd soon get tired of them, I can tell you. What were we talking about before they came?'

'You were telling me about Charles.'

'Oh yes, so I was; well, our dear brother Charles has bolted.'

'Bolted? How, when, who told you?'

'Freddy, you remember Freddy, one of his disreputable acquaintances. I hadn't seen Charles for ages, and one day became full of remorse for neglecting him, so I went to his lodgings – a beastly place in Bermondsey. He wasn't there, hadn't been for weeks. Anyway I thought, that's that, he'll be in touch when the going gets bad, and told my coachman to drive home; that's when I saw Freddy, just passing Southwark Cathedral. So naturally I stopped, and got all the news. Apparently Charles' money-lending friends closed their hands on him. No more post-obits. They if no one else take this famine business seriously. Know that rent rolls are down, that inheritances may not be what they were in Ireland. So no more money. And worse, they threatened Charles that unless he coughed up something on account they would take proceedings. Freddy said they wouldn't, they know they are on to a good thing with the estate to come. But you know Charles. He got on his high horse, came the "I am the son of Lord Kilgoran, how dare you talk to me like that", and then attacked one of the men. Fortunately he escaped before the police were called. He holed up with Freddy. And from him borrowed the passage money for Australia. Poor old Charles, still I suppose it was that or Botany Bay.'

'I've no longer any sympathy for him, he's ruined Papa. Have you written to tell him?'

'What would be the point – I told you, Papa seems to have gone crazy, I showed you his letters.'

Catherine thought about the strange jumbled letters from her father, the crossed out sentences that were not rewritten, the blots of ink. References to a disgrace involving Charlotte petering out in a muddle of disjointed words. Her father was obviously not himself. She should never have agreed to attend the ball. But now it was too late to change her mind. Olivia was in a fever of excitement about it, she would have hysterics if the arrangements were altered. There was nothing to do but hope that, if her father was indisposed, his condition wouldn't worsen during the time she spent in Dublin.

Catherine and Olivia crossed from Holyhead. Before the boat sailed Olivia was sick. In the open sea the wind shrieked, the ship pitched and tossed, the structures groaned and shuddered as the wind and waves buffeted them. The sound of crashing glass and china reverberated throughout the vessel.

Olivia lay on the bunk, her skin pallid, sweating profusely, her hair that had been beautifully arranged, ruined. 'Oh dear God, I want to die. I feel so wretched, I want to die. I hate the sea. It terrifies me. I wish I'd never come. I'll never . . .'

The ship dipped steeply, Olivia retched and was sick again. While the maid cleaned up, Catherine bathed her sister's forehead with cologne, and spoke soothingly. 'Close your eyes and try to sleep. Let yourself go with the motion of the boat, don't fight it.'

'Fight it, I haven't the strength to move, never mind fight.'

After several more bouts of vomiting, Olivia, exhausted, at last fell asleep. Her maid dozed in a chair beside her, and Catherine lay down on her bunk watching the level of the porthole change as the storm continued to pound the ship. Eventually she too slept and when she woke everything was still. She got up and went to look out of the porthole. The sea was calm, there was a faint light in the sky, and on the horizon a mass just visible. She wasn't sure if it was land or cloud. Then she saw the lighthouse beam. 'The Kish,' she said, 'we're nearly in.'

Lady Rose Martin, with whom they were to stay in Dublin, had sent her coach to Kingstown. It awaited them, Catherine and Olivia got in and sat waiting while Olivia's maid and the coachman saw to their luggage.

'I can still feel the wretched motion of the boat. It will be with me for days,' Olivia complained, while Catherine looked through the carriage window noticing that the number of beggars had increased since her last visit. There was a different air about them, a dejection not usual in the ones who frequented the harbour, jostling the disembarking crowd.

The carriage moved off, and Olivia continued to complain. 'My complexion will be ruined, it always is after a bad crossing.'

Catherine murmured sympathetically, her mind preoccupied with the memory of the beggars, whole families of them huddling together, their imploring eyes. She wondered if they were people up from the country. Were the people in Kilgoran being forced to leave, too?

As the carriage neared the city, Catherine saw many more beggars as wretched-looking as those at Kingstown; people barely able to walk, clutching at railings for support, children and old people, women carrying babies. Several times she drew Olivia's attention. 'Look! Have you ever seen anything like it? Look at their faces, the colour of them, they seem half dead!'

For a while Olivia made the appropriate noises, then complained of a headache, closed her eyes and went to sleep.

The carriage slowed and stopped as it neared Ballsbridge. 'There's something blocking the thoroughfare, ma'am,' the coachman who had alighted and come to the window explained. 'I'd say we'll be stuck for a while.'

Olivia opened her eyes and looked through the window. 'Oh!' she said disappointedly, 'I thought we'd arrived at Rosie's,' and closed them again.

Catherine shifted along the seat, looked through the window and saw the woman. She was sitting outside a large red-bricked house, her back against the railings. Beside her were huddled four children, and on her lap a baby. She saw that the woman's clothes were disarranged, her legs exposed to the knees, and thought what a strange thing that was for a woman, even a beggar-woman, to be so immodest.

Then looking more closely she realized that the woman was either asleep or unconscious, dying perhaps. For how could she live, her face had the appearance of a skeleton, her exposed legs were devoid of flesh, her breast at which the baby's claw-like hand pumped hung flaccidly, a fold of grey skin crumpling in the child's fingers. She stared incredulously at the child, at the monstrous head, the bald patches on its scalp, the crusted yellow sores. Then Catherine realized the head seemed monstrous only because the body was emaciated. Her eyes moved over the other children, they too had all the signs of starvation, swollen stomachs, stick-like arms and legs protruding from their torn, filthy clothes.

She must do something. She couldn't just sit and stare. She couldn't look on while a woman and her children died from hunger on the pavement. But what? Take them into the coach and on into Dublin? Call the attention of someone passing? But as she pondered what was to be done, the coach moved off. She lowered the window and continued to look back to where the group huddled. With relief she saw that a man was approaching. He would help, surely he would. The passer-by took a snowy handkerchief from his pocket, covered his nose and mouth, and stepped off the pavement, not stepping back until he was well past the woman and her children.

Catherine closed the window and sat in the warm interior that smelled of leather and the musky scent of her sleeping sister. – So it is true, she thought, people are dying by the wayside. It isn't an exaggeration.

By the time she arrived at her hostess' residence in one of Dublin's fashionable squares, she had decided to remain in Ireland indefinitely. She would organize relief. She could not help everyone, but she would ensure that at least in Kilgoran people would have food. She would see to that first thing in the morning, contact one of the Bible Societies, they would help. And tonight she would tell Olivia of her plans, perhaps she, too, would assist.

Lady Rose Martin, a tiny bird-like creature, very fashion-conscious, and reputed to be one of Dublin's best hostesses, gave a small dinner party to welcome back Catherine and Olivia. Olivia, who had spent the afternoon resting, and whose maid had worked wonders with her hair, looked completely recovered from her journey, and ate heartily of the game soup, cold salmon, and roast quail.

Catherine had little appetite, and when she began to dismember the frail bird was reminded of the frail bones she had seen sticking from beneath the tattered clothes of the dying woman's children, of the baby's claw-like hand. She felt nauseated, and pleaded biliousness. A servant removed the offending dish. Rosie said she often felt indisposed, unable to face food after travelling, but Catherine must try the delicious water ices, they were so refreshing.

After dinner when the women withdrew to the drawing-room, the conversation centred on the Clanbrasil Ball. Who would be there, and how much was likely to be raised. Then Rosie complained how tiresome it was that primary colours were no longer fashionable. 'Pastels do nothing for me. But, as they say, one might as well be out of the world as out of fashion.'

They talked of dressmakers, of hair styles, and who made the best dancing slippers in town. Catherine listened, pretended interest, until she could no longer contain herself, and when there was a lull in the conversation, commented on the numbers of beggars she had noticed on her way in from Kingstown.

'My dear,' Rosie said, 'the place is overrun with them. The situation is ridiculous. Do you know last week I could not get into Brown Thomas', Grafton Street was awash with them. Martin says law and order is breaking down. It's too tiresome, really.'

'Then it's true that conditions are serious? That there is starvation?' Catherine inquired gravely.

One of the guests laughed. 'A complete exaggeration. They always exaggerate. The truth is a rumour got round that free food was to be had in Dublin, and people from the country just poured in. My dear, you should know what they're like. You were reared with them, we all were – they just won't work if they can get for nothing. Charming people, but workshy I'm afraid.'

'Absolutely,' agreed another woman. 'We get so annoyed with our ghillie in the west. Lazy fellow. Not at all like ghillies in Scotland. As Freddy says, a ghillie should be rather like a superb batman. But not a bit of it in Ireland. You'd think they owned the lakes, and were doing you a favour rowing the boat.'

Rosie and Olivia looked bored with the turn the conversation had taken. An elderly woman sitting next to Catherine said, 'Don't worry, dear, things are not as bad as they seem. And people are helping what distress there is. The Quakers are doing splendid work, and the Bible Societies, too, so I believe.'

'But I can't help worrying. This is Ireland not India, one doesn't expect to see such sights here. Why, this morning I saw a woman dying in the street. Can you imagine that?' She described the scene in detail.

'Really, Catherine!' Olivia said reprovingly, 'you make me feel quite faint.'

'A tinker, dear, drunk probably. They often are, you know,' Rosie said dismissively.

'A tinker, maybe, though surely that matters not. The woman was dying, not drunk. Dying in the street – her children too – from starvation.'

'Dear Catherine, you are overwrought,' Rosie said soothingly, and adroitly changed the conversation.

Later, when Catherine and Olivia were in the latter's bedroom, Catherine told of her plans to organize some sort of relief in Kilgoran.

'How? What will you do, you've hardly any money and Papa has none.'

'I'll contact one of the Bible Societies, their offices are here in Dublin. We'll start a soup kitchen.'

'A Bible Society!'

'Yes, why not?'

'They make conditions, didn't you know? They are evangelical. The tenants won't take their soup.'

'Of course they will. They must be starving – like the woman I saw today. Katy and her sweet children, Statia, all starving.'

'And Father Bolger, have you forgotten him?'

'Why do you ask that?'

'He won't let them take your soup. Don't you realize that? Don't you know that much about the tenants? They'll do what he says, not what you or Papa tell them. And he won't let them take soup from the Bible Society.'

'You're wrong. Of course he will. He'll be delighted that they won't starve.'

'How little you know them or their clergy for all that you love them. You're a sweet trusting girl. Don't you know they only tolerate us? Oh, they're civil and charming, but that's all on the surface. Their secret selves we know nothing about, couldn't begin to understand. They're not like us, they're not rational. If the priest tells them to starve, they will.'

'I'll never accept that. Father Bolger is a reasonable man, an educated man. You talk as if he was a fool who'd let his people die rather than take the soup. You're wrong, Olivia.'

Olivia was no longer interested. She yawned, then said, 'If you're so sure, go ahead. Now I'm going to bed. I came over early to be well rested before the ball.'

'I don't suppose you'd cancel your arrangements for going back with Peter and come down to see Papa and help me get things organized?' Catherine asked.

'Sorry, darling, I really couldn't. I never liked the place when things were normal, I wouldn't venture near it now. And in any case I couldn't, we are spending the rest of September in Scotland, there's some good cubbing.'

After she had left, Catherine thought how wrong her appraisal of the situation was. Of course Father Bolger wouldn't interfere, but before she went to sleep decided that as a matter of courtesy she would consult with him.

In Kilgoran, Charlotte continued to fast, and Hannah to lament the fact to Jamsie, Peader and Katy. Katy felt not an atom of sympathy for Charlotte, though her heart was touched by the sight of Peader's haunted look. But Charlotte, she thought, was a spoiled crot of a girl, her starvation was from choice. And let her keep it up, for the more she fasted the more food there was for Hannah to bring.

And without that, her children, who had no choice in what was happening to them, would starve.

As the days passed and Hannah's reports of Charlotte were the same, Peader became desperate. He had to get word to her, force Hannah to take a letter. He had to let Charlotte know he loved her, more now than ever. Tell her she was never from his thoughts. That he still intended taking her to America. Convince her he loved her, that she had something to live for.

So on the day that Catherine and Olivia were preparing to attend the Clanbrasil Ball, he wrote Charlotte a letter and set out for Kilgoran House, risking the possibility that Lord Kilgoran might spot him from a window, maybe, in his demented state, fire on him. Praying that he wouldn't, and that Hannah could be persuaded to give Charlotte the letter.

Hannah moved aimlessly round the vast kitchen talking to herself. 'Look at the state of the place and Miss Catherine coming home.' She rubbed ineffectually at grease embedded on the wall by the range, blew at the dust thick on the dresser, and stared despairingly at the kitchen table ingrained with dirt. 'I remember when you were as white as the driven snow, scrubbed every day, sand sprinkled on you and brushed with the grain. And look at you now, yellow as an old woman's tooth. What will Miss Catherine think at all?'

She found a damp rag and dabbed at the table, still talking to herself. 'Everything gone to wrack and ruin. The kitchen that was my pride and joy destroyed with dirt and neglect, cobwebs as big as any Nan ever had in the dairy, hanging from every corner. But with the best will

474

in the world, one pair of hands can't do it. A battalion of servants was ever needed to keep order. It takes all my time and energy making a bit of food and running up and down the stairs, that I'm not able for, trying to stop that child killing herself, nothing but water passing her lips.' She gave up her attempts at cleaning the table, stopped talking to herself and sat down by the range.

Peader came quietly into the kitchen and was beside her before she knew it. When she saw him, her hand flew up to her mouth and her eyes were fearful. 'What are you doing here? Have you gone mad? Don't you know the Master could come in this minute and find you?'

'I don't care if he does. In a way I wish he would. Maybe I could talk sense to him. Tell him the fever's raging. That if Charlotte gets it she hasn't the constitution to fight it. That locking her up is wrong. That I . . . Anyway that isn't what I've come to say.'

'What was it then? And with the help of God she won't get the fever. Miss Catherine's coming. She'll eat then. Everything will be all right when Miss Catherine comes.'

'It won't. She still won't eat. I know her. She thinks I've deserted her. And can you blame her? All this time and not a word from me. You should have taken in a letter, you've got to take this one.' He held out the note. Hannah shook her head. 'Don't refuse me, Hannah. If you don't take it Charlotte will die. Maybe she still will, maybe I've left it too late. But give it to her, please.'

'I won't. I won't take it up. You don't know what you're asking.'

'Then you'll help her to commit suicide. Do you realize that? You'll be helping her to commit a mortal sin. Don't shake your head, it's the truth. Suicide's a sin whether or not you're a Catholic. If she dies it's because she's lost hope. And if you don't bring up the letter you're encouraging her despair.'

Hannah said nothing, and Peader continued, 'Please, Hannah. I love her. Don't let her die on me.' Hannah looked away from him, she couldn't bear to see the grief on his face. To see a man like Peader, his eyes swimming with tears, pleading with her like a little child. It was heart-breaking.

'Don't refuse me, Hannah. I know you love Charlotte too. I know you don't want her to die. Don't let her. You'll be doing the right thing. She'll eat, she'll live. Take it to her.'

They were both crying, Peader silently, Hannah sobbing openly. 'Oh, Peader, son, I don't know what to do for the best. I'm that afraid. Afraid for her, and for the Master. Now you've made me afraid of something that never crossed my mind. Sure I never thought of suicide. Would it be the same sort of sin and Miss Charlotte a Protestant? Are you sure about that?'

'Isn't it the same God, Hannah? Wouldn't He judge the taking of your life that He gave you, the same way?'

'He would, I suppose,' Hannah said with not a lot of conviction. 'It's a thing I never pondered, that Protestants might have the same Maker as ourselves, and be judged the same.'

Hannah looked confused and frightened. Peader regretted causing her bewilderment, putting a new fear into her mind. But his main concern was that Charlotte should get

476

the letter, and he pressed his advantage. 'A terrible sin it would be for her as much as you. Will you take it?'

'All right, I will.'

'Miss Charlotte, 'tis for you, a letter from Peader. Read it now quick before your father comes back, and let me have it immediately.'

She was so weak, Hannah had to lift her up on the pillows, unfold the note and place it in her hands. 'Read it now quick,' Hannah urged, 'and let me have it back.'

My Love,

I can't come to you today no more than I could this long time, but I'm thinking of you as I always am. Every morning when I open my eyes I see your face. It's before me all day, and God is sometimes kind and sends you into my dreams.

I see you as I did at our first meeting in the little wood. There was holly, full of scarlet berries, like your lips, and your hair was like a robin's wing. You smiled, and said, 'I'm Charlotte, Charlotte Kilgoran.' I fell in love with you then and have loved you every minute since, and will love you for every minute to come until eternity. And soon we will spend all the minutes, the hours, and years together.

God will send a way for me to come to you. You must be ready. You must be strong, able to fly with me. And then we'll be united for ever and ever.

I know your sister is coming soon. When she does, don't fight her. Don't get angry if she talks of taking you far away. Remember I won't let her. No one, only me, will take you.

When you've read this give it to Hannah to burn. Promise me you'll do that. For only if Hannah can destroy the letter will she bring in others. You'll do that, won't you, my little brown bird? And when the letter is taken care of Hannah will bring you food, and you'll eat it. And every day until I come for you you'll eat and grow strong for we have a long way to fly.

I love you.

Peader

'Oh Hannah,' Charlotte held the letter to her breast. 'Oh Hannah, he never stopped loving me, never for a minute.'

'Sure I told you that. Come on now, hand it over. Your tears won't move me, not one bit,' Hannah said wiping away her own, taking the paper out of Charlotte's hands. 'Lay back and before you know it I'll be back with a mug of bread and milk mashed that soft you won't feel it going down.'

Chapter Twenty

Across the street from the early Georgian mansion, watching the guests arrive for the ball, stood the crowd. Catherine saw them as her carriage drew up. It was dusk, and she could not discern them clearly, but imagined their pallor, the thinness of them, the cold they were feeling, their hunger. They reminded her of the dying woman, and she shuddered as she followed Olivia up the broad flight of shallow granite steps into the warmth and brilliantly lit hall of Clanbrasil House.

In the salon with its stuccoed mouldings of exquisite birds, garlands and cornucopias spilling fruit and flowers on walls and ceilings, its vast expanse of gleaming wooden floors scattered with brightly-hued oriental rugs, and its elegant furniture, Lord and Lady Clanbrasil waited to receive their guests.

Lady Clanbrasil, a tall, fair-haired woman, wore a gown of pale pink satin, a tiara of rubies and diamonds, on her neck the same precious stones shone. Lord Clanbrasil, as dark as his wife was fair, and several inches taller, had on the dress uniform of a Colonel of Hussars, his red tunic laced with gold braid, his epaulettes of fine chain mail.

Catherine and Olivia joined the line waiting to be presented. 'The Honourable Mrs Peter Melrose. Mrs Edward

Synge,' the butler, resplendent in the Clanbrasil livery, announced. The sisters were greeted by their hosts, exchanged pleasantries, and moved on.

Halfway down the room on gilded chairs that looked too fragile to support their stoutness, sat two elderly women. One wore a short-sleeved, low-necked dress of ivory-coloured silk. Her exposed arms and bosom were creased and crumpled, the skin like old used tissue paper. The other woman's dress was fuchsia pink and clashed horribly with her dyed red hair. She held an ear trumpet close to her head to hear what her companion was saying.

'The Kilgoran gels.' They both raised their lorgnettes to inspect the approaching young women. 'She's barren, you know, a dreadful blow that for young Synge.'

'You can't say it runs in the family. Her brother's by-blows are all over the place. Rosie tells me he's made a bolt for the colonies. Run out of moneylenders before they ran him out on a convict hulk, eh,' the deaf woman said, and cackled.

'Not so loud, dear, they're coming,' her friend warned.

The two women gushed over Catherine and Olivia, said how delighted they were to see them, inquired after their father, and were most distressed he could not attend the ball. Then they admired Olivia's gown, exclaiming how beautiful was the pale lavender silk shot with silver; how cleverly it was cut, such a long narrow waist. They wondered how such fullness could be gathered into it.

'Ten yards at least,' the woman in fuchsia said.

'Twelve actually,' Olivia replied and made an attempt to move on. But the woman was fingering her gown, admiring the flounced hem, caught up at half-yard intervals by velvet bows a shade darker than the dress itself.

'And such a beautifully pleated bertha, how becomingly it frames your shoulders. What a clever choice, silver and lavender. Do show me your slippers.'

Olivia impatiently displayed a foot. 'Absolutely divine, what beadwork, and exactly the same shade as the velvet.' Then the one with the ear trumpet said in a very loud voice, 'Ah, what it is to be young and have a London dressmaker. Dublin's never been the same since the Union.'

Then they turned their attention to Catherine. Telling her how becoming was her pale primrose gown, how it suited her colouring. But before they could elaborate further, Olivia made an excuse and left them.

'Dreadful old witches,' she said, pulling and patting at the places on her dress where the woman had fingered it. 'I'd rather die than become old and horrible like them.'

'I can't imagine you ever being old or horrible,' Catherine said as they entered the ballroom.

It was ablaze with light. Hundreds of candles burned in French crystal chandeliers, the faceted droplets sparkled, and from large mirrors at either end of the room, the brilliance was reflected.

'I had forgotten how beautiful it is,' Catherine said, stopping to look round her, to gaze at the rows of white and gilt framed, blue upholstered chairs lined along the walls, the sumptuous velvet hangings trimmed with gold and caught back from the long sash windows with silken cords. Raising her eyes to the painted ceiling where rosy cherubs with dimpled hands offered posies to a goddess reclining on a cloud formation, a swirl of gauze flowing around her. Thinking as her gaze shifted that so real did the flowers, features, limbs and flesh appear, if you could reach to touch them they would feel soft, formed, yielding and warm.

Olivia moved on from her staring sister, down the room and joined a group of young men and women. Slowly Catherine followed, noticing as she did so the flowers arranged on side tables, banked in every recess, surrounding the raised dais where the musicians waited. Flowers from the garden, from the hot-houses. Roses and dahlias, carnations and freesias, white, yellow and pink, massed greenery and trailing ferns spilling from the container, the fragrance mingling with that of the guests' perfumes and powders.

She joined Olivia and the group. Everyone was talking excitedly. The women blushing, smiling, using their fans, offering their programmes to men requesting dances. The musicians tuned their instruments, the sound of music heightening the excitement. All of Catherine's dances, except one before supper, were claimed. She was glad of the blank space in her prettily-decorated booklet, wished there were more. For despite being surrounded by opulence and gaiety, she was not in the mood for merry-making. The sight of so many men in uniform reminded her of Edward, and how much she missed him. And now and then she thought of the crowd outside, and wondered if they were still there in the cold night, watching the lighted windows, hearing the strains of music, smelling the aroma of food wafting up from the basement kitchens.

Suddenly there was a silence in the ballroom, the musicians ceased their tuning, breaths were held, fans remained motionless, nothing moved except the quivering flames and their reflections in the mirrors, and Lord Clanbrasil walking to the dais to announce that the ball had begun.

Then the music floated forth, a Viennese waltz, lilting and lovely. Lord and Lady Clanbrasil led the floor; silks whispered, and taffetas rustled as couples followed them into the dance. The room became a sea of swirling colour, of pinks and lilacs, of rose and cream, palest yellow, peach and apricot, of billowing silks and muslins, shimmering satins, silver shot materials rippling like water beneath the moon.

The women's feet shod in slippers of softest kid, or fabrics, beaded and embroidered, danced as though on air. Their sleek hair was centre-parted, ringleted below the ears, fair and chestnut, blue-black, it gleamed on their slightly tilted-back heads. Golden chains and silver bracelets shone, diamonds caught the light and flashed. Like swallows in graceful flight the dancers moved round the room, a swirling mass of movement and colour.

Their short-gloved hands were held by men equally as adorned as they. Men in coats of blue, burgundy, and claret colour, in scarlet tunics emblazoned with golden braid, worn over black kerseymere trousers held taut with straps beneath their feet, or pantaloons displaying shapely calves and multicoloured stockings. All had fashionable hairstyles, some wore it straight, others had curls round their heads, side locks thick and also curled. They held their partners at the correct distance, guiding them, gliding with them, reversing, swirling, some looking adoringly at the tilted-back faces.

483

The waltz finished. Young girls were returned to their chaperones, men sought their partners for the next dance. Dainty lace-edged handkerchiefs dabbed discreetly at perspiring foreheads and cheeks. Larger round-cornered handkerchiefs were taken with a flourish from the pockets of men releasing breaths of perfume. Women whose ringlets were artificial nervously fingered the combs and pins holding them in place, digging in more securely their hold before joining partners to dance a polka.

Long-legged soldiers in tight-fitting trousers, hopped one, two, three and gyrated, the women hopped with them, their heads bobbing from side to side, their ringlets bouncing, their faces flushing beneath the pearl powder. Round and round the room the couples hopped and twirled. When the polka finished they clapped enthusiastically. The women, panting from their exertion on the dance floor, tight lacing, and the weight of skirts and petticoats, finished clapping before the men. Some slid hands amongst the folds of their skirts to feel the reassuring shape of smelling bottles hanging by silken cords from their tiny waists.

The dancing continued. Waltzes and polkas interspersed with quadrilles, sets of eight and sixteen couples forming squares, executing steps and movements with grace and precision.

Into the ballroom began to drift the delicious smell of food being brought to the supper room. It mingled with the scent of flowers, of hot wax from the candles, the men and women's perfumes, their fresh clean sweat, the combination producing a perfume that had luxury as its essence.

The music stopped. Catherine was conducted from the floor, her partner thanked her and excused himself. She consulted her programme, and thankfully saw that the next dance was the one she had free. She went to the window and looked out. Below in the street she saw some figures staring up at the window. Were those the ones with no shelter for the night, the people who had come into Dublin looking for succour? A voice interrupted her thoughts.

'My dear girl, how nice it is to see you after all this time.' She turned to see an elderly man, not unlike her father, genial-looking, silver-haired, pink-cheeked, smiling at her. She knew his face, but couldn't remember his name. She greeted him warmly, hoping he wouldn't notice the omission of a title. He inquired about Edward, about India, and her father. In the middle of the conversation he beckoned a young officer standing a little way off, who came and stood by him.

'Catherine,' the old man said, 'this is my nephew Robert.' Catherine looked at the tall young subaltern, and felt a little faint – he was the image of Edward, much younger, but still the likeness was remarkable, striking enough to make her heart pound.

Robert bowed, and they chatted until interrupted by his uncle. 'Be a good chap, Robert, and remind Clanbrasil he's lunching with me tomorrow, the fellow's very absent-minded.'

When Robert had gone to do his bidding, the old man caught hold of Catherine's arm and said, 'I had to get rid of him for a minute, wanted to ask you a favour. Are you booked for the next dance?' Catherine said she wasn't.

'Good, then take him up for it, otherwise he'll stand about all night. Break the ice, don't you know. An old man's privilege, arranging these things. You're a sensible gel, give him a bit of confidence.'

'Oh, but I couldn't, really, it's not . . .'

'Nonsense! of course you could,' the old man cut her short. Robert was returning, the music beginning. 'Off you go now,' he propelled her in his nephew's direction.

'Your uncle . . .' she began to explain.

The young man smiled. 'He's always doing it, arranging for me to dance. Very bad form, annoys the ladies, I think he's mad. I don't like dancing.'

'Of course . . . I'm sorry. I didn't . . .' She was furious with this grinning boy, with his lunatic uncle, embarrassed, hovering on the edge of the dance floor.

'Except with beautiful dark ladies in primrose dresses. May I have the pleasure?'

Before she could refuse, he took her hand and led her on to the floor. In his arms, waltzing, she forgot her resentment. Was unaware of everything except the music and movement as round and round they glided. Her body relaxed on to his arm. He was smiling at her. She was dizzy, intoxicated with pleasure, with the rhythm, the melody.

His face became more like Edward's. She lost all sense of reality. He was Edward. And after the ball she would lay in his arms. She would taste the wine of his breath. His hair would smell of pomade, and faintly of cigar smoke. His heart would beat above hers.

Round and round they danced. His mouth was soft and red, his teeth gleamed. His eyes never left her face. On her waist his hand tightened, moving her towards him. She went willingly. In her mind she spoke to him. 'Oh darling Edward, it's been such a long time.'

Then they were spinning, the world was spinning. Her blood raced. Everything was going round and round and round. Then everything was silent except for the exhalation of breath. And from far away she heard the voice. 'I could die like that. I could die waltzing, couldn't you?'

She looked at the dark smiling eyes, at the face of Edward, only it changed and it wasn't Edward. And she saw it was Robert and that he didn't look at all like Edward. His hand was at her elbow, escorting her from the floor. He was saying, 'I hope your programme has a space.'

'It hasn't. I'm sorry.'

'So am I, you waltz divinely. Are you coming in to supper?'

'Well, actually I must find my sister, perhaps I'll see you later.'

'Of course,' he bowed and left her.

She went out on to the balcony, it was cold and she shivered. The stars were very bright. She wondered was it night-time in India? Was Edward looking at the stars? They were bigger there, she remembered. Was he thinking of her? 'Oh my darling, I love you. I miss you so much. What shall we do? How shall we live for the rest of our lives? All the thousands of nights? How could we?'

'I've been looking everywhere for you.' Olivia's voice was annoyed. 'You are an idiot, it's freezing, and you out here talking to the stars. You'll catch a chill. Are you coming in? Supper is being served.'

The supper tables were covered with white damask

cloths, spread with silver platters of lobster salad, galantines of ham and fowls, baskets of fruit, pyramids of black and white grapes. There were crystal goblets of champagne, glasses of sherry, and of warm water, and after the meal and shellfish were eaten, vanilla ices would follow to cleanse the palate.

Catherine and Olivia sat at a table across from the two elderly women who had earlier spoken to them. They asked if the sisters had enjoyed the dancing, lamented that their own dancing days were done. Now they spent their time in the card room, and tonight they hadn't been lucky, had lost a small fortune.

Then they returned to a conversation in progress before Catherine and Olivia arrived, at the same time cracking lobster claws, scooping out with silver implements the succulent flesh and noisily chewing it.

'Not a word of truth in it,' the one with red hair, her mouth full of food, said to her companion.

'Absolutely not,' the other shouted. 'It's all because they ate the seed potatoes. They're so feckless.'

'Indeed they are. Eating the seed, that's the truth of the failure. After all if you don't sow you shan't reap.'

They both laughed, and dug into their plates of salad. Olivia chattered about who she had danced with. Teased Catherine about dancing with Robert, warned her he had a dreadful reputation, no woman was considered safe with him. Catherine blushed, recalling her fantasy while she had waltzed with him, and was relieved she had no dances available on her programme. Loneliness and longing for Edward she knew were responsible for her flight of fancy, but Robert had held her too close and it had been very pleasant. She was sure his reputation was well deserved.

Olivia ate too much, and Catherine had to go to the cloakroom with her to loosen her stays. Olivia sighed with relief. 'Phew, I thought I should burst or faint.'

'I'll fasten them not so tight, shall I?' Catherine asked.

'No, I'll be all right in a moment. Pull them as tight as you can, I'd be a show if my waist was half an inch bigger. Hurry, the music is beginning, I mustn't miss a single dance.'

Everyone agreed it had been a wonderful ball. They shook hands, kissed cheeks, reminded each other of forthcoming events where they would meet again, and cocooned in their warm wraps and capes, settled sleepily in their carriages for the journey home.

Catherine travelling to Rosie's thought with pleasure that tomorrow she would be on her way home to Kilgoran. She wished Olivia would change her mind and come too. But knew it was a vain hope. Olivia on the opposite seat was snoring softly. Catherine looked at the passing houses, the private railed squares, the tall churches, and thought with joy of the reunion with her father.

The Dublin coach dropped her at Carey's, but the Kilgoran one wasn't waiting. Carey came out of the public house, saluted her, and said it would be along any minute. Asked would she like to come in, 'Not into the public house,' he added, 'into the parlour, Ma'am.'

Catherine thanked him, but refused. She had been sitting for so long, she welcomed the chance to stretch her legs. 'If you change your mind, you're very welcome,' Carey said, tipping his hat, and went inside.

She walked up and down, looking at the blackened potato fields; she had seen the same all along the journey, patch after patch with the appearance of places that a fire had raged through. And the dreadful stench was everywhere. But all of it was as nothing compared to the sight of the people on the roads. Barely able to put one foot in front of another, eyes sunken in the backs of their heads, or burning with a kind of mad glare, some shaking their fists after the coach.

The carriage came after a while. The coachman got down. She vaguely remembered him, he came after O'Donnell died, she had met him when she came on holidays, but surely he wasn't always so slovenly, his livery so stained, the nap worn, a green tinge showing through? And the carriage was spattered with mud, old mud, dried, it had been there for a long time. And only one horse, not a carriage horse at all.

'I've been down this three days to meet the Dublin coach,' he said, opening the door for her.

'I sent word from London that I wasn't arriving until today. Didn't my letter come?'

'Letters is it? They're a thing of the past. Gone to hell like everything else, Ma'am. Sure there's that many of the fellows on the mail dying the same as everyone else you'd be lucky if the letter came a week next Friday.'

The coach bowled along the familiar road, and her heart was beating fast, at the next bend, the gap in the trees, she would see the House, and in a very short while enter the gates. The gates were swinging open, one not level with the other. She saw with a shock that they were rusting, great flakes peeling from them, tall stinging nettles and docks growing by the sides of them. – What was Papa thinking about to let such neglect happen?

The rooks were flying overhead in the elms lining the drive, hundreds of them, more than she ever remembered at this time of the year. There couldn't have been a spring shoot. She looked from side to side as the carriage proceeded towards the House. The grass was knee-high. Where were the horses, the cattle? There wasn't a single thing grazing.

Around the last bend of the drive and the House was in view. It looked the same, thank God. Then she saw that it wasn't, as the coach turned into one of the half-circles of gravel. Weeds were sprouting through the paved path leading to the bottom step, growing in profusion up the steps. The windows were dull, a few broken, jagged panes of glass still in place. And only Hannah stood waiting to welcome her.

Where was everyone? Her father? Charlotte? The other servants? No one arrived home after a long absence without the staff, never mind the family, assembling to greet you.

The coach pulled up, the coachman opened the door, Catherine got down. Hannah came down the steps, arms outstretched. She was crying. 'Oh Miss, welcome home, a thousand welcomes.' Dabbing at her eyes with the hem of her skirt, fighting back the tears. 'Come in, astoir, and amn't I glad to see you. Amn't I glad you're back.'

'What's happened? Where is everyone, my father, Charlotte, the servants?'

'Ah, sure they've gone this long time,' Hannah was telling her, leading them into the hall. 'Them and the horses, the poor Master had to let them all go.'

Catherine was staring round the Great Hall in disbelief. Thick dust coated everything. The remains of a fire, half-burned logs, turf ash, charred sods were spilled out of the enormous grate, as if someone had started to clean it, and then forgotten to finish. She closed her eyes, picturing the room as it had been, as it was on the morning she got married. It was a bad dream. When she woke all would be as before. There wasn't a broken fanlight, patches of damp on the walls, the pennants weren't drooping, mildewed.

She opened her eyes, it wasn't a dream, and Hannah's eyes were swollen from crying. And she was urging her to come into the kitchen. Telling her not to look round, not to mind the state of it. At least it was warm and she'd soon have a sup of tea wet. And they'd let the Master doze a while longer.

It wasn't happening, none of it was real. She wasn't allowing Hannah to lead her into the kitchen. This wasn't the kitchen, not this. The kitchen smelled of good things, never of stale fat, there were never mice droppings on the dresser, it never smelled of cabbage that had boiled too long, boiled over and filled the air with the acrid smell where the water had sizzled on the hob.

And all the time Hannah never stopped talking. 'Sit down now. You'll see a terrible change in the Master, and Miss Charlotte, though she's on the mend, thank God.'

Catherine couldn't bear another minute of it. What was the matter with her? What was she doing, listening to

Hannah's prattling, and Papa and Charlotte waiting? What was going on in the House?

She got up from the chair where Hannah had put her. 'Don't bother with tea, Hannah, I'll ring for you later. No, don't come,' she said, as Hannah prepared to accompany her.

– What was Hannah thinking of, attempting to come with her? It wasn't like her. Hannah never forgot her place, Catherine thought as she went to the main part of the house. Hurrying up the stairs, along passages, her feet leaving imprints in the dust that lay like another carpet on the floors. Every room was dilapidated, and all over hovered the smell of mould and damp.

Papa would be in the library, asleep at his desk, taking a little nap. He would explain everything. Tell her not to worry, not to be alarmed. It was all just a temporary setback – soon put right. He would engage new staff. The House would be put to rights in no time. She mustn't worry, she mustn't take everything so seriously.

The library door was open – she stared in disbelief. Her father's sanctum, the room he didn't like disturbed, always slightly cluttered. But never like this. Never great gaps in the shelves, the rare, exquisitely bound books face down, fallen awkwardly, their spines strained. She knelt and picked one up, rubbed at the green fungus growing on the finely tooled leather cover. The mould came off on her fingers. She wiped them on her skirt, began to rub again, willing herself to concentrate on the task, not to see any further. To ignore the desk piled high with papers, with ledgers. Not to see the blackened silver, the fly-blown picture glass, the broken window where the curtain flapped.

But like someone mesmerized she put down the book, rose and walked to the desk. She blew, her breath sending the dust in a cloud into the air, it made her sneeze, dislodging more from the top ledger. Why wasn't it with the agent, the rent was his concern? Why were they here, laying for so long on her father's desk? She bent to look closer, and saw in her father's hand columns of figures scribbled in the margins. Additions and subtractions, sums multiplied, crossed out, begun again. 'Oh Papa,' she whispered as the meaning of the arithmetic became clear. His income balanced against his expenditure, and always, no matter how many times he added it, the same answer, there was almost no income.

She ran from the library, along the corridor and up the stairs to her father's room. He wasn't there. The room was relatively clean and tidy, unused-looking. 'Charlotte! Papa! Where are you? Answer me. Where are you?' Her heart was pounding, her voice panic-stricken. She turned the handle of Charlotte's door, it was locked; she was amazed, then terrified.

'Charlotte!' she called, pounding on the door. 'Are you in there? Open this door at once.'

'I can't.' The answer was faint. 'It's locked. I'm locked in.'

'Where's Papa?'

'Asleep.'

'Where is he asleep? Charlotte, what are you playing at? Where is he? Waken him. Do you hear me, waken him at once.'

She put her ear against the door, straining to hear. Charlotte's voice was raised. 'It's Catherine. She's on the landing. Open the door. The door, Papa, open it.'

Then the key was being turned in the lock, and the door opened narrowly, so all Catherine could see was a section of a face, an eye. Cautiously, inch by inch, the section was widened.

'Papa! It's me, Catherine. It's only me.' Her heart broke when no light of recognition dawned in the rheumy, vacant eyes. The door began to close again. She pushed against it, forcing her way in. 'It's me, it's Catherine,' she kept repeating.

Her father looked at her long, then shook his head. 'Catherine's in India. You've come to trick me. You're in league with O'Hara.'

Catherine moved close to him, holding out her arms. 'No I'm not. I'm not trying to trick you. I'm me.' She spoke very quietly, gently, as if her father was a frightened child, a startled horse. She was crying for him. Tears running down her face. Crying for this sick old man in his crumpled clothes, food-stained, food encrusted. With unkempt hair yellowing like smoke-stained paper, hair that had been silver, that now was being combed by shaking fingers with long dirty nails.

She put her arms round him and held him close, kissing his unshaven face. Telling him again and again patiently, 'It's all right. I'm Catherine. I love you. I came back from India to see you, to make you better.'

'Yes,' he said, shaking his head approvingly. 'Oh, yes, that's fine,' said this sick old man to Catherine. She kissed his cheek again.

'Now you know me, don't you? I'm Catherine. Sit down and have a little rest.' She led him to a chair, then was about to go to the bed, talk to Charlotte, ask for an ex-

495

planation. Find out when her beautiful father had become a shambling old man, who stared and stared and never saw that she was Catherine. But before she could move, he was out of the chair, clutching her arm, his voice frantic.

'You didn't lock the door. He'll come. She won't be safe, he'll take her. The door's not locked, Where's the key?'

'There now, Sir. The key's in the lock where you left it. Look at it.' Hannah was in the room, leading Lord Kilgoran to the door, helping him to turn the key. 'Now, Sir, isn't that grand.' She helped him back to the chair. 'Sure it's only Miss Catherine come to make you well. Have a little doze now. Put the key in your pocket and go to sleep.'

Catherine was trembling, looking from the madness of her father to Charlotte, a Charlotte she wouldn't have recognized. Thin and pale, not dressed, her nightgown several sizes too big on her wasted body.

'What happened, Hannah? What ails them?' She looked to Hannah, her eyes imploring an explanation.

'Miss, 'tis a long story. It's why I wanted you below in the kitchen, to prepare you so it wouldn't come as a shock, and you only arriving.'

Then Hannah told Catherine all she thought it necessary for her to know. Blaming Mary Doyle, safe from questioning in America, with having told Lord Kilgoran that Charlotte was seeing a young man.

'So he wasn't rambling, then. He was right about an O'Hara.'

'Ah, not at all, Miss, your poor father's terrible confused. Sure there's only Jamsie O'Hara happily married to Katy, the other two long since gone. It was a different man.'

496

'But who?' Catherine looked inquiringly from Hannah to Charlotte. Charlotte cast down her eyes and said nothing.

'Ah Miss, sure what do names matter when the thing is finished and done this long time. Anyway the name escapes me, and the man isn't hereabouts.'

Catherine, convinced that Hannah was lying, didn't pursue the man's identity, later she would ask Charlotte. 'And was it that, finding out about Charlotte and whoever it was, that caused my father to be how he is?'

'It was not. That started last year with the first failure. Maybe the beginnings of it were there long since. Maybe like many another man it would have come anyway. Who knows that, only God. Though I daresay Master Charles didn't help. But one thing is certain, Miss Charlotte wasn't the cause.'

'Catherine, you haven't kissed me. You haven't spoken to me.'

'Oh Charlotte, darling Charlotte, I'm so sorry. Forgive me. It was such a shock finding you locked in, and then seeing Papa. My love, how are you? I expected such a different homecoming.' They embraced each other. 'Let me look at you.' Catherine held Charlotte away from her. 'You're so pale and thin, you look so ill. Oh, my poor little love, what ails you?'

'She's better than she was, Miss. She's made a grand improvement. She had a chill, and then lost her appetite, from being imprisoned, you know.'

'Poor child, we must stop that. We can't have that,' Catherine declared. Lord Kilgoran shifted on the chair, opened his eyes and closed them. Catherine talked in a whisper. 'Is he like this all the time?'

497

'No,' Hannah said, 'he could wake up and be himself, it might last for an hour, a day or two even. And you'd almost think he was his old self. What ails him comes and goes, but you never know the minute when the change is going to come on him.'

'And the House, his clothes, the library, is there nothing to be done about them?'

'I'm sorry about that. You know it wouldn't be my wish to see them so. I do my best, Miss Catherine. I can do no more.'

'Dear Hannah, I'm not criticizing you, only trying to see all the problems. Isn't there anyone who'd come in to help?'

'There isn't. Half the parish is dead and the rest gone to America. And besides, if there was anyone how would we be paying them? The likes of Katy who out of love for the family would work for nothing hasn't the strength to draw water from the well.'

'Never mind. I'll begin cleaning things up, we'll manage. But the first thing we must stop is this locking up of Charlotte. That's monstrous. Papa must not continue to do that.'

'I wouldn't rush him, Miss,' Hannah cautioned. 'It might be better to make a start on her clothes. If you can get him to let the child have her clothes, 'twould be a start.'

'Come and sit here.' Catherine patted the side of the bed. Hannah sat down and in whispers they planned how they would get round Lord Kilgoran to let Charlotte have her clothes.

Lord Kilgoran stretched, yawned and opened his eyes.

'I must have dropped off,' he said. Then he saw Catherine. 'Why, darling, you've come. You're here. Why didn't someone call me? Welcome home, my dear girl.' She went to him. He put his arms round her, kissed her, and talked as if she had just arrived. Telling her how delighted he was to have her home. To see her looking so well.

She was beginning to think that all that had gone before was imagined. Then Hannah said, 'Sir, Miss Catherine will be wanting her tea, if you'll let me out I'll make it.'

'Of course, Hannah.' He unlocked the door, held it for Hannah, instructing her to serve tea in the bedroom, and immediately she left turned the key in the lock. Catherine shivered, she had imagined none of it.

'Well now, tell me, how is Edward?' Catherine answered her father's question. And he continued talking as if everything was normal, the locked room, having afternoon tea served in the bedroom. Appearing to be his old self, sitting in his filthy clothes, stained and torn, his elegant hand poised as he elaborated a point.

– Where has my beautiful, immaculate father gone, where has his wonderful mind flown? Oh God, what a cruel thing to do, why didn't You just let him die? He was kind and good, he deserved a better end, Catherine thought, as she poured tea from the blackened silver service into cups not properly washed.

Hannah told her her room was ready, hot jars had been in the bed for days, it was well-aired. And dinner would be served at six o'clock. Hannah was let out, and the door fastened. Her father became silent and sat staring into space. After a while Catherine said she would go to her room, unpack and bathe.

'You do that. I'll sit with Charlotte. She's been very ill, you know. I was quite worried, not eating. But there's an improvement.'

Hannah came to Catherine's room while she was changing. 'The dinner won't be much,' she said apologetically. 'Not like the dinners we used to have. But it'll be nice for the Master to have company at that great big table. I do look at him there of a night, and see the ghosts around him.'

During dinner and afterwards, when they were back in the locked bedroom, Lord Kilgoran continued to behave with a kind of normality. Lamenting the loss of the potato crop, his failure to relieve the distress. Catherine asssured him there were hundreds, many friends of his, in the same predicament, unable to help their tenants. He seemed consoled.

She told him about the soup kitchen, but remembering Olivia's forecast of how Father Bolger would react, did not mention that the organization was run and founded by a Bible Society, her father had never approved of proselytizers.

'Good,' he said, 'soup will help. They need help, they need something to help them. Damned Government, damned man Trevelyan, has made a botch of things. Food in plenty being imported – all useless – all in the hands of merchants, and the people with not a penny to purchase it.'

Catherine agreed with him that the situation was distressing. It was possible, she thought, as they talked, to believe her father was perfectly normal, so pertinent were his observations, his summing up of the situation. How long, she wondered, would this respite last? While it did, she must take advantage, suggest that Charlotte should be allowed to dress.

'Papa, wouldn't you say Charlotte was well enough to get up for a little while? Get dressed?'

Lord Kilgoran appeared to consider the question. Charlotte caught hold of Catherine's hand, and they waited for his answer.

'Yes, I don't see why not. The bed is weakening. Yes, I suppose so. Get dressed tomorrow. But not out.' A perplexed expression crossed his face, lingered in his eyes, as though his mind searched for something. Then he shook his head, clearing the worried look away, and smiled. 'Yes, that's an excellent idea. Good girl, always a sensible girl, I could always rely on you.'

Charlotte squeezed Catherine's hand. Lord Kilgoran beamed at his two daughters. 'Yes, I'll have Hannah see to it. And in no time you'll be as right as rain, Charlotte.'

'Of course she will,' Catherine said. 'Then you know, Papa – a holiday might be a good idea. Perhaps you and Charlotte could travel back to India with me. A lovely long sea voyage. Just think of that.'

Charlotte's grip on her sister's hand slackened, let go.

'India? Not sure I'd fancy it now. Did at one time,' Lord Kilgoran said.

'Oh you would, Papa. Come just for a while. You and Edward could have such fun. You like hunting. You could hunt tigers. It's only a suggestion, you don't have to come, but think about it.'

'Wouldn't want to leave the house. Charles could come, no one here.'

Carried away with visions of her father settled and safe in India, properly taken care of, Charlotte removed from the danger of forming another unsuitable liaison, meeting suitable young men, Catherine blurted out what Olivia had told her. 'Charles has gone, left England, he's gone to the Colonies.'

Her father looked as if he had been struck, the colour left his face, the hands in his lap trembled.

'But of course Olivia wasn't positive. I'm sure it's not true. Not true at all. You know how people gossip,' Catherine said, attempting to reassure her father.

'He probably has. It's a long time since I heard from him. It's the truth no doubt,' he said resignedly, and seemed to have recovered his composure. 'Now my dear, if you'll stay with Charlotte for a while, I have to go downstairs for a moment.'

He left the room and locked the door after him. Catherine shuddered. Charlotte noticed, and said wryly, 'You get used to it.'

'I'll never get used to it. It's like a monstrous nightmare. Oh Charlotte, what possessed you to become involved with a tenant, it must have aggravated Papa's condition, no matter what Hannah says.'

'It didn't, and it wasn't a tenant,' Charlotte lied.

'Well, who was it then? Where was he from? How did you meet him? And why won't you tell me?'

'He was from another village. He came to work for Driscoll. There's nothing else to tell. It was a moment of madness that came over me. It wouldn't have lasted, even if Papa had never found out. I don't want to talk any more about it.'

502

Believing her, and crediting her with a reticence she understood, Catherine pursued the matter no further. Talking instead about the Clanbrasil Ball, Olivia and her children, the voyage from India. And when their father returned she kissed them both fondly and went to her own room.

Hannah had lit the fire, it smoked, but she was glad of its warmth, the living flame distracting her from examining too closely the dilapidation of the room. She undressed, sat before her looking glass brushing her hair, telling herself that the mildew on the glass could be treated, the green bloom on the dressing table removed. In time it could all be put right.

Tomorrow she would see the priest. She got into bed, the linen was spotless, the hot jar comforting at her feet. She must not dwell on her demented father, on the disintegration of Kilgoran House, her energy must be conserved, put to a better use. Soon she slept.

Chapter Twenty-One

'Miss Catherine! Come in. Sit down.' Father Bolger was ill at ease, taken by surprise, never in all his years as parish priest of Kilgoran had the gentry come to call. What brought them now? It could only be to complain about Peader and the business with the young woman.

'Here, let me shift that. Mary Doyle left this long time and I'm not much of a hand with the housekeeping, you'll have to excuse it,' he apologized, shifting an accumulation of clothes and books from the chair.

Catherine watched him look for somewhere else to lay them. – He has aged, she thought, more than the years warrant, his back is very stooped. 'Perhaps they could go on top of the press,' she suggested, pointing to the bundle he held.

'Oh aye, the very place.' He smiled, looked relieved at having a solution found, the smile made him appear younger, more relaxed. He was a nice man, Catherine was sure, and Olivia surely wrong in her estimation of him.

'There now,' he said when his hands were free, and waited for Catherine to speak.

'I wanted to talk about the hunger. I thought we could discuss ways of relieving it.'

'God bless you, what sort of thing have you in mind?'

'A nourishing soup, easy to digest and prepare.'

'Soup would be the answer. But how would you manage that – yourself and Hannah only?'

She felt her way. 'I'm sure it could be handled. It has to be. If the suffering here is anything like I saw in Dublin something must be done. I'd hate to think our own people were enduring similar hardship.'

'They are. It's a sin against God such things are allowed to happen. Trevelyan will have a lot to answer for when he meets his Maker.' Then he repeated his earlier question, inquiring how Catherine and Hannah would manage.

'I made inquiries in Dublin about the possibility of a soup kitchen being set up in Kilgoran, and I've had the promise of help. These people would come here, bring the equipment, supply ingredients, we could use the outbuildings.'

'I see,' Father Bolger said.

Catherine felt an unease. His eyes appeared to probe her. She remembered what Olivia had said.

'Who are these people?'

'Does that matter?'

'Oh yes, it matters very much,' the priest replied.

'They are just people renowned for their charitable works.'

'Would it be the Quakers, the Quakers do grand work, I'd have no objection to them.'

'I don't think you're in a position to choose. If people are starving does it matter who feeds them?' Catherine could feel hostility rising in her. Surely he wasn't going to object – he couldn't in all humanity do that. 'Keep calm,' she told herself, 'you came to discuss something, do just that. Use reason.'

'The group I contacted is the British Bible Society, and they've kindly offered their assistance.'

'They are proselytizers!'

Catherine was startled by the vehemence of the priest's exclamation, the expression on his face, such anger. She tried to keep her own in check and argued. 'They have sincere beliefs, perhaps not in accordance with yours, but after all it's soup we're concerned with, not religion.'

'Proselytizers!' Father Bolger said again. 'The people will not take their soup. I'll forbid it.'

Catherine's poise deserted her. 'You have no right! They are starving! They are my father's tenants, don't forget that.'

'They are. And he was a good landlord. I have never interfered in his affairs nor he in mine. Until recently he saw to the needs of their bodies; their souls are my affair. They will not take the soup. And I'll not discuss it further. I'm sorry, for I know you mean well.'

Rising, Catherine spoke. 'I came to ask for your co-operation. You've refused it, nevertheless I shall go ahead with my plans. The people are starving – I think they will accept.'

'You must do what you think right, and I must do what is right. I'll show you out,' he said, and opened the door.

– Dear sweet Catherine, how good it was to have her home, Lord Kilgoran thought as he sat in the bedroom watching Hannah carry in armfuls of Charlotte's clothes and hang them in the wardrobe. He felt very happy. It was good to see Charlotte dressed, she had been sick for such a long time. A severe chill was all it could have been, not after all the decline he feared she had gone into. Perhaps a holiday in India would benefit her. Put the roses back in her cheeks. She would meet young people. A young man. It was time she found a young man. Poor child had never had a beau. A vague memory of something unpleasant, something that threatened her, stirred in his mind. He felt frightened, and glanced apprehensively at the open door. Something to do with the door, he concentrated for a moment trying to resurrect what it was that troubled him, but couldn't, shook his head, and chided himself that he was growing old.

– Yes, he continued to think, India would do her good. But he wouldn't go. He wouldn't leave Ireland. In a day or two he would explain to Catherine. Tell her about his headaches, he wasn't well enough to travel. He might die on the journey. And that was unthinkable. To die away from Ireland, be buried at sea, or in some foreign place. Not lay beneath the springy turf with his wife and ancestors. Catherine would understand.

And besides, Charles was coming back. There was something he had meant to do about Charles. What was it? Growing old was dreadful, you forgot so many things. He was sure it had been important, but like so much else it eluded him. The colonies, Catherine said. Must have got it wrong, Charles wouldn't go to the colonies. He was coming home. Definitely, India was out of the question, couldn't have Charles arrive and the place locked up. That would never do.

'We've finished, Sir, the clothes are all back. I'll go down to the kitchen, if there's nothing else,' Hannah said.

'Good, well done. Nothing else for the moment.' Lord

Kilgoran came out of his reverie and locked the door after Hannah.

During the week two vast cauldrons arrived from Cork, brought out on carts. The drivers and their helpers pushed and shoved the famine pots into a shed near the stables, prised up the cobbles to make holes deep enough for fires, erected a platform from which the pots could be raised and lowered over the heat. On another day members of the Bible Society came with the soup ingredients: oxheads, turnips, carrots, pea meal, and meal ground from Indian corn. Catherine, Hannah and the men who had driven the carts carried buckets of water to fill the pots.

'A very thin sort of a broth it'll be, if you don't mind me saying so,' Hannah remarked to Catherine.

And to her astonishment Catherine replied shortly, 'It's better than nothing, which is what they have at present.'

'Begging your pardon, Ma'am, I meant no offence, 'twas in my capacity as a cook I was speaking.'

'I'm sorry, Hannah,' Catherine apologized. 'I didn't mean to snap. But I'm worried. I want this venture to succeed. I want the people to have nourishment, and I'm afraid Father Bolger will forbid them to take it. Do you think he will?'

'I couldn't say, Miss Catherine. Mind you if he saw all them tracts and Bibles he might well forbid it. Wouldn't the ladies have been better advised to buy a few more cows' heads, and a few onions, instead of them things?'

'Soup!' Father Bolger's voice thundered. It echoed round the little chapel. 'Protestant soup to take the hunger off you. To save your bodies at the expense of your souls. For make no mistake about it – that's the price you'll pay. Take one spoonful, one mouthful, and you'll have sold your immortal soul. Forfeited your right to Heaven for a mug of greasy water, and the right of your innocent children. The little children you carried here to this very chapel for me to baptize, each and every one of them that from that moment became one with God. Don't risk their most precious possession. Don't,' his voice lowered, became imploring, 'allow yourself to be bought. Don't let the devil whisper in your ear, "It's all right. Take the nourishment for the sake of the children."' His voice rose again and thundered forth. 'It – is – not – all right. Not if you and your children were stretched dying.

'These people who have come with their pots and bones are doing the devil's work. They have always done his work. Down through the centuries he has come in many disguises. He came with ropes to hang you, ropes to bind you two by two and throw you into the swirling torrents at Drogheda. In Wexford he used guns. And now it's soup.

'Through all of that we kept our faith. Your fathers and mothers, them that went before them, risked their lives to hear Mass in the shelter of a bush, under an outcrop of rock. The priests daily took their lives in their hands to minister to the people, to baptize the infants, give the sacrament of penance and communion, anoint the dying. Don't dishonour all that. Don't sacrifice your immortal soul for a bowl of broth. Don't play into the hands of the proselytizers.'

He paused and looked round his small congregation. He remembered faces that were no longer there, the faces of the dead, dead of starvation and fever. He saw Katy's face and those of her children, pale and gaunt, hollow-eyed. Statia and Jamsie, the flesh melted from them. While he looked his parishioners shifted uncomfortably under his scrutiny. An awful thought occurred to him. Was he right? Was this the message God wanted him to preach? Was the Holy Spirit talking through him? Or did the devil have a hand in him, too, twisting his reasoning, preying on his hatred of injustice, and bitterness against the English. 'Oh dear God, direct me,' he prayed silently. 'Show me what is right.' The answer came to him. Their bodies were temporal things, it was their life everlasting he must protect. He cleared his throat and spoke again.

'Go from here and ask God to give you strength to withstand temptation. Think of the Day of Judgement when you shall stand before him and have to answer, "Yes, I renounced my faith, I took the proselytizers' soup." And He will say to you: "Depart from me into the flames of everlasting Hell." In the Name of the Father, the Son and the Holy Ghost.'

Only a handful of people turned up at the Lodge Gates on the first day the soup was being given out; some brought jugs, but the others were empty-handed, come to taunt. 'You'll roast in Hell and drag your infants with you,' one shouted as the gates opened and the women with the jugs filed in. 'Soupers! Turncoats!' The shouts followed them up the drive, and stones flew in their direction. The next day no one came for the broth, and the hecklers having no one to heckle went away. Each day the great vats were reheated, towards the end of the week the members of the Bible Society announced their intention of leaving. There were people starving in other districts. They would move on. Catherine persuaded them to delay their departure by one more day. 'I'll ride out, talk to the tenants myself, you'll see, they'll come tomorrow.'

She had the horse yoked to the dog cart and went from cottage to cottage, amazed to find so few occupied. But where there were occupants the answer was always the same: 'Thank you very much, Miss Catherine, but sure we can't take it.'

She was shocked by Katy's appearance, her drawn haggard face, her beautiful hair lank and lifeless. 'You'll take the soup, won't you, Katy, for the sake of your children.' She looked to where the children huddled listlessly round the fire.

'I know you mean well, Miss Catherine, but I couldn't take it. It wouldn't be right.'

'Why that's nonsense, Katy, and you know it. You can't sit by and let them starve.'

'Sense has nothing to do with it, Miss. It would be a sin, that's not the same as sense.'

'Look,' Catherine pleaded, 'I could arrange for Hannah to bring it to you every day. No one would be the wiser. Say you will, Katy. You have often taken food from the House. It isn't any different really.'

'I have indeed, and been grateful. But the soup is different. But sure you wouldn't understand that. I can't take it.'

There was a finality about her tone, and Catherine realized it would be useless to try further persuasion. She wished she had money on her. Maybe Katy would have taken that. Then remembering Olivia's words the night of the ball, she wasn't sure, perhaps Olivia was right and she didn't know the people, didn't understand them, knew nothing about their inner lives. She bade Katy goodbye and went back to the soup kitchen, but didn't inform the helpers that her mission had been a failure, evading direct questions. Let it stand for one more day, then if no one came they could dismantle it.

After Catherine left, Katy went out to scour the bushes for berries, searching for hips and haws, sloes, blackberries, ripe, worm-infested, red and hard, anything that was remotely edible. There were few. She pulled stinging nettles, raising white blisters that burned and throbbed on her hands. Boiled them and fed the children the mess. No sooner had they eaten than the purging began in their bowels, and they had to go outside. She called after them, reminding them not to go far and come straight back. Then returned to the kitchen, rage and frustration at the intolerable situation she was in making her cry aloud and pound the wall with her fists. 'What is to become of us?' she spoke aloud. How were they to exist? When the berries were all picked and the nettles finished how would she feed the children? Why couldn't someone other than a Bible Society have brought the soup? Her arms ached from the pounding, her fists were sore. She sat down thinking of the nourishment that was available for the asking. That could be brought to her. Considered changing her mind, running after Miss Catherine, telling her she would take it. But the words of the priest's sermon came into her mind, and she saw the dancing flames and her children's bodies writhing in them for ever and ever. 'Oh God,' she prayed, 'look down and pity me and mine.'

At that moment Jamsie came in, and at the sight of him resentment flared again. And with her tongue she attacked him. 'Isn't it well for you, out rambling around with Peader while he makes arrangements to run with her. Not a care on you, and me nearly driven mad with worry. Why aren't you looking for work? Trying to get the passage money to take us to America.'

'America? I never thought you favoured America,' Jamsie said.

'Well, it's America or Hell, for I've a good mind to take the soup. You're driving me to it.' In her heart she longed for him to take her in his arms, hold and hush her, stroke her hair. Tell her it would be all right. Something would turn up. They would be saved. She needed to lean on someone, have someone take care of her. The burden was too great and she didn't think she could carry it for much longer. Yet she knew that if he so much as laid a finger on her, she would fight like a wildcat and spurn any tenderness he might show. She hated him, hated herself, her body that was scrawny, her dirty clothes, her hair that hadn't been washed for weeks. She didn't love herself, she couldn't love anyone else. But she found some relief in berating him. And started again about America.

'There's passages from Cobh – £3 16s for a grown man or woman and all you can eat, and sure it would be cheaper for children. If we had £20 we'd be safe.'

'And pigs might fly,' Jamsie laughed. 'What do you want me to do – go out and rob someone, knock a farmer coming back from market over the head and take his purse?'

'God forgive me, I wouldn't care if you did. At this very

513

minute if you came in here with the money I'd ask no questions.'

He said no more, knowing she didn't mean it, no more than she meant to take the soup. Looking for twenty pounds was like looking for a crock of gold. He would just sit and listen, let her have her say. What else could he do?

Charlotte, up and dressed, watched her father come out of the dressing-room and, without saying anything to her, leave the bedroom. In amazement she noticed that there was no sound of the key turning on the outside. She sat still for a moment, thinking he was fumbling, or had dropped it. But when after a while she heard his footsteps walk away she got up and tried the door. – He's forgotten! He didn't lock it! Oh please God don't let him remember and come back. She cautiously opened it, peered round the edge; there was no sign of him, but the sound of footsteps coming the other way quickly made her close it and return to sit on the bed.

Then the voice of Hannah called, 'Miss Charlotte, the Master's gone for a walk and forgotten to give me the key. I don't know, dotey, what you'll do for your breakfast.'

Charlotte tiptoed to the door, opened it quickly and said, 'Boo.' Hannah jumped with fright and clutched at her heart. 'He forgot. Oh Hannah, isn't it wonderful, he forgot.' She caught hold of Hannah and twirled her round.

'Miss Charlotte, stop it! Stop it, you're making me dizzy.'

Charlotte let go of her and asked, 'Where is Papa?'

'Gone out for a walk, something he hasn't done this long time.'

'Then I'm coming down. I'll eat breakfast in the kitchen.'

'You will not.'

'I will so. I'll be back up here when he returns.'

She raced down the stairs pursued by a panting, protesting Hannah. 'Quick, quick, let me eat quick. Oh isn't it heavenly. I'm free. Isn't it marvellous?'

'He'll walk in on top of us and you'll soon see how wonderful it is. Then your clothes will be out of the press before you can say Jack Robinson and you back in the nightgown,' Hannah said, ladling out porridge. 'Oh, Sacred Heart of Jesus! you're caught. Listen! that's him whistling, he's coming.'

Charlotte jumped up, looked round for a way of escape. There was none. The door opened, her father came into the kitchen.

'Good morning, Charlotte, you're down early. Hungry, eh? Couldn't wait. Having a snack before breakfast?' He looked from Charlotte to Hannah and smiled. 'Always one for spoiling her, letting her raid the kitchen. Right then, see you in ten minutes in the dining-room.'

Hannah made the Sign of the Cross in a small motion across her face. 'God bless the poor man, what turn has his mind taken now? Go you, Miss, to the dining-room, and I'll lay another place.'

'What'll I say to him?'

'Nothing, let him do the talking. Take your lead from him.'

'Do you think he's forgotten about me and Peader?'

'Don't be mentioning his name and Miss Catherine likely to arrive any minute. Even if some cloud has come into your father's mind and blotted out the business with you and Peader, at the drop of his name your sister would put two and two together and have you off to India in a minute.'

During breakfast Lord Kilgoran talked to Charlotte and Catherine as if the three of them sitting down to a meal happened every day. 'There's nothing like a walk to sharpen the appetite. Fresh air, that's the thing. More of that for you, Charlotte, soon have you like your old self.'

Catherine allowed herself to believe something miraculous had occurred. Her father was better, no doubt about that. Apart from the state of his clothes he looked quite like his old self. She congratulated herself, that perhaps her arrival was responsible for his improvement.

After breakfast, Lord Kilgoran suggested another walk. Charlotte asked would he mind if she didn't come, making an excuse that her legs still felt a bit wobbly.

'Of course not, my darling. You were laid up so long, take it easy for a while,' her father advised, and she hurried to her bedroom to write to Peader. Catherine accompanied her father on the walk.

Darling Peader,

I'm so strong and fat you won't know me. And the greatest thing has happened – a miracle. The night Catherine came home Papa agreed to let me have my clothes back. And now, this morning, he has forgotten to lock the door. He even saw me in the kitchen, and it didn't strike him as odd. We had breakfast together. He asked me to go for a walk. So you see, he has forgotten.

Isn't that wonderful? I'm free. Your little bird is free. Only I'm afraid. So please come soon in case he should suddenly remember. I couldn't bear to go back in the cage. I would die.

I love you

As she folded the letter, into her mind came the first feeling of remorse she had experienced for deceiving her father.

516

She had done so from the moment she met Peader, was doing so now. Taking advantage of his troubled mind. Not once had she felt sorry for him. Then she reminded herself that she had been concerned. Hadn't she postponed her flight to America when he first became ill? She had, it was true, deceived him. She was sorry for that. She loved him very much. It broke her heart that she was forced to choose between him and Peader. Nothing would have pleased her more than to live in Kilgoran for always. How wonderful that would be. Her father accepting Peader, coming to love him, approving of her choice. – Dear Papa, I hope one day you'll come to understand why I have to do this. How much I wish it could have been otherwise. But I would die without Peader. I have to go with him. But I'll always love you, and always hope that one day you'll forgive me. She was crying, her tears had fallen on to the letter. She dabbed at it with her handkerchief, making the ink run. Then went down to the kitchen.

'You must find him, Hannah. Go quickly and give him this. You know what will happen if Papa suddenly remembers and locks me up again. This time I would die. Even Peader's letters couldn't save me. Please take it to him.'

'I believe you would, for the life you've led in the last months is against human nature. I'll take it for you, and may it all work out.'

Hannah found Peader at his house and gave him the letter. 'How long will this change last, do you think?' he asked when he had read it.

'That no one could say. To see him this morning he

looks as normal as anyone. Yet the queer thing is he never mentioned a word about not seeing a horse in the park on his walk, nor noticed the state of the kitchen, nor the ruin that the house has become. I'd put no faith in the change at all. If you were planning on anything I'd do it as quick as you can.'

Peader thought for a while, then caught hold of Hannah's hand. 'Listen,' he said, 'there's a fellow passes the Lodge Gates before it gets light. He has a yoke full of turf, taking it into Cork. Tomorrow is the day he comes. I knew him well, he'll give us a lift. You have Charlotte down by the Gate between three and four, I'll be waiting for her, and by the time she's missed we'll be miles away . . . Will you do that for me, tell her all, and make sure she's there?'

'I will so. Take her and may God go with you.'

Hannah hurried back. Passing the Great Hall she heard what sounded like the rattle of a chain. Something blowing in the draught, she thought, and was about to pass the door. Then she heard it again and went in. Where was the wind coming from at all, she wondered, for suddenly she felt very cold, shivers running up her back. I know the place is draughty, but never so bad as this. Then she saw the figure under the gallery, moving slowly in her direction, chains hanging from the outstretched hands, dragging from the ankles.

She blessed herself. 'God between us and all harm,' she said out loud, as the figure came nearer. 'Once before I saw you on a night long ago. It was dark then, and I couldn't see plain. But I can now. I was right, you are a man. A fine big man. You're wearing the clothes from the olden times, not trousers, but a kind of skirt and a tunic. And

I can see the sore places on your arms from the chains.' She became aware of her voice talking out loud, and that she wasn't shivering, nor feeling cold. And she wasn't frightened, for the man's face looked only sad. She felt pity for him. For his restless wandering.

She began to walk in his direction, and made the Sign of the Cross towards him. 'May the Lord rest your weary spirit. Go now in His name.' Before her eyes the figure vanished. Then she felt the power drain from her, she clutched the wall for support as the realization of what had happened struck her. It was the ghost of the O'Sullivan. He came to warn of death. 'Sacred Heart of Jesus,' she prayed, 'protect everyone under this roof.' After a while when she felt calmer she went and found Charlotte, but said nothing about the apparition. After she passed on Peader's message she warned Charlotte not to let excitement get the better of her. 'Take deep breaths and drinks of water, your face is red as a turkey cock's, and if you don't calm down Miss Catherine will want to know what ails you. And before she comes back from her walk throw a few things in a bag, not much mind you, and I'll hide it in the kitchen until it's time for you to leave.'

Charlotte after much indecision packed only a change of clothes, an extra woollen shawl, her mother's silver-backed brush and mirror, and Katy's medal. She took the bag to the kitchen, then returned to her room and lay on the bed, thinking about Peader, and praying that her father wouldn't come back from his walk and lock her in.

The further they walked the more troubled Catherine became, the more doubts came into her mind that her father was far from well. He seemed totally unaware of his surroundings. Blind to knee-high grass, the profusion of weeds choking the flowers, the dahlias and chrysanthemums unstaked, the piles of rotting fruit in the orchard. A remark that he had let the place go, that next year if the potato crop thrived and rents came in, things would improve, anything to show he was conscious of his surroundings, would have lifted the dread that was descending upon her that her father had lost his mind.

'Where's the smoke coming from, Catherine?' Lord Kilgoran's question broke in on her forebodings.

'From the cooking fires, you know, where they are making the soup. I showed you yesterday, down by the stables.'

'By the stables! Fires by the stables! You can't have fires near the stables. Madden the horses, terrify them. You can't have that.' He began to run.

Catherine ran after him, calling, 'Wait, Papa. Don't run. The ground's uneven. Be careful, mind those wheels, you'll fall over them.'

Lord Kilgoran talked aloud. 'Dreadful smell. Pig swill. Who's cooking pig swill in the stables?' He hurried on, shaking his fist, threatening what would happen to whoever was guilty of lighting fires in the stable yard. Catherine, behind him, attempted to calm him.

Pigeons pecking old hayseeds from between the cobbles flew away as Lord Kilgoran and Catherine came into the yard. He stood still for a minute then went from loose-box to loose-box, talking to the non-existent horses, calling their names, making soothing noises. Telling them not to be frightened, he would soon put out the fires.

Catherine followed him. A host of chestnut heads, dappled mares, black stallions, her mother's hunter, her own pony, her father's horse that had recently been put down, flashed before her eyes. She could smell them, see their glistening coats, the gold of the straw on which they were bedded, feel their soft mouths nuzzling her. She closed her eyes to blot out the vision, and when she opened them again saw the reality, row after row of empty stalls around the three sides of the yard, pigeons flying in and out of the harness loft. And the only smells were of mouldy hay and re-heated soup, and her father was looking at her with mad, staring eyes.

'You're not well, Papa. Let me take you back. You must lay down.'

He allowed himself to be led away, leant on her arm. Let her help him upstairs, remove his boots, settle him on the bed, cover him. She sat with him until he fell asleep.

When he awoke his head ached. Hannah came and asked if he wanted lunch. He said, no, he was going to the library. He wasn't to be disturbed.

While she served lunch Hannah passed on Lord Kilgoran's message. Catherine said she would look in on him after she had helped the members of the Bible Society pack, they were leaving this afternoon.

'Try not to disturb him, Miss, he'll potter about in the library for hours, and come to not a bit of harm, and maybe tomorrow there'll be an improvement,' Hannah said, before she realized that tomorrow Charlotte would be gone, and it might be as well for the poor man to stay in his lost world. Tomorrow she would have to face Miss Catherine, lie to her, or make a clean breast of her part in

521

the affair. But, whatever the outcome, Charlotte would be away, thank God, she was only a child and deserved her chance of happiness. Miss Catherine had a life of her own, and she would face her when she had to; so long as nothing interfered with Charlotte getting out of this unhappy house, she could face a lion.

Down by the stables the vats were being lifted from their platforms, turned over, the soup draining into the ground. Catherine thought of the stomachs that could have been filled, and blew her nose to prevent crying. One of the drivers gathered the mess of bones and pulped vegetables, dug a hole and buried them. Catherine helped the women wipe and scald the vessels.

When it was time for them to go, one of the women said, 'If you had the time, Ma'am, there's plenty of work to be done in other places, in other soup kitchens and the fever hospitals.'

'Unfortunately I haven't. My father is ailing and I'm needed here.'

'Well, goodbye, Ma'am, you did your best, no one can do more than that.'

Several times during the afternoon she quietly opened the library door, and saw her father moving about replacing books on shelves. Each time she left without drawing his attention. Hannah went to ask if he was coming to dinner, or did he want a tray? A tray would do nicely, he told her. And when she served dinner to the two sisters she told them he was working wonders in the library. The desk was clear, all the books picked up from the floor, the room tidier than she had seen it for many a day. 'I'd leave him alone if I were you,' she advised the sisters. 'Don't even go in to kiss him goodnight. Leave him to his pottering, that's what I'd do.'

'Perhaps you're right,' Catherine said, though she was reluctant to take the advice. It seemed callous to leave her father alone so long. But then, she supposed, Hannah knew his ways better than anyone.

Charlotte, terrified that sight of her might remind her father that she wasn't locked up, was only too eager to comply, and said, 'I shall go to bed in a little while; you should, too, Catherine, you look very tired.'

'I'll come up with you,' Catherine said when Charlotte made to leave the room.

'No, don't do that,' Charlotte said quickly, afraid Catherine might notice the empty spaces on the dressing table where her mother's brush and mirror had been, and ask questions. 'You know what'll happen if you come with me, we'll gossip all night, and tomorrow won't be worth a light.'

She was sorry for lying, sorry for the disappointment she saw on Catherine's face. 'Oh, darling, I'm sorry, it's mean and selfish of me. But I can't help it. Say you forgive me.' She went to Catherine and put her arms round her, and kissed her fondly. 'I love you very much.'

Catherine returned her kiss. 'I love you, too. Don't sound as if it's the end of the world. You're only going to bed. And I don't mind postponing our gossip. There's tomorrow, and three months on the voyage to India. Off you go now, and sleep well.'

On the way up to her own room Catherine paused outside the library door. She could hear her father moving

523

about. She thought about going in, placed her fingers round the handle, then decided against disturbing him, and went on.

Charlotte lay on the bed fully dressed beneath the quilt and listened. She heard Catherine come up to bed, the sound of her footsteps going down the corridor to her room. Then all the familiar creakings and groanings of the house, occasionally an owl hooted, and from far away came the noise of the dogs, demented wailing that she had become accustomed to in the last few months. Hannah had told her it was because they were starving, that they were skin and bone, and didn't bark like dogs any more.

She counted the strokes of the clock, it was midnight, and still her father's footsteps had not passed her door. – Supposing, she thought, he doesn't come to bed, is still in the library when I go down? Supposing he opens the door and sees me. Her throat contracted with fear, and her heart beat so loudly she could hear it. 'Dear God,' she prayed, 'don't let him hear me. Please don't let him hear me. I couldn't bear it if Peader and I were separated again. Make Papa fall asleep.'

Then she became afraid that she might fall asleep and miss the hour she was to meet Peader. She got up and sat on the side of the bed, lit a candle and counted the beams on the ceiling, and flowers on the carpet, the tassels on the curtains, and when she had finished began again in an effort to keep awake.

The clock chimed once. – One o'clock, he must surely have fallen asleep by now, she thought. He was asleep in the library. She got off the bed and tiptoed round the room, went to the window and looked out. Everything was pitch black, but after a while she began to discern the shapes of trees, then the wind rose and the trees waved, and she was afraid at the thought of the long walk down the drive in the dark. 'I'll run all the way,' she told herself. 'I'll run and sing, the way I did when I was small and frightened passing something.' She came away from the window, and it seemed to be forever before the clock struck two. Only another hour, she thought, and hugged herself.

In the kitchen Hannah watched the clock and tried to keep at bay thoughts of O'Sullivan's ghost and what its appearance meant. The Master was still in the library, the last time she had crept to the door he was talking to himself. She regretted that earlier she had not warned Miss Charlotte that at the very minute she came down the stairs her father might open the library door. She hadn't, foolishly hoping he would go to bed. Now it was quarter to three, and any minute Charlotte would be coming down the stairs. She offered a silent prayer that whatever was occupying the Master would occupy him for another while. Or that he fall into a doze. Anything rather than come out and catch Miss Charlotte leaving. She watched for the hands to move on the clock, not taking her eyes from its face, they stayed motionless. She was convinced it had stopped. She looked away for a second and when she looked back the big hand was on twelve. And from another part of the house a clock chimed three.

Charlotte heard it, and left her room, crept down the stairs; when she reached the bottom, she heard the shot. Then Hannah was running along the passage holding out her bag, saying, 'Go, Miss Charlotte, go. Run all the way. Peader will be waiting.'

'But the shot, it came from the house, what was it?'

'Ah, nothing, Miss, maybe a farmer putting one of the oul dogs out of its misery. Go quick now, love, for fear you'd miss the cart.'

A terrible fear took hold of Charlotte – Hannah was lying – the shot had come from the house. She had heard too many guns not to know that. 'It's Papa. It's Papa. I must go to him.'

Hannah squeezed her arm tightly. 'How could it be him? Sure he's fast asleep this long time. Didn't I bring him in warm milk well-laced with whiskey. He's unconscious with sleep, isn't that why he didn't hear any oul shot.' She looked unblinkingly into Charlotte's frightened brown eyes. 'Would Hannah lie to you?'

'No,' Charlotte said, not very positively, but desperately wanting to believe. 'No,' she said again, and this time her tone was less hesitant. 'No, you wouldn't.'

'That's my good girl. Away you go now quick.' She reached up and kissed Charlotte, who then went running into the night, tears streaming down her face.

Hannah went slowly towards the library. She knew the Master was dead, wasn't that why the O'Sullivan had walked? She was afraid, not of the dead, but of how the Master had died, what way she would find him ... Then an awful thought occurred to her. He had killed himself! And hadn't Peader told her that, Protestant or Catholic, taking your own life was a sin? He would go to hell. She began to hurry, calling on God to forgive him. 'Sweet merciful Jesus grant him pardon. He was the kindest man, the gentlest of creatures. He didn't know what he was doing. It wasn't like Miss Charlotte starving herself. He didn't do it on purpose. You wouldn't judge him too harshly, sure you wouldn't.'

She thrust open the library door, her fear of what she would find forgotten before a greater fear. He was laying face down on the desk. The case that held the duelling pistols was there too, open, the crimson velvet lining the same colour as the blood spreading in a pool from beneath Lord Kilgoran's head, and she saw only the one pearl-handled gun in the box.

She bent over him, whispering an Act of Contrition close to where one side of her Master's face should have been, 'Oh my God, I am heartily sorry for having offended Thee.' She knew it was into the ear you were supposed to whisper it. She hoped that God would understand, there wasn't an ear. Not unless she turned him over, then she'd be losing time, the prayer had to be said immediately, to stop him going to Hell. The ear that wasn't there would have to do. She bent closer, closed her eyes and finished the Act of Contrition. She made the Sign of the Cross over him. 'I haven't a drop of Holy water, but you'll understand, Jesus, by the time I'd get it his soul might be gone. You'll go easy on him. He didn't know what he was doing, he didn't mean it.'

Then she left him and went out. Catherine was coming down the passage, her hair loose, rubbing the sleep from her eyes, reminding Hannah of the little girl from long ago. – Oh, if only God could give back the happy years, if it was only from a troubled sleep you were wakening, and me not having to break this terrible news, she thought.

527

'I heard something. It woke me. It sounded like a shot.' Catherine was shivering, it was cold in the passage. Hannah told her the best way she could, and afterwards said, 'Do you want me to go in with you?'

Catherine shook her head and went into the library, closing the door after her. Hannah waited for her. She was a long time in the room. When she came out her face was white, but composed.

'We had better tell Charlotte, or maybe, maybe we should let her sleep a little longer.'

'Miss Charlotte's not here. She's gone away. Went away with the man she's to marry.'

'And my father found out – that's why he killed himself, is that what you're telling me?' Hannah was afraid Catherine was about to collapse, her skin had gone grey and she was sweating.

'Come away from here, Miss, you've had a terrible shock. We'll go into the kitchen, you'll get warm, stop that oul shivering.' She reached out a hand to touch Catherine, who moved to avoid the contact.

'I'm all right. I want to know about Charlotte. It must have been the reason for what happened.'

'It was not then. Miss Charlotte was on the stairs with me when we heard the shot. She wanted to stay. I wouldn't let her.'

'You mean you encouraged her to go and her father dead, though you couldn't have known for sure that he was dead, if what you're telling me is the truth. For all you knew he might have been only injured, needing help, and you wasting time with Charlotte.'

'I knew he was dead.'

528

'How could you? That's not possible unless you looked.'

'I didn't. But I knew all the same. You could say I was expecting it.'

'That's nonsense, Hannah. But never mind that, I'm not interested in your premonitions. But I want to know what right did you have to encourage Charlotte?'

Hannah saw beneath Catherine's imperious expression the frightened face of a child, heard the grief disguised by the overbearing questions.

'It was this way, Miss,' she explained quietly. 'I was mother and father to her once you left. She was a lost wee thing. My heart went out to her. She was good and biddable, but a want was there. She needed more than the love of an old servant woman. And your poor father, Lord rest him, was always busy, Miss Olivia wrapped up in her own affairs and you gone. She'd wander round the house, and out in the fields and beyond. And when she grew up it was worse still. All the changes there were by then, no dances, nor parties, never meeting people of her own age, never a young man, and she the beautiful girl.

'Then she met Peader. Peader Daly, a decent man. He loved her and she him. In the beginning I thought it was infatuation and would blow over, but it didn't. And she blossomed, grew happier and lovelier. Sometimes in my mind I wondered if I was doing the right thing, deceiving your father by helping them. But in my heart there was never a doubt. And in the end I only did what anyone who loves another would. I helped her to be happy. I've taken liberties, you may well be thinking. And if you see fit to punish me or dismiss me, well, Miss, that's your right.'

They stared at each other. Hannah's eyes fearless, full

of love for this girl who confronted her, not sure which role she should play – the mistress irate with an old foolish servant, or the young, frightened woman, broken-hearted by the sudden, horrible death of her father, and desertion by a sister.

'Think of her, Miss,' Hannah broke the silence. 'What was in front of her? Buried alive here, maybe for the rest of her life, for she mightn't have liked India, and come back. In Kilgoran she could never have married Peader. Think of her. She'll be happy now with a good man to cherish her like you have yourself.'

'Oh Hannah,' she reached out her arms, and laid her cheek against the old soft creased cheek, the familiar smell of Hannah's body rolling back the years, so that once again she was a child, and she cried.

Hannah brought her to the kitchen, sat her down and put a shawl round her, comforting her, telling her not to fight the tears, to let them come, they'd ease her heart.

At last she controlled herself and asked Hannah what should they do now? What was to happen to her father, shouldn't someone be seeing to his body? 'I don't know about such things, but shouldn't we wash him, or something? Always before, no matter what happened there were people, servants to take care of everything.'

'It'll soon be morning, and then I'll go down to Katy's. Jamsie will go to the barracks, we'll have to let the police know.'

'The police?'

'When it's a thing like this you have to tell them, child.'

'I suppose you do. Yes, I suppose you would have to let them know.'

530

'But it'll be all right. Don't you be fretting yourself. And Statia will come to make everything tidy.'

– And please God, Hannah thought, they won't take away the Master's body or anything like that.

'Now, will you do something for me like a good girl?'

Catherine nodded her agreement.

'Will you go up and lay down for half an hour. I'll give you a hot jar. You'll feel the better of the sleep, and the minute I come back from Jamsie's I'll waken you.'

'But how could I sleep and poor Papa laying alone in the library?' Catherine began to cry again. But Hannah was insistent and made her go to bed.

'Oh my little love. My little bird.' Peader caught hold of Charlotte and held her close, showering her face with kisses. 'Why, you're crying. Don't. Don't cry any more. It's all over. We'll never be parted again. There's a boat sailing from Cork on tomorrow night's tide, we'll be on it. Now don't cry. Did you have any trouble getting out of the house?'

She wiped at her tears. 'No,' she said. 'No one saw me, only Hannah. There wasn't a sound.'

They stood in the shelter of the hedge, his arm round her, holding her close. She forced herself to believe what Hannah had said about the shot, it was only a farmer after a wailing dog. That's all it was. Hannah wouldn't tell her a lie. She would write to her father from America. Everything would be all right.

The cart came and Peader lifted her up amongst the pile of turf, then climbed in himself. The cart drove off. Peader shifted the sods until he had a hollow made. 'Lay in there,' he said. 'I'll pile a few more round you, so you won't be seen, and I'll sit here by the side. To anyone curious I'm only a poor man having a lift into Cork.'

Chapter Twenty-Two

Every time Catherine closed her eyes she saw her father's face, the gaping hole, the scorched flesh. She wanted to go to him, cradle his broken head against her breast. But she was afraid, knew she could never look upon him again, and guilt consumed her that she felt such fear, such revulsion at the sight of her dead father.

Her feeling of guilt worsened as she remembered the long hours he had spent alone in the library before the shooting. How, though she had gone to listen by the door, she had been too easily dissuaded by Hannah's warning that he wasn't to be disturbed. And she asked herself, had she heeded it from consideration of him, or because she found him tedious?

Had he been aware of that, of her impatience? Of the shame she experienced in the stable yard, concealing it as fear for his safety, when in reality all she feared were the people in the soup kitchen seeing a mad, old man who was her father?

She buried her face in the pillow to stifle her sobbing. 'Oh Papa, I'm so sorry. I didn't mean any of it. I never meant to hurt you, to tell you about Charles in such a way. Oh why did I do that? Why did I badger you about coming to India, about Charlotte and her clothes? You weren't well, and I made you worse.

'I came to you. I wanted you to comfort me. I needed you. I wanted to be a child again. I needed you and you weren't there. You failed me. Did I let that show? Did you see your failure in my eyes?

'Oh, Papa, if only I could have back the days, how differently I'd use them. I'd be kind to you, gentle, not bully or be ashamed of you. I'd have lied more convincingly about Olivia's reasons for not visiting.'

'Miss Catherine! Miss Catherine, stop that now! Stop that crying or you'll be sick. Sit up like a good girl and drink this.' Hannah was by the bed, holding a tray laid with tea things. 'Drink it and then come down. Statia and Jamsie are below, and I'm expecting the sergeant any minute.'

Catherine sat up and Hannah placed the tray on her lap, then went and drew back the curtains. Sunlight flooded the room. Catherine thought – this morning shouldn't be so fine, there should be clouds and rain falling.

When she came down to the kitchen the police sergeant was there. He was a youngish man, not very tall, thick-set with sandy hair and a freckled skin. She remembered hearing that the old sergeant had died. Statia and Jamsie said they were sorry for her trouble, and the sergeant added his sympathy. Then he said, 'If it's all right with you, Ma'am, I'll go and have a look at the ... go and see your father.'

'Yes, of course, Hannah will show you to the library.'

'He's new, that fellow, an improvement on the last one. They say he has a kind heart, though I've yet to meet the policeman with one,' Statia said when the sergeant left.

534

Jamsie said he had heard the same thing, then the three of them sat in an uneasy silence waiting. The policeman came back followed by Hannah. 'The poor man,' he said. 'Lord have mercy on him.'

'Will there have to be an inquest?' Catherine inquired.

'Ah no. Sure as far as anyone is to know he died of the fever. I'll make no report. But you know he'll have to be buried quick.' Catherine nodded, and the sergeant continued, 'There'll be no problems, haven't you your own burial ground on the estate?'

'We have,' Hannah answered for Catherine, 'where every one of the Kilgorans have been laid to rest, going back this long time.'

'I was thinking if there was enough wood, there's a fellow below in the barracks that's handy with the carpentry, he could make a coffin, a proper one, Ma'am. I'll send him up right away. Tomorrow then the funeral will be. I'll give a hand, and you too Jamsie.'

Jamsie nodded his agreement.

'Right then, Ma'am, I think that's all.'

'What about a clergyman to say a prayer after the Master?' Statia asked.

'A minister, yes, I'd forgotten, we must have a minister,' Catherine said slowly, for she was dazed with the speed at which the sergeant had arranged things, and overcome with gratitude for his decision to hide her father's suicide.

'Now there I can't help you. The nearest Protestant clergyman died himself this week. And I don't know where we'd get another in time. Time is very important.'

'Well, thank you very much for all you've done. I'm most grateful.'

'Sure it was nothing, Ma'am. I'd like to think someone would do the same for me or mine one day. Goodbye to you now.'

'There'll be no time to let Miss Olivia know,' Hannah said when the sergeant had gone.

'Isn't that a crying sin, the poor man buried with only one of his children here, and no time for a friend or relation to come. God's curse on the same famine,' Statia said.

'Miss Olivia will be heart-broken,' Hannah said. No one made reference to Charlotte, though she was in all their minds. And Catherine did not mention that Olivia was in Scotland, she wasn't sure where, so that even if her father's funeral was not such a hasty affair, Olivia wouldn't have been attending.

'Who'll follow him to the churchyard?' Hannah asked, then realizing it was something better not discussed, not yet anyway, began apologizing to Catherine.

'It's all right, Hannah, I understand. I know you're not allowed to attend Protestant funerals.'

'Well, may God forgive me,' said Statia, 'but I think circumstances alter cases, and it would be more of a sin not to folly the Master's remains, and folly it I will.'

'I'll be there in any case, so what difference does it make if I stay?' Jamsie said.

Hannah remained silent, her mind grappling with the situation. Would attending the Master's funeral be a mortal sin – the way drinking the soup was, or helping Miss Charlotte commit suicide? Knowing which sin was what was the hard thing to be sure of. She would risk purgatory rather than desert Miss Catherine, but Hell was a different thing altogether.

But it might only be a venial sin, only standing by the grave, out in the open, not putting her foot inside a Protestant church, and there'd be no minister saying prayers. And come to think of it, she had never heard a priest denounce standing in a Protestant graveyard. It could be only a venial sin. She would risk it.

Katy went to the priest's house and told him Lord Kilgoran was dead.

'The poor man. God have mercy on him. What happened?'

'He took his life, Father, he shot himself, and Peader has run away with Miss Charlotte.'

'The poor man found out, I suppose?'

'He didn't then. It was before she left. She was on the stairs with Hannah when the shot rang out.'

The priest shook his head. 'I warned him, I told Peader no good would come of it.'

'But it wasn't them, Father. The Master knew nothing about them going,' Katy said, and then wondered what was she doing defending that pair.

'Maybe not. But one way or the other it's a bad business for all concerned. Do you realize that Master Charles comes into his inheritance now, and the men he owes to will be waiting to claim it. There'll be a reckoning, and the rent arrears looked for, has that thought crossed your mind? If the Master had lived, however he managed, the back rent could have stood, and he wouldn't have been after you for the November Gale.'

'Oh Father, what'll we do?' Katy was consumed by fear. What would happen to her family if they were evicted

537

with the winter coming? There was nothing in front of them but starvation. All her striving to keep them safe would have been for nothing. They would die by the side of the road, or if pity moved the hearts of them in the workhouse, they would be separated, sent here and there amongst them that might be carrying the fever. Her children torn from her side, Jamsie in one place, she in another.

'Pray for a miracle, Katy. Pray that from somewhere you'll find the means of leaving Kilgoran. Kilgoran is finished. Ireland is finished. It'll be many a long day before she rises again. I had hopes of great things when I came, and now I'll be sent away.'

'Away! Sure they couldn't do that. What would we do without you, Father?'

'It's numbers the Bishop considers, Katy, and there isn't the numbers here any more. I'll be sent where there's more people. Now in the name of God I'll go up to the House and express my sympathy for Miss Catherine's trouble. If you wait till I harness the horse I'll give you a lift.'

He felt awkward, as he always did in the presence of the gentry.

'It was very good of you to come,' Catherine said.

'Not at all,' the priest said. 'I'm sorry it's on such a sad occasion. Your father was a good man, and I'm sure he's in heaven; God is merciful and takes all things into consideration. He'll be sorely missed. Well, I'm sure there's a lot you have to do, so I won't delay you.' He held out his hand and Catherine took it.

'Thank you again for calling, I'll show you out.' She went with him to the door. – He's a minister, she thought. I would wish for someone to pray for Papa. But he might refuse. It might not be allowed for him to pray over someone not of his calling.

He bade her good day and was halfway down the steps when she ran after him. 'Father Bolger, there is something I'd like you to do for my father. Would you pray for him?'

'Why, of course I will.'

'No, I mean now, would you come and pray over his body. There isn't a minister available, and I'd like Papa prayed over.'

'Indeed I will. The thought had occurred to me, but I didn't like to suggest it.'

He went back with her up the steps, and then upstairs to the bedroom where Statia and Jamsie had laid out her father's body. 'He's in there,' Catherine said, opening the door but keeping her head averted.

The priest held back, waiting for Catherine to enter. When she made no move, he asked, 'Aren't you coming in?'

She shook her head, and lied. 'No, I've been in several times already.'

'All right so,' Father Bolger said. He took a stole from his pocket, draped it round his neck and went in to pray over her father.

A week after the funeral Hannah watched the family solicitor drive away from the House. He had come the previous day, stayed overnight, and for hours had been closeted with Catherine in the library. Hannah wondered what the outcome of his visit would be. Not long after the solicitor's departure Catherine came to the kitchen to tell her.

'I'm afraid, Hannah, what the solicitor had to tell me was bad news.'

'Is that so, Miss Catherine, I'm sorry to hear it,' Hannah replied.

'Very bad news indeed, much worse than I expected.'

Hannah sat nervously rubbing one hand in the other, and waited for Catherine to speak again.

'The estate will have to be sold to pay the debts accumulated. I'm sure you know all about my brother, Charles, that he incurred many. Then of course, since the failure, there were other losses. You probably know all that, so there's no point going into details. I doubt if you'd understand the half of it. *I* found it hard enough to follow.'

'It's the land, the farms and that, that'll be sold then. Not the House, Miss?'

– Oh, not the House, please God, Hannah thought, while Catherine seemed to consider her question. My days are numbered, please God let me end them here.

'Dear Hannah, the House too, I'm afraid. The House and maybe all the contents, that won't be known until the valuers come down from Dublin. It will take a couple of weeks before things are finally settled. But of course you're welcome to stay until the last minute.'

'I know that, Miss Catherine, wouldn't I have to stay anyway? If I didn't, who'd mind you?'

'I won't be here, Hannah. I'm going, the day after tomorrow. I've decided to help in one of the fever hospitals in Cork until it's time to return to India. Do you under-stand what all this means for you?'

'Don't you be worrying about me. It's been in my mind this long time to go back to Connemara. Though to tell you the truth I never thought I'd get the chance. For who'd have looked after the Master, Lord rest him, and Miss Charlotte? But now there's nothing to stop me, so don't you be worrying about me,' Hannah said in what she hoped was a convincing manner.

'Hannah, it shouldn't have ended this way. You served us for so long, we should have been able to take care of you, instead of sending you off with a fare to Connemara, and your wages to the end of the year.'

'I know well if things had been different, taken care of me you would, the way your family always looked after the people. But the times are not the same. 'Tis no one's fault, and we must take what God sends,' Hannah said, determined not to shed a tear, not to cause one more minute's worry to Catherine. 'Tell me now, what'll we do with all the things, the clothes belonging to Miss Char-lotte, all them books and letters, and things that should belong to no one but the family?'

'I don't know. I can't think. I couldn't face touching any of them for the time being. Maybe tomorrow you'd see what you could do. Parcel up what you think fit, and we'll put them to one side, then before I go to India I'll go through them. Come over one day from Cork, maybe by then I'll be able to bear the sight of my father's personal possessions and Charlotte's. Poor Charlotte – I wonder where she is?'

'Wherever it is she'll be in good hands. Now, Miss, I'll

go and make a start on that packing,' Hannah said, for she knew if she stayed a minute longer she would be crying like an old fool, and upsetting Catherine.

Hannah packed boxes, folding gowns belonging to Charlotte, books from which dried flowers fell, the contents of her work table, silver thimbles, and scissors in an embroidered case, skeins of silks and wools, wrapped her painting brushes in an old petticoat, placing everything carefully in the boxes. Recalling times when she had seen Charlotte wear such and such a thing, her delight on the morning of her birthday when her father had given her the set of brushes.

She went from Charlotte's room to the nursery. No one, she thought, had set foot in the room for years. She closed her eyes and heard the voices, children laughing, quarrelling as to who should ride the rocking horse. Olivia scolding Charles for breaking her doll. Catherine sitting on the window seat singing to sleep her own family of wax-faced dolls. She opened her eyes, the voices faded, the dolls looked back at her, the horse was still. She walked into the room, into the dusty sunbeam and touched the horse's head, making him rock; she pushed harder on his head until he was galloping, and she went away from the room, hearing the sound of the horse growing fainter and fainter.

She emptied the presses in Lord Kilgoran's room, folded and packed the clothes. Cleared his dressing table, anything that was small and movable and personal she put into the boxes. They were her Master's things, not for the eyes or hands of the men from Dublin.

When it was done, the man from the Lodge came and shifted the cases to a small room. 'And don't you let them put a hand to what's in them,' she told him. 'You'll be here till the end, maybe after if you're lucky. But you remember, them things belong to the family, and no one but the family is to lay hands on them.'

From the kitchen she collected what little food remained, the heels of bread, a few handfuls of meal, scraps of meat and a marrow bone, they would keep Katy for another day.

Soon it was time to go. The fires were put out. In the drawing-room dust-covers draped the sofas and chairs. The mice came out of their holes, behind a wainscot a rat gnawed its way further forward. The wind blew and sent showers of soot down the chimneys, rattled the jagged panes of glass; they fell in shards on to the floor, and the weather entered the House. Catherine and Hannah walked away without looking back. Catherine got into the coach, and Hannah went to say goodbye to Katy.

'Don't go, Hannah,' Katy pleaded when the time came for her to leave. 'They might all be dead and gone in Connemara. You could get there and not know a living soul. The fever's been bad there. You've been in Kilgoran so long, you'll be a stranger in the west. I'll make room for you.'

– If only I could, Hannah thought, if I could end my days with you, Katy, isn't it me that would die happy. But how could I throw myself on you, haven't you enough of a burden as it is?

'You kind creature, God bless you for the offer. But I've a longing to go back. I'm a Connemara woman, and there

543

I want to die and be buried. Sixty years I've been here and it's time I went back.'

'Sixty years, is it that long, Hannah?' asked Statia who had come to say farewell to her.

'Sixty it is. The Master was no more than a child when I arrived,' Hannah replied, her voice had a note of pride in it. 'And if I don't get up from this settle and make a move it's another sixty I'll be here. Commere and let me kiss you.' She held out her arms to the children. 'God bless and spare you, be good now, won't you, and say a prayer for Hannah every day.'

Thomas wriggled out of her embrace, red in the face with embarrassment. Bridget and Mary Kate returned Hannah's kisses affectionately. Danny refused to have anything to do with Hannah, a scowl on his thin pale face, and buried his head in his mother's lap. But the twins were lavish with their kisses and hugs, twining their arms round Hannah's neck, squeezing her until Katy told them that was enough, and if they didn't stop they'd be strangling Hannah.

'Leave her alone now, you'll have the head pulled off of her, and wouldn't that be a nice sight arriving in Connemara. And when me and Daddy and Statia go up the road to send Hannah, don't one of you come after us.'

Katy and Statia stood at the top of the boreen watching Jamsie walk Hannah to catch the coach from Carey's. Jamsie carrying her black portmanteau that Katy recognized as having come from the House, containing all that Hannah possessed in the world. Thinking that she had a long way in front of her. A long ride to Galway, and many a mile before she reached Clifden, and maybe a bitter end to it all, if no one belonging to her still lived.

Statia's voice broke in on her thoughts. 'Wasn't I right? I'm no fool. Sixty years in Kilgoran, did you hear her admit that. So much for pink ribbons in her hair the day the French war ended. An oul wan, didn't I tell you all along.'

– Poor Hannah, giving away the secret of her age. But this wasn't the time to make a mock of her. Katy turned to say the same to Statia, to tell her a kinder word should be spoken, and saw to her amazement Statia's face wet with tears – Statia that she had never known shed a tear for anyone. 'An oul wan,' Statia repeated, angrily knuckling her eyes. 'Everyone's gone. Everyone we called our friends. All gone, Katy. And she the last of them.'

'Come back with me,' Katy said, taking hold of Statia's arm, 'we'll have a heat of the fire, and make a pick to eat.'

With a long thin twig, Katy scooped marrow from the beef bone and melted it in the pot. The smell of the sizzling fat filled the kitchen and made them weak with hunger. Katy broke one of the ends of a loaf into pieces, dipped it in the pot and offered a bit to Statia.

'I couldn't touch it,' Statia refused, 'fat never agreed with me.'

'You're only letting on, I never knew fat to turn your stomach before. Have a little taste.' But Statia stuck to her excuse and wouldn't accept the bread, glad she had had the strength to hold out when she saw the ravenous way Jamsie, who had returned from seeing Hannah off, devoured it.

When the food was eaten they talked about the estate, wondering who would buy it, and when.

545

Jamsie said the land could be broken up, sold off in lots maybe. And Statia said at this very minute Dano would be counting out his money to buy any lots that were going.

'Oh no! Not the Driscolls, not Dano taking the place of the Master. Not them in the House!' Katy was aghast.

'Not in the House, nor the Master neither, he hasn't come that far yet. But he'll plant his arse in some of the fields. It's not his pedigree they'll be looking at, only the colour of his money,' Statia said. 'It's the likes of him and Connolly the robber that'll grow fat out of the famine.'

Jamsie walked Statia home, and Katy put the children to bed, then returned to sit staring into the fire. Seeing in its glowing heart, pictures. Hannah trudging from Galway to Clifden. Hannah teaching her the lacemaking. Hannah running down from the House with leftover food. Hannah, who had been part of all her days from the time she could first remember.

The sobs burned, were consumed, collapsed, and the pictures vanished. In Katy's mind they were replaced by other visions, other thoughts. Peader and Charlotte on their way to America. Happy with each other. Making a new start where there was full and plenty. Weren't they the lucky ones? For the first time ever, she admitted to herself that maybe Charlotte really loved Peader, and he her. And she no longer cared. There wasn't room in her heart or mind for anything but the desire to save her children, to keep the life in them. But how could she succeed in the winter that was coming? With the House closed and what Hannah used to bring finished? Unless they got away from Kilgoran, all her efforts would have been in vain. She could stop the children going up on the road, that way maybe keep the fever at bay. But in the months, even weeks to come, she could not prevent hunger coming to claim them.

She remembered Father Bolger telling her to pray for a miracle – a happening to take her away from Kilgoran, out of Ireland. And sitting by the fire she now began to pray fervently. Telling God if it was pleasing to His will to let them go. Explaining that everyone else was gone. Only herself and Statia left. The priest himself was soon to leave, and how would they manage then? They'd be forgotten. So even if they sickened and died, no one would know or care. They could lie for days, even months and not one to come and bury them, make the Sign of the Cross over them. – It happened in other places, Lord, don't let it happen to me and mine.

Jamsie came back. He said it was a cold night. And she said, it was. She looked at him and thought – I feel nothing for him, not even pity that he's blue with the cold, and that thin, a puff of wind would blow him away. If he was a stranger I'd be more concerned, ask him to sit up to the fire. But I don't care if he sits or stands, sleeps or doesn't. There's no feelings in me any more, where he's concerned my heart is dead.

The Dublin singing tavern was crowded, the lights dim, the air thick with tobacco smoke.

'Give us another song,' a drunken voice called, 'one with a bit of life in it this time.'

'You dirty lot of bowsies,' Johnny O'Hara's wife said to herself, as she moved between the tables, then began to sing the Waxy Dargle. The light was so poor she could hardly distinguish one face from another, but she felt the groping hands stroke her thighs and pinch her buttocks. The ones that attempted to reach under her skirt she slapped away, That sort of caressing cost money.

A few discordant voices joined in the song she was singing about Donnybrook Fair, then she heard another voice call her name, and her heart stood still.

'Josie,' the voice hissed again. No one in Dublin called her that, and only one person in the whole world spoke like that. Again her name was repeated and at the same time a hand reached out and imprisoned her wrist. 'You hoor! I've been watching you sporting your charms. Come away with me this minute.'

'Johnny! Oh Johnny, you gave me a terrible fright! Sure I thought you were dead this long time.'

'Did you now, well I'm not.'

'What happened to the singer?' a man shouted. Another took up the cry. 'Whare's the singer?' Soon there was a lot of shouting, and banging of pots on tables, and calls for the Waxy Dargle.

'Let go me wrist, Johnny. I'll have to finish the song. Wait there till I finish, I won't be a minute. I'll be with you then.'

'You better had. It's taken me this long to track you down, you won't escape again.'

– I'm done for, she thought while she finished the song. He'll want to know about the children. He may even have heard tell about the other child. Well, that she could lie her way out of, but what was she to say about his own?

'So that's where you finished up – in a den of thieves

and prostitutes!' Johnny said when they were making their way through narrow streets towards the alley where Josie lived.

'What else was I to do? Wasn't I run out of the bog because of your affair with the Society?'

'Was that why, or was there another reason? I heard tell there was a child, a child that wasn't an O'Hara.'

'May God forgive you for saying such a thing about your wife. Listening to lies, and accusing me.'

'What sort of a kip is this?' Johnny asked as they stumbled through the filth of the narrow court and Josie stopped before a door.

'It's all I could get. Whisht now, there's an old woman living above, don't waken her. Who told you such terrible things about me? Sure don't you know me, Johnny, I never in my life looked at another man.'

'You were looking at plenty tonight.'

'That's all a cod, you have to do it in the job. Here, have a sup of this.'

He drank from the whiskey bottle, then looked towards the bed in the corner. 'Where's the children?' he asked.

'There's a woman minds them. You'll see them in the morning, you'll stay the night. Say you will.' She was undoing his coat, caressing him, pressing him to drink more whiskey. 'Never in all my born days did I look at another man, and that's the God's truth.' She had his coat off and was beginning to unfasten his trousers. 'I missed you terrible, Johnny, where were you this long time?'

'Hiding, running. Over in England, everywhere except Kilgoran.' He pulled her down on to the bed. 'You're a fine woman, not a girl any more.'

'Ah sure, don't be talking, Johnny.' She fastened her mouth on his, thinking while he mounted her, – I'll get him stocious, I'll get him that drunk he'll fall into a stupor, then I'll run for the polis. For if I don't he'll kill me when morning comes and he learns the truth of the children.

'Oh Johnny! My darling Johnny! My lovely man!' She held him tight, feigning cries of delight.

He got off the bed, his trousers concertina-ing round his feet. 'What happened to your mother?' he asked.

'Lord have mercy on her, she died last year.'

He pulled up his trousers, tucked in his shirt, watching her all the time. He fastened his trousers then grabbed hold of her and yanked her from the bed. 'If you scream I'll kill you.' He punched her in the face. 'Where's the children?'

Blood spurted from her mouth and nose. 'I told you, with a woman, honest to God.'

He hit her again, she fell. He bent over her, raining blows on her face, on her head. 'What did you do with them, answer me?' His fist punched her stomach.

'I . . . couldn't help it. They were starving. I had to put them in the union.'

'You rotten cow! You rotten tinker's bitch! You put my children in a foundling hospital! God's curse on you!' He battered her senseless, and even when she lay still continued to punch and kick her. When he had exhausted himself he sought the whiskey bottle, drank from it, then returned to Josie and searched amongst her clothes until he found money, which he pocketed. Only then did he lay a hand on her breast, place an ear to her mouth. He could feel no heartbeat, nor breath. 'You're dead, it's what you

550

deserved, may you roast in Hell,' he said, and pushed her aside with his foot.

He lay on the bed, but didn't sleep. Before daylight he left the room and made his way to the quays. Already there was a crowd waiting to board the boat for England; he went amongst them and waited until it was time to embark.

Chapter Twenty-Three

The woman with two children came down the boreen and knocked on the open door. 'God bless you, Ma'am,' she said when Katy came to see who had rapped, 'I've walked a long way. We were in the workhouse. My husband died there, and I ran out of it before we all died. I'm walking the road and would be obliged for a drink of water.'

Katy was repulsed by the appearance of the woman and the children. She had never seen anything like them. She thought it unnatural that they had the power to stand, to speak. They seemed to her as people who had been dead, and risen from the grave. Their skin with a greenish pallor scarcely concealed their bones, great clouts of downy hair sprouted from the children's faces, yet parts of their heads were bald, and their jawbones thrust forward, so their chins were inches out in front of their faces.

She was repelled and frightened. Her instinct was to slam the door in their faces. Shout to them, she had nothing for them, to go away. But the woman beseeched her, 'Just a cup of water, Ma'am, and we'll be on our way.'

'I've no food,' Katy said. 'But you're welcome to a heat of the fire, and there's plenty of water, come in.'

They came into the kitchen and it was filled with the smell of their filthy clothes and their sick bodies. 'Get up from the fire,' Katy told the children, 'and go out to play. Get up now and let the woman sit down.'

Thomas, Bridget, Mary Kate and Danny did her bidding, the twins stayed where they were, looking curiously at the strangers. Katy was too tired to insist that Peg and Nora obeyed her, and left them where they were. Katy gave the woman and her children a mug of water between them, and said there was more when they finished. The woman took the shawl from her head, and Katy saw the lice moving through her hair, some crawling on her forehead, and when she looked at the children saw that they too were infested. 'Go on out, you two,' she shouted at Peg and Nora.

'Ah leave them, sure they're doing no harm,' the woman entreated, reaching out a hand to touch Peg, then Nora. 'They're beauties, God bless and spare them to you.'

Peg responded as she always did to praise and attention, and Nora copied her. Before Katy could shift them they were talking to the strange children, lolling beside them, their red hair touching the scant hair of the other children.

The woman thanked Katy, and got up from the fire. 'You're lucky to have a shelter and turf to burn.'

'We are, thank God.'

'May you be rewarded for your hospitality and get it back on the treblefold,' the woman said when she was leaving.

'What ails the pair of you?' Katy asked the twins, who were unusually quiet, sitting together on the settle, ignoring Bridget's request that they should come out to play, unmoved by Prince licking at their hands.

'Do you hear me talking to you?' Katy's voice was harsh to hide the unease she felt, an unease that had troubled her since this morning when she noticed that the twins weren't their usual selves.

They didn't answer. Peg sucked her thumb, and Nora had a finger wound in a red curl listlessly twirling it. Katy wiped her wet hands down the side of her petticoat and placed one on each child's forehead. They were burning. Two pairs of glazed eyes looking up at her, and their cheeks were unnaturally rosy.

'Go in and lay down – you're chilled. I told you you'd get your end the way you go in and out, running like wild things, and it freezing yesterday.'

She helped them down from the settle and with her arms round them took them into the bedroom. They stood by the bed shivering. ''Tis a chill, that's all,' Katy said loudly, trying to convince herself that was all that ailed them.

She put them into the bed the way they were in their ragged clothes, pulled the one remaining blanket over them, and piled the few coats and her shawl on top of them. Their bodies were convulsed by rigor, their teeth chattering in their heads.

'Lay close to each other to keep warm, there's good girls. Shut your eyes and try to go to sleep. 'Tis only a chill, you'll be as right as rain when you wake up. Go to sleep now.' She stayed by them until they fell asleep, then ran to Statia's and asked her to come and see them. 'I think they've got the fever. Oh Statia, I'm sure they have. No chill would make them so bad. That woman who came last week brought it with her. I kept them close to the cottage, I wouldn't let them stir from the door. And she brought it down the boreen and into the house.'

'Go back to them,' Statia said. 'I've got a few coppers, I'll go to a farmer's wife for a sup of milk, it might only be hunger that ails them.'

They wouldn't drink the milk. They lay still in the bed, gazing at Katy and Statia. To moisten their cracked lips Katy dipped a rag in water and wiped them. For days they never spoke, only made whimpering sounds when Statia lifted them as tenderly as newborn babies, while Katy folded the sheet to make a dry place for them to lay.

'My little lambs, Statia won't hurt you, lay easy now my little beauties that Statia had the great hopes for,' she crooned to them, cradling the wasted bodies against her own.

They were very sick, Katy knew that. But they wouldn't die. God wouldn't let them die. She pleaded with Him not to. They had grand constitutions, never sick a day in their lives. No, God wouldn't take them from her.

Statia tried to dampen her hopes, 'They're not improving, child, and I don't like their colour.'

'They're only pale, that's all.'

'They're saffron-coloured, Katy. They've got yalla fever.'

She could see the colour on them, but wouldn't admit it, not to Statia, not to herself. A week after they had first sickened, their fever dropped, and although they still looked very ill, Katy saw an improvement in them. They were getting better, she was convinced. 'Run quick,' she told Bridget, 'and tell Statia, Peg and Nora are better.'

555

And when Statia came and told her the improvement was the course yellow fever ran, and maybe tomorrow, maybe next week, they would relapse, Katy turned on Statia, and told her not to wish ill luck on her or the twins. Anyone with eyes in their head could see they were getting better, though in her heart she feared that Statia spoke the truth.

The next day the twins relapsed. Through the day while Katy foraged for something for the other children to eat, Statia sat with them. Jamsie stayed away from the house for long periods. Katy didn't know where he went, and didn't care. Walking, she supposed he was, running away from trouble, not able to face it unless he had a drink, which he nor no one else had the price of. Father Bolger came in the night and brought more milk, and blessed the twins. Katy and Statia sat by them, and in the small hours, almost at the same instant, Peg then Nora took a long shuddering breath and they were still.

'Easy now, Katy,' Statia said when the cart came to collect the bodies of Nora and Peg. 'God only lent them to you, He's taken them back. They're in Heaven this minute, two little angels, looking down, interceding for you. What's on the bed 'ithin is only their shells.'

The coffin with the sliding bottom was laid outside the door. Jamsie carried out Peg and placed her in it. Katy went and knelt by the side of the box. Jamsie came back with Nora, and arranged her beside her sister.

'It's too big for them. They'll be jolted, the road's uneven, they'll be bumped and banged from side to side,' Katy said as if talking to herself. 'I won't let them go like that. Wait!' She ran into the cottage, found the twins' bodices and petticoats, packed the clothes in round them, wedging them in the spaces round the edges, but still there were gaps. She took off her shawl, and bent to arrange it in the coffin.

'No!' Statia said, taking it from her. 'Not that, it's your only covering. Peg and Nora don't need it. Peg and Nora aren't there. They're in Heaven, they won't feel the cold, nor the heat, nor the bumps in the road. Keep it, tomorrow you'll have to go to the well, you'll need the shawl.'

Katy let Statia drape the shawl round her. 'Kneel down and take your last of them,' Statia said, and Katy knelt, kissed each little girl, touched their hair and their cold yellow cheeks. 'Wasn't I right?' she whispered. 'Do you remember when we found the rabbit, and I told you Heaven was a lovely place. Well, wasn't I right?'

'Take them now,' she said, rising from her knees. The lid was closed and the coffin carried away by Jamsie and the cart driver, Statia walking behind them.

Katy went into the bedroom and stood looking at the pillows with the imprint of Peg and Nora's heads still upon them. She looked at them for a long time, then picked up each pillow in turn and shook them. Then she knelt and brought from under the bed the box that had once held her treasures. Nothing remained inside it, only the piece of rag in which the cauls were wrapped. When she undid the cloth the membranes were brittle and crumbled. Her lovely children that Statia said would grow up to be lucky and beauties, she thought as the tissue disintegrated between her fingers. Peg and Nora going over the hillocky road, being emptied from the box, their clothes falling down on top of them. She ground the cauls until they were

557

only dust, and her nails tore the palms of her hands. And she reminded herself that they weren't there going up to the graveyard at all, they were two little angels in Heaven – that was lovely. And she went from the room and threw the cauls into the heart of the fire.

That night in bed Jamsie put his arm round her, and she let it stay, was comforted by it, and fell asleep. When she woke she forgot that the twins were dead. Then she remembered, but not that they were buried. She got up and went into the bedroom. The bed seemed vast with only the four children in it. She went closer to see why it seemed so vast, and she remembered why. She bent to look at the faces of her other children. Thomas and Danny at the foot of the bed, Bridget and Mary Kate at the top. And she thought how the dead had made more room for the living. And what a terrible price it was to pay so that the others could stretch out in comfort. And she wanted to scream and beat her head on the wall, and curse God for taking her little girls. And she wanted to stop seeing them tumbled into the clay with nothing between them and it. And then she told herself they were in Heaven, and that she believed that, for if she didn't she would go mad.

When she returned to the kitchen Jamsie was up and dressed. 'I'm going to Cork,' he said. 'I'm going to work, and if I can't get work, then I'll rob, but one way or the other I'll get the passage money for America.'

'Do so,' she said listlessly, not believing him. Knowing if on the way he met anyone with the price of a pint he'd be easily distracted from his purpose.

*

Jamsie chose the coast road, it was the longest way and few if any would travel it. But a cart might stop to pick up a lone man, though he knew there were few carts, and fewer still that stopped, everyone afraid of the fever, and the crazed eyes of people mad with hunger.

He began the climb to the road that ran along the cliff, stopping every few yards to get his breath, thinking how once he would have strode with ease to the top, glorying in the movement, the power of his body. Now every step, every breath was a conscious one, his bones ached, his eyes were sore and watered, there wasn't an atom of his body that didn't protest.

When he got to the top he leant on a drystone wall and looked down on the sea; it was smooth and changing colour, slatey grey, with patches here and there of pale green. It came in slow and easy, breaking in little waves down below on the shingle. His mind went to Katy, he wondered how she would fare while he was gone. She looked terrible bad. Maybe he shouldn't have started out, not so soon after the twins. He thought of them in his arms carrying them to their coffin, and how it was a hard thing for a man to have to do, but harder still for Katy to watch. Would she have strength to draw water from the well? Should he have left her so soon after her grief? But if he hadn't, the winter would be on top of them, and no boats going to America. America, what was that like? So far away did his mind wander he didn't hear the horse and cart approach and pull up, not until a voice said,

'`Tis you must be the contented man, gazing out at the ocean; or was it America you were contemplating?'

'`Twas more for the rest I stopped,' Jamsie said to the

little withered-looking man on the cart. 'I'm heading for Cork.'

'God bless your ambition, you've a fine long way ahead of you.'

'I have that.'

'I'll give you a lift. Get up.'

'Thanks very much,' Jamsie said and got on to the cart.

In Cork fever was reaching epidemic proportions. Sheds had been hastily erected in the grounds of workhouses and hospitals to accommodate the sick. There was a shortage of doctors and nurses, aggravated by the number of them who got fever and died. Many people volunteered their help, people of all denominations, of all classes. Among them was Catherine.

She nursed the sick and dying, and from a small office attempted to keep a record of those admitted. On the day when Jamsie was riding on the cart towards the city, Catherine was at her desk. Someone, she believed, had to attempt keeping track of the men, women and children coming into the fever sheds. Often it was impossible, they were half-dead before arriving, no one to speak their names. But it was important to do what she could. There might be someone, somewhere who one day would seek information about a husband, wife, parent or child.

– If only, she thought, I wasn't always so tired, if only there were more people to help. If only I could walk out of here this minute, catch the Dublin coach, the boat to England, return to India. Leave all the sickness and death. Go away, forget it existed. Often she felt as she did now, almost succumbed to the temptation, but always resolved to stay until tomorrow. To work one more day. Only one more day to endure, the thought gave her hope, lent her enough strength to carry on. And when tomorrow came, she said again, – tomorrow I will go. And so, taking it a day at a time, she had been at the hospital three weeks.

She pushed back a strand of hair that escaped from her carelessly arranged knot. There was barely time to keep herself clean, never mind paying attention to hairstyles.

'Ma'am,' said the young girl who helped clean and cook, coming into the tiny office, 'there's a lady coming up the path. A beautiful lady, Ma'am, all dressed up, and a fella carrying that much baggage.'

'Well, he can take that back, volunteers I'll welcome, but not their baggage, we haven't room to move as it is. Go and meet her, bring her in.'

The maid went out and Catherine ran her hands over her head, attempting to smooth her hair; she didn't wish to appear slovenly before this woman, whoever she was.

The door opened and Olivia's radiant face appeared round it. 'It's me. I've come to help.'

Catherine gasped. 'It can't be. Oh, but it is. Darling, it's really you.' She got up from the desk, was halfway round, then stopped. 'I mustn't touch you. I must wash my hands. I'm so overjoyed I don't know what to say.' She scrubbed furiously at her fingers. 'Yes I do. You shouldn't have come. Why didn't you stay where you were safe? Turn round and go back. You've no idea what it's like here. No one has.' She emptied the basin into a pail, dried her hands and approached her sister. 'You were mad to come.'

'Fiddle! I've never been sick in my life except on a boat

and when it suited me to pretend I had the vapours. Anyway it's the least I can do after missing Papa's funeral, leaving you to cope with everything.'

They embraced each other, cried and laughed, then separated, and sat either side of the desk. 'Now tell me what's the latest on the estate, does it have to be sold?'

'I'm afraid it does. MacNamara, he was so upset giving me the bad news, you'd have thought it was his property being lost.'

'Poor Catherine, how ghastly. It meant such a lot to you. Of course I loved it, in a way, and hate the idea of strangers having what was ours for so long. But it won't grieve me in the same way. I'm truly sorry. And I wish that years ago I had taken Charles' escapades more seriously. Perhaps if I had and spoken to Papa he might have disinherited him. The place should have been yours. But it's too late now. I wonder who will buy it?'

'MacNamara thinks it will take a long time to sell, years maybe. I think in a way that's worse, the thought of it standing empty and neglected. No one caring for it,' Catherine said.

'The tenants I suppose will suffer too with no one interested in their welfare.'

'There aren't any tenants, only the O'Haras and Statia, everyone else is gone. You wouldn't recognize the place, it's deserted.'

'Isn't it awful what a few years can do. It seems such a short time ago we were all happy there. The House full of people, parties, balls, the hunt. It seems as if then it was always summer. The fields were full of men and women working, they seemed happy too. I suppose they were.

562

There was Papa, and Charlotte, me and you. Charles before he went up to Trinity, he wasn't too bad then. I was bored and wanted to escape, but none of us were really unhappy. And look at us now. Papa dead, Charlotte God knows where, and Charles in Australia. I don't suppose we'll see or hear from either of them again.' Olivia took off her bonnet, the sunlight shining through the window made a halo round her head.

'I don't suppose so. There's only the two of us,' Catherine said, and began to cry.

'Now for Heaven's sake stop that or I shall go straight back as you advise. Anyway you have Edward waiting for you, and soon you'll have a family. We must look to the bright side. No more crying now.'

'I'm sorry. I won't.' Catherine dabbed at her eyes. 'I still can't believe you're here, that you crossed the sea alone. I didn't think you'd do that for anyone.'

'Ah, but you're not just anyone. And God obviously approved – the sea was like a mill pond.'

'Your courage was rewarded. It will be again.'

'Just once more and I'll be grateful. Then I'll say goodbye to Ireland forever. It would be asking too much of God to still the waters more than twice.' She laughed her beautiful laugh. Like a peal of joybells, Catherine thought. And felt that she could move mountains with that vitality of Olivia's to sustain her.

It was dark when the man dropped Jamsie from the cart. He took shelter for the night in a ditch. He rose before daylight and walked on a few miles. When dawn broke he saw a farm, there were cabbages in a field and he stole one.

It was small, but the heart was good, he tore off the outer leaves, broke the root to which clay still clung and discarded that with the leaves. He munched the heart, the stalks were juicy and quenched his thirst.

In the city he looked for work, but everywhere he asked, the answer was the same. Looking him up and down, the employer said he had nothing. He asked at public houses where barrels were being unloaded from drays pulled by horses bigger than Jamsie had ever seen, in builders' yards, down by the docks, wherever work was being done, but without any success. In a side street he came upon a man shifting a mound of coal, shovelling it into bags, weighing it, and he asked him for a start.

The man laughed outright, contemptuously.

'You hoor, what are you laughing at?' Jamsie demanded to know, incensed by the laughter and derision in the man's eyes.

'A start is it. Be Jasus you couldn't shovel feathers, never mind coal. Have you looked at yourself lately? You're like a walking corpse.'

'Mister, I can still handle a shovel.'

'Not mine you can't.'

'I've a starving wife and children. Give me a try anyway.'

'Everyone has a starving wife and children. I'm sorry for them. I can pick and choose from ten or twenty big strong men. There's nothing for you here. Away now and don't be wasting my time.'

– The bastard, Jamsie said to himself walking away. But I'll show him. I'll get work. I'll get money to take back to Katy. He walked back towards the river. There he saw

564

ships and carts pulling up beside them, carts piled high with grain being sent to England. – The bastards, he said again to himself. Even so I'd help unload and carry it on if someone paid me. He stopped to ask for work and watched, smelled the tar of the ship, the ropes, and the grain, and the green weedy smell of the water. A big burly man with a full sack on his shoulder told him to clear off, they weren't looking for casual workers on the docks.

He went back towards the city, climbing a hill, coming down it was another cart piled high, heading for the docks, with a crowd following it, shouting and shaking their fists. The driver turned in his seat and lashed out at them with his whip. A big, gaunt man ran to the front of the cart, up to the horse's head, and caught the bridle in his two hands, stopping the horse. Another man pulled the driver off the cart, kicked him as he fell. 'Good on you,' someone in the crowd shouted, it was taken up, then another one filled the air. 'Pull down the sacks, split them open.'

A woman ran forward, she had a knife and slashed the sack. The grain spilled out in a golden shower. The cart was surrounded, sacks pulled down, ripped open. Jamsie joined in the melee, pushing and shoving, picking up handfuls of grain, stuffing it into his pockets. A man beside him took off his breeches, tied knots in the legs, and began to pour grain into them until they took on the appearance of gross limbs from which the trunk had been severed.

'The polis,' a voice shouted, and from the corner of his eye Jamsie saw two things, a truncheon descending towards his head, and Catherine Kilgoran getting down from a coach. The truncheon descended and he lost consciousness.

'That man, constable, that man you struck – he works for me at the fever hospital.'

'He was plundering the cart, Ma'am.'

'Nonsense! He's one of my father's tenants. My father's Lord Kilgoran. The man you appear to have gravely injured is an upright, honest fellow. He volunteered to come to Cork and help me with my work. If anything he would have been attempting to protect the cart.'

The policeman looked from the prostrate Jamsie, grain trickling from his pockets, to the severe, commanding expression of the woman. She was gentry, no doubt about that. And God only knew her reasons for protecting this fellow: anyone but a blind man could see the evidence that he'd been implicated in robbing the cart. 'Ah, to hell with it all,' he said to himself, 'I haven't time to be arguing, or the others will make away with every sack on the cart, and besides there's something about the gentry that unnerves me.'

He touched his cap. 'Begging your pardon, Ma'am, I'd no idea he was a decent sort of man. I'll give your driver a hand to put him in the coach.'

– That's odd, Katy thought, two days and no sign of Statia; with Jamsie gone I was sure she'd be on top of me every five minutes. 'Run off, you,' she called to Bridget, 'and see if she's all right.'

'You're to go down, she's very sick,' Bridget said when in no time she was back.

'Statia! What ails you?' Katy asked in alarm at the sight

566

of Statia in bed, something she had never seen before. 'Are you not well?'

'I'm finished. I took this fit of shivering after the funeral, and I haven't been right since.'

Katy went closer to the bed. Statia's eyes were far back in her head, her face yellow, and a pinched look about it. 'Indeed you're far from finished,' Katy said, trying to hide her fear. Knowing well Statia had whatever it was the twins had died from. Avoiding the hand Statia was reaching towards her. She didn't want to touch her, she didn't want to get the fever, die and be buried in a grave from someone else's coffin. She couldn't die. She was on her own. She couldn't die and leave the children.

'Katy,' Statia's voice was hoarse, not much above a whisper, her hand was raised still reaching for Katy. She sighed, and the hand fell on to the blanket.

'Oh Statia! Don't die on me, Statia! What would I do without you?' Her fear forgotten, Katy took hold of the thin, wasted hand. 'Don't you die on me.'

''Tis not my wish, but His will.' For an instant there was a flash of the old mocking smile, then it was gone, and Statia was making an effort to talk. 'Under the bed ... in a piece of flannel ... there's money ... it's no use to me, take it.'

'Whisht now, don't be talking. I'll bathe your head, it's very hot. Whisht now and be a good girl,' Katy said, and thought her heart would break as she repeated words that Statia had said many times to her in the hours of travail. She brought water and wrung out a piece of rag, wet Statia's lips, wiped her face and laid the cold cloth on her burning forehead.

567

She appeared to sleep for a minute, and Katy sat by the bed. But soon Statia's eyes were open again, and her rasping voice was saying, 'Get word to them, I'll have to be shifted, to the fever shed, but take the money first. Let me see you take it. It's long ago I should have,' her voice was barely audible, and Katy had to bend close to her what she said. 'Under the bed, pull it out.'

'All right so, if it pleases you,' Katy bent and felt under the mattress, found the piece of flannel and held it up so Statia could see. She nodded her head, feebly, approving. The cloth felt heavy and Katy knew from its weight there were many coins in its folds. She undid it, it was long, like a belt, folded in two and the raw edges had been secured down with running stitches close together, and by more stitches it was divided into pockets, each one with coins in them.

She pulled at a corner, but the thread was strong, the sewing fine, it wouldn't give. She looked round the room for something with which to unpick it. There was nothing. Not a knife, nor scissors, nor a hair pin in her hair or Statia's. Everything they had possessed, worn out, sold, nothing replaced.

Statia watched Katy's efforts, then began to gesture feebly to the old coat folded beneath her head. 'Me beads, there, me beads.'

Katy slipped a hand beneath the makeshift pillow and found the cloth purse, opened it and tipped the rosary into her palm. A twist of paper fell with them. She knew what it was, a needle, wrapped to stop it rusting. It was a thick one and didn't snap when she levered the coarse thread holding the money in place. One by one she released the coins, gasping at the amount. 'You have a fortune, Statia! Why didn't you spend it, buy milk, a bit of meal for yourself? There's nearly twenty pounds.'

'Me burial money, for a decent send-off.' Again, briefly, Katy saw the old mocking smile. 'To have a good keen set up, and a coffin that would last. Little did I know the send-off I'd be getting.' Statia waved her hand towards the money spread on the bed. 'You take it, for the children, for America.'

'Whisht now, don't be talking so. You'll be up and about in no time,' Katy said, and thought bitterly of how long the silver had lain under the bed. Lain there while Statia starved, while the children starved, then reminded herself she had no right to think such things. It was Statia's earnings, and wasn't she entitled to be buried decent? Before the famine wasn't it everyone's ambition?

'Take it,' Statia urged, catching hold of Katy's wrist, attempting to squeeze it.

She could buy new milk, meal, build up the children, and there'd still be enough for the passage to America, in case Jamsie didn't succeed in Cork. In her excitement, Katy was shouting at Statia. 'I'll mind it for you. I'll account for every penny when you're better,' she said, and a part of her mind thought, – and God forbidding all harm, if you die, we'll go to America.

She took her hand away from Statia. 'Lay still now,' she said. 'I'll moisten your lips again. And I'll see to the fire, then I'll run Thomas up for the priest. You'd like that, wouldn't you?'

Statia nodded her agreement, and closed her eyes. Katy fetched fresh water and again wet Statia's cracked mouth

569

and bathed her forehead. She built up the fire, collected the money, tied it in the flannel, put it under her shawl and went home.

'Go you, Thomas, to Father Bolger and tell him Statia's dying,' she said when she arrived.

She unwrapped the coins, took five shillings from them, tied the remainder up again, and went to the garden where with a piece of stick she dug a hole under the box hedge and buried them. Marking the place with a stone so she shouldn't forget their whereabouts, nor Prince uproot them. She had just finished when Thomas came back. 'The priest is queer. In the bed. I shook him, but he didn't waken. His face was red, but he was sweating like Peg and Nora.'

'Sacred Heart of Jesus, he has the fever too! What'll I do? There's not a soul for miles. Only Carey and Dano, neither of them fond of the clergy, and both I suppose afraid of the sickness. What'll I do about Statia, and who'll mind the priest? Oh, if only Jamsie hadn't gone. I'll go anyway to Connolly's for food, and milk. Statia and the priest might take milk. And if she gets better I can't go to America. But I can't let her die.' Thomas looked on as she talked aloud.

Then she went into the cottage and he followed her. The other children were huddled round the fire. 'I'm going to Connolly's. I'll bring back food. Shut the door after me, and don't open it to anyone until I come.'

The road to the shop seemed never-ending. When at last she came to it the smell of provisions nauseated her shrunken stomach. She had forgotten, except in hunger-crazed dreams, that such foods existed.

Her head was light, and her bones ached. Cold sweat broke out on her, and she told herself, ' 'Twas the walk, six miles, I wasn't able for it. Milk I want, and I brought nothing to carry it in. Milk and meal. I want milk and meal,' she repeated, like a child memorizing messages it had been sent for.

The man behind the counter, she couldn't tell who he was, the father or son, for his features kept blurring, said, 'What do you want?' His tone was surly, she was aware of that. – He thinks I have no money, and knows we've had the fever.

She put the money on the counter. He drew back from her hand. He was afraid, like she had been afraid to touch Statia. 'What do you want?' he asked again.

'Meal. I want meal. Meal,' she said again, 'and milk. A drop of new milk, only I've nothing to carry it in. I forgot. Could you oblige me with the loan of a can?'

'Shops don't sell milk. 'Tis a farmer and a cow you want.' She heard him laugh, but couldn't see his expression, his face was out of focus. He brought the bag of meal and pushed it towards her. She put her two hands round it. It felt grand, her fingers kneaded it. He took four of her five shillings. She picked up the bag, there was a terrible weakness in her legs, and it took her a long time to reach the door.

Slowly she began to walk away. 'Sweet Jesus assist me,' she prayed. 'Give me the strength. Don't let me fall by the wayside. Don't let me die and leave my children. Bring me home safe.'

Many times she had to stop, stand still until her breath returned, and her heart calmed. – If only, she thought, it

571

was long ago, someone might have passed to lift me part of the way. Tim with his cart and jennet. A neighbour going out to the bog with an ass. Taking pity on me and letting me ride. My father could have come with the Master's coach.

Confused thoughts chased each other through her mind. Maybe Miss Olivia and Miss Catherine in the dog-cart, or the Master himself exercising the mare, Master Charles, even Driscoll, any one of them would have pitied her, carried her home. Jamsie would have picked her up in his two arms – 'You're like a feather,' he would have said. – Oh Jamsie, Jamsie, where are you? There was no need to go. Statia had money. The money to bury her – she gave it to me. Come back to me. Help me, someone help me.

She heard the voice crying out. She stopped walking, her mind cleared. 'It was me,' she said, 'talking to myself. Talking and screeching out loud like a poor mad woman. Sacred Heart of Jesus don't let me fall. Oh, don't let me die and leave my children bereft.'

It grew dark and the wind rose. It moaned in the trees. She was frightened, and thought of the bean sidhe. The weight of the meal was a burden. She changed it to the other arm, and forced herself to go on, putting one foot in front of the other, willing herself not to fall. At last she came to the top of the boreen, and turned into it. Clutching at the hedge for support, staggering and stumbling like a drunken man until she came to the cottage, called to the children within, and when the door opened collapsed across the threshold.

*

When Jamsie came to, in the closet next to Catherine's office, he thought he was dead, and in Heaven with an angel bending over him. And the angel was saying, 'Come on now, keep your eyes open, don't close them again.'

His sight was misty so that the angel's face was fuzzy. But, he thought, maybe that's how angels look, and her hair was golden and curled like the pictures and statues of all the angels he had ever seen. He blinked his eyes, his vision cleared and he looked again. 'You're not an angel at all, you're Miss Olivia!' he said.

'Yes, that's who I am.'

'Then I'm not dead, nor in Heaven?'

'You're not. You're in Cork in a sort of hospital, a fever hospital.'

'Have I the fever?' Suddenly he felt very sick.

'No, only a cracked head.'

'What happened?'

Olivia told him what she knew, and he asked how long he'd been unconscious.

'Off and on for over a week,' she replied. 'Now, no more questions for the time being. Drink this water, and my sister will be along to see you presently.' She went then, and left him to his thoughts which came slowly and with no great clarity. He remembered the man with the coal, then the cart and the grain. And then why he was in Cork. Katy! She'd think he was dead. Whatever possessed him to leave her? To think he could earn enough for the passage. Even if he'd got work, it would take a month of Sundays to earn that much money. And as for robbing it, as he had threatened, he couldn't succeed in robbing a handful of grain without landing up with a cracked skull.

573

He wasn't much use for anything, no wonder Katy despised him. But still, she'd be better with him than without, if it was only to cut turf and draw water, he could do that. – And besides, he thought, I'd rather be dead than deprived of sight of her.

He got out of the bed, his legs felt weak and his head throbbed. Holding on to the wall he got as far as the door, opened it, and the cold air hit his face. He gasped, but after a moment the fresh air made him feel better, and he looked out. Across the way was a big shed. Where the fever patients were, he supposed, God help them. It wasn't a healthy place to be, and he wasn't staying. This very minute he was getting out of here, going back to Katy. But first he would have to find his clothes, he couldn't go out in a shirt, which was all he had on. He shut the door and looked round the room, there was no sign of them. Then he looked under the bed and saw them, and his brogues too. He dressed himself and went to the door again.

This time when he opened the door, he saw that the one in the fever shed was also open. He could see in. See Miss Catherine, and Olivia moving about, bending, doing things to what he supposed were people laid on bundles of straw. He heard voices asking for water, and the sound of someone vomiting, a dry retching sound of a person being sick on an empty stomach. And all the while as he looked Miss Catherine and her sister were attending on the people. Miss Olivia, like an angel, wiping faces and holding mugs to lips. Then he realized if either she or Miss Catherine was to glance in his direction, they'd have him stripped and back in the bed. He closed the door. He was trembling, and he knew it wasn't only his weakness that caused it.

He waited for what seemed an age to him, his hand on the door handle, wanting to make a run for it, afraid that any minute the knob might turn from the other side, and someone discover he was up and dressed. Then he decided to risk opening the door. He peered round its edge and there was no one about, and across in the fever shed, Miss Catherine and Miss Olivia were busy by a bed, their backs to him. He went out and walked as fast as he could, down a laurel-lined drive and through a pair of iron gates.

Between them, Bridget and Thomas dragged Katy from the door. 'She's like the priest, that's how he was, sweating and roasting. What'll we do with her?'

'We'll give her a drink of water, maybe that'll make her better. Fill the mug, Thomas.'

Bridget raised her mother's head and held the water to her lips. 'Mammy,' she said softly. 'Mammy will you have this.'

Katy opened her eyes. 'I'm sick, astoir, very sick.' She drank a mouthful of the water. 'That'll do now. If you and Thomas catch hold of my arms I could rise. If I can get into the bedroom and lie down I'd be better in no time.'

They linked her in and helped her on to the bed. Katy closed her eyes, and Thomas whispered to Bridget, 'Maybe she'll die, like Peg and Nora.'

'Shhhh. Don't you say such a thing. She will not,' Bridget responded in a fierce whisper.

'I'm terrible cold,' Katy's teeth were chattering. 'Put the shawl and coats over me.'

They piled all the ragged garments on top of her. Thomas awkward and clumsy in his arranging, so that Bridget had to rearrange them.

'Make the meal, let it steep a while, bring it to the boil ...' Katy's voice petered out, and she began to shiver violently. Thomas looked terrified, and began to cry.

Bridget grabbed him by the arm and dragged him from the room. 'If she sees you crying, she'll get a fright. You're not to be crying. Mammy will be all right.'

'But what'll we do if she dies? There's no one. Maybe even the priest is dead, and Statia too.'

'They're not! And Mammy won't die. We'll mind her, we'll mind her until Daddy comes back, he'll be back soon. I'll make the meal, and feed her. You and Mary Kate will bring the water, and carry in turf, and keep an eye on Danny. We'll go in now to see if she's asleep, and don't you cry.'

They stood by the bed looking down on their mother. She was moaning, and tossing restlessly. 'She's only having a bad dream, that's all it is,' Bridget said. 'We'll leave her for a while.'

Katy was in Hell, and the Devil was dragging her to where thick yellow plumes of smoke waved above a deep chasm. 'Don't take me,' she pleaded. 'There's no one to mind the children. No one to give water to the priest or Statia. And what'll Jamsie do when he comes back? I loved him all the time. The blue-black of his hair, his beautiful face and body. Drunk or sober, I loved him. From the minute I raised my eyes in Mass and saw him. He was my miracle. And if you keep me in Hell I'll never see him again. He'll never know I loved him all the while.'

The Devil laughed, and so did the little devils dancing round the edge of the chasm. Katy saw them, and opened her mouth again to scream at them, but the smoke went into her mouth, filled her nose, snaked down into her lungs and she couldn't speak. Only hear and feel. The pains in her arms and legs where the Devil prodded with a long fork, and the agony of her head being pierced by the fork's prongs. And in high, delighted voices the little devils chanted her sins, 'You took Statia's money. You didn't bring her the milk. Nor water to the priest. You left them both to die.' They laughed and pointed at her, dancing up and down exultantly, shouting, 'God didn't want you! We got you. We got you, Katy, for telling lies to your mother and father. For loving Peader and not Jamsie. For making false promises to the priest. And God wouldn't forgive you. God wouldn't forgive you for being jealous of Miss Charlotte, and doubting that the twins were in Heaven. We got you and we'll keep you forever and ever.'

The big Devil had a black face and horns growing out of his head. His eyes looked into Katy's and she saw that they were black and yellow and the shape of a long flat bead, like the eyes of a billy goat. The breath coming out of his mouth was hot and seared her face, the heat ran up into her head, and she wanted to scream but could make no sound for her tongue was swollen and her lungs choked. The Devil pushed her nearer to the edge of the pit, and with his cloven hoof sent her over. She fell down and down, spinning over and over, and the fire rushed up to meet her. Then she was in it and being consumed for all Eternity. But the agony of her body was as nothing to the certain knowledge that she would never see the faces of those she loved who were in Heaven, and never look upon the face of God.

Outside the gates of the fever hospital Jamsie looked hurriedly around. Down below in the distance he saw the river, the road home lay that way. He set off, walking as quickly as he could to put distance between him and the hospital. Afraid that any minute his departure would be discovered and someone come after him. But after a while he reasoned that Miss Catherine and Miss Olivia had enough to do without bothering about him, and he relaxed. Then he began to worry in case the police might be keeping a lookout for him, and when he heard a voice behind him call 'O'Hara', he was sure his fears were founded, and stopped, waiting for a hand to descend on his shoulder.

'I thought it was you, though with the look on people since the failure it's hard to be sure,' the voice said, closer at hand. Jamsie turned to look. The man like himself was dressed in flitters, whoever he was he wasn't a policeman.

'Did you want me?' Jamsie asked, stopping for him to catch up. 'Do you know me?'

'Only that you're an O'Hara – Johnny's brother. I often saw the two of you together years ago.'

'Is that so? I don't remember your face. Where are you heading for?'

'Home, halfway between here and Kilgoran. If you're going in that direction I'll walk with you.'

'I am,' said Jamsie. 'I've been away more than a week, and God knows what I'll find when I arrive.'

'I'm in the same boat myself, though it's longer than a week I've been gone.'

'Come on then,' Jamsie said, 'let's foot it out.'

They walked on, and after a while the man said, 'I saw Johnny not a month since.'

'You saw Johnny?'

'I did,' said the man.

'He's been gone that long we didn't know whether he was alive or dead. Tell me now, where did you see him?'

'In a place beyond called Woolwich, over the other side. I was waiting to be discharged. I lost this in India.' Only then did Jamsie notice the empty sleeve of the man's short coat.

'You were a soldier then?'

'I was and so is your brother, he was waiting to go foreign.'

'Isn't that the dangerous place for Johnny to be – in the army, won't he be found out?'

'Not at all, sure isn't the army full of O'Haras, O'Briens, Flynns and Carthys? Anyway he was under a different name. Don't call me O'Hara, he told me the first time we met. I'm Michael O'Brien now, that's what he said.'

It began to rain, and the two men quickened their pace. 'Johnny a soldier, after taking the Queen's shilling. Him that was the great patriot. I wouldn't have thought soldiering would have suited him.'

'And why wouldn't it?' said his companion. 'Hasn't he the grand training for the work he'll be doing in foreign parts? Only now it'll be legal.'

'You knew about his trouble, then?'

'I did indeed, all about it, and the bits I didn't he told me in Woolwich and a good laugh we had over it.'

'I don't suppose he mentioned his wife. The neighbours ran her out. I often wondered what became of her and the children.'

'He never said a word about her, and I didn't think to ask.'

There was a crossroads becoming visible. 'That's the turn I take,' said the man. And when they came to it, he stopped and bid Jamsie goodbye. 'Thanks for your company. Goodbye now, and I hope your family's been spared.'

'Yours, too,' Jamsie replied and they parted. It was getting dark, and the rain heavier. He wasn't sure if he had the strength to keep walking through the night, but was afraid to lay down in a ditch for fear he'd never rise again. So he kept going.

Chapter Twenty-Four

'Jamsie O'Hara's gone! I've been into the room and he's vanished, clothes and all!' Catherine exclaimed, coming into her office where Olivia was sitting.

'I spoke to him not an hour since. He thought I was an angel.' She shrugged. 'I suppose you can't blame him. I think he was terrified when he heard this was a fever hospital.'

'The silly man, he could collapse in the street. Be picked up by the police. Anything could happen to him.'

'Haven't you enough to worry about? You can only do so much, Catherine. And now it looks as if you'll have to manage alone for a day or two. I feel wretched, sick, my head aches, my bones hurt.'

Immediately Catherine forgot all about Jamsie, and felt sick herself, an awful fear clutched her as she paid full attention to Olivia and saw that she did indeed look ill. Surely she couldn't have the fever? It was a chill, no more than that. Please God, no more than that. Not so soon after she had arrived. Not the fever.

'Go and lay down,' she said, disguising the concern she felt. 'You're over-tired, you've caught a chill, the weather's been so changeable. I'll help you undress.'

Olivia allowed herself to be taken to the room they

shared, and stood shivering while Catherine removed her clothes. 'Sleep, dear, you're exhausted, you've worked like a horse, not rested, not eaten properly. Have a good sleep and you'll be fine.' She tucked Olivia into bed, kissed her cheek and waited for her to fall asleep.

By evening she knew Olivia had fever, but consoled herself that she was a strong, healthy woman. She would get over it. Others had. Not many, but some. Half-starved wretched creatures, and they had survived. Olivia would too. Night and day she would nurse her. She would not let her die.

Towards midnight Olivia became delirious. She threshed in the bed, entangling herself in the bedclothes, attempted to get up, and Catherine, amazed at her strength, struggled to restrain her. She talked incoherently, of her father, saying she hadn't loved him. She was jealous of how he favoured Catherine.

Catherine held her close, bathed her face, fed her sips of water, and spoke soothingly. 'Hush, my darling, it's all right, everything is all right. Don't talk, don't waste your energy. I've sent for a doctor, he'll give you something. You'll be better.'

The doctor didn't come. 'I tried, Ma'am,' the servant girl said, looking fearfully at Olivia, making the Sign of the Cross. 'There wasn't one to be found. The only one's the fella who was working here till he went down himself with the fever, and he's at death's door.'

Catherine thanked and dismissed her. She felt Olivia's pulse, it was weak and her breathing shallow, the strength she had displayed during her delirium all gone. 'Oh God, why do You do it? Why do You allow it? Why have You stricken her?' Catherine asked in a voice choked with grief. She looked at the face of Olivia and remembered her the night of the ball – a vision of loveliness in her lilac and silver – the most beautiful woman there. How she had danced. She could hear the tinkle of the bracelets she had worn that night, see them round the firm rounded arms that now lay so still outside the sheet.

'Please don't let her die, please God, not Olivia. She had so much to live for. Let her live and I'll never question You again. I'll accept my childlessness. I'll go back to Edward and be a wife to him, and if it means I forfeit my life, I'll do it gladly, if You save Olivia.' Catherine prayed with fervour, her head bent, her eyes closed.

When she raised her head and opened her eyes Olivia was looking at her, and for one minute she thought God had answered her prayers. 'I always loved you, even when I mocked and teased. I wanted to be like you.' Olivia was gasping for breath.

'Hush, darling, you mustn't talk.'

'Why not?' Olivia asked, making a desperate effort to be light-hearted. 'Why mustn't I talk?'

'Save your strength, you'll need it.'

'For the grave? No strength needed there.'

'Don't talk so. Don't say such things.' Catherine was holding Olivia's hand; it felt very cold. And she saw that her face had changed expression, and didn't look like Olivia's at all. It had in seconds grown old and long and tortured-looking.

Olivia attempted a smile that on her altered features was a grimace. 'I'm dying, Catherine. After all I'm to remain in Ireland, me that couldn't . . .' She gasped. Cath-

583

erine leant over her, her face close to Olivia's, trying to hear the choking voice. 'Look after,' she sighed, 'my children,' she whispered and sighed a long sigh.

Catherine stroked her hair in a way she remembered Olivia had liked when they were children and her head ached. 'Don't you worry about anything. I'll look after them. I'll treat them as if they were mine.' She made promises, soothing and talking, stroking and talking, and holding Olivia's hand for a long time after she realized that her beautiful sister was dead.

'She looks lovely now, Ma'am,' the servant girl who had assisted Catherine to lay out Olivia said. 'Not the same person I saw last night suffering.'

'Thank you very much for helping me. You must be tired, go to bed now.'

After the girl left Catherine looked again at Olivia, and thought, at peace, composed, but not lovely. Loveliness was life. Olivia had been life, radiant, beautiful, and she had taken that with her.

'That's how I'll remember you,' she began to talk. 'Not this way, this isn't you. You aren't here. Where are you? Can you hear me? I'll pretend you can. You'll laugh at me, you always laugh. Sometimes that irritated me. I thought you never took anything seriously. That's why I didn't tell you my real reason for coming home. It wasn't just concern for Papa or the tenants. You see, Richard, he's my doctor in India, he said I mustn't have another baby, that I could die. So I wasn't to, well, you know.'

She began to cry quietly. 'Oh Olivia, are you laughing at me again, the way you did the day before I was married? Do you remember? I couldn't find the words then either.

584

How I wish I could hear you. You had such a joyous laugh.

'I wasn't to sleep with Edward, that's what the doctor said. I was so frightened. Frightened of dying if I did, of losing Edward if I didn't. So I came home to think about it. Then Papa was ill, and all the other terrible things happening ... I didn't have time to think. Though I did dream about it. Sometimes I dreamt about Edward, but the strange thing was I saw only his eyes. They were filled with reproach, then his eyes would change, become hard and cold like the eyes of a reptile. In other dreams I saw myself as an old woman, a widow being dragged to a funeral pyre, resisting, not wanting to die.

'Death is terrible. I've seen so much since I came here. But now I know that death would be preferable to living without Edward's love. So, I've made my decision. I love Edward more than anything else. I'm going back to him. I'm going to be his wife.'

She bent and kissed Olivia's forehead. 'Goodbye,' she whispered. 'I'm glad I talked to you. I've found the calm I came to look for.' She thought she heard a faint laugh, a joyous one that had nothing irritating about it, and smiled as she left the room.

She wrote to Peter, and made arrangements for Olivia's funeral. And then a letter to the family solicitor instructing him to have the boxes left at Kilgoran shifted into storage, as the new-found calm wasn't strong enough to endure a visit to the House. And then she set about finding someone to relieve her at the hospital, she wanted to return to India as soon as possible.

*

Katy in her delirium struggled and writhed in the tongues of fire. For Eternity she burned, her body was consumed, and as consummation was completed, so again she was made whole, and the flames licked round her. And all the while she heard the demonic laughter of the little devils, and saw their gloating eyes peering over the edge of the pit. Then from far away she thought she heard another sound – the voices of Thomas and Bridget. But she knew that couldn't be. She was in Hell, separated from all those she loved. The sound of her children's voices was a trick played by Satan, another torment to agonize her. It was the cruellest of all. She could still hear them. Hear Bridget tell Thomas to lift up her head, to hold it still. Then her face felt cold as if water had splashed it. The shock made her gasp, and water flowed into her mouth, cooling her swollen tongue and parched throat. And she saw that the fire was going out, and the devils slinking away, though their yellow and black eyes glared malevolently, and their forks pointed to her. But they were going, light was filtering into the pit, and the flames were quenched.

She had to escape. Climb up the steep side of the pit, escape from Hell before they came and pushed her down again. It was a hard climb, but she fought and struggled to reach the top, up and up she clambered, and then she was free.

'Mammy, you're awake!' Bridget was bending over her.

'Am I?' she said, not recognizing the face above her. Then she saw who it was and reached a hand to touch Bridget, feeling her to make sure she was real.

''Tis you, love. I had a terrible dream. Was I asleep for long?'

'Oh you were. Wasn't she, Thomas? Wasn't she asleep for a long time?

'A terrible long time.' Katy looked in the direction from which the voice came and saw Thomas, and Thomas was crying.

'Where's Daddy and Mary Kate and the child?'

'They're asleep at the foot of the bed, but Daddy never came back.'

'Never came back? Where did he go?' Katy asked.

'To Cork City, for to look for work, don't you remember, Mammy?'

'Oh, I do, of course I do,' Katy lied for she could remember nothing. 'He won't be long now I'd say.' The children looked relieved. 'How long have I lain?'

'Six days, maybe more. 'Tis hard to tell for no one comes, nobody passes.'

Katy's mind was working, things coming back. Jamsie went for work, to get money for their passage to America. Six days, maybe more. Where was he, what had happened to him?

'Nobody came, only the constable,' Thomas said. 'He asked for you, Bridget said you were asleep.'

It was all coming back – the money – Statia. 'Oh my God,' Katy said out loud. 'Statia is sick. Statia is very sick.' She struggled to get out of the bed. 'I have to go to her, help me, love.'

'Statia died, Mammy. That's what Thomas was trying to tell you. The day the constable came, we went after him to the top of the boreen. Down on our hands and knees so he wouldn't see us. We hid in the hedge on the top road. And he went down to Statia's. He wasn't there long. We took turns watching and after a good while the cart came, the one that took Peg and Nora. We said a prayer for Statia every night.'

'Don't be crying, Mammy.' Thomas put an arm round Katy. 'You'll be sick again, don't be crying now.' He was crying himself.

– My poor Statia that was as kind as a mother to me. And I never brought you the sup of milk. God knows you didn't deserve to die alone, you that brought ease to so many. She gave me her money, her few shillings that was for the grand send-off she wanted. The grand funeral she was going to have with everyone in the parish there. The best keen that was ever set up. Poor Statia, little did she know her end.

'We never saw Father Bolger either, maybe he's dead too,' Thomas said, and Katy saw Bridget give him a dig with her elbow. And despite her grief she couldn't help smiling. Poor Thomas who couldn't keep a thought or a question to himself. She wiped her eyes. She had done enough crying in front of the children.

She lay back on the pillow. 'I'm all right now. I'll just close my eyes for a minute. Tomorrow I'll be well again. And tomorrow Thomas you'll go to the priest's house, just in case he's alive but still sick. Go you now and sit by the fire.'

Her thoughts came back to Statia. She would be in Heaven now, please God. She had the yalla fever, the one Peg and Nora died from. And she remembered that sometimes you got better, and then relapsed. Maybe it was the same fever she herself had. Maybe tomorrow she, too, would relapse. Then what would happen to her children?

'Oh Jamsie, Jamsie,' she said to herself, 'where are you? Don't be dead on me. I need you. Don't you be dead and not knowing that I loved you. I love you as I did on the morning I raised my eyes in Mass and saw you. I loved you drunk and sober. Sometimes I hated you the way you would a fractious or unbiddable child. But that had nothing to do with not loving you, though at times I thought it had. But it was no more than me lashing out at Peg or Nora, screaming at Thomas or Bridget. It was only that sometimes a person displeases you, but it didn't mean you wanted someone else in their place. And I was the foolish woman to have thought so.

'If you were spared to me I'd never think so again. I'd never turn from you. Oh Jamsie, don't be dead on me. Don't leave me. I sent you away without a kind word. I'm sorry. Maybe I have the relapsing fever, and will be dead before you come. But come, if you don't what will happen to the children?'

'Are you better now?' Bridget had come back into the room, was bending over Katy.

'I am, astoir. I'm better. Tell me, how did you manage, is there a bit of food for you?'

'There's the meal you brought from Connolly's. I boiled it, and gave it out a bit at a time. But it's nearly all gone.'

'We'll buy more. Tomorrow we'll get more. I might eat a spoonful now. If you and Thomas help me I'll put my feet to the floor.'

They helped her out of the bed, and linked her into the kitchen. Her head was swimming, and she was glad to sit down. 'Aren't you the great girl, you kept the fire in.'

'And I brought in the turf and the water from the well,' Thomas said.

'You were good children, God bless you.' Bridget ladled out a spoonful of porridge, and Katy ate it. From the other room came the sound of Danny crying, and Mary Kate came out bringing him by the hand. He was half naked, only a flannel bodice over his chest. Katy saw that his buttocks were red raw, and the insides of his thighs. She ran her hand over his flesh, it was burning to the touch. – It is so, she thought, from all the purging, and I've nothing to soothe the scale. He was filthy, and so was Mary Kate, her hair matted, bits of porridge in it. God look down on them, they're lucky to be alive with only Thomas and Bridget to mind them and me as well. She clasped them to her, kissing their pinched faces, her hands caressing them.

– If I had the strength I'd put on the kettle and wash them, and wash myself. Make us all clean and sweet-smelling. If only I had the strength, but I haven't. What is to become of them? She began to cry. Thomas and Bridget, who had thought once she was out of the bed she was better, looked on in bewilderment.

'Everybody in the whole world's dead,' Katy cried. 'Statia is dead, and Father Bolger's dead or he'd have come before now. What'll I do? What'll become of us?'

'Daddy'll be back soon. You'll be all right then, won't you?'

'I will, aghille, I'll be all right then, Bridget. I'm only tired, that's all,' Katy said, and wiped her eyes with the back of her hand. And thought – I'll never be all right again. I'll bury every one of you. Every one of my lovely children. Like Peg and Nora you'll die on me. I've the money I robbed from Statia, more money than I ever saw in my life, enough to buy food, to take us to America, and not the strength nor the will to do anything with it. She looked at her hungry, dirty children, at Thomas and Bridget who had nursed her through the fever, little handfuls, not much more than infants, and they had done all that for her, and kept in the fire, and fed Danny and Mary Kate, and told lies to the constable. And now they were doomed. Like Peg and Nora they would be snuffed out.

Her head felt like a ton weight, there was a sickness in her stomach, and she was sure this was a relapse. Like Statia and the twins she had the yalla fever. Terror engulfed her, her heart pounded, her mouth went dry and cold sweat broke out on her body.

'Bridget,' she called, and the child came to her. 'What colour am I?'

Bridget peered at her mother. 'You're white,' she said.

'Are you sure, not yellow?'

'No, 'tis white you are, very white, like a sheet. Are you sick?'

'No, not sick, it's only weakness after laying so long. You mind the children and I'll go into the bed for a while.'

She slept, and when she woke it was daylight. The children were in the bed with her, Mary Kate laying between her and Bridget, Thomas with Danny beside him at the bottom of the bed. His feet were against her legs, her hand reached and held one, her fingers touching the rough calloused skin, the hot broken chilblains. – His poor feet, she thought, the feet that were beautiful, that I'd kiss and want to bite lumps out of.

She looked at the two little girls beside her. Mary Kate with her dirty face and matted hair, the sound of her breath wheezing, her mouth open, not able to draw air through her congested nose. And Bridget, her golden-haired doll, her first born, the child of her wondrous love, a little girl who'd done the work of two women in the last week, purple stains beneath her closed eyes from hunger and exhaustion.

– Wouldn't they all be better off dead, she asked herself? Then they'd be in Heaven with the angels and saints, with God smiling on them. If only they could stay sleeping, and she with them, and never waken up. Bridget stirred, opened her eyes and smiled at her mother before closing them again. And Katy thought, but maybe you wouldn't want that, you smiled at me then as you did long ago. Maybe you were dreaming that the starvation never came. That the beggar woman never walked down the boreen and brought the fever. That tomorrow you'd go running up to the Hazel Grove, you and Thomas, with your golden hair flying behind you. Your poor lovely hair, that's as dull and lifeless as my own.

– What sort of a woman am I, laying here wishing you all dead? Looking for the easy way out. Of course I'll folly every one of you to your grave, or worse still you might folly me, and be left to the winds of the world. What else is there in front of you if I lay here and commit the sin of despair? God spared me, and it was for a purpose. Statia died and I have her money. I can just imagine what she'd say if she saw me laying here giving in to myself.

For the first time since the fever left her a smile crossed her face as she remembered Statia. 'Get up off your arse,

Katy, and see to them children or I'll haunt you,' that's exactly what Statia would be saying if you could say such things in Heaven.

Gently, so as not to disturb the sleeping children, she manoeuvred her way out of the bed. She was still weak and light-headed, but determinedly she ignored it, holding on to the wall for support. She re-kindled the fire and thanked God she still had the kettle. Every one of the children needed washing, as she did herself. Her own clothes were filthy, they smelt, she had slept in them all the while she was sick. Only fit for burning they were. But she had no others, they would have to do. When the room was warmer she would strip off and wash her body. Then cook the last of the meal. With a bit of that inside her she'd get the strength to go to Connolly's, but first Thomas had to go to the priest's house, maybe he was still alive and in need of something, though she doubted it. How could he have lasted with no one to bring him a drink of water even?

She quickly became exhausted and had to sit and rest. While she rested she thought about Jamsie. Maybe God had spared him. She would wait for another two or three days, but no more than that. If she kept breaking into the money for food, there wouldn't be enough for the fares to America. She did calculations in her head, please God if Jamsie came back, at £3 16s each for the two of them, and half price for the children, they had more than enough, there'd even be a few shillings when they got to the other side. But not if she waited too long. – Please God, let him come. Let him come and take us to America. I don't want to go on my own, but if I have to I will.

593

She got up from the stool and went out to stand by the door. The fresh air was reviving after her confinement. The hills were covered by low grey cloud, everywhere she looked were the signs of desolation. Untilled fields, rank with weeds, not a spiral of smoke from one of the cottages. Everyone gone, silence everywhere, not a breeze or a bird on the wing. Maybe, she thought, there was no one in the whole world alive, only herself and her children. Maybe everywhere the fields and houses were deserted and silent, the roads empty, and the boats still at their moorings, no one to sail them.

Prince came out of his upturned barrel and licked her bare feet. She had forgotten all about him. She bent and stroked him, he was a riddle of bones. – Poor Prince, what'll I do with you when the time comes to go? Then she heard the sound of horse's hoofs. There was someone alive, after all. She went up the boreen, and looked down the road. Her eyes were deceiving her, she thought, it couldn't be Father Bolger driving the horse and trap, it couldn't be. But she saw that it was and in the trap was a man with him. And her heart nearly stopped with joy, for the man was standing up and waving, and calling, 'Katy, oh Katy!' And she forgot about the lightness in her head and the weakness of her legs and went running.

Jamsie was out of the trap and she was in his arms, crying and talking, holding him away to look at him, and pulling him close again. 'You came back, oh thank God, you came back. We'll be all right now, won't we? We can go to America. I have the money. Statia gave it to me. Oh say we'll be all right.'

594

'I thought you'd be dead,' Jamsie said. 'I was afraid to come down the boreen in case you were gone.'

'I thought you were too. I thought you were dead and you'd never know how much I loved you.'

He looked down at her thin white face, her eyes sunken, her lank and lustreless hair that was once the colour of ripe corn, and he saw her as beautiful as the first time he had laid eyes on her. And she gazing at him saw not the signs of his recent illness, nor the haggard face, only blue, blue eyes with the light of his soul and his love of her shining from them. So enchanted were they with each other they forgot all about the priest, until a discreet cough reminded them and quickly, even guiltily they separated.

'Father, how are you? You were sick and I couldn't come. I had the fever myself, today is the first time from the bed.'

'Thank God who spared you for your children and to Jamsie. I had it myself, what sort I don't know, there's that many fevers. I managed to crawl into the kitchen where thankfully there was plenty of water.'

'Did nobody come to you at all?'

'Sure there is no one, Katy, only Carey, and he as you know hasn't much time for the clergy, and besides like everyone else he'd have been in mortal dread of catching it. It's the brave man or woman that goes to anyone with the fever.'

'You shouldn't be out so soon, and you just up from a sick bed,' Katy admonished.

'Well, do you see, I had to. The way it is the day before I got sick I had my marching orders, a letter from the

Bishop. I'm going to a parish in Limerick. I'm going the day after tomorrow, and I had to see if you were alive and well. Then on my way who did I bump into, only himself,' the priest said, nodding at Jamsie.

'You'll come in, Father, won't you?' Katy asked.

'I will indeed, hold on now till I secure the horse.'

Katy and Jamsie helped him down from the step. He was very bent and frail-looking after his illness. He let them help him down the boreen.

'Father,' Katy said when they were inside and sitting down. 'Statia is dead, Thomas and Bridget saw the cart come for her, and I have the burial money.' She began to cry. 'The last time I saw her she was dying, maybe her senses had left her, but I don't think so. She made me take the money. I promised to bring her milk and I never did. Would it be wrong of me to use the money for America?'

'What better use could you put it to, unless you thought of scattering it over the pit where she's buried. Spend it to save yourself and your family, isn't that why Statia parted with it? And stop crying, there's a good girl, or Statia will haunt you, she had no time for tears. Pray for her, that's more fitting. And I'll go to the graveyard and do the same. Now tell me this, what way were you thinking of going?'

'From Cobh, for three pounds sixteen shillings they'll take you and feed you,' Katy said.

'Do you know if you went on a smaller boat it might be cheaper, then you'd have more when you arrived in America?' the priest said.

'Do you tell me, and where might the other places be?' Jamsie inquired.

'Off-hand I couldn't say, but I'll find that out in Bandon. Now I'll be on my way.'

'Father, I was thinking could you give Jamsie a lift to Connolly's, we want more meal.'

'Getting rid of the man already. Come on then, Jamsie, you're not wanted.'

When they left Katy fed the children, sent them into the bedroom and stripped off to wash herself, avoiding looking down at her breasts or body for it was that thin it reminded her of a skeleton she had seen once in an old sunken grave. She dressed and did what she could with her hair which wasn't much for there were few teeth left in the comb. Then she called in the children and one by one washed them, too.

Jamsie came back with the meal. The children gathered round him, kissing and making much of him. He told Katy about Cork, about Catherine, and thinking Olivia was an angel, but how he had seen them working in the fever ward.

'God bless and spare them, they were ladies,' Katy said. Then Jamsie told her the news of Johnny.

'I don't suppose you heard anything else about Peader and Miss Charlotte?'

'Sure how would I? It wasn't a subject you could mention to her sisters, and the fellow who knew Johnny wouldn't have known anything about them.'

She cooked the meal and served it, giving a share to the dog. The fire burnt brightly, and she thought how if you didn't look too closely at anyone's face and for an instant could forget Peg and Nora, it might have been a night long ago. A night before the hungry months, when there were potatoes instead of meal. And in a little while Hannah would come, followed by Statia, Dinny would drop in, Mary Doyle and Tim Coffey and they'd sit by the fire talking until all hours.

And afterwards you'd walk to the top of the boreen to send them. All about you would be the smell of burning turf, smoke going up from the chimneys and the sound of talking and laughing as the neighbours wended their way home. Hannah going up the drive to the lovely big House, spick and span, every room in it gleaming, lights shining from the library window where the Master would be reading. Everything in the world was right then. But tonight was no ordinary night, and outside everywhere was desolation. And after tomorrow her light and fire would be quenched, nothing would remain to show anyone had ever lived here, loved and been happy, nothing, only the brown stain over the chimney breast to show that a fire had once burned on the hearth.

The priest called in on the way back from Bandon. He told them they could get a boat from Kinsale. 'And I'll tell you what I'll do,' he added.

'What's that, Father?'

'I'll take you there for it's a long old walk, and after the fever you might not be able for it.'

'But you're going to Limerick, wouldn't you be getting the coach from Carey's?' Jamsie asked.

'Sure there's more ways than one of getting to Limerick.'

'But what about the horse, isn't it Dano's?'

'Dano can whistle for it,' Father Bolger said. 'God will forgive the theft for a good cause. I'll pick you up at daylight the day after tomorrow, and before we set off I'll give you both confession and communion. Goodnight now, and God bless you all.'

'I love you,' Jamsie whispered when later he and Katy lay on the straw pallet. 'When we get to America I'll make it up to you. I'll work till I drop and never let a drink pass my lips, as true as God.'

'And I love you. And I'll be cross no more, nor turn from you in the bed.'

Jamsie kissed her, and his hand was underneath her shift, circling her belly and moving up to caress her breasts, and she felt beautiful and desirable and responded as passionately to him as she had on the first night he brought her as a bride to the cottage.

On the morning before Jamsie and Katy were to leave Kilgoran, Catherine was on board a ship sailing down the Lee towards the open sea. She watched the river banks slide by, and said farewell to Ireland, to its green fields and soft skies, and to all those she was leaving there forever.

She thought about Peter in London and Olivia's children, and wondered if the news of Olivia's death had reached them yet? Poor Olivia, buried amongst strangers. Olivia, who had never wanted to remain in Ireland, there now forever. The strange turns life took, she herself, who had never wanted to leave, might never come again. The House, her beautiful home, passing into the hands of strangers, soon too, from what MacNamara had told her just before she left. A wealthy Englishman, in business, was very interested, but didn't intend living there. He would be what her father had detested – an absentee landlord. She must, she knew, put such bitterness from her mind. Ireland was no longer her home. That was wherever Edward was. She was returning to him. She was lucky, God had spared her life. It was there before her to live and enjoy with the man she loved.

Katy rose before daylight. She revived the fire, boiled the kettle and put on the meal to warm. She had a terrible thirst and longed for a drink of water, but food nor water could not pass her lips until she had received the Sacrament. She called Jamsie and the children, fed them and moved about the room wrapping the spare rags of clothes into a bundle.

Thomas talked excitedly about Kinsale, reminding Katy that once long ago she had promised to take them there. She remembered the day well. The day before the terrible weather and thunderstorms. She thought of all the things she had promised they would bring on the picnic, salmon and sweet cake, fruit cordials and cold chicken. But it didn't do to look back, she told herself, and said to Thomas to hurry up with his food, she wanted the table tidy before the priest came with the Blessed Sacrament.

When they had finished eating, she sent all the children out. 'Up behind the bushes now, I don't want you stopping the priest every five minutes along the way to Kinsale.'

She was fidgety, not knowing what to do with herself, wanting to be gone, and not wanting to go. Afraid of what lay ahead of them, of the strange land, of the time they would be on the sea. And beneath it all was a worry as to what she should do with Prince. – Why weren't you dead when I woke up this morning? she thought when he came in the door barely able to walk. 'Here, eat this bit of porridge,' she said to him. She cleared the table, putting the two remaining tin mugs in her bundle. They might want water on the way.

Then she heard the horse above on the road. 'While the priest is hearing our confession, be good,' she warned the children.

The priest came and she showed him into the bedroom. Jamsie went in first and made his confession and received Communion. When he came out Katy went in and offered up the Sacrament for all those dead and gone. Kneeling on the floor her eyes kept straying to the two old pillows and when her mind should have been filled with thoughts of God and the miracle that had taken place, all she could see was the imprints of Peg's and Nora's heads on the pillow.

At last it was time to go. Jamsie collected the children; they were crying because Prince couldn't come.

'Who'll mind him?' Thomas demanded to know.

'Carey will come up every single day,' Father Bolger lied.

Katy put down the pot with the remains of the porridge, placed the bucket of water on the floor and piled sods on the fire. 'There now,' she said, 'you'll be grand.' She took a last look round the little kitchen and went out to the trap. Jamsie gave her a hand up and they set off.

'He's running after us, look at that now,' Thomas called out, and there was the dog trying to catch them up. But as the horse increased his pace Prince dropped further and further behind. The children began to cry and Katy to scold them, glad of the opportunity to take her mind off her own sorrow.

There was a light in Carey's. 'I suppose I should say goodbye to him all the same,' the priest said when they came near the public house.

'You should, and so should I,' said Jamsie. 'Many's the pint he gave me on score, he's not the worst in the world.'

'Get down then like a good boy and save my legs.'

Jamsie got down and knocked on the door. Carey opened it. 'What are you doing here at this hour of the morning?' Then he looked out, saw the priest and the trap full. 'Where are you all off to?'

'America.'

'The best place for anyone to be heading, I'm telling you. You're going, too, Father?'

'I'm not, I'm away to Limerick, another parish. I stopped to say goodbye and God bless you.'

'I'll tell you this,' said Carey, 'I need someone's blessing. The clergy didn't succeed in putting me out of business, but the potatoes did all right. Well, goodbye so.' He shook hands with the priest and Jamsie, inclined his head to Katy, and gave a little wave to the children.

The priest gave a tug on the reins when Carey raised a hand and slapped himself on the head. 'Don't go for a minute. There's a fool of a man I am, didn't I forget the letter.'

'What letter?' asked the priest.

'Oh, 'tis not for you, but for Jamsie. It came a while back. I was meaning to bring it up, but between the jigs and the reel, forgot about it till this very minute. Hold on now and I'll get it.'

'For me?' Jamsie stared incredulously at the letter Carey handed to him. 'Do you know I've never had such a thing in my life.' His hands were shaking as he tore open the envelope, and took out the folded sheet of paper. 'There's something in it,' he said, his thumb rubbing the raised bump in the notepaper.

'Open it, Jamsie, we're dying of curiosity,' Father Bolger urged.

'It's a sovereign! It's from Peader! It's his name on the bottom,' Jamsie said, his eyes scanning the letter. 'It's from him all right.' He studied the sheet of paper for a moment, then handed it to Father Bolger. 'Would you read it to us, the writing's awful small.'

'The date's two weeks ago, and it's from Liverpool. Wait now and I'll tell you what he says.' The priest took out his spectacles, put them on, and read:

Dear Jamsie and Katy,
By the time you get this we'll be on our way to America. We missed the boat from Cork and came over here, afraid to delay in case Charlotte's father came after us. Once I arrive and get settled I'll write again. I hope you are all in good health, and that the few shillings will be a help. Remember me to everyone, and tell Father Bolger I'll not forget to write to him. Mind yourself and Katy.

Peader

'Poor Peader,' Katy said, 'he was ever generous. And God help her, too. Like myself she's going far away from home.'

The priest gave back the letter. Jamsie folded the notepaper back into its exact creases, put it in the envelope and into his pocket. 'I wonder,' he said, 'if we'll ever come across him over there.'

'You might very well indeed. And in any case he'll write again, and you'd be good enough to send it on to me or Jamsie if we post you our address, wouldn't you?' the priest said to Carey.

'Oh, I would that. I would indeed,' Carey promised.

'Right then, we'll be off. May things improve for you, and don't forget about the letters now.'

'Goodbye, Jamsie. Goodbye, Katy, God go with you, and you too, Father.'

The trap drove off, the children kept waving until they could see the Cross no more. Jamsie and the priest were talking about Peader, how he didn't know Lord Kilgoran was dead, or the House shut up. They drove past the gap in the hedge and Katy caught a glimpse of it, and thought how even from this distance you could sense the loneliness of it, know that it was no longer lived in, or cared for. She said farewell to it, and to the fields, and the hills, the river and the lake, and the little cottages with grass sprouting through the thatch. Gazing intently at all of them, fixing them in her mind's eye, for she knew she would never look on them again.

It was dark before they reached Kinsale. Father Bolger advised them to spend some of their money on a night's shelter. He would drive on himself, he said, to a friend he had beyond the town. 'In the morning make your way early down to the harbour, you'll find the boats and men selling passages. Goodbye now and may God guard you every step of the way to America. I'll remember you always in my prayers, and you pray for me, too.' He shook Jamsie's hand and then Katy's, touched each of the children's heads and gave them all his blessing. 'You'll be all right,' he said, before leaving them. 'There's love in your hearts for each other. You'll be all right.'

The sea was rough, the little ship swaying at its moorings. While Katy waited for Jamsie to buy the passages she looked out at the grey churning mass of water beyond the harbour, and was filled with apprehension. Never in her life had she stepped into a boat, the thought of it terrified her. She wanted to run away, take the children, call to Jamsie and go running back to the cottage. There at least the ground was firm beneath her feet.

Then Jamsie was coming. He was smiling. He had the tickets. It was too late. She couldn't turn back. He was beside her, taking Danny from her arms, telling Thomas things about ships, about the sea. And Thomas was looking at him with shining eyes. And Bridget was explaining to Mary Kate that they were going to America, and America was the grand place. And Katy remembered what the priest had said. 'There's love in your hearts, you'll be all right.' And there was such love in her for Jamsie and her children, she would face the sea, face anything on earth for them.

They moved along in the crowd waiting to board, and soon it was their turn to go up the gangplank. And there was a man shouting directions as to which way they went when they were aboard.

'Wait!' Katy called to Jamsie who was obeying the man's instructions, shepherding his family and her towards the steps leading into the hold of the boat. 'Wait!' she said again. 'Let me look for the last time.' And she fought her way back through the throng to stand by the rail and take a last look at Ireland. The tears washed her face as she thought of all those she was leaving. Peg and Nora, her mother and father, Statia, even the poor dog. Never again would she tread the paths their feet had known. Never again would she see her green fields and the mist on the low hills. But she would remember Ireland until the day God closed her eyes in death. And in Heaven she would meet again all those she had loved on earth.

Jamsie was calling her. Telling her to come on, they had to go down below. She wiped her eyes and turned from the rail. He was waving to her. He was smiling at her. He was waiting for her. She went to him. It was going to be all right. She had him, and her children, they were safe now, and, please God, America would be kind to them. She took his arm and together they went down the steps into the hold of the ship.

MORE ABOUT PENGUINS, PELICANS
AND PUFFINS

For further information about books available from Penguins please write to Dept EP, Penguin Books Ltd, Harmondsworth, Middlesex UB7 ODA.

In the U.S.A.: For a complete list of books available from Penguins in the United States write to Dept DG, Penguin Books, 299 Murray Hill Parkway, East Rutherford, New Jersey 07073.

In Canada: For a complete list of books available from Penguins in Canada write to Penguin Books Canada Ltd, 2801 John Street, Markham, Ontario L3R 1B4.

In Australia: For a complete list of books available from Penguins in Australia write to the Marketing Department, Penguin Books Australia Ltd, P.O. Box 257, Ringwood, Victoria 3134.

In New Zealand: For a complete list of books available from Penguins in New Zealand write to the Marketing Department, Penguin Books (N.Z.) Ltd, Private Bag, Takapuna, Auckland 9.

In India: For a complete list of books available from Penguins in India write to Penguin Overseas Ltd, 706 Eros Apartments, 56 Nehru Place, New Delhi 110019.